# Awards for *Flight to Destiny*

2016 — The Eudora Welty Memorial Award in Fiction from the National League of American Pen Women;

2013 — The Greyden Press Book Competition Grand Prize Winner, Fiction;

2000 — Pikes Peak Writers Conference First Place in Historical Fiction.*

*Sarah won Back-to-Back First Places in Historical Fiction at the Pikes Peak Writers Conference in 1999 and 2000, first for Flight From Fear and then for its prequel, Flight To Destiny.*

# Flight to
# Destiny

## A WASP Story

# Flight to
# Destiny

## A WASP Story

by
Sarah Byrn Rickman

*Foreword by Trish Beckman*
*Commander, US Navy (retired)*

**Braughler Books**
braughlerbooks.com

# TABLE OF CONTENTS

# DEDICATION

This book is dedicated to the nine members of the Women's Auxiliary Ferrying Squadron (WAFS) of World War II who were alive in 1999: Nancy Batson Crews, Barbara Jane "B.J." Erickson London, Teresa James Martin, Gertrude Meserve Tubbs LeValley, Florene Miller Watson, Barbara Poole Shoemaker, Barbara Donahue Ross, Phyllis Burchfield Fulton, and Bernice Batten.

All 28 of the Original WAFS have now taken their final flight.

# FOREWORD

*Strap into your pursuit plane and prepare for air combat maneuvering.*

Our lead pilot (author) Sarah Rickman will be taking us on a fast-paced and historically accurate mission with the Women's Auxiliary Ferrying Squadron (WAFS) of World War II. Along the way Sarah will introduce us to three fictional "wing-women" who will help us get inside the thoughts of the main characters in their history—Nancy Love and Jackie Cochran.

Because I know the history of the WAFS, I originally thought it would be difficult to suspend disbelief of Sarah's additional fictional characters. However, Sarah has developed them so they are superbly believable as young women and as aviators flying military aircraft in support of World War II. Sarah injects just enough realistic romance, plus relationship issues, to create well-rounded 20-something women who also happen to be patriotic, talented pilots.

Through the eyes and hearts of the fictional characters, Sarah has creatively added dimensions to the main characters—Nancy Love and Jackie Cochran—who have often been portrayed as one-dimensional (classy/crass, patriotic/ambitious, "for the common good"/"my way or the highway").

For those who know the story, Sarah's approach will add substance to the main characters, our role models.

For those just beginning their journey learning about the WAFS, this entertaining approach will provide insight beyond the mere statement of facts regarding their incredible stories.

Every time I read *Romeo & Juliet* or see it in theaters, I never give up hope for a different, more positive outcome. This story is much the same for me. Like *Romeo & Juliet*, I know the ending but I keep hoping that it will end differently—that the WAFS had continued flying for the military!

In spite of how the real story ends, Sarah weaves an optimistic future for these World War II women aviators who continued to contribute to our country's success in many ways, including being role models for my generation of military women aviators and many generations to come. I hope she is setting the stage for a follow-on book to tell the post-WAFS story.

Thanks to Sarah's expertise both in subject knowledge and in story-telling, I now feel more connected to the main characters—Nancy Love and Jackie Cochran.

*Lead on, Sarah!*

**Trish Beckman**
**Commander, US Navy (retired)**

# CHAPTER ONE

Annie Gwynn nudged the control stick to the left, touched her foot to the left rudder pedal, and put the small, single-engine airplane into a shallow bank. The right wing lifted and traced an invisible arc across the sky as the aircraft swung through a 180-degree turn.

The early morning mist had vanished from the green valleys between the rugged mountains that looked down on Pearl Harbor. In the two months she had been there, Annie had learned that the seasons in Hawaii didn't change like they did in Tennessee. Back home, by early December, the trees on the gentle, rounded Green Hills south of Nashville were bare, and the sky had taken on that slate gray monochrome that comes in mid-November and stays until March. Here, in this tropical paradise, the world brimmed with sunshine, gloriously brilliant blossoms of red, purple, orange and yellow, and smiling brown-skinned people who seemed to have not a care in the world.

Annie bit back a yawn. She had been up since five. Both she and her roommate, Cornelia Fort, had students scheduled to fly at sunrise — not unusual for a busy Sunday at Honolulu's John Rodgers Civilian Airport. She could see her friend's yellow trainer flying a half-mile away. Cornelia had taken off first and already had her student doing turns and stalls.

When a scan of the sky told her no other airplanes were in the practice area, Annie turned to eighteen-year-old Tom Witten, who sat behind her in the enclosed cockpit. "OK, Mr. Witten," she yelled over the noise of the engine, "let's try some power-off stalls. Carburetor heat on, power off, stick back, nose up, back pressure, back, back. When the controls get mushy, stick forward to neutral, power on. Carb heat off. Gentle but firm."

She watched the nose of the plane climb the sky, her hands and feet resting lightly on her own set of controls, ready to take over in an instant if the young man sitting behind her failed to perform the maneuver correctly. To land an airplane, the pilot first has to put it into a stall. But a fledgling pilot learns how to stall by practicing high in the air where a mistake results only in a little loss of altitude, not an uncontrolled flight into the ground.

Tom did well for a beginner, she noted. You never could tell with students. The ones you expected to be bold often turned out to be the most timid once in the air, whereas the poor soul you thought was afraid of his own shadow might turn out to be a roughneck who tended to jerk the plane around all over the sky.

"My grandmother gave me the money for my birthday. I'll be eighteen on the seventh," the eager young man told her when he signed up for lessons. His broad chest puffed out just a bit. "I'm gonna join the Air Corps and be a pursuit pilot."

Annie smiled at that. When she graduated from Ward-Belmont College last summer, Gramma Gwynn had given her the gift of money to get her instructor's rating. Now, barely twenty-two herself, she taught eighteen-year-olds how to fly.

And she loved flying the little J-3 Cub, single-engine trainers. Like many small, modern airplanes, they were made of heavy cotton fabric stretched taut over an aluminum skeleton of fuselage and wings, and painted a bright, distinctive yellow. She thought it the spiffiest airplane around.

"Very nice, Mr. Witten," she called out when Tom had three reasonably successful stalls under his belt. Then she put him to work negotiating 360-degree turns, first to the right and then to the left — to be accomplished without gaining or losing altitude. "Keep your eye on the altimeter." She tapped her finger on the instrument panel.

Below lay the jungle — so dense, so verdant, so intense in the early morning sun, it almost hurt to look at it. Mesmerized, lulled by the drone of the engine into a momentary complacency no flight instructor could afford, Annie forced herself to look up and out beyond the crests of the hills in front of her to the brilliant gem-blue of the Pacific Ocean. Having lost track of Cornelia's plane, she began to search for it. Instead of her friend's yellow trainer, in the distance Annie saw moving specks — specks that caught the rays of the rising sun.

A flock of birds? Too big. Airplanes? Maybe she and Cornelia weren't the only ones flying this morning. She squinted through the windshield. The specks — yes, airplanes — were coming toward her, closing on her. And now she could see a formation of dozens, maybe hundreds of planes. They resembled a swarm of angry bees. Seconds later, the lead aircraft banked right and turned south and she caught sight of a red ball on the wing. The other airplanes followed the leader. All but one.

The last plane peeled off and flew toward her. With the sun behind her and shining right into the other pilot's eyes, maybe he couldn't see her. Nevertheless, they were on a collision course with Annie's much smaller, slower aircraft the vulnerable one.

Alarm bells were going off in Annie's brain. Red ball. The Rising Sun? Japanese? Impossible. But that sleek silver airplane was closing on her fast.

"Let's get outta here." She yanked the controls from her student and shoved the throttle in full. Her stomach did a rollercoaster flutter as she put the airplane in a sudden dive, mindful that she didn't have a lot of altitude to lose in these hills. But Annie knew she had to do something to evade the silver menace that came straight at her.

She heard what sounded like machine-gun fire and bullets whining overhead. Keep the nose down, she thought. She swung first left and then right, hoping to spoil his aim.

"Where is he?" she yelled. "For god sake, find him. Tell me where he is." She knew any minute a burst of those bullets could rip through the fabric of the little Cub and tear them to shreds.

"H-h-h-he's gone, Miss Gwynn," Tom Witten stuttered.

"What?"

"Flew over us, turned, followed the others — straight south," he yelled over the engine roar.

She turned in her seat and saw him pointing back toward Pearl. She eased back on the stick and banked right, beginning a gradual climb to regain her lost altitude.

They saw the smoke from the direction of the harbor — columns of it rising from behind the hills, fouling the bright blue morning sky with a dirty pall that threatened to obliterate the few fleecy clouds that floated high over paradise.

Now what? The airport lay right next to the harbor.

Tom tapped her shoulder, his mouth next to her ear so she could hear him. "Who were they, Miss Gwynn? Why d'ya suppose he shot at us?"

"Japanese. Trying to kill us. Damn near succeeded."

Where the hell was Cornelia? Annie hadn't seen her friend's plane since before she spotted the Japanese formation. Again, she scanned the sky for the other yellow airplane. The blue expanse above and around her appeared as empty of airplanes now as it had been full just moments ago.

Hopefully, Cornelia had landed safely. Besides, Annie had other worries right now. She had an airplane and a student she needed to get home safely. If that fighter came back looking for her, he might bring a couple of his buddies along. A 50-horsepower Cub against high-speed Japanese warplanes? No thank you! She didn't like those odds one bit. That he had missed her the first time and not stayed around for the kill constituted a major miracle. He wouldn't miss a second time.

Maybe she should fly to the other side of the island. But land where? Eventually, she would run out of fuel. No, she had to get back to Rodgers.

Blood still pounding in her ears, Annie realized she and her student had barely escaped that encounter with their lives. But hot on the heels of the fear, yet another emotion welled inside her, vaguely familiar, and yet far more intense than she had ever felt before.

Big and awkward as a child, she had discovered acting the part of daredevil blunted the teasing inflicted by the other children. At age eight, she rode her bike at breakneck speed off a crudely constructed ramp and jumped Overall Creek. The split second she hung suspended over the water electrified her inner core. "I'm flying," raced through her mind.

She crashed in a heap on the far side, but outdistanced even the most athletic boy in the forbidden competition. A broken collarbone was followed by a scolding from her mother, but a new respect from the boys and girls she played with was her greatest reward. Deep within came the realization that, finally, here was something she could be good at.

When the government-subsidized Civilian Pilot Training Program opened to college women in 1939, nineteen-year-old Annie was a junior at the University of Tennessee. She signed up immediately — the first girl admitted to the program that allowed one woman for every nine men enrolled in a class. The first time the high-winged trainer lifted off the ground with her in the back seat of the tandem cockpit, Annie knew she had forever left behind life as she knew it.

The instructor let her fly straight and level and then handle the stick and rudders for two sweeping 180-degree turns, one in each direction. Though danger was distinctly absent from that tame, twenty-minute introductory flight, Annie felt thrust into a new dimension. She was one with the airplane, the sky, the universe. Time stood still — ceased to exist. And now she would do anything to capture that rush that waited for the moment the wheels left the ground and the little airplane surged upward, no longer connected to the earth, held back by such puny notions as human frailties, family allegiances, or worldly pursuits like school and job.

That an error in judgment could send her hurtling earthward never occurred to her. That engine failure or myriad other mechanical problems inherent in flying above the earth could send her into an uncontrollable flat spin — the death spin to inevitable oblivion — was worth the risk. Flying meant living on the edge. And Annie liked living on the edge, something hard to come by in her sheltered, Southern middle-class life.

Now, there she was in the skies over Oahu, having come face-to-face with the knowledge that danger made her feel very much alive. No matter how bad the situation might be, she had to see, wanted to see, what was happening beyond those mountains, back at Pearl.

"We're going home," she shouted over her shoulder to Tom, pleased at the measured composure she heard in her voice. Already the rapid heartbeat had slowed, her breathing returned to normal, the electric charge of danger replaced by an almost eerie calm. She checked the altimeter and her airspeed and shoved the throttle to the firewall. "Keep your eyes open for planes — any planes. Tell me the minute you see one."

Annie flew lower than usual, dropping down just above the treetops as she made her way between two hills. As they came through the gap, she saw flames towering higher than a multi-storied building and leaping from listing ships in the middle of the harbor. Smoke billowed wherever she looked. Plumes of water from fire hoses shot skyward then fell as millions of droplets that turned to steam when they contacted the molten metal of the burning ships that lay dying amidst what had been the United States' Pacific fleet.

Pearl Harbor spread out in front of her now and the water itself appeared to be on fire. Japanese planes zoomed back and forth, diving, climbing, turning, shooting at everything that moved — planes, boats, trucks, cars, bicycles, people.

Please don't let them come after me, Annie thought, as she came out in the open — once more a target. I'm small potatoes compared to those battleships and destroyers. A stab of guilt caught in her stomach. She knew some of the officers on those embattled ships.

With the northeast-to-southwest runway in her sights, she dropped even lower and swung in an arc, keeping the airplane below the horizon. The rounded line drawn by the crests of the hills would make her bright yellow aircraft easy to spot on such a sunlit morning. She said a silent prayer as she throttled back and prepared to land.

No landing pattern for her this time. She'd be a sitting duck for some trigger-happy Jap pilot who might decide a pretty Cub would be an extra trophy to brag about. She set up a straight-in approach, totally disregarding wind direction, and aimed the little airplane straight at the runway. Staying only high enough to clear a couple of outbuildings and the vegetation that lay at the near end of the runway, Annie chopped the throttle, pulled back on the stick, executed a flawless flare, and stuck the wheels solidly onto the gravel of the runway.

"Greased it," she shouted, triumphant in her power of concentration. Not touching the brakes, she taxied the plane full speed along the runway toward the hangars in the distance. Then she felt a shadow cross over her like a vulture looking for its dinner. She saw the silver and black gas-powered, prop-driven bird streak ahead. Almost in slow motion, the climbing fighter wheeled 180 degrees and started back toward her, flying low. Now Annie hit the brakes, swerving for the side of the runway where high grass and a stand of palm trees grew. The little Cub slowed and stopped.

"Run for it."

"I see him," Tom shouted as they scrambled from the plane and dove for the high grass at the side of the runway.

Bullets beat a tattoo sending gravel flying and ripping the fabric airplane to shreds in a split second. The Jap plane flew off down the end of the runway, banked and began to turn again.

"He's coming back," Annie yelled, oblivious to the sharp-bladed grass lacerating the side of her cheek where she lay. She got up and started running for the cover of palm trees twenty feet away, Tom Witten following, breathing hard behind her. She reached the cover of the palms just as the plane came at them again — so close that she saw the goggles and leather helmet and, she swore, a grin on the pilot's face. She tripped and heard bullets thudding into the ground behind her as she fell forward, striking her head into the trunk of a palm. She laid there, stunned, her head bleeding and throbbing, her eyes pulsing with blood-red cobwebs.

The inferno that was now Pearl Harbor still roared in her ears, but close around her there was not a sound. No airplane. No buzz of a homicidal Zero searched her out. She shook her head and the cobwebs receded. She was face down under the stand of palm trees, her body encased in flight coveralls and bathed in sweat... but she felt cold.

"We made it," she said, finally getting some semblance of control over her trembling body. "We made it!"

She pushed herself upright with hands and arms that didn't feel like hers and twisted around into a sitting position where she could see back to the runway, the ruined airplane, and the firestorm that engulfed what had been a beautiful harbor. Tom Witten lay face down just beyond the circle of sheltering palms. The back of his white T-shirt oozed pools of red.

Annie stared as comprehension seeped into her brain and an overwhelming sadness crept into her heart. She dropped her head back to her knees, let out a shudder and then a sob, and began to rock back and forth, her body racked with uncontrollable spasms.

# CHAPTER TWO

Clare Varsky sat in the co-pilot's seat on the right side of the cockpit and watched as her friend Nancy Love throttled back and eased the twin-engine Lockheed Hudson bomber into the downwind leg, paralleling the runway on which they were about to land. S.O.P., Clare thought, standard operating procedure on an approach to a strange airport. But she noted Nancy's knuckles were taut as she lowered the flaps, no doubt remembering their hurried instructions back in Boston that morning.

Moments later, turning to base leg, Nancy kept the ball centered in the glass tube of the turn indicator and negotiated the 90-degree turn. Then, with the near end of the runway coming up off her left shoulder, she made her second 90-degree turn, placing the big bomber on final approach. She lined up the nose with the runway, headed in and, moments later, set the airplane down as if she had been landing twin-engine bombers all her life.

Damn, Clare thought, Nancy always makes everything she does look so damn easy. She had only checked out in the bomber that morning, now here she had completed her first flight in it with a flawless landing.

Nancy taxied the plane to the spot near a fuel truck where a crewman in flight coveralls and a bulky jacket signaled her to stop. Two men in flight gear stood near him. Clare helped Nancy shut down, as per their checklist, and then they waited while the two replacement pilots climbed aboard. They handed over their clipboards, gave up their seats to the men who wore the uniform of the Royal Canadian Air Force, and disembarked through the same hatch the men had used to enter the airplane. Clare checked her watch. Just past two in the afternoon. The 450-mile flight from Boston to the small airfield outside Halifax, Nova Scotia, had taken just under three hours.

The women stood on the tarmac and watched as the co-pilot climbed back down and performed a quick pre-flight of the bomber's surfaces while the gas jockey topped off the fuel tanks. A few minutes later, having deemed the airplane still airworthy, the co-pilot climbed back in and the two men taxied the plane to the end of the runway and took off. The December sun, well past its zenith and heading for the horizon, resembled a silver disk behind layers of overcast clouds so thick the heavens looked like a roiling chowder. Not unlike the clouds Clare knew so well that brought blizzard conditions to the mountains surrounding Florissant on the backside of Pikes Peak.

"Unless we want to spend the night in this god-forsaken place, we'd better get to Operations and arrange for transportation home," Nancy said.

"Gawd, it's cold here." Clare hunched her shoulders and turned up the collar of her leather flight jacket to keep out the biting northeast wind. She fell into step with Nancy down the long taxiway to the Operations office adjacent to the hangar.

Clare pushed open the door and held it for her friend. A hush settled over the dimly lit interior and all eyes focused on them as they entered a space not much bigger than the miners' shacks Clare was used to in the Colorado Rockies. One man stood behind the counter; two others sat with their feet propped on the lone desk. Ground crew on break, they wore the uniform of the job — oil-stained coveralls, fleece-lined jackets, and caps with the earflaps pushed up and out of the way for indoors — and all three seemed to be drinking coffee from thick brown earthenware mugs. Clare followed Nancy to the counter, curious to see what kind of reception they got.

Two men were scheduled to bring the bomber to Halifax, but both the pilot and co-pilot had come down with food poisoning. Robert Love's Boston-based flight service had received an urgent call the night before, and he had come through with two veteran pilots to ferry the airplane on to Halifax — his wife, Nancy, and their weekend houseguest, Clare Varsky.

The men at Halifax knew, before they landed, that the incoming pilots were women. They had heard the voices on the radio. With the plane's arrival imminent and two RCAF pilots hanging around waiting for it, the fact that two women flew it in still caused a stir.

The men gaped now at Nancy. She was, Clare was sure, the classiest lady this crew had seen in a long time in spite of her flight coveralls and windblown hair. Young — twenty-seven, same as Clare — and pretty, would she get deferential treatment or would the men be rude or, worse, crude? You never knew how men would react to a female pilot — hell, to a female in general, Clare thought. She had surprised a lot of Fixed Base Operators at airfields in her day, and she knew how to talk to them and get what she wanted. So did Nancy.

"I am Mrs. Love," she said, in her low, carefully modulated, Vassar-tinged voice. "I'm closing my flight plan. The RCAF has possession of the airplane. My co-pilot and I will need transportation back to the closest bus or train station or, if you have an airplane going back to Boston, we need to secure seats on that." She handed him the travel voucher signed Bob Love, Boston Inter City Airways.

Clare smiled to herself. Nancy had the man eating out of her hand. He picked up the phone and called a taxi for them.

"It'll be awhile," he said, apologetically. "Only one cabby works on Sundays."

Both women poured cups of coffee from the half-full pot on a hot plate and sat down at a pockmarked wooden utility table. "Too bad they wouldn't let us fly it on to Gander," Clare said.

"Fly the plane to Halifax and turn it over to the Canadians. Those were our orders," Nancy said. "Something like when Bob and I ferried those Stinson 105s to Canada, June a year ago. We had to push them across the border in Maine and then fly them on to Halifax. Of course, I never flew anything as big as that bomber before."

"A real coup for us," Clare said, "adding an A-28 to our log books. I'll bet we're the only two women in the country who've flown one."

Nancy took a swallow of the coffee. "Nope. Jackie Cochran did it last summer."

"Gawd, I'd forgotten about that. Where'd she go? Over the pond to England, right?"

Nancy nodded, "Bob figured it to be a publicity stunt. She checked out on the multi-engine equipment, but they wouldn't allow her to handle the airplane alone. Rumor is, she didn't have the strength to operate the braking system. So a male pilot did the takeoff and landing and set the course. She handled the controls while they crossed the Atlantic."

"Wouldn't she just have a fit if she knew what we just did today? Of course, we didn't fly it over the big pond. And this thing is so hush-hush, nobody but us will ever know we did it anyway."

"Nothing wrong with that, Clare. Doing the job right is what's important, not getting publicity for it."

"I don't know… Cochran sure takes things into her own hands. Now I hear she's going to recruit women to go to England and fly for the Air Transport Authority."

"Well, British women pilots are already ferrying airplanes in England for the ATA. A woman by the name of Pauline Gower is heading it up."

Clare looked hard at her friend. "Whatever happened to your plan to organize a group of women to ferry airplanes for our Army?"

Before Nancy could answer, the door to the Operations hut blew open, allowing a gust of Arctic wind to stir the dust on the floor and rattle the papers on the desk. A crewman strode in, pushing the door shut behind him with his booted foot, extinguishing the shaft of twilight that had crept momentarily into the dusky room. "Turn on the radio!" he shouted.

One of the men reached over to a small black box sitting on the desk and flipped the knob. A lot of static and a droning voice filled the room as the men moved in closer and clustered around the desk, listening.

"Sonofabitch!" one exclaimed.

"Those bastards," shouted another.

"Hey, guys, what's going on?" Clare called out.

"Quiet!" One of them waved his hand at her.

The women watched as the four men bent over the black box, listening. Then one of them detached himself, strolled over to their table, pulled a chair out, and sat down straddling it, leaning his elbows on the back. "You ladies 're Yanks, ain't cha? Just brought in that A-28?"

"That's right." Nancy gave the man her sweetest, most genuine smile.

He cocked his head toward the men and the radio. "The Japs attacked a bunch of your ships at some place called Pearl Harbor, over in Hi-wa-yah."

Nancy and Clare stared at him.

"What?" Clare finally managed to say.

"So it's begun," Nancy whispered.

"Yeah, less than an hour ago, according to the guy on the radio. Japs came in right after dawn. Lotsa airplanes. Bombers 'n' fighters. The guy on the radio is callin' it a sneak attack."

"How much damage?" Nancy asked.

"Don't know. They ain't sayin'."

"It's war. I've got to call Bob." Nancy pushed her chair back and headed for the pay phone on the wall.

Clare had a sudden, jealous, gut-wrenching need to talk to Will. The shooting war had just widened to include the U.S. and Will would be down knocking on the door at the enlistment office when it opened tomorrow morning. How could he possibly have come to mean so much to her in such a short time?

She remembered when she first laid eyes on him just over a year ago. A year and what seemed to her a lifetime ago. So young and cocky, so full of himself. No taller than her own five-foot-six, he wore cowboy boots to add height. Clare knew aviation drew short men — maybe because they fit more readily into cramped cockpits; maybe because they, more so than the tall guys, thought they had something to prove. And this young pup had proving something written all over him.

"I'm here to take flying lessons from that world-famous girl stunt flyer Clare Varsky. I do believe I may have just made her acquaintance."

The brass of the kid, she thought. "I'm Clare Varsky. Who might you be?"

"William Page Webb, ma'am, but I prefer Will. And I am most gratified to meet you." He grabbed her right hand and shook it, holding it a fraction of a second longer than necessary.

Now she had him pegged. She knew what he was after, and it wasn't flying lessons. She extracted her hand and growled, "Yeah? Why?" He was kinda cute.

"Because I've heard about you from everybody who's anybody in the flying world east of the Front Range. They say you're the best dang instructor around and I want to take from the best."

"How old are you?"

"Twenty." A grin, accented by a deep dimple on the left side of his mouth, split his fresh, not-quite-handsome face. Far too young to be flirting with a woman six years older, she thought.

"How old are you?" he asked.

"That's none of your business, hot shot."

"Miss Varsky, you are every bit what I've been told you are. Now…" He reached in his back pocket and pulled out his wallet. "I've got a brand new, crisp one-hundred-dollar bill right here and I want as many flying lessons with you as it will buy."

Even though it was 1940 and the worst of the Depression had begun to fade from people's minds in the face of Roosevelt's New Deal and increased prosperity, the attitudes of people like Clare, who had lived through it, hadn't diminished all that much.

"Whadya do? Rob a bank?"

"No, ma'am. My gran'pappy died and left it to me. I told the bank to give it to me in cash. One century note."

"That's crazy." She stared at the bill in the young man's hand like it represented money from the devil himself.

"Not really. Before he died, the old man told me what all he'd done in his life and made me promise to do something I really wanted to do with my own life. 'You're only young once, Will,' he said. 'Lots a' time to make a buck and be responsible.' So, here I am, Miss Varsky. I want to learn to fly. With you."

Clare found herself speechless — a rarity — but she recovered quickly. "A hundred dollars will buy you a hefty amount of flyin', son. Let's get down to business."

Will Webb stepped forward and laid his hand gently on her arm. "Miss Varsky, I'm not your son by a long shot, so don't talk down to me, okay?"

His mild gray eyes, serious and not the least bit mocking, stirred something inside her. He immediately dropped his hand from her arm but his eyes never left hers, and he remained very near, his presence filling the small space between them.

Clare Varsky didn't back down from anybody, certainly not this fresh kid. He made her uncomfortable, but it was a pleasant discomfort, she had to admit. She knew already that she liked him.

"Like I said, let's get down to business." She raised her chin and gave him back an equally steady look. She had a momentary flight of fancy that he was about to lean over and kiss her and that silken twinge deep inside caught her by surprise at the thought.

Nah, she reasoned. I'm an old woman to him. My imagination.

The crewman who sat across the table from her seemed to be waiting for her to speak. Clare wrenched her mind back to the present and said, "So, I guess we're in the war now, too."

"Yup. Sure sounds like it."

Nancy returned to the table. "Bob says all hell has broken loose in Washington. He's been called down there. He's in the Reserves, you know, and they've already put him on active duty. We've got to get back to Boston. Where is that taxi?"

On the long train ride back, neither the darkness nor the monotonous clacking of the coach car's wheels on the iron rails could lull them to sleep. Clare heard Nancy's voice from the seat beside her.

"Clare?"

"Yeah."

"Back there, you asked me about my idea to use women pilots to ferry airplanes."

"Yeah. I remember you were really high on that. What happened?"

"Back in May of last year, even before I flew that Stinson to Canada, I wrote to Colonel Olds —head of Air Corps Plans Division.

I told him I knew of forty-nine women pilots capable of handling pretty complicated stuff. Told him most of them had several hundred hours, two-hundred horsepower ratings, and enough cross-country experience so that they could ferry anything the Army needs moved."

Clare felt a stab of interest. Surely her name had made the list. "What happened?"

"He promised to take the idea to his boss, General Hap Arnold. I waited and waited to hear from him. Nothing. I wrote again and offered to come to Washington and talk to them, personally. Then finally, oh, it must have been three or four months later, Olds wrote that Arnold had rejected the idea. But he told me he'd keep the suggestion on file."

"And that was the end of it?"

"Yes." She paused. "Until now…"

Something in Nancy's tone caused Clare to sit up, shift in her seat, and turn to look at her friend. Nancy stared straight ahead, as if trying to see into a not-too-distant future.

"What do you mean?"

"I've been thinking. About us delivering that bomber today. We did it in a pinch, when they couldn't find anyone else. Did the job without a lot of fanfare. Quickly and efficiently. Right?"

"Yes."

"Colonel Olds told me that Hap Arnold turned down my suggestion because the United States Army had sufficient manpower to supply its flying needs. I took that to mean the Army didn't want to bother with women pilots. That may have been true last year, but not any more. Heck, with all these supposedly available pilots, civilian and military…on a weekend… they couldn't come up with anybody but us to fly an airplane four hundred and fifty miles."

Clare caught her breath and let it out slowly. "I think I see where you're going with this."

"They need us, Clare."

Clare nodded. "They just don't realize it yet."

"Right. As of today, the U.S. is in this war. The Army is going to need every available pilot it can get — male or female. And I'm going to help them see beyond the noses on their faces. I'm going to convince them that there's a willing group of pilots out there who want to fly for their country. They just happen to be female." She beamed a smile and nodded. "You and I are going to war, Clare."

# CHAPTER THREE

Midge Culpepper awoke to the ringing of the telephone. She rolled over and extracted herself from beneath the heavy-armed embrace of the sleeping man next to her, sat up and reached for the receiver.

"Hello, this is Midge Culpepper," she said in her most clipped, professional voice, the one Jacqueline Cochran had taught her to use whether the call was business or personal.

"Midge?" The voice at the other end of the line had the usual imperious tone. "Do you have your radio on, Midge? Have you heard the news?"

Midge pulled the sheet up to cover her bare breasts and mentally shook both sleep and sex from her eyes. "What news, Miss Cochran?"

"The Japs have bombed Pearl Harbor!"

"The... the," Midge stuttered and turned, trying to collect her thoughts. Captain Barry Metzger's brown eyes were open and staring at her. "The Japs have bombed Pearl Harbor," she repeated aloud for his benefit. "No, I hadn't heard." She watched Barry's eyes widen.

"It's two o'clock in the afternoon, girl." In her excitement, Jacqueline Cochran occasionally slipped back to her native Southern drawl. "Aren't you up yet?"

"No, I mean, yes Miss Cochran, I'm up, I just don't have the radio on." Barry rolled over, his back to her, put his bare feet to the floor, and stood up.

"Well, now you've heard it from me. We're at war, or will be once Franklin gets to those damned isolationists in Congress. He's been trying to warn them," the woman snapped. "That's why I'm calling you. We have a lot of work to do. And we must be quick about it. Meet me at the office in an hour."

Midge looked at the figure of Captain Barry Metzger, now standing in the bathroom doorway, tall, sinewy, naked. The black hair on his chest and abdomen was curly and matted down — silent testimony to their earlier lovemaking. Afterward, they had both fallen into a deep, exhausted sleep only to be awakened by the ringing telephone. He closed the door and a moment later she heard the shower running.

"In an hour? But, I have company." She couldn't let her boss know she had a man in her apartment, particularly one known to Jacqueline Cochran — cosmetics queen and friend of the rich, famous and powerful, including General "Hap" Arnold, Barry's boss. "I'll have to get rid of them." She emphasized the lie — them. "I'll be there as soon as I can. A little over an hour." Barry opened the bathroom door, toweling beads of water from his chest. "Dragon lady?"

"Don't call her that, Barry. Someday you might say it when someone else could hear you. Miss Cochran's all right. She's just," Midge paused, "very determined. She's going to be the commander of an all-women's air force or die trying."

"Shit! And she wants you to come in to work, now? It's Sunday, for God's sake!"

"Yes, and I told her I'd be there. You heard what she told me. Pearl Harbor's been bombed. We'd better turn on the radio."

CBS News confirmed what Cochran had just told Midge. The announcer went on to inform servicemen that all leaves had been cancelled and that they were to return to base immediately. Barry tried to call his commanding officer in Washington D.C., but the phone lines were jammed. Now he stood at her dresser, looking in the mirror. He set his cap on his head and straightened his tie.

"When will I see you again?" she asked.

His hand was on the front doorknob and he looked impatient. To get away from her or to go to war? She wasn't sure.

"I don't know. This changes everything."

"You said you were about to get orders to go to California."

"We'll cross that bridge when we have to. You could go with me, you know."

"That would be cozy. Me and your wife."

"Connie won't go to the West Coast with me. She can't be that far away from her mama. As usual, she'll find every excuse. Besides, you're the one I want with me."

God, the man knew how to get to her. "I can't leave Miss Cochran, Barry. You know that. She handpicked me for this job. She could have taken any secretarial school graduate in New York, but she picked *me*, a hairdresser off the line at Antoine's, to be her administrative assistant. And now she's taught me how to fly so I can be her co-pilot on cross-country trips. She's paid for all that. I can't leave her in the lurch."

"Somehow I don't think you'll be making so many cross-country trips for Jacqueline Cochran Cosmetics now. War will put a crimp in civilian flying. Fuel will be hard to come by because the military will take it all." He paused, "Well…I've got to get out of here or I won't make the last train back to Washington."

"Look both ways before you go out in the hallway, then take the stairs just in case someone is in the elevator. I don't want anyone to know what floor you were on or whose apartment you were in."

"You worry too much."

"No, you don't worry enough. I have a reputation and you have a wife. Now, go, Barry. We both have jobs to do."

An hour later, Midge let herself into the Manhattan office of Jacqueline Cochran Cosmetics. Miss Cochran sat behind her ebony desk, tapping her fingernails — professionally manicured but short and blunt and sporting only clear polish — on the shiny black surface. Her large brown eyes bore into Midge like twin magnets. As she did every time she entered this office, Midge felt herself being drawn by those eyes into the circle of power that surrounded her boss and all she did. Cochran's honey blonde hair was drawn back in a full but neat chignon and she wore a tailored navy blue wool serge suit and high-necked, white silk blouse. Ready for a day of business at four o'clock on a Sunday afternoon.

"You're late." The tone was accusatory, impatient.

"Yes, ma'am, I'm sorry. I had to see my company off and they didn't go right away," Midge said, taking off her coat.

"Someone from your family in town, Midge?"

"No, Miss Cochran, just a couple of friends."

Cochran eyed her. "You weren't entertaining a young man, were you, Midge?"

Midge's hand flew to her carefully repinned hair. Barry took such pleasure in removing the pins, letting her long brown curls fall free so he could run his fingers through it.

"You must be careful, my dear. I warned you when you wanted to get involved with that two-bit hairdresser at Antoine's, a woman's reputation is all she's got. Once lost, it cannot be retrieved. No man is worth the price of the loss because you will lose him in the process and then no self-respecting gentleman will ever look at you again — other than as a plaything to be discarded at whim. Mark my words, Midge. Listen to what I'm telling you."

Midge squirmed inwardly. "Where do you want to start, Miss Cochran?"

"It's a new game, Midge." Cochran waved her hand expansively in the air. Midge knew those hands. She had seen them handle the controls of her elegant Beech Staggerwing and knew that she had flown the swift P-35 to victory for the Bendix trophy.

"As of today, and thanks to the Japanese, there are new rules for everybody to play by. And, by God, we are going to make some of those rules ourselves. Remember my idea for using women pilots? We need to draft a letter to Bob Olds. It must be on his desk no later than Tuesday morning."

The previous summer, Midge had overseen seven employees from Jacqueline Cochran Cosmetics, handpicked by her boss to go through the records of the Civil Aeronautics Administration to determine how many licensed women pilots there were in the United States. Jackie had just had lunch at the White House and boasted to President and Mrs. Roosevelt that there were 1,500 to 2,000 women that she could put at the Army's disposal for a variety of pilot duties in order to release men for combat duty, should America get into the war. War was a certainty! Only a matter of time, her boss insisted.

Midge and her staff actually found 3,000 women licensed to fly, but only 131 of them had the minimum requirement for a commercial license, which was more than 200 solo hours. And of those 131, only about fifty were between the ages of twenty-one and thirty-five and could also meet the 200-horsepower rating requirement.

"We'll just have to train the rest of them," Cochran had announced to Midge.

Ultimately, General Arnold had turned down her plan. But the Japanese attack had catapulted the U.S. into war and changed everything. Jackie Cochran, Midge knew, was an opportunist of the highest order.

"We're at war now, Midge, and I'm going to get my women's flying corps and the school to train them. And you'll be one of the first graduates."

"Me, Miss Cochran, what about you and our work here?"

"This war is going to take all of our time and energy for the next few years. The cosmetics business will almost run itself. I've got bigger plans. I'm going for a commission in the Army. The Army will be taking men with business and management experience and giving them commissions. Why not a woman? Yes, General Arnold will see it my way. Colonel Cochran, Director of Women Pilots, U.S. Army Air Corps. How does that sound?"

Midge thought that even for someone with an ego as insatiable as she knew her boss's to be, what she had just heard sounded audacious, if not ridiculous. But she had worked for Jacqueline Cochran for a year and a half and knew how the woman's mind worked. She also knew her boss nearly always got her way.

"Wonderful, Miss Cochran! But why do you want me to go to this flight school? I already know how to fly."

"You're going to have to learn to fly the Army way. So will all those young women with fifty to a hundred hours who qualify for my program. And it will be tough. They'll have to pass my requirements first, before they even get to the army's."

Jackie's brown eyes sparkled with excitement and then took on a dreamy quality. "They will be the most deserving, hard-working girls in America — the cream of the crop. Any girl with a private pilot's license can apply and have a chance to be accepted, but I will take only the best! And they will be officers — officers in the Air Corps Specialist Reserve, from second lieutenant to captain, with all the privileges of that rank and station."

She stopped. "But first we've got to get this letter drafted. Start typing, Midge. Oh, and by the way, we've got to move immediately to get experienced women pilots to England. I promised Lord Beaverbrook we'd help out their Air Transport Auxiliary. We'll go for the oldest of the group for that assignment. It will take more mature girls to go overseas."

A few weeks later, on January 8, Midge was just getting ready to leave for lunch when the inner office phone rang. "Get in here, now!" Cochran's voice startled her with an intensity greater than usual.

Midge entered to find the usually self-contained Miss Cochran striding around her office, waving a cigarette in one hand and a letter that Midge had delivered to her less than ten minutes earlier in the other.

"You won't believe what that idiot has done! He's suddenly decided to go ahead with a plan to use only a few women, twenty-five to fifty, and as civilians, in the Ferry Command! Not MY plan. No! Nothing about my flight school where thousands of young women can learn to fly and be of service to their country. Nothing about militarization and commissions. Nothing about order and rank and supervision. Civilians! And a salary of three hundred dollars a month — equal to the men."

"Who, Miss Cochran," Midge ventured, "who says they're going to do this?"

"Olds, that's who! He completely ignored my letter last month and came up with this cock-and-bull plan instead. And you know what's worse? This is coming *now*, just as I'm getting ready to go to England. I need to take twenty-five of our best women flyers over there to work with the ATA, *now*. I can't afford to lose them to this civilian squadron. I promised Franklin. And Lord Beaverbrook is counting on me. I just got General Arnold's backing on the England project yesterday. *Yesterday!* Don't these men talk to each other? Don't they think? They certainly don't listen!" She stamped out her cigarette in a nearby ashtray.

"Why… these girls won't go to England now, not if they think they can fly in this country. Why risk going to where the war is only a narrow strip of water instead of an ocean away? And the living conditions in England! You wouldn't believe them, Midge, you just wouldn't believe what they have to do *without*."

Midge held her breath and waited, saying nothing. Her job was to listen, not comment.

"And nothing about me heading up this group. Apparently they don't think that's important. Well, they've got another thing coming. Sit down and take a letter to General Arnold himself. I'm not bothering with any junior officer."

And she began to dictate as fast as Midge could write.

> *General Olds has informed me that he is planning on hiring women pilots for his Ferrying Command almost at once. His plan, as outlined to me, is not only bad in my opinion from the organizational standpoint, and contrary to what you told me yesterday but is in direct conflict, in fact, with the plans of a women's unit for England. In addition, it would wash me out of the supervision of the women flyers here rather than the contrary as we contemplated.*
>
> *General Olds intends to hire the women without having any organization of them just as he would a male pilot in any particular unit. This will bring disrepute on the Services before very long and injure the interest of women flyers themselves. Here just as in England a woman in charge of women is essential. His plan should be put on ice for at least the next six months or my program in England should be stopped!*

"Now, Midge, type that up and I'll sign it. I want you on the next train for Washington where you will deliver it, in person, to General Arnold tomorrow morning."

In the outer office a few minutes later, having secured a seat on the afternoon train to Washington, Midge called Barry Metzger's office in the Pentagon. She hadn't seen or heard from him since the attack on Pearl Harbor.

Maybe we can spend a few hours together, she thought. I can talk Miss Cochran into letting me stay over tomorrow night, too.

"Yes… Captain Metzger, please."

The voice at the other end told her what she didn't want to hear. "*Major* Metzger has been assigned to the West Coast. May someone else help you?"

Midge thought fast. "This is a friend of Mrs. Metzger's. I tried to call her at home and got no answer. I thought he could tell me when I might reach her."

"Mrs. Metzger has gone to the coast with Major Metzger, ma'am. If you wait a moment, I'll give you her forwarding address."

Cold gripped Midge's stomach. "No, that won't be necessary. I hoped to invite her to lunch. Obviously, she won't be able to come." She hung up and gripped her desk with both hands until her knuckles turned white. Then she began to gather what she would need to make the trip to Washington. She wouldn't need that additional over night after all.

# CHAPTER FOUR

Nine months after Pearl Harbor took away her innocence, Annie Gwynn walked into Nancy Love's sparse outer office at New Castle Army Air Base, Wilmington, Delaware. The desk outside the door to an inner office was neat and orderly, with a half-drunk cup of coffee placed next to the telephone and an empty ashtray. The owner was nowhere to be seen.

A woman with abundant red curly hair, wearing slacks and a well-worn leather flight jacket, lounged in one of the two gray institutional chairs. She looked up from the letter she was reading, glanced at Annie with a look of open appraisal in her large brown eyes, then returned to her reading.

Annie's suitcase thumped softly on the linoleum floor as she took the chair opposite the red-haired woman. Moments later, a plump young woman emerged from the inner office.

"I thought someone else came in. I'm Miss Colsen, Mrs. Love's secretary. And you are…?"

Annie rose. "I'm Anne Gwynn. Cornelia Fort told Mrs. Love about me. I have her telegram here." Annie fumbled in her purse trying to find the yellow paper bearing Nancy Love's name that had arrived at her home in Nashville three days earlier. Out of the corner of her eye, she saw the other woman glance up at her at the mention of Cornelia's name.

"Yes, Miss Gwynn, welcome to New Castle. Mrs. Love is expecting you today. I'll tell her you're here." She turned to the other woman. "Miss Varsky, she knows you're waiting. I expect she'll be out in just a minute." And with that, the young secretary quickly disappeared behind the door. Annie returned to her chair.

"You're a friend of Cornelia's?" The woman hit the "r" in Cornelia's name, whereas Annie — and Cornelia herself — pronounced it with only a bare inflection, so that her name sounded like "Cawnelia." Both she and Cornelia had taken a lot of teasing about their Southern accents in Honolulu.

"Yes, we used to fly out of the same airport in Nashville."

"I'm Clare Varsky. You were flying that day, right? She told us all about it."

Annie nodded. "They closed the fields to civilian instruction immediately afterwards. Cornelia and I were out of a job. Then it took several weeks to get transport back to the mainland. And it took me awhile to find a job, but I've been teaching future fighter and bomber pilots how to handle a J-three Cub." She paused. "Well, that's what I was doing until I got a letter from Cornelia... followed by Mrs. Love's telegram."

The shared experience of December 7, 1941, had kept Annie and Cornelia close during their remaining days in Honolulu. Cornelia was the one who wrapped her long arms around the sobbing Annie — held her, talked to her, rocked her — when, after the attack was over, the field personnel at John Rodgers Airport began searching for their own missing, dead and wounded.

They had found Annie after somebody spotted the ruined Cub on the runway. Alone and forlorn, she sat beside young Tom Witten's lifeless body, staring, Annie remembered, into nothingness. Her life had turned to nothingness right in front of her eyes. She still couldn't shake the feeling.

The waste of a young man's life weighed heavily on her, though, God knew, nobody twisted his arm to sign up for those flying lessons and get in her airplane that morning. Sitting there under the palm trees that had sheltered her, she thought fleetingly of the grandmother, somewhere on the island, who soon would learn that her loving generosity had been repaid, courtesy of the Japanese, with the death of her grandson.

"It's not fair!" Annie kept repeating to herself, as Cornelia soothed her and coaxed her away from the lifeless form now covered by a Red Cross blanket. And she had repeated it many times since — when the nightmares awakened her, drenched in sweat and trembling, and when her days weren't busy enough to prevent her from thinking too much, and remembering.

When they finally got her into the Jeep that December morning, Annie stammered and tried to tell them what had happened in the air and what she saw when she came out of the hills beyond the airport and landed, only to be chased from the Cub by the Zero.

"I made the fastest landing I've ever made in my life," Cornelia drawled. "Some of the others apparently weren't so lucky. We've still got two instructors missing. And Bob Tyce was killed when they strafed the hangar."

"The airport manager? Oh, Cornelia!"

The bodies of the missing instructors and their students washed ashore several days later on the leeward side of the island. And the fear of imminent invasion hung like a pall over the Islands. Cornelia and Annie began the tiresome process of finding passage home amidst frantic telegrams from their families back in Tennessee. They spent many an evening in a bar near the airport, in the company of the other out-of-work instructors, bemoaning their fate. One by one, the men enlisted in the Air Corps, anxious to use their hard-won flying skills and knowing that if they didn't, they'd be drafted into the walking army.

Cornelia and Annie had no such solace. Overnight, they had become expatriates — unwanted baggage, useless, and in the way. Annie learned to drink Cuba Libras during those dark weeks, courtesy of Cornelia, who claimed to have acquired a taste for them while attending Sarah Lawrence College in Bronxville, New York. "If you've got to drown your sorrows, might as well do it with something that tastes good."

But they couldn't forget. Nor could they truly ignore who they were and where they came from. "It's that damn Southern guilt our mammas laid on us, Annie," Cornelia would say, peering through the boozy atmosphere and the smoke from dozens of cigarettes. Neither could let herself drown the memory to the point of oblivion, so both churned increasingly under a worsening depression, exacerbated by the guilt of trying.

"I knew someday flying on Sunday would get me," Cornelia said. "My mother would never have consented to me flying on Sunday, so I kept it from her that Sunday *was* traditionally our busiest day at the airport. How could I tell a woman who doesn't understand women working for a living that my job required me to do just that? Well, she finally caught me breaking the Sabbath. Pearl Harbor — Sunday, December 7th — did it. Now she knows."

Annie and Cornelia considered joining the Red Cross and putting on a uniform in order to be part of the frenzied war fever that swept the Islands, but, as they admitted to each other in the dark, smoky confines of that bar, they still wanted to fly more than they wanted to conform to someone else's idea of patriotism. But for women pilots, right then, the outlook was dismal and they knew it. Bored, they took jobs with the Army in Honolulu taking workers' applications for jobs being supervised by the Army Engineers. And they waited for evacuation from the Islands.

When they finally did return to Nashville in early April, they found that friends and family were aghast that the girls were nearly shot down by the Japanese, yet no one truly understood the trauma or what the aftermath felt like. As local celebrities, they were asked to speak at War Bond rallies and at Civil Air Patrol meetings. The local newspapers interviewed them and wrote heroic stories about them. Cornelia, Annie noticed, was always gracious and accommodating and seemed to take it in stride, but then she had been to finishing school and raised to accept, without question, her public responsibilities.

Instant celebrity unsettled Annie. Her wallflower days in high school and college, and the feelings of inadequacy anywhere but in the cockpit of an airplane caused her to shrink from crowds. She froze in front of cameras and reporters with pencils and notebooks and barely endured the frenzied weeks after their return in a state of shock and despair. To her relief the fickle public eventually moved on to other heroes. In her own eyes, she wasn't a heroine, rather the instrument of death of another innocent human being.

Instead of remaining close because of the bond they'd forged, she and Cornelia drifted apart and saw little of each other once the initial crush of publicity was over. Cornelia's social calendar, further enhanced by her celebrity status, continued to pull her out into the public eye — a place Annie did not want to go. Then Cornelia, too, seemed to tire of the merry-go-round. She called Annie the middle of May to tell her that she had enrolled in a three-month aircraft instrument-training program in New York. Not long after that, Annie finally landed a job teaching primary training to Army cadets. Then on September 6, Cornelia called from New York to say she had just received a telegram from a woman pilot named Nancy Love asking her to join a group of women pilots being formed to do ferrying for the Army's Air Transport Command.

"I think I can get you in," Cornelia said when Annie admitted she hadn't received one. "I've looked at the requirements and you fulfill them all. You not only have a high school education, you're a college graduate. You're at least twenty-one and you certainly aren't anywhere near thirty-five. You have a commercial license and a two-hundred-horsepower rating. And you were getting close to five hundred hours the last time I talked to you."

"Yes, I've got more than five now," Annie said, thankful for the instructing job she had finally landed.

"How about cross country? You'll need recent cross-country experience."

"Yup, I did some this summer."

"Then you qualify. I'll speak to Nancy Love about you the minute I get to Wilmington." Confident Cornelia, raised with noblesse oblige, seemed to have little doubt that she, herself, would be selected, Annie noted.

A few days later, Annie received a letter from Cornelia about the great things Nancy Love, Colonel Robert Baker, and Colonel William H. Tunner were doing in the organization called the Ferrying Division of the Air Transport Command. Several women already had passed their flight tests and physicals, and more were due at New Castle momentarily. The squadron was to be twenty-five strong. She knew there was a spot for Annie. Watch for a telegram, she added.

Annie checked on train schedules to Wilmington, Delaware, and did a thorough washing and ironing of the clothing she might need to take. Concerned over what her boss at the airport might say if she departed with no notice, she sought him out and explained the situation. Inside, she churned over his potential ire but, worse, she worried how mortified she would be if she told him she hoped to be called and then the invitation never materialized.

"You do what you have to do, Annie," he said, and she read no rancor in his eyes.

When the telegram arrived, Annie was ready. The very next day, she took the train out of Nashville Union Station bound for Wilmington. Her mother cried, of course. Her father looked very proud, but a frown had deepened his brow — a frown almost non-existent before she left for Hawaii.

"I thought when you came home from Hawaii that you would stay," her mother said, her handkerchief held tightly to her lips. "You were almost killed. Please don't go, Annie."

"Mother, I'm not going anywhere near the fighting. All I'm going to do is ferry airplanes from one place to another right here in the States."

"Now, Mother, don't fret over the girl," her father said. "She's doing what she has to do. We're at war, and everybody has to do what they do best so that we can beat those devils in Europe and the Pacific. She'll be fine."

Annie realized that Clare Varsky was looking at her, waiting for her to finish. "Yes, I'm the one. Cornelia and I were together at Pearl Harbor."

With that, a woman who Annie knew immediately had to be Nancy Love, walked through the door. Though her face was young, a maverick streak of gray hair swept back from her right temple, in sharp contrast to the rest of her light brown hair.

"Clare, so good to see you. I knew you'd come." And they shook hands warmly.

They're old friends, Annie thought. Clare Varsky is a shoe-in, like Cornelia. But what are my chances?

When Nancy Love turned to her, Annie felt the power that radiated from those luminous eyes that were the grayish-green of a troubled sea. Nancy's gaze was one of cool appraisal, but Annie thought she detected interest behind it.

"Miss Gwynn." The elegant lady extended her hand. She was a good five inches shorter than Annie's five feet eleven, but Annie felt totally engulfed by the personality of the commander of the women's ferrying squadron. "I'm Nancy Love. Cornelia has told me so much about you."

Then she looked from Annie to Clare and back to Annie and made up her mind. "Tell you what. Do you have your log books, transcripts, recommendations?"

Annie nodded.

"Let me see them. Clare, wait just a minute, will you, sweetie? Then we'll talk." Nancy Love took the documents Annie handed her and disappeared back into her office. Clare and Annie looked at each other.

"How long have you known Mrs. Love?" Annie asked, hoping to overcome the lump that had lodged in her throat and the sudden realization that she wanted this more than anything she had ever imagined. She also knew she was up against women with far more flying experience than she had at this point in her career.

Clare told her how she and Nancy had met while working for the Airmarking Program for the Bureau of Air Commerce. In the fall of 1935, Nancy had been assigned to travel the northeastern section of the country trying to persuade mayors and city councilmen to paint the names of their towns on water towers as a navigation aid to airplanes. When she left at the end of 1935 to marry Bob Love, Clare was hired.

"If anybody'd told me, way back then, that I'd be consorting with the likes of a lady like Nancy Love, I'd have laughed myself silly," Clare said. "Just look at her. They coined the word *class* for her. But for some reason we clicked. She accepted the horse manure on my cowboy boots, my western ways and the fact that I didn't go to Vassar — hell, I didn't go to college, period. Barely made it out of high school. Me, I accepted that she was perfect and could do no wrong."

Five minutes later, Nancy was back. "Everything's in order Miss Gwynn. I've called for Lieutenant Tracy to get you set up for a flight test right away. He'll be here in ten minutes. Do you have slacks and low-heeled shoes with you?" She glanced at Annie's standard traveling outfit of tan jacket and skirt, white blouse, brown high heels and a tan felt hat perched on her brown hair.

"Yes, in my bag."

"You can change in the bathroom down the hall. Disregard that it says Men on it. Meet Lieutenant Tracy back here when you're ready. I'll talk to you after your flight test." Then she turned her magnificent eyes on Clare. "Clare, it's been *too long*. Come on in and tell me what you've been doing." And the two of them disappeared into the office.

Annie stared after them. They belonged to a sorority she wanted very badly to join. This was her ticket out of the inertia that had plagued her since Pearl Harbor. Her life could have meaning again.

As she went down the hall to change, she vowed her outfit wasn't all she was going to change. She was going to become one of them. Her upcoming flight test was just the beginning.

# CHAPTER FIVE

Settled behind the closed doors of her office, Nancy offered Clare a cigarette from a crumpled Chesterfield package and lit up then leaned back in her army-issue desk chair and took a long drag. Clare, seated in the straight-backed chair facing Nancy's desk, leaned forward expectantly.

"So, how did you finally swing it, Madam Director of Women Pilots?"

Nancy smiled slowly. "You mean the squadron?"

"Yeah. The last I heard, Bob Olds was ready to do this back in January and Cochran threw a monkey wrench. Then right after that, she started recruiting girls like mad to go to England and fly for the ATA. Come on now, Nancy, give — tell me what happened?"

"Well, of course, I was furious when I heard that Jackie had sabotaged what Olds and I were trying to do. She went straight to Hap Arnold and he nipped our plan in the bud. It wasn't her program so she was determined that no one else would get their ideas through either. Bob advised me to 'lay low' — as he put it — for a time and see what transpired. A few days later I saw an article in the paper saying that Cochran was recruiting women to fly for Great Britain and I put two and two together."

Clare nodded. "I admit, I thought about going when she contacted me early in February, but I had too good a job as a flight instructor by then."

"She did get her twenty-five, though they went to England in small groups, by convoy. Some awfully good pilots were in that group. Helen Richey for one."

"Yeah, I know some of them."

"But then things began to move here. Olds became ill and had to be replaced. General Arnold named General George head of the Ferrying Command, which almost immediately became the Air Transport Command. That's where Bob — my Bob — ended up, assigned to the ATC. He's a major now. After he was activated, you may recall, we closed the business in Boston and moved to Washington. After Pearl Harbor, all flying within fifty miles of the coast was restricted, so we had to close Inter City Airways."

"Sounds like a lot has happened since the last time I saw you two."

"That's not the half of it. Before he became ill, Bob Olds, who was a general by then, saw to it that I got a civilian administrative job with the Ferrying Command operations office near Baltimore. Guess he still had my best interests at heart. What with gas rationing, I ended up flying from Washington to Baltimore to get to work.

"Being at ATC headquarters put Bob close to Colonel Bill Tunner, who George appointed to head the domestic Ferrying Division. He's the one who had to go out last spring and find ferry pilots and he was desperate. You won't believe this, Clare, but one day Bill Tunner and Bob were talking — at the water cooler, no less — and Bob happened to mention that I commuted to work every day in my Fairchild 24. Tunner said 'Your wife flies?' So Bob said yes and told him how many hours I had. Then Tunner said, 'I'm looking for pilots. Are there any more like your wife around?' Bob told him to talk to me and he did."

"Gawd, what luck!"

"Well," Nancy waved her hand expansively, "this is the result. He gave me the job of writing the proposal and recruiting the women pilots. He got everything pushed through the various Army channels. And so here we are, the Women's Auxiliary Ferrying Squadron."

"Incredible. After all that work you put into two different proposals for Bob Olds, it happened almost by accident."

"Exactly! The final decision was to station us all here at New Castle under Colonel Robert Baker, as part of the 2nd Ferrying Group. It's close to the manufacturers of the primary trainers and liaison planes we're being hired to fly."

"Jackie's just back from England and hopping mad, I hear," Clare said. "You don't suppose she could still mess things up here, do you? Or get her expensively manicured hand on this throttle?"

Nancy sighed. "I don't have time to worry about that. I'm sure she'll use every tool at her disposal to worm her way in here. All I can do is trust that Baker, Tunner, George, and Arnold will remain firm."

"I think you're OK with the first three, but I don't know about Arnold. Word is he listens to her."

"I know, but I can't let it bother me. We've got too much work to do here." Nancy reached for the telephone. "Which reminds me, we need to get you a flight test straight away."

Clare held up her hand. "Answer me something first. What do you know about the new pursuit planes in the works — the fighters? Is it true one of them is based on that prototype P-35 Cochran won the Bendix in back in '38?"

Nancy glanced at the closed door, leaned forward over her desk and lowered her voice. "Yes, it's true. The P-47. And if we play our cards right, Clare, eventually we'll get our shot at flying all those hot numbers. But first, we've got to prove ourselves." Nancy leaned back and pulled on her cigarette, pursed her lips and blew a near-perfect ring into the air before letting the remainder of the smoke escape slowly through her nostrils.

"Most of these men are scared to death of us. They're afraid we'll prove to be capable of flying their big, powerful airplanes. But they need us right now and they know it. They've seen the numbers and ratings in our logbooks and they've seen us perform on the single-engine planes they expect us to fly. So, it's just a matter of time and waiting them out."

She ground out her cigarette. "Listen, Clare, they need to move three thousand airplanes a month. Eventually that will include twin-engine stuff and pursuit. They don't have nearly enough pilots to accomplish that. That's why they need the women. The really good, dedicated women pilots — you, Cornelia, Del Scharr, Teresa James, Helen Mary Clark, Betty Gillies."

"I hear Betty Gillies is your exec."

"Yes. First one here. She came immediately, bless her heart. Was I delighted to see her — and relieved when she promised to be my second-in-command. She's thirty-five, a little older than the rest of us, and certainly more settled, what with young children at home."

Clare wondered if she had gotten there sooner maybe she would have been Nancy's number two. "I hear Betty's mother-in-law is taking care of the kids?"

"Yes, Mother Gillies and Bud. He's a top executive with Grumman Aircraft. Betty says he'll spend the war right where he is."

"She's had a rough go, losing her youngest to leukemia," Clare said, remembering the news that had rocked the last meeting of the Ninety-Nines, the national association of women pilots.

"Well, personally, I think this is the break she needs to get herself together after that. Take her mind off it. Betty's a determined gal. She does what she puts her mind to. She adds the maturity we need when the younger, unmarried girls — like this Annie Gwynn — start showing up."

"For sure. Gawd, I remember when Betty fought the CAA over the regulation saying that a pregnant woman couldn't pilot an airplane. She lost that round, but she's right. If a woman can't fly while she's pregnant, she can't get in her required hours to keep her commercial license. Then she has to take the test all over again after the baby comes. That's not fair. And it's damned expensive."

Nancy's eyes took on a dreamy quality and she said, "You know… there's no telling what we, as women, can prove, starting with flying airplanes while this war is on. The barriers are there just waiting to be broken. But we must use this opportunity in the right way. We can't afford to lose our femininity while doing it."

Clare frowned. "We're damned if we do and damned if we don't, aren't we? We act too feminine — be women — we get accused of being soft, not strong. Show emotion and we're crybabies. But then if we stray from the prescribed narrow path — as in morally — we're dismissed as camp followers, good-time girls, not much better than prostitutes."

"Precisely," Nancy agreed. She started to light another cigarette and changed her mind, tossing the pack back on the desk. "You know, now that I think about it, pregnancy just may be the easiest, most real problem we might have to deal with. Most of us here, now, are married and several who are still expected are as well. Of course, I don't want an unmarried pregnancy on my hands — that would really give the women who think we're stepping out of our rightful place something to use against us. But so far, you, Cornelia and this Annie Gwynn are the only unmarried ones. Cornelia has a reputation as spotless as a nun's and I know I don't have to worry about you.

Clare fidgeted with the decorative button on her sleeve. "Uh, Nancy, there's something I think I should tell you."

Nancy looked at her, and Clare felt those inquisitive eyes boring into hers, probing, questioning. She could almost see Nancy's shield go up — the one she used for strangers or people she didn't trust. And behind it there was a touch of fear of what she was about to hear.

"What is it? If it affects your standing in this program, Clare, you'd better spit it out now."

"I wasn't going to tell anyone, but you deserve to know. Will and I were married two months ago."

"Good lord, you're not pregnant are you?" Nancy's question fired across the desk and rocked Clare back. She started to laugh and stopped when she saw Nancy's frown deepen.

"No, no, I'm not pregnant. That's all we'd need right now. Me try-ing to join the Ferrying Division and him already gone off to flight training and destined for overseas." She paused again as she saw a look of pure relief spread across her friend's lovely face. "No, I wasn't sure what the regulations would be, whether you would even allow married women in at all. I should have realized that you, being married, and Betty, that you would make sure that it didn't interfere. But I wasn't sure. And there's the talk of militarization. I don't know their regs on marital status. Besides, we didn't want to broadcast the marriage because people ask stupid questions and it's none of their business."

Now Nancy's smile beamed. "Well, congratulations, sweetie. That's wonderful news. I wondered if you were ever going to do it. Will is a lucky guy and I think he knows it…"

A knock at the door interrupted Nancy mid-thought.

"Come in," she called, and Lieutenant Tracy appeared in the door-way. Annie Gwynn stood behind him looking sweaty and apprehen-sive.

"She did fine," he said, cocking his head toward the tall girl.

"Thanks, Lieutenant," Nancy said. "Come on in, Miss Gwynn."

Tracy stood aside and let her pass into the office.

"Congratulations," Nancy said to the girl.

Clare watched as a relieved smile creased the younger girl's face. Her dark blue eyes — so wide and wary when they had been talking in the outer office — were now more trusting. No, Clare thought, make that believing, as if she couldn't believe she was really here until now.

"Thank you, Mrs. Love," Annie said softly.

"I'll have Miss Colsen call the infirmary and see if we can sched-ule your physical this afternoon." Then Nancy turned to Clare. "Why don't you go on with Lieutenant Tracy now and do your flight test. On the assumption that you'll pass — can't imagine that you won't — I'll have Colsen schedule your physical after Miss Gwynn's. We'll probably have a board meeting to review the latest candidates first thing in the morning, if we can get all the officers together."

Clare rose to leave.

"Let's have dinner together tonight, sweetie," Nancy said to Clare as she started to follow Tracy out the door. "Oh, and Miss Gwynn, you're welcome to join us at the Officers Club. We'll meet in the lounge there after you and Clare have finished your testing."

Clare had taken a real liking to Annie at dinner that night and thought the younger girl handled herself very well in Nancy's presence. The following afternoon, Nancy summoned them after lunch to tell them that the board had accepted them into the Women's Auxiliary Ferrying Squadron and that they could, officially, move into the newly renovated BOQ 14, which had been strictly male quarters until workmen had converted the most important areas to accommodate the women pilots. That meant tearing out the urinals, installing doors on the showers and the commode stalls, and hanging Venetian blinds, all to give the girls privacy the men of the army apparently didn't want or need.

Clare and Annie carried their suitcases across the wooden planks that led over a muddy ditch and made their way up the wooden stairs to the second floor where those already accepted for the mandatory thirty-day trial period had taken up residence. Annie first checked to see if there was a room down by Cornelia, but those had been taken by the earliest arrivals. Clare realized she might be second choice, but then Annie had known Cornelia for some time and looked upon her as a mentor of sorts. Eventually they chose side-by-side rooms facing the southwest, hoping that location might be warmer during the winter, which would be arriving soon enough.

Clare's choice was a far cry from her old room in her parents' home. And since Will left for training immediately after their honeymoon, they'd not yet had a home together. She couldn't help thinking of her husband as she put her suitcase down on the flimsy mattress on a narrow metal cot and began to unpack. She hung her two dresses, two pair of slacks and five blouses in the two-by-four framing that substituted for a closet. In the drawers of the cheap maple-finished chest on the opposite wall went her underwear, socks, a couple of sweaters and pajamas. She and Annie were scheduled to go to the sub-depot for GI flight equipment once they got moved in. Somehow she had to leave room for that in the closet and drawers as well.

Everything stored, she gingerly sat down on the cot — there were no chairs, something she decided she must remedy immediately — and then stretched out.

"Gawd, this is uncomfortable!"

A few seconds later, Annie stood in her doorway. "I know, mine's terrible, too."

"None of the rooms downstairs are being used," Clare said, "and probably won't be. There are only supposed to be twenty-five of us and there must be fifty or more rooms in this building. Let's go see if we can find better mattresses."

What they found were more mattresses in a similar state of use as theirs upstairs.

"I've got it," Clare said, "let's double up. We'll use two mattresses on our cots. That's got to help."

"Good idea."

They picked the two best they could find and, working together, dragged them upstairs one at a time. Soon, they each had a bed made with a double thickness of mattress.

"Can't be any worse," Clare said, admiring her handiwork. Then she called out to Annie, "Let's go get our equipment. I've been looking forward to owning one of those spiffy goatskin jackets with the ATC emblem and an Army-issue flight suit I can call my own."

# CHAPTER SIX

"I did it! They weren't going to give it to me, Midge. They were going to let that Love woman walk away with *my* idea. *My* program. But I wouldn't let them get away with it! I made them give me my flight training school." Jacqueline Cochran's brown eyes danced with triumph.

"I thought Mrs. Love's program was simply to form one squadron of experienced ferry pilots, and a small one at that. Scuttlebutt is that she only has nine women at last count."

"Don't be impertinent. No, it's not a school, but, more important, she has my title. They named her Director of Women Pilots — the title Hap Arnold promised me — and all she really is is a squadron leader. That upstart Ferry Command clerk tried to steal my idea and my title from me. She pushed herself in while I was away in England fulfilling a promise I made to the President and to the British people. Well, nobody gets the best of Jacqueline Cochran. Mark this day, Midge. This is the dawning of a new age. There will be a woman's air corps and I, with the rank of full colonel, will be its commanding officer."

The calendar on Miss Cochran's desk read September 15, 1942. Midge knew Nancy Love was an experienced pilot and had heard that she had presented an idea for a squadron of women ferry pilots as far back as 1940. But Midge decided not to mention that in the face of her boss's obvious agitation. "So what does this mean for you, Miss Cochran? And for us?"

"It means that I can put my plan into action. I am the Director of the Women's Flying Training Detachment. We will begin recruiting our first class immediately. All those women we found in the CAA files a year ago will be eligible to apply. But it will take a special kind of woman to be accepted. Our requirements will be stringent."

"I thought you were looking for a way to give the women with just a few hours a chance to prove themselves. If the requirements are too stringent …"

"Not flying requirements, my dear, personal attributes." She ticked them off on her beautifully manicured fingers. "Good moral character, sufficient education, from a nice family, and a willingness to work hard. No, just because a girl has money and her father has bought her an airplane and expensive flying lessons that will *not* get her into my school. She will have to qualify like all the rest. We'll have no prima donna debutantes at our school — unless, of course, they can measure up. They will be girls like you, Midge, and like me. Girls who want to make something of themselves."

As Jackie quietly stared off into the middle distance, Midge took the moment to collect her thoughts. She had often heard Miss Cochran rail against the privileged few who, she thought, ran the Ninety-Nines. But she had been elected president of the women pilots association a year earlier when one of her main rivals, Betty Gillies, stepped down after two years in office. Miss Cochran seemed particularly proud of being a Ninety-Nine and delighted to be its president.

Midge kept hoping her boss would take her to a Ninety-Nines meeting and let her meet some of the well-known women pilots — the ones, like Betty Gillies, who had known Amelia Earhart and helped her found the organization. Midge joined as soon as she had earned her license, but Jackie had yet to take her to a national meeting.

Not for the first time, Midge questioned what made this proud, vain, wealthy, yet beautiful and charismatic woman tick. She knew the official rags-to-riches story of Jacqueline Cochran — the name was her own creation — in which a poor girl makes good by becoming a beautician at thirteen and works her way out of Florida canebrake poverty all the way to Antoine's Salon at Saks Fifth Avenue in New York City. There Jackie met and married millionaire Floyd Odlum after Odlum divorced his first wife. Rumor was, Mrs. Odlum got the department store Bonwit Teller in the divorce settlement.

Then Floyd helped Jackie set up her own cosmetics business, bearing her name, and convinced her to learn to fly in order to more easily get around the country to call on her customers. Floyd financed the prototype P-35 that Jackie flew when she won the prestigious Bendix Air Race Trophy in 1938. From such success in the aviation world — coupled with her husband's money and the added cachet of their friendship with Franklin and Eleanor Roosevelt — Jackie found it a short leap into the power structure with Hap Arnold and the others in Washington's military establishment.

The woman definitely had vision; Midge gave her credit for that. Who else would have dreamed up the potential of an all-woman air corps, superbly trained, ready and willing to give all for their country in time of war? God, the woman was made of the stuff of greatness, all right! And she had chosen Midge as her administrative assistant.

"Yes," Cochran was saying, "clean-cut, ambitious, all-American girls, Midge. Those who are accepted will be paid one hundred fifty dollars per month during the training course, which is projected to last four months."

"Miss Cochran, where is this school to be located?"

"That's still to be determined. In the meantime, I'm beginning to recruit for our first class."

"And am I to be a member of that class, Miss Cochran, like you said back in December?"

"No, Midge, I have other plans for you. You are going to spend the next month flying. We need to get you up to five-hundred hours so you'll be eligible to apply for Mrs. Love's WAFS. I need to know what's going on in Wilmington."

The sun was just beginning to burn off the October morning fog when two taxicabs arrived at the guardhouse almost simultaneously. The sharp smells of aviation fuel and metal, the musty odor of dampness, and the crisp, clean aroma of autumn competed for air space as Midge watched a tall, attractive blonde climb from the cab that had pulled up in front of hers. The young woman wore a stylish brown herringbone suit and matching hat. Though slender and not particularly big-boned, the girl had large hands, Midge noticed. Hands capable of wrestling three suitcases out of the cab. Hands probably capable of controlling a balky airplane in bad weather.

Midge sensed the girl had to be a WAFS candidate. She certainly looked like a pilot. Besides, why else would she be getting out of a taxicab at New Castle Army Air Base with three suitcases?

Good, thought Midge. They're still taking candidates. They aren't full yet.

As Midge got out of the second cab, she watched the MP in the guardhouse giving the other girl the once-over as she strode toward him. Midge knew she presented a contrast to the leggy blonde. Short and petite with small hands and small feet, she did not look like a woman who could wrestle an airplane around the sky. As she got within earshot, she overheard the MP speak into the telephone. "Miz Love. Looks like I got two more for you."

Half an hour later, the blonde — Nancy Batson, of Birmingham, Alabama — exited Nancy Love's office. "She says for you to go right in," Nancy said to Midge in her lilting Southern accent. "I'm going with that gentleman for my flight check." She tilted her head toward a lieutenant in flying gear who was waiting for her.

Inside the Director of Women Pilots' office, Midge looked Nancy Love over as closely as she dared without being obvious. She had no idea if Mrs. Love would know who she was. Nowhere in her credentials was Jacqueline Cochran's name mentioned. They had gotten around her employment for the last year and a half by listing Antoine's and the beauty school and salon where she trained in Saint Louis as her work references.

Midge was handed a completely new logbook. Miss Cochran had worked some magic and Midge was now credited with taking and successfully completing the CPT courses at Harris Teachers College in Saint Louis. All her hours flying the Staggerwing were gone, replaced by hours in an assortment of small airplanes with just enough 200-horsepower time to qualify her for the WAFS.

The biggest question she might be asked would be how, on her salary, could she have afforded the flight time and ratings she now possessed? Midge decided to claim a rich grandfather if asked.

She wasn't asked. Nancy Love didn't even linger over her previous employment record. She did compliment Midge on her hard work accumulating those 502 hours in just over two years. "You've done a lot of flying," was all she said.

Climbing up into airplanes was the most difficult part of flying for Midge. Her short legs and lack of height put her at an immediate disadvantage when trying to lift a booted foot to the trailing edge of the left wing root — the first step up on a low-wing or bi-wing aircraft. To make matters worse, she now wore a heavy parachute strapped to her thighs and over her shoulders, and it tended to pull her backward as she tried to step up and bend forward at the same time in order to get her momentum going in the right direction.

On her third lunge, she grasped the handhold on the side of the fuselage and pulled herself the rest of the way up. The front cockpit was hers as the student on this flight. Lieutenant Tracy, who would be her judge and jury that day, took the back seat in the silver open-cockpit PT-19A. She had seen similar planes, though they were the black and orange Fairchilds the Civil Aeronautics Administration inspectors flew around the country to meet their exam appointments.

"I can talk to you through the Gosport tube," Tracy said to her. "But you won't be able to talk back to me."

Midge listened as he went through all the startup maneuvers and ran the checklist. Soon they were taxiing into takeoff position and awaiting the green light from the tower. Then she felt the surge of power supplied by the Fairchild 175-horsepower engine and, moments later, they were in the air.

Tracy took the airplane to 1,300 feet and then turned it over to her with the orders to "keep this heading and make forty-five degree turns until we get to 3,000 feet."

Midge shook the control stick to indicate that she had control, checked the wingtips and nose relative to the horizon, and began the climbing turns.

"Let's see your power-off stalls," Tracy said, after they achieved altitude.

Midge pulled out the carburetor heat lever, pulled the throttle back to idle, and started to bring the stick back.

"Stop!" Tracy's voice came sharply through her earphones.

Midge jerked the controls as she stopped mid-maneuver. The airplane settled itself back to level flying.

"You forgot something."

Her mind felt like a sieve. She knew what he wanted her to do, in fact she could anticipate most of the test flight ahead of her because she had done it a couple hundred times in the last year and a half as she learned to fly bigger, heavier, more complex airplanes — all at Miss Cochran's bidding. She shook her head trying to clear her mind and remember what she had either failed to do, or what she had done that she shouldn't have.

Finally, Tracy's voice came through her earphones again. "OK. Think. You're up in the air and you're about to start some maneuvers. What is the absolute first thing you must do. This is elementary stuff, Miss Culpepper." His voice carried a warning tone.

Midge's heart was in her throat. She was going to flunk out on her first maneuver. Miss Cochran would never forgive her. Think! Think! "Oh, my God," she said aloud as she realized what she had forgotten.

She quickly began a 90-degree turn to the left, her head moving up, down and around to check the airspace above, below, in front of and behind her. Then she repeated the maneuver to the right. Clearing turns. Elementary! Safety first. Never forget that, Culpepper, she said to herself. Satisfied that there were no other airplanes in immediate proximity, she leveled off and, once again, pulled the carburetor heat lever, came back on the power, and began to bring the nose of the primary trainer up to begin the power-off stall.

"That's more like it," Tracy said when she had completed the maneuver.

He continued to put her through her paces and Midge knew that she had made the one mistake she would be allowed. From that moment on, her performance had to be letter-perfect. She felt sweat popping out under her helmet, in her armpits, along her back, and in her crotch where the parachute straps clamped tight against her thighs. Soon the sweat was running. The tickling sensation in the small of her back and her armpits was only a distraction. But a stream trickled down her forehead and into the rubber rings that formed the goggles. She feared that some of the moisture would get through to the lenses and cloud her vision so that she would be unable to see the instruments or to land properly.

For a split second, she took her hand off the throttle and pushed the goggles tighter against her face. Then, quickly, she returned her hand to the throttle, remembering her first instructor's admonition when they were flying in the J-3 Cub — "Keep your hand on the throttle at all times. Power."

Lieutenant Tracy had her lose altitude through gliding turns until they reached 800 feet. "The army doesn't take a chance with glides at idling speed. If you have power available, never cut it off," he warned.

Midge waited, breathlessly on edge, for him to give her a simulated forced landing order and continually scanned the ground below for a potential put-down spot. When he did, she was ready and responded by pulling the carb heat on immediately. Then she proceeded to set up her glide and aimed for the spot she had selected for an emergency landing. When it was obvious that she had the maneuver under control and had picked a good spot, he said, "OK, return to normal flight." She breathed a sigh of relief, glad he couldn't hear her, pushed the carb heat off, the power back to full, and put the aircraft into a climb.

Finally it came time to do landings. He made the first traffic pattern and landing, she did the second. He had her takeoff without flaps and land with half flaps. After that landing, he took the controls back and ran the plane to a taxi strip where he said, "OK, you take it now and do a go-around."

He had taxied the airplane much faster than Midge was accustomed to doing, but, assuming that's what he wanted her to do, she began to taxi at the same speed he had. Then she felt him hit the brakes and chop the throttle.

"Never, never taxi fast like that. If you ground loop or damage an airplane, you can be court-martialed and made to pay for the damages."

That's it, she thought. I'm done for. I'll wash out before I ever begin. Miss Cochran will probably fire me, too, for letting her down.

This time she taxied slowly, swinging the airplane in S-curves in order to see what was in front of her. She performed the takeoff and go-around to perfection. She had to.

After they had parked the plane and shut it down according to the checklist, Midge climbed out of the front cockpit. Then, head down, feeling totally dejected, she followed Lieutenant Tracy back to Nancy Love's office. They had to wait in the outer office because, Miss Colsen told them, Colonel Baker, the base commander, was conferring with Mrs. Love.

Midge listened as Colsen and Tracy kept up a running dialogue about Colsen's fiancé, who Tracy knew and who had been accepted for flight training and sent to Texas. Colsen shared her concern with Tracy that though she worked with pilots and knew he wanted to be a pilot, she'd be a lot happier if he were destined to be a ground crew member, preferably there at New Castle.

Tracy laughed. "Once you've got the bug to fly, not much will keep you on the ground. And that goes for these women coming in here as well. There's no difference in their attitudes from those of the men — except that I've found they are a lot more serious about it. They want to fly in the worst way. Not much difference in the skill levels either, I've discovered. These women can handle anything the boys can. I'm convinced of that after checking out the fifteen or so who've already made the program."

When Colonel Baker came out, Lieutenant Tracy motioned for Midge to follow him into Mrs. Love's office. Here it comes, she thought. Wash out time. She didn't know if she could face Nancy Love's penetrating eyes that seemed to know what was going on in Midge's head. Worse, how would she explain it to Jacqueline Cochran?

"She's a little rough around the edges, Mrs. Love," she heard Tracy saying. "Forgot some of the basics. But I'm chalking that up to nervousness because she handled the airplane flawlessly during the maneuvers themselves. I think the four weeks of training will help her remember those little things. As far as I'm concerned, she passes."

"Thank you, lieutenant. Miss Culpepper, please sit down. We can finish talking now that you've passed your flight test. And I'll have Colsen schedule your physical."

Midge listened as Mrs. Love explained the program. All volunteers — that's what they were — had to sign a ninety-day contract of which the first thirty was a pass-or-fail trial period. At the end of thirty days, if a WAFS's performance was not up to snuff, she washed out. If she was satisfactory, she completed the ninety-day contract and was accepted as a civilian Service Pilot.

They were to attend ground school in the morning and evening, if necessary. Flying was done in the afternoon after the fog had burned off the Delaware River. And they would be given Link trainer time — an aid to instrument training.

She would be paid $250 a month and $6 per diem while on a mission.

Finally, Mrs. Love told Midge to get her gear together. Once she passed the physical, she could move into BOQ 14 right away.

She was in.

That night, Midge put through a call to Washington. Cochran had just returned from Fort Worth, where she was moving quickly to establish the Flying Training Command School for women pilots. Midge passed along the good news of her acceptance and decided that Cochran sounded quite pleased.

# CHAPTER SEVEN

On October 20, Nancy Love called nine of her squadron members into her office with orders for the first deliveries to be undertaken by WAFS. First, on October 22, Betty Gillies was to lead Teresa James, Del Scharr, Helen Mary Clark, Pat Rhonie, Clare Varsky and Midge Culpepper on a flight from the Piper factory in Lock Haven, Pennsylvania, to Mitchel Field on Long Island. Their mission: deliver seven L4-Bs. Nancy explained that Midge, who had yet to complete her thirty-day training period, was to go along to gain needed cross-country experience under Betty's tutelage. Then, on October 23, Annie Gwynn and Cornelia Fort were to take two Cubs already there at NCAAB and deliver them to the 346th Base Headquarters and Air Base Squadron at Nashville.

Annie decided that it was Nancy's plan to give Cornelia and her a chance to spend a few hours at home after making the delivery. Betty, Rhonie, and Helen Mary were being offered a similar opportunity. Betty's family lived in Syosset, Long Island; Rhonie's in the New York area; and Helen Mary's husband and two sons — ages twelve and ten — lived in Englewood, New Jersey.

After Nancy explained the logistics of flying a ferrying mission, she emphasized that they were to stay at least five hundred feet away from each other and anything else, including clouds, and high enough over towns that if they lost the engine, they could deadstick to the outskirts and land in a field, not on somebody's house. Since Cubs were not equipped with radios, they decided on some hand signals to use in case of trouble.

Then Nancy dismissed them. "The men say 'good hunting' when they leave on a mission. I'll just say 'fair winds and blue skies.'"

The prospect of an overnight at home delighted Cornelia, but not Annie. That night, Annie sought out her friend and, seated on a battered card table chair Cornelia had liberated from one of the empty rooms downstairs, she tried to explain how she felt.

"I don't want to go home. This didn't just happen — I've had these feelings for a long time. Back in Hawaii, when I began living on my own for the first time, I realized I had escaped from something. I found I really liked being on my own and secretly I wished that I would never have to go home again and live within the confines of my family."

Annie paused, looking at Cornelia as if trying to read her thoughts. "I didn't know you well enough then to confide in you. But after Pearl Harbor, I began to think that what happened to me during the attack was retribution for these terrible thoughts I had been having, like some vengeful God was out to teach me a lesson.

"Now it's happening again. I've made the transition to another life that I really like and I don't want it disturbed. I live only for today. I want to be left alone and not have to think forward to a future I don't believe exists or look backward to a way of life that's gone forever. And I don't want to go home and see my family because if I try to tell them, they won't understand and they'll be hurt."

Cornelia sat on her cot with her back against the wall and listened without comment. Then she stood and walked over to the card table that served as her writing desk. She picked up the diary that lay surrounded by letters bearing postmarks from around the country and a half-written letter to one of her many correspondents.

"When I'm confused about my own feelings, I write in my diary. Surprisingly enough, when I go back and re-read it later, I find a pattern to it and make sense of what has happened to me. I've done this since I was a little girl. Someday, I hope to use what I've written about my WAFS experiences to write a book."

She leafed through the pages until she found what she was looking for and handed the diary to Annie.

> *December 6, 1941.*
> *I'm caught in a cocoon of my own spinning. I'm happy, carefree, on my own. I don't ever want to go home. I want to stay, forever, here in Paradise. No one would understand if I did such a rebellious, thoughtless, irresponsible, inconsiderate thing. My family would shake their collective heads and say, "the old girl's finally flipped her cork." And they'd be right. But life can be or seem so simple here, I wonder why it can't last forever?*

Annie looked up. "You've felt this way, too?"

Cornelia smiled and nodded.

"You're the last person I would ever expect it of, Cornelia. You seem to have the perfect life."

"I do, in many ways, Annie, and I have no complaints. Still, my dear mother hovers. Always has, but even worse now since my father's death two years ago. She tries, bless her heart, but she has never and will never understand my love of flying. Do you know what she said to me the day I soloed and arrived home in that state of absolute elation that only another pilot can understand? I quote: 'How very nice, dear. Now you won't have to do that again.'"

"None of them understand, do they?" Annie said. "That's what's so nice about being here. We *all* know. We've all been there and we can talk about it, or not talk about it, if we choose."

"This is a unique time, place, and circumstance, Annie. Women have not really had an opportunity like this before and if we don't do it right, it will be a long time before women have such an opportunity again. All of us, I think, realize what a terrific spot we're in and draw closer together as a result, often to the exclusion of others, like our families. Because this is a miracle, women working together in cooperation and friendliness toward a common goal — the end of the war. We know that what we do will affect generations of women pilots yet to come. Will affect whether or not they are ever accepted in and by the military."

As Cornelia talked, Annie watched the inner light spread across her face. When Cornelia talked about things she loved, she truly glowed from within. She was not, by Hollywood standards, beautiful. At five feet ten, she was far taller than most women and many men. But when her gray eyes sparkled and her long patrician face achieved that glow, crowned by her lustrous brown hair with its red-gold highlights, Cornelia was, Annie thought, lovely. Hers was truly that inner beauty of song and story.

"I can't even write home any more," Annie said plaintively, willing herself out of the spell Cornelia cast, and confessing, finally, the worst of her terrible secret. "I've cut myself off from them. I don't want to hurt them. But I want them to understand."

"That may be the one thing they can't give you, Annie. But they won't stop loving you no matter what you do or don't do. You should go home. Act as normal as you can and remember, the next day we'll be on our way back here."

Annie smiled. Cornelia was right, of course. She must do this in order to avoid deeply hurting her family. Surely she could manage for one night. Surely she could hide the fact that she no longer looked beyond today.

"Cornelia, do you ever wonder if you'll survive this war?"

Her friend looked thoughtful for a moment, then answered. "I did when we were back in Honolulu, waiting for passage home. I feared the ship would be torpedoed before we could reach San Francisco. I even wrote my mother a farewell letter and my last will and testament before we left, just in case."

Early the morning of October 23, dressed in flight suits, helmets, boots, jackets, gloves, and silk scarves, and lugging their parachutes and B-4 bags, Annie and Cornelia walked into Operations. They "bought" their Cubs — meaning they signed them out, received the paper work, and each officially took responsibility for her aircraft's safe delivery — then began their preflights.

Cornelia plotted the course. Their route would take them to Pittsburgh, then on to the flatter terrain of Ohio — Columbus and then Cincinnati — to Louisville and into Nashville. Cornelia thought it far safer than flying over the Appalachians almost the entire route. Besides, the weather report said fog in the mountains.

The Cubs, which averaged eighty miles per hour, had limited fuel capacity and range. Fall meant they had fewer hours of daylight and ferry pilots could only fly during daylight hours. This necessitated frequent landings for fuel and to "remain over night," which the army, Annie had learned in ground school, called RONing. So they would RON in Columbus, barring problems, and make Nashville the following afternoon.

Several male ferry pilots were leaving at the same time to deliver trainers to bases further west in Tennessee and down in Alabama. Annie encountered two of them in the Ready Room.

"Well, look-a-here, Al, we got us a real, live girl pilot, though it's hard to tell inside all that gear," said the shorter of the two.

"Wimmen don't belong in airplanes," said Al. "Some dame named Cochran says they can fly as good as men. What they're doin' is takin' jobs away from guys who need 'em. Bunch of society wimmen, do-gooders."

"Hey, they're dames, ain't they, and they're gonna be in Columbus tonight, same as we are."

"Hey, Georgie, you got that right. We gonna have us a fine ol' time. Nothin' you can tell the wife about, 'course," said Al, as he sidled closer to Annie. She towered over him as he rocked back on his heels and said, "What's your name, little lady pilot?"

"She's WAFS Gwynn to you, brother, and I suggest you back off," Annie heard Cornelia's soft, low-pitched Southern drawl behind her.

Al's mouth dropped open. "I thought it was two dames taking those trainers to Nashville."

"I think it is, Al," George snickered, "but they both look like guys."

Annie felt her face go hot. She and Cornelia — both tall and encased in the bulky flying gear — might appear a bit formidable to these two shorter-than-average males, but the men's behavior was totally unacceptable. She started to respond but thought better of it. Instead, she tried to breathe deeply and push the heat of her anger inside. She said nothing, but watched the two of them disappear out the Ready Room door leading to the flight line, laughing.

"Low-life scum," Annie said between clenched teeth.

"They're afraid we might really be better than they are and show them up. We're a threat to their self-esteem. Fortunately, not all men feel that way." Cornelia pushed the door open and they followed the men out toward the flight line.

But Annie's temper had been piqued and she found she couldn't swallow the insults as easily as Cornelia appeared to have. She watched the two pilots pre-flighting their airplanes. The one called Al kept looking over at her and Cornelia. Once, she saw him walk over to his buddy, whisper something to him and then poke him in the ribs with his elbow. The one named George laughed at whatever Al said and glanced over at them as well.

Inside her heavy flight gear Annie felt a trickle of sweat start down her back.

Later in the air over central Pennsylvania, Annie — the navigator and therefore in the front plane —saw another airplane approaching from east by southeast. Trained to stay five hundred feet away from all other airplanes, she watched warily, ready to move her aircraft if necessary. The other plane seemed to be coming straight for her. Maybe the pilot didn't see her.

But as it kept coming, an uneasiness settled over Annie. She had been here before. She remembered all too well the Jap Zero bearing down on her. Though the terrain had changed — bare trees on coal-mine-ravaged hills instead of lush green jungle — she was back in the familiar Cub. An involuntary shiver shot through her. She tried to shake off the memory.

Turn off, you fool, she muttered to herself, watching him come on. Can't you see me? This is my airspace. Are you looking for a mid-air?

When he got to within five hundred feet and kept coming, she realized it was a PT-19. It had to be one of those guys they had the run-in with. She put her aircraft into a climbing 45-degree turn to the right and looked back. Cornelia, flying a good five hundred feet behind her and a couple hundred feet above her, put her craft into a climbing right turn as well, then they both came back around, leveled out, and picked up the course they were flying.

The intruder plane dropped back a little, but as Annie swiveled her head around to the left, she saw him zooming up to sit off her left wing tip. Her heart started to pound. As the aircraft drew up next to hers, only about ten feet off her wing, she looked. It was Al.

In a flash of brilliance, she memorized the numbers on his airplane. At least she could report the infraction to Nancy Love.

Then the intruder did a barrel roll to the left, came back to sit almost on her wing tip again. After a few minutes, as he moved off, he waggled his wings, taunting her.

Annie kept her eyes on the horizon, trying to keep her airplane flying straight and level, and trying to ignore the harassing tactics. It wasn't easy because the intruding airplane kept feinting toward her, which quickened her heart rate every time he moved closer in.

"Idiot," she screamed out loud, watching him speed up and pull into a loop.

She lost him for a moment, ducked as his shadow crossed over her. She saw his wheels within what seemed like inches of her wingtip. "Stop it, you fool!" she screamed. He had nearly clipped her wing. Certain death for her and maybe for him as well.

Then, some distance away by now, Al put his plane into another barrel roll to the left and was gone. When she allowed herself a look around, she saw him flying off Cornelia's wing. They flew like that for several miles with Al showing off more of his aerobatic skills before he finally tired of the game and flew off to the south. Guess he's had his fun for the day, Annie muttered to herself, her face flushed, her body tense and sweating profusely.

When they landed in Pittsburgh, Annie made the call back to New Castle and reported the incident to Nancy Love, including the tail number of Al's plane.

"RON somewhere other than Columbus," Nancy said.

"She wants us to RON someplace else," Annie said.

"Ask her if Patterson Field, Dayton, would do?" Cornelia suggested.

Annie repeated that to Nancy who answered yes to Dayton.

"I have an old friend stationed at Patterson. If he's on base, he'll take us to dinner," Cornelia said, grinning.

They refueled at Lockbourne Air Base in Columbus and flew on another ninety miles to Dayton, landing just as the sun sank in the west.

The next day a front moved through and they were weathered in at Dayton. Annie was glad that Al and George weren't around. Cornelia's friend, a major she knew from "the old days in Nashville," not only took them to dinner the first night, he entertained them the second night as well. Annie thought the major and Cornelia seemed quite glad to see each other and tried to beg off the second night, but Cornelia wouldn't hear of it.

"We're in this together, Annie."

Still, Annie felt like a third wheel. Pleading a headache, she finally managed to leave them alone for a while.

The following morning the weather had moved on east and Annie and Cornelia took off for Nashville by way of Cincinnati and Louisville. They saw no more of George and Al.

Annie's father met her at Berry Field. Cornelia's mother had sent the family chauffeur to bring her home. Her mother didn't drive, Cornelia explained.

As Annie hugged her father, she felt a tug of regret for him. He had flown in a small plane only once — with her, but he had long since given up any thoughts of learning to fly himself. His daughter had been in the right place at the right time, learning to fly while in college. The time and place had never been right for him to take it up. Family needs always came first.

As they drove home over the familiar roads of Davidson County — Thompson Lane, Granny White Pike, Hillsboro Avenue — Annie remembered the day she and her father had both fallen in love with airplanes.

It had been fifteen years ago and in a world that now seemed lost forever. Annie's whole family was packed in the car and on their way to Berry Field to see Charles Lindbergh, Lucky Lindy everyone called him, and hear him speak. Seven-year-old Annie wasn't really sure why her father wanted to see this man, but she knew he had done something special and it had to do with an airplane.

The car rounded a bend in the road and there in front of them, just beyond the road, was a wide-open green field. Then they heard the noise! What sounded like a great tractor a few feet away was closing fast!

And then she saw it. Approaching from the right, flying ever lower and right at them, was a silver airplane. Annie gasped. Her father jerked the steering wheel to the right, braked, and stopped the car, two wheels still on the road and two on the narrow shoulder. "Everybody out," he hollered, opening his own door and bolting.

Annie, squeezed in the middle of the front seat between her mother and father, slid under the steering wheel and clambered out after him. She stood with her head thrown back like his and watched as the airplane flew directly over them, the silver underbelly and the extended black wheels clearing them by what seemed like inches. The turbulence whipped her hair into her face and, for an instant, Annie felt the dark shadow of the sleek craft slide over her, then it was gone.

She held her hands to her ears to block the deafening scream of the engine and squinted to keep out the dust stirred up by the massive movement of air kicked up by the spinning propeller. But the pulse of that great engine was already surging in her blood and she refused to shut her eyes, so struck was she by the singular beauty and grace of the winged machine.

She and her father spun around in concert, one hundred and eighty degrees, to watch those wheels settle on the grassy strip across the road and beyond the fence. Annie couldn't take her eyes off the aircraft as it rolled away in the distance toward a low wooden building where a crowd of people waited.

"Let's go, or we won't get close enough to see him," her father called.

When Annie turned back, she saw that no one else had followed her father's command and climbed from the car to watch. Her mother sat stolidly in the front seat, clutching her purse to her stomach as if it, too, would take flight if she let go. Her sister and two brothers were all rooted to their seats in the back, mouths agape.

But her father had a faraway look in his eyes as he glanced from her to the retreating airplane and then once again at her. The gleam she saw there matched the pulsating excitement she felt in her stomach, the racing of her heart, the dryness in her mouth.

# CHAPTER EIGHT

Midge could hardly believe her good luck at being allowed to go on a mission, and one to New York, no less. The evening Nancy assigned her to the Cub flight, she put in a call to Jackie Cochran to see if she was, by chance, in New York. She was.

"I'll be at the office. Come see me," Cochran told her.

"I'll be with the others," Midge said, hesitantly.

"You'll have to get away from them for awhile," was the reply.

On the morning of October 22, with no fog reported at their destination, the seven WAFS assigned to ferry L4-Bs to Long Island climbed into the 2$^{nd}$ Ferrying Group's twin-engine C-60, carrying their B-4 bags and dragging their parachutes. Getting to Lockhaven was so complicated, Colonel Baker had opted to fly them there and he, himself, was at the controls.

"I had no idea what to pack," Midge said to Clare, who happened to be walking in front of her.

Clare turned and gave Midge a withering glance. "Common sense. That's all you need whether you're packing for two days, two weeks or two months."

Helen Mary sat where she could see out through a small porthole and kept her charts out so she could navigate all the way to Lock Haven. Rhonie sat next to her and Del Scharr sat near the porthole on the opposite side of the transport. Betty sat next to Del for take-off, then got up and went into the cockpit to watch what was going on. Sensing that Clare was either in a bad mood or didn't want her around, Midge sat by Teresa for the duration of the flight.

When they walked into the factory, Midge noticed that people halted their work to turn and stare at the seven women pilots in full flight gear. But soon the women were inspecting their seven khaki-colored planes — aircraft they knew in civilian life as yellow J-3 Cubs.

Midge did a quick mental calculation. The Cub had a maximum speed of eighty-seven miles per hour, which meant they would probably cruise around eighty. With a nine-gallon fuel tank, the range was only two hundred and six miles.

Betty appointed Clare navigator for the first leg, which would take them to Allentown, Pennsylvania, where they would refuel. Then, together, Betty and Clare laid out the route with Betty purposefully pointing out things to Midge as they worked.

They took off, circled "Cubhaven" once, and then turned east. Since Lock Haven was in north central Pennsylvania, flying to Allentown meant establishing a heading east by southeast over the hilly terrain of the Alleghenies. But the earth dropped away to lower elevations as they neared Allentown and the eastern edge of the state. The flight lasted all of seventy-five minutes.

Betty went to check weather and close that leg of the flight plan while Midge oversaw the gassing up of both her plane and Betty's.

"You know the rules," Betty told them when she returned. "We're supposed to be in an hour before sundown. We can't get to Mitchel by then, so we're going to RON here. I've already got us rooms in town."

Midge and the others went back and tied down the tails, wings and sticks of their airplanes. Betty had made sure a night watchman was on duty to keep an eye on them.

After dinner, the women gathered in Betty and Helen Mary's room. The tailor had called earlier in the week to let them know the first uniforms were ready. That meant everybody but Midge had one. Hoping to wear them in New York and on the return train trip, they had brought them along to try on. And now the moment of truth had arrived. The fashion show was about to begin. The tailor, used to fitting men, was way off in his measurements. The trouser legs were far too generous, the waists gapped and the seats sagged.

"There's room for two in here," Clare complained.

The next morning, as they pre-flighted their airplanes, Betty gave them an update on the flight into Mitchel.

"I talked to Bud last night. He says flying is grounded along the New York waterfront today because they're doing aerial target practice with defense gun positions. I just wired Mitchel Field base operations to let them know we're coming and to tell them to call off the guns for us. Helen Mary is going to navigate until we get over the water, then I'll take over. Here's the route."

Again, Betty worked carefully with Midge. "I'm going to put Teresa behind you this entire leg in," she said.

An hour later, they were ready to go. It had started to drizzle, but Betty's check of the weather indicated that no rain, only smoke, lay in front of them to the east. Midge stowed her B-4 bag on the front seat in the tandem cockpit and climbed into the backseat, the preferred seat from which to fly the J-3 Cub. A line boy pulled the prop for her and she felt the small engine catch and rumble to a start. She taxied into line behind Clare, and then they were off.

Visibility was poor from the start. Midge remembered from her days as a student pilot that, thanks to all the factory smoke, conditions could get pretty ugly around New York City. Mentally, like Betty had told her to do, she checked off each of the points she had marked on her chart as they came up every few miles. When they passed over Plainfield, New Jersey, nothing but city stretched ahead. Row after row of box houses, row after row of smoke-belching factories, and between them and interconnecting them, the arteries of urban life, the system of streets and highways that carried cars and trucks in and out, feeding and clothing the population trapped within.

Midge had learned to love New York in a way she never thought possible. Theaters, museums, fine restaurants, clothing and department stores that sold only the best — and Jacqueline Cochran knew them all and was known in all of them. When Midge was with her, she was recognized, too.

Midge knew she was a long way from the little barefoot girl who waded in the backwaters of the cove formed by a configuration of jutting rocks and the Missouri River that was her front yard. She remembered the warm ooze of the mud between her toes, the cut and sting of a sharp rock on the bottom of her foot as she walked, and the way her footprints disappeared behind her as the mud and water conspired to tell her how unimportant she was — a mere trifle in their timeless existence.

Midge didn't realize until much later how that mirrored the opinion of her held by her stepfather. To him she was a necessary, but irritating, presence — right up until the day when, at age fourteen, she carried her only pair of shoes and walked barefoot down the sun-baked road into town, right into her aunt's beauty parlor and a job shampooing the ladies' hair, getting it ready for other women to cut and set.

But I showed 'em, she thought, hauling her attention back to her airplane and the job at hand. Still, just now, hanging above the urban sprawl she had most recently called home, she longed for the lush, uncluttered green of Missouri and the muddy ribbons of brown that were the Mississippi and Missouri Rivers, that brought life to Saint Louis and the small towns beyond.

Then, through the windshield of her airplane, the water appeared, the Atlantic Ocean where it collided with New Jersey and Long Island, and Betty moved forward, taking over the lead. Midge noted, with relief, that they were ahead of any weather. Now they moved into what Nancy had called echelon flying — in a straight line but strung out to the right. Teresa brought up the rear behind her.

Midge's vantage point near the back of the line reminded her of the game "crack the whip." She barely managed to keep the next Cub in front of her in sight. She wondered how Teresa kept up.

The sight of all that water made her apprehensive. Her first instructor had told her that he never let a student get any farther out of sight of land than she had altitude to get back should an engine quit and she needed to make a forced landing. But then many areas around New York City were restricted and she figured Betty knew better than she did where they were.

She pushed the throttle forward a fraction to maintain cruise speed, which in a Cub wasn't much less than full throttle. She recognized Coney Island. Then they flew over south Brooklyn and kept going until Midge could see two airports in front of her. Familiar territory — Roosevelt, where she took her instruction, was to the north and Mitchel to the south. Soon they were circling Mitchel. One by one, they went in to land.

The officer who greeted them grumbled, "We asked for these two months ago. We don't need them now."

Midge noticed that didn't faze Betty in the least. "Well, they're here now and you will please sign for them," she said as she walked off toward Operations leaving the man gaping after the five-foot-one-and-a-half-inch dynamo encased in a flight suit and a parachute almost as big as she was.

Then Betty did the impossible, considering that everyone else stared at the seven of them like they were from Mars. With a big smile and her most polite voice, she asked one of the men to order transportation for them to the Aviation Country Club, of which she and Pat Rhonie were members. Betty had a way about her that Midge admired. Direct, forceful, but with a gentle restraint, always in control.

As they picked up their B-4 bags and got ready to depart, the telephone rang in the Operations office. Moments later, the Operations chief called Betty back into his office. Midge and the others watched as the man spoke to Betty. When she joined them again she took a deep breath. "That was the telegram I sent this morning. Rather tardy getting here." Her voice was calm, but her mouth was set in a grim line and a telltale muscle pulsed at the side of her jaw.

Midge felt a quiver of panic rise in her stomach when she heard the news. But she noticed that Betty's outward composure never slipped — characteristic of the woman she was getting to know better each day. The muscle in her jaw was the only sign of upset and that was involuntary. She doesn't take things quite as coolly as she would like us to think she does, Midge thought. But she never lets her feelings show.

"No one ever told the officers to cease firing the guns because nobody knew we were coming," Betty told them.

The other women looked at each other, eyes wide at the news that they could have been blown out of the air. That they, just as easily as not, could be dead now. A few more war casualties to add to the list.

"Whew, we were lucky," Midge said to Clare, finding her voice.

"Yeah, we're lucky all right," Clare responded, "but somebody ought to get his ass chewed out good for not responding to that message immediately."

Wartime, Midge thought. Accidents did happen. But this was too close to home. She wondered if the others felt the same unease she did at the thought.

Once at the club, Betty called Nancy Love in Wilmington and got them the afternoon off. Then they laid out their plans for the day. "If we meet at Grand Central Station at six o'clock, we can catch the train for Wilmington tonight," said Betty, who knew the train schedules. "In the meantime, you're on your own to do what you want. Have fun."

Betty and Helen Mary left for home. The other five took the subway into Manhattan. There, Rhonie parted company with them, saying she had friends to visit.

Teresa, Del and Clare wanted to spend the day "doing Broadway" as Teresa put it. "Take in the Rainbow Room for lunch and then Radio City Music Hall. Come on with us, Midge, or is that too mundane for a New Yorker."

"No, it's not mundane. I've lived here just a year and a half. I've only begun to see the sights of this city, but I have an old friend I'd like to catch up with, if you don't mind."

"We don't mind," Clare said.

"I'll try to catch up with you at Radio City."

"Just be sure you're back at Grand Central by six," Del added.

"Don't worry. I will be." And with that, Midge left them standing at the entrance to the subway station.

"So, Midge, how are things going in Nancy Love's cozy little nest?" Jackie Cochran leaned back in her white leather desk chair, but to Midge she appeared more like a cat ready to pounce than a woman asking a simple question. The skin around the signature brown eyes showed tiny worry wrinkles her careful makeup couldn't conceal, and her mouth had a hard line to it.

Midge felt a stirring of resentment at her boss's attitude. She had learned to respect Nancy Love in the short time she had been at New Castle, and she certainly liked the girls she flew and lived with, particularly Betty Gillies and Annie Gwynn. They were all competent flyers. Now Midge felt uncomfortable, cast in a "kill the messenger" trap.

"Reasonably well, from my perspective," she answered.

"Meaning?"

"Well, with the addition of Nancy Batson and me, Mrs. Love has twenty toward her goal of twenty-five. Two have gone back to get higher horsepower ratings and will join once they complete those, and she has a line on a couple more who want to come but are still under contract elsewhere."

"Do you think she'll have her twenty-five by the end of the year?"

"I think so, yes."

"Hmm." Jackie brought her blunt fingertips together to make an inverted V where she momentarily rested her chin. Midge noticed a slight frown crease her forehead, as if she were considering her next move on a chessboard. Then she dropped her hands and leaned forward, her elbows on her desk.

"General Arnold is backing my plan and I have his complete support." She had bargained for and won her independence from any Ferrying Division authority over her training program, she added.

In her own mind, Midge could almost reconstruct the tide and tenor those discussions and negotiations must have taken. Jackie Cochran was a powerful adversary and when she set her mind on something, she went at it with single-minded tenacity and cunning thoroughness. Midge had seen her do it many times before. She almost felt sorry for General Arnold — a mere man caught in the snare of the Dragon Lady, as Barry Metzger had called her.

Jackie continued, "My task now is to find and train a minimum of five hundred women pilots. We aren't publishing minimum requirements for admittance. Qualification for the program will be on an individual basis. Meanwhile, I've been in Fort Worth buying civilian airplanes and negotiating a contract with a civilian aviation company to run the training school. As of now, the plan is to locate the school next door to Ellington Army Air Base at Howard Hughes Field, Houston Municipal Airport. That's the future home of the 319th AAF Women's Flying Training Detachment."

She went on to tell Midge that the first class would be called 43-W-1 — which meant the first women's class to graduate in 1943, and they were due in Houston on November 16.

# CHAPTER NINE

As tired as she was, Clare's heart beat faster and she felt chills run up her spine. The buildup of excitement began with the pre-breakfast march in review of the personnel stationed at New Castle Army Air Base (NCAAB). The *Star Spangled Banner* followed, played by the base's marching band and sung by the assemblage, all standing at attention. As soon as the strains of the stirring music died away a B-24 — its four big 1200-horsepower Pratt & Whitney engines roaring with every ounce of torque they possessed — took off right in front of them and headed for England. But the roll of thunder that followed the bomber was even louder as six sleek P-38s streaked down the runway and launched into the air behind it.

Clare and the other six WAFS who had flown the L4-Bs to Mitchel Field had gotten back on the train late the night before, but, as per Colonel Baker's standing orders, they were up for roll call and the Saturday morning breakfast march. That October morning, the twenty who currently made up the squadron stood at attention near the flight line and saw history made. They found out later that morning, that they had witnessed the first flight of P-38s to attempt a trans-Atlantic crossing. As the twin-engine pursuits formed behind the lumbering four-engine B-24 and headed northeast, the NCAAB band struck up the Air Corps song, "Off We Go Into the Wild Blue Yonder."

The review over, they were dismissed. Clare caught Nancy's eye and nodded to her. Nancy motioned her into the office.

"You were right," Clare said, as she settled in the chair across from Nancy.

"Damn!" Nancy brought the flat of her hand down hard on her desk. "And she's such a good pilot. Good instincts. Perceptive. Steady. Her instructors give her rave points."

"What are you going to do?"

"Tell me what you found out."

"Well, Midge, Jamesy, Rhonie, Del and I rode the subway into town together. Rhonie had planned to meet friends, but we asked

Midge to go to lunch with us at the Rainbow Room and see a show at Radio City. She said she had an old friend to look up — but that she would try to join us at the Rainbow Room in time to go to Radio City. So then she took off and I let her get a fifty-pace start on me. I told the other two to go on to lunch and save me a seat, that I had forgotten to give Midge something. I'm not sure they believed me, but you know Del and Jamesy, they were full of being in New York and went along with it. Then I took off after her."

Nancy nodded, a slight smile crossing her face as if she could see the puzzled looks on the faces of two of her crack pilots. "Go on."

"I could have really messed up, gotten lost. But I managed to stay on her tail. I hung as close to the inside of the sidewalk as I could so I could duck into a shop or something if she turned around, but to my knowledge, she never looked back. I followed at what I hoped was a safe distance, but close enough to see her disappear into the skyscraper on Fifth Avenue — just like you suspected. When I got inside, she was just getting into an elevator. I held my breath, raced over and watched the floors that it stopped on.

"I looked at the listing of the offices in the building. Sure enough, there was Jacqueline Cochran Cosmetics — eighteenth floor. I figured I was on the trail of the fox."

"Clare, this is incredible," Nancy said, offering her a cigarette before taking one herself. She leaned across the desk, snapped the Zippo, and lit first Clare's then her own.

"I rode up to the eighteenth floor and when the door opened I prayed that she wouldn't be standing right there. I don't know what I would have told her if she had been. But the doors opened onto a space with a big glass door and there was the company name. There were some chairs outside the door, so I sat down for a minute to think about what to do next and just like that it came to me. So I walked in and right up to the receptionist — who looked like a younger version of J.C. herself — and said, 'I'm Teresa James, a friend of Miss Culpepper's and a member of the women's ferrying squadron.'"

"You told her you were Teresa James?"

"I thought I'd better cover myself somehow. If Midge said anything to Teresa, ol' Jamesy would tell her she was nuts and rib the life out of her — lead her on. She'd treat it like one big joke."

"Go on," Nancy said.

"This girl is looking me up and down, but she hasn't blown the whistle and called building security, or Jackie Cochran — yet. So I lied. 'We're having a surprise birthday party for Midge at the Rainbow Room,' I tell her. 'I wanted to be sure we have time to get everything set up before she gets there. Is she in seeing Miss Cochran now? If so, do you think they'll be at least a half an hour?'

"Well, she smiled and relaxed and said, 'Oh, Miss Culpepper just got here and Miss Cochran's been expecting her. I'm sure she'll be in there for quite awhile. Would you like to wait? If it's really important, I can tell her you're here.'

"Get that, Nancy? 'Miss Cochran's been expecting her.'"

Nancy nodded and chuckled.

"'No, no,' I said, 'that will spoil the surprise. You've told me what I need to know. By the time she gets back to the Rainbow Room, we'll be ready for her. Don't breathe a word about me coming in. And don't wish her Happy Birthday. It will spoil *everything*.'"

By then, Nancy was laughing so hard, tears ran down her cheeks.

"Anyway, I gracefully excused myself and said that I had to go back and get the party organized. 'Remember, not a word,' I told her as I fled and prayed the elevator would come before Midge waltzed out of that office."

Nancy wiped the tears from her eyes, shaking her head. "Clare, you're a genius!"

"OK, so do you mind telling me what's going on?" Clare asked. "And what tipped you off to Midge?"

"First of all, Midge's credentials were too good to be true. I had her checked out. I couldn't figure out where she got the money to pay for it all and in such a very short time. Her family has no money and, in fact, is in pretty dire circumstances if my sources got the facts straight. She's earned the ratings all right, but it seems that the number of hours in her logbook have been doctored. Apparently she flew Cochran's Staggerwing a lot, but that aircraft is not listed. Her list of aircraft flown is right in line with our other gals."

"Oh, boy. But what made you think she might be connected to Cochran?"

"She's sleeping with a married major on Hap Arnold's staff, my confidential source tells me, and she worked at Antoine's hair salon in Saks Fifth Avenue in New York. I recognized the name because that's where Jackie got her start. I put Arnold and this major and Jackie all together and wondered if, maybe, Midge also knew Jackie."

"Gawd almighty, Nancy… and you thought…?" Clare shook her head.

"Yes, I thought she might be a plant."

"I knew I didn't like that girl."

"I couldn't believe it at first, but it seems to be the only answer. That's why I asked you to follow her. Just a hunch. I wanted proof."

"And it paid off. So what are you gonna do?"

"I'm weighing my options, trying to decide what is the best course to take. Jackie's preparing for the opening of the Women's Flying Training Detachment in Houston. She's got much more grandiose plans than I ever dreamed of, Clare. She wants to command an entire corps of women pilots, and, by God, I think she's going to do it. She wants to train them to do far more than ferry airplanes. She wants them to tow gunnery targets, fly radar testing missions, be test pilots, fly personnel around... in general do everything but fly combat."

"Oh, my. Well, we know she thinks big."

"I don't know how much of this comes from Colonel Tunner's insistence that all women pilots entering the Ferrying Division *must* have the same three hundred hours currently required of entry-level male ferry pilots. He says if Cochran doesn't hold to that requirement by the time they graduate, he will only let a handful of her most experienced and proven pilots ferry airplanes. On the other hand, she's saying she can take a girl with a private pilot's license and the required thirty-five hours and put her through fifty to seventy-five hours of training and stick her in the cockpit of a P-40."

"Ohmigod!"

"Yeah. And you know what? She's just about to do it. She's cut her way through red tape like it's butter. She just walks over people. When I think of how long and hard Bill Tunner and I had to work last summer to get permission to try to find and employ twenty-five women, God, it infuriates me!" She took the last puff of her cigarette and ground it out before continuing. "All she has to do now is get her school up and running. The only thing she doesn't have right now is students. But if I know Jackie Cochran, she'll have enough for that first class that is slated to begin November 16th. Oh, one other thing. Once her school is launched, and once we've got thirty firm commitments on our roster, we can't grow anymore except by taking in graduates of *her* school."

"The woman's got balls."

"Well, Clare, we always knew that, didn't we?"

"How will all this affect us here?"

"I'm not sure, to tell you the truth. But I have some pretty good ideas about how to combat the worst of it. First, we're going to have to grab opportunities for ourselves to fly bigger, faster airplanes. Otherwise — hours aside — Jackie's graduates are going to come out with higher horsepower ratings than we've got and twin-engine experience we don't have at all. We'll be overlooked, shunted aside, and passed over."

"Good Gawd in heaven, then she's won! She'll gradually take us over with her graduates."

Nancy looked pained. "Don't say that, Clare, please don't say she's won. It's not a contest. Besides, I'm convinced her first graduates will be the women who only lacked a few hours or sufficient horsepower rating to join us in the first place. Remember, she's already got the required hours dropped from five hundred to two hundred to enter training. That lets in several more women we know." Nancy paused, brow furrowed. "I've still got a couple of cards up my sleeve. I'm just wondering when and how to play them."

Clare had suspected that Nancy — or Bob — had sources inside Hap Arnold's command.

"I don't think Midge can tell Cochran anything she doesn't already know. And right now I have no secrets. Besides, Midge shows considerable promise as a pilot. I'm going to keep her on where I can watch her."

*****

*On November 8, 1942, Operation Torch, a land, sea and air offensive, began when the Allied Expeditionary Force— units from the USA, the UK, and the Free French — landed in North Africa. With the landings on the shores of Morocco and Algeria, the first major offensive by the Allies against Hitler and the Axis was on its way. On November 10, British Prime Minister Winston Churchill issued the following statement:*

*"This is not the end. It is not even the beginning of the end. But it is, perhaps, the end of the beginning."*

*****

Early in December, Nancy called Clare into her office again. "I'm getting cabin fever. I haven't been flying enough. You girls are having all the fun."

69

Clare wondered about the fun part. Yes, they were flying a lot, but she wasn't sure she'd call flying putt-putt Cubs and open-cockpit PT-19s in wintertime "fun."

The weather had turned unusually cold in November and looked like it had no intention of letting up. The squadron had marched itself down to Supply early in November to be outfitted with winter flying gear — bulky fleece-lined leather jackets and high-waisted fleece-lined leather pants that zipped from the shinbone, up one leg to the sternum, and were held up by suspenders; and underneath all of that, woolen long johns. Chin-strapped leather flying caps, gloves, and wool-lined boots completed the ensemble.

"You may think this is a lot, but it won't be enough," the equipment officer told them.

Feeling like a cross between a sausage and a balloon wearing all that gear, Clare made her first PT-19 trip from Hagerstown to Chattanooga. The supply officer was right. It wasn't enough. The cold seeped under the considerable bulk and lodged next to her skin, chilling her through and through. Sometimes she couldn't feel her feet when she had to use the rudders. Her face had a red, wind-burned look requiring gallons of cold cream to take the sting away, and she had a constant runny nose.

On that memorable trip, as she had ascended to 3,000 feet above the Appalachians, she clocked the air flow by the open cockpit at better than one hundred miles per hour and the temperature at ten degrees. Clare lashed her charts to her leg so they wouldn't blow away, a trick she had learned flying in open cockpits in Colorado in the wintertime.

The six-hundred-fifty-mile trip to Chattanooga normally took eight hours flying time — with stops every two and a half hours to refuel, get rid of the hot coffee they had drunk at the previous stop, and drink another cup to get warm again — and that was just about the amount of daylight they had to make it under the "down-an-hour-before-sundown" rule. One overnight of RON was the rule en route to Chattanooga — more if the weather turned sour.

"Oh, yes, Nancy, we certainly are having fun," she answered, "freezing nose and toes and everything in between."

"Well, you and I are going to make a delivery to Dallas."

"Oh, goody. What are we flying? Cubs that go so slow into a west wind that the cars running below on Highway 40 pass you, or that ice bucket also known as the PT-19?"

"Neither. We have a Lockheed Hudson that needs to go to Dallas, ASAP. All the men are out making deliveries. Most of the women are out, too. Besides, none of them have checked out in it and we have. Remember Pearl Harbor?"

Clare nodded her head. "Do I…"

"Well, get your gear. We're going now."

"Uh, Nancy. Will's stationed outside Fort Worth."

"I thought of that, too. Wire him. See if he can get a twenty-four-hour pass while we're there."

"You are a very good friend, my dear," Clare said, grinning.

Once in the air, Clare realized that Nancy needed a confidante more than she needed a co-pilot. Once they were settled into their course, Nancy started talking.

"There's some good news, Clare. Bob told me this morning that our B-17s and B-24s were part of a big Allied raid over Holland, yesterday. Biggest series of daylight bombings yet over targets in Europe. And three of our fighter squadrons were part of the diversionary activity."

"So maybe the tide is turning?" Clare had to raise her voice over the thrum of the engines.

"That may be a bit optimistic, but at least we're striking back. And word is that pursuit —you know, fighters — production is really gearing up. With any luck along with careful planning, someday we'll be ferrying them."

"Now that would be a *real* coup."

"We need to get our girls transitioned into bigger, more complex airplanes. Make them more useful *before* Cochran's graduates start swelling our ranks."

"How?"

"Well, first of all, New Castle isn't the only location in the country that's close to factories that build trainers. There's Dallas. The 5th Ferrying Group is located there, near several aircraft factories building trainers as well as bigger stuff. Those trainers have to be delivered to training bases — all located in the South where the weather is better year round. Ferry pilots, preferably stationed nearby, are needed to fly them. And then there's Long Beach, California, which is located in a hotbed of factories — Lockheed, Douglas, North American and, more important, Consolidated Vultee that builds basic trainers. I'll eat my hat if the 6th Ferrying Group there doesn't turn out to be the busiest squadron of all. And there's Romulus, Michigan, outside Detroit. The 3rd Ferrying Group stationed there does all the ferrying for Bell in Niagara Falls. Speaking of pursuits, they make the P-39 Airacobra there. And they all want us."

"Want us? You mean they want *women* ferry pilots?"

"Yep. I showed them our delivery records so far and they're impressed. Where we've sent both women and men ferry pilots to the same factory to make the same deliveries, the women have been getting planes delivered faster. Now, granted, we've only been doing this a few weeks, but they like what they see. I tried to tell them it's because women have more to prove, therefore they just want to get the job done. Whatever it is, they're willing to give us more ferrying flights. So those three other bases might be willing to house small contingents of female ferry pilots. Five or six to start with. If we continue to do our job well, and as Jackie's graduates become available sometime around March, we'll increase the size of each squadron."

"So this trip to Dallas is to finalize the deal?"

"More like starting the ball rolling. It's where we'll establish the first squadron away from New Castle. I plan to bring five or six of the girls here the first of January and stay with them until they're established."

"When will the others start up?"

"The plan is Romulus mid-January and Long Beach mid-February. Of course, I haven't told the girls yet that they're going to be broken up."

"Think Midge has gotten wind of this yet?"

"Had you?"

"No."

"Then I don't think she has either. And since we've been keeping such a lid on the idea in the planning stage, I doubt Cochran has heard either. From what I gather, she's busy right now beating the bushes, filling up her future classes."

Clare stared out the cockpit window. The lush green trees of Kentucky and Tennessee had finally dropped their leaves, leaving only the dusty green of an occasional stand of evergreen trees on the hills.

"You said we're going to transition into the bigger airplanes. How, unless the men running these bases are willing to let us do it?" she asked.

"Well, for weeks now we've all been watching the men check out in the P-47 there in Wilmington. I asked Colonel Baker about checking out in it and you know what he said?"

"I'm afraid to ask."

"He said he didn't think women could handle pursuits — this after all he's seen us do and after all he's been part of in getting the WAFS up and running!"

"You know, I've noticed that it's the smaller guys who fly those pursuits. I looked inside a P-40 cockpit the other day. It's tiny. I thought a woman would fit in there real nice."

"My thoughts exactly. Well, I figured we needed to spread that word around. As the commanders at these other bases get to know our girls and see what good pilots they are, pretty soon they'll start to bend. But just in case, I'm going after a check ride in a pursuit. I don't know where I'm going to get it, but I will. And once I've done it, the door should be open for the rest of you. I'm also going after more big twin-engine stuff. By summer, the WAFS should be ferrying a lot more than Cubs and primary trainers."

Will stood at the counter waiting for them when they walked into the Operations Office at Love Field.

"You children run along and have a good time," Nancy said with a wink, after giving Will an enthusiastic hug. "Mother will take care of everything. Clare, call me at seven tomorrow morning and I'll tell you when we depart for Wilmington. It'll probably be American Airlines. Now go! I've got paperwork to hand in and a meeting to get to."

Clare and Will had spent a total of three nights together since he left for flight training two weeks after their wedding in June. They hadn't seen each other since she arrived in Wilmington to join the WAFS. Now, as they rode the bus to the hotel where they would spend the night — agonizing at each bumpy, time-consuming stop that kept them merely holding hands and not in each other's arms — Clare remembered their first night together.

They had been alone in the hangar, hunkered over a work bench where pieces of a torn-down engine lay scattered in what Clare considered organized chaos. Two months into his flying lessons with her, Will was now busy absorbing everything she could teach him about aircraft maintenance. Both had been leaning over the cylinder head they were cleaning for so long that Clare's back began to bother her. She straightened, stretched, and wiped the back of her hand across her sweaty cheek leaving a grease smear. "Ugh, that gets to me after awhile," she said.

Will glanced up and smiled.

Then Clare saw a different look come into his eyes. He straightened and reached in his back pocket, pulling out a clean white handkerchief. How on earth had he kept it so pristine working at grease-monkey chores?

Before she knew what was happening, he moved to her, wet a piece of the cloth on the end of his tongue and gently wiped the grease from her cheek. Clare felt that silken explosion again as his fingers touched her cheek and lingered. But she abruptly backed away, denying what she had just felt and what she had been feeling all too regularly in his presence — every time their elbows or hands or fingers touched performing the little tasks necessary in the close quarters of a cockpit or working on a small piece of airplane hardware.

Will stood his ground, smiling. His eyes, she thought, had a knowing look. "What did I do," he protested. "I just wiped grease off your cheek."

He had her there. That was all he'd done. But what she felt in the process was what concerned her now. And she couldn't let him know. Her mind raced. All the snappy little comments that she kept at the ready had suddenly deserted her.

"Clare?" He stepped toward her.

"No!" She backed up again and put her right hand out as if warding him off. Her shoulder bumped solidly into the wing of the airplane they were working on and she started to move sideways, but he covered the distance between them and leaned forward, placing his hands against the wing — one on either side of her. She was trapped.

"Don't do this," she said, her voice a whisper.

"Why not?"

"Because…"

He moved against her, leaned in and touched his lips to hers, barely brushing them.

"Oh, God!" This was what she had wanted so much to avoid. Or was it? She really wasn't sure anymore. OK, so she had had a long dry spell when it came to men. But this was not a man, this was a boy. A boy who looked very much like a man now standing there so close, trapping her, kissing her, for god's sake. And the sensations inside her were not those generated by contact with a mere boy.

She started to put her hands to his chest to push him away, but he pulled back and watched her, mild amusement on his lips. Her hands fell back limply to her sides. She shook her head. "Will, this isn't right…"

His hands left the wing and cupped her face as he brought his mouth against hers again, seeking, hungry. Clare groaned and, to her utter surprise, met his mouth with equal hunger. The hardness of the wing bit into her shoulder. The unmistakable hardness of him pressed against her thigh. And she knew right then she was falling into a hole she could never climb out of.

Will lived up one of the canyons west of Colorado Springs. On snowy nights, he slept on a cot in the makeshift, ceilingless room at the back of the hangar. They got that far, all the while peeling each other out of their greasy coveralls and their flying clothes beneath. At Clare's prompting, Will put a chair against the door for privacy should anyone inadvertently wander in.

In the morning, Clare had to think fast about how to explain to her frantic parents why she hadn't come home last night or at least called. In the end, she told them the truth — more or less — that she lay down on the cot in the hangar and fell sound asleep and, of course, couldn't call until morning when she awoke. She gently reminded them that she was twenty-six years old, to which her father exploded that as long as she lived under his roof, she was still his responsibility no matter how old she was.

She let it go at that and didn't argue.

It took almost two years of stolen nights together, the declaration of war on the part of the United States, and his enlistment in the Air Corps before Will broke down her resistance and talked her into marriage. She worried about their age difference and knew people would talk. They already were.

"Why don't you find someone younger, Will."

"Because you're more woman than any of these gals around here. And besides, I told you from the beginning, I want to make an honest woman out of you."

Just as she predicted, the Monday after Pearl Harbor he had enlisted. When he got the call to leave his defense plant job for boot camp, she wavered. When he came home on leave before going for flight training, she gave in and they were married. Two months later, after she got the telegram from Nancy Love, she, too, went to war flying airplanes.

And now it was December 1942, and, thanks to Nancy Love, they were about to spend one more night together, this time in a posh, downtown hotel in Dallas.

By Christmas, the squadron numbered twenty-eight. Then Pat Rhonie ran afoul of Colonel Baker over unauthorized time she spent away from the base. She left New Castle on December 31, at the end of her ninety-day contract. By then Nancy also knew that she had the potential of three more members waiting in the wings: Sis Bernheim, Helen McGilvery and Lenore McElroy, a high-time flight instructor who lived near Romulus, Michigan.

Nancy gathered the girls for a meeting and told them they were being split up and where they were going to be stationed. She would take Dorothy Scott, Florene Miller, Helen Richards and Betsy Ferguson to Dallas the first of January. Del Scharr would take Barbara Poole, Barbara Donahue, Kay Thompson and Phyllis Burchfield to Romulus mid-January. Nancy would come there and check out Lenore McElroy once they were settled. B.J. Erickson would take Bernice Batten, Cornelia Fort, Barbara Towne, Annie Gwynn and Evelyn Sharp to Long Beach in February. The rest — Nancy Batson, Gertrude Meserve, Dorothy Fulton, Teresa James, Helen Mary Clark, Esther Nelson, the recently married Esther Manning-Rathfelder, Midge Culpepper and Clare Varsky, as well as Sis Bernheim and Helen McGilvery — would remain in Wilmington with Betty Gillies in charge. By late January 1943, the WAFS squadron would number thirty.

# CHAPTER TEN

"Now that Nancy checked out in the P-51 last week, what have you heard about the possibility of us flying pursuit planes?" Annie asked Cornelia as the two of them lounged in Cornelia's room in the WAFS's quarters at Long Beach. Annie sat in the lone chair, tilted back, her feet propped on the side of the cot, where Cornelia sat with her back against the wall, her long legs stretched out in front of her. They had been in California barely three weeks and, on February 27, Nancy Love had become the first woman in the United States to fly a pursuit aircraft — a 1200-horsepower, North American A-36-A/P-51A.

"Well, I know she's been busy getting checked out in everything they'll let her fly — sixteen different planes, she told me, including the C-47 and, finally, that P-51," Cornelia said.

"Did she say what it felt like — the pursuit, I mean?"

Cornelia laughed. "She said it was the most incredible experience she'd ever had in an airplane but, once aloft and she got the feel of it, that it flew just like any other airplane."

Annie grinned. "I would love a chance to fly one of those. Four hundred miles an hour… I can't imagine."

"Well, if Nancy has her way, you'll get your chance. Just be patient. Right now, the BT-13s look pretty good after all the open-cockpit flights we made in the cold back east."

"I thought we were busy in Wilmington," Annie said. "Since we've been here, we've made so many trips to Texas, I feel like I know Guadalupe Pass more intimately than the green hills around Nashville — and the route on to Dallas is more familiar than the back of my hand."

"Ah, but once we get there, the steaks are worth the whole trip. Last time I was there, I had dinner with friends and they served the biggest juiciest T-bones I've ever had. And, speaking of Dallas — oh-silent-one-who-keeps-everything-to-herself — what's this I hear about a certain second lieutenant who seems quite taken with you?

Sounds like you made a conquest. Are you looking forward to another BT-13 delivery to Love Field?"

Annie blushed. "Florene introduced me to a friend of hers."

"Florene! Well, she certainly has enough to go around. That girl has more smitten suitors than Scarlett O'Hara."

"She told me about this cadet she's known since grade school. Charlie Richardson. He's real tall — 'just right for you, Annie,' she said. He's going to fly B-17s."

Annie had tried very hard to get out of partying with the group in Dallas that night. She had pleaded the onset of cramps as the reason. Memories of her wallflower days at Ward-Belmont made her leery of such functions.

"Oh pooh, Annie, take some aspirin and come along. Once you get out of here, they'll go away real quick," Florene had said. "We're meeting some good looking boys and I have a particular one in mind for you."

Annie rolled her eyes. Still... the other WAFS were going, so maybe it would be all right.

"OK, I'll go, but what do I wear? All I have is my uniform."

"Good heavens, girl, I always carry a party dress and heels when I go on a trip. Just in case. But never mind. We'll all wear our uniforms so you'll feel more at home. That ought to dazzle these boys plenty — nine WAFS, all in uniform. A sea of gray-green gabardine and silver ATC wings."

Barely fifteen minutes into the party, Florene made good on her promise. "Annie, I want you to meet Charlie Richardson."

Much to her delight, Annie was looking *up* from her five-feet-eleven perspective for a change. And what she saw was a very tall young man with piercing blue eyes set deep in what were obviously premature laugh lines — tanned crinkles that come early to both men and women growing up in the sun and wind of west Texas. With his hawkish nose and high cheekbones, he looked like an aviator. But under the tan, she could see that he was blushing. "Hey," she said, holding out her hand in best Ward-Belmont fashion, "I'm Annie Gwynn."

He wore the standard crew-cut fashionable among the young flyers and had an appealing smile. He took her extended hand. "Nice to meet you, Miss Gwynn," he drawled, the flush deepening on his cheeks.

Instinctively, she liked him. Thank you, Florene, for picking a tall one. She liked the feel of her hand in his. What a grip! Feels like he can handle the controls of a four-engine bomber, all right.

"Would you like something to drink?" he said.

She nodded, and as they made their way to the bar, she tried to think of something witty to say, but nothing came to mind. Damn, she thought, it's Ward-Belmont all over again. Get a hold of yourself, Gwynn. He's cute. Don't drive him away with your undazzling personality.

When she realized he was waiting for her to tell him what she wanted, a sudden burst of exotic sophistication overtook her. Remembering the smoky-sweet taste of the rum drink she had discovered after Pearl Harbor, "Cuba Libra," she replied in a low voice she hardly recognized. To Annie, the name conjured warm southern nights, palm trees and romance. She knew about the first two. She wanted desperately to learn about the third.

Charlie ordered a beer for himself.

As they walked together back to the WAFS's table, he guided her by the elbow. Then he held the chair for her and they sat down together.

Now comes the hard part, Annie thought. Small talk. How long before he becomes bored with her and frantically looks around for one of his buddies to come to his rescue? Annie, herself, felt the urge to flee before the humiliating scenario could play out. But instead of the standard "Where are you from, where'd you go to school?" the first question he asked her turned out to be, "What made you decide to learn to fly?"

Soon they were comfortably smoking cigarettes and comparing first flights, first solos and other airplanes they had flown. She wondered why he didn't ask her to dance. Then it dawned on her that the dance floor was packed with couples jitterbugging. Fast music was her downfall. She never could master those intricate steps even when several friends tried to teach her one night on the third floor of the Tri-Delt house in Knoxville, her lesson brought to an abrupt end when the housemother made them turn down the Victrola and act like proper young ladies.

Now the question was, would he try to dance when the jukebox played a slow, romantic song? She got her answer when the strains of *Smoke Gets In Your Eyes* floated across the dance floor and he said, "Miss Gwynn, would you like to dance?"

"Charlie... please call me Annie. And yes, I'd love to." She hardly recognized the girl who said that. She sounded so confident. Thank you, Mother, for the seventh-grade dancing lessons at Miss Tuttie's, she thought, remembering how her rudimentary knowledge of the foxtrot had gotten her through the rare high school dances she had attended and then a few more at college as well.

Tall, shy, and awkward, Annie learned early that being asked to dance by any young man would be a rarity in her life — even by the tall ones. They, too, seemed to prefer the petite girls who made them look, and feel, even taller. And invariably, the little girls were pretty. But more important, Annie learned, they tossed their heads just the right way. When Annie practiced that in front of the mirror, she knew she looked ridiculous.

She had learned the steps in dancing school playing the role of the boy — because of her height and because of the dearth of boys. She would carry *that* secret to her grave rather than reveal it to her popular-with-the-boys fellow WAFS.

Charlie's big hand closed over hers — taking command of it much like, she was sure, he took control of the stick of the AT-6 trainer he currently flew. He led her to the dance floor and then held her close enough to dance comfortably to those sultry tones, but not too close. And when the song ended, he did not let her go; rather, he held her in a state of suspended animation. Neither of them spoke. She liked the feel of his arm around her.

When the sugar trumpet began to play the romantically familiar *Stardust*, they began to move again in time to the music. He pulled her a little closer and she sighed, relaxed, and felt her hair graze his cheek. Seconds later, his cheek pressed lightly against her hair. Annie had the sensation of floating. Only his arm held her to earth.

*Stardust* over, he released her slowly — reluctantly, she thought — but kept her right hand. Their eyes met and her heart did a stutter step. As the band launched into the *Boogie Woogie Bugle Boy from Company C,* he laughed, shook his head and directed her off the dance floor and back to their table.

Seated again, he began to tell her about his family and their ranch near Amarillo, all about learning to fly at fifteen and how he proved to be so good at it, his father made him the official family pilot once he turned seventeen and could get his license. He talked not in the boring, bragging way she had learned to expect, from her limited dating experience back home, but quietly and sincerely. Heads bent close to hear better over the loud music and the buzz of others' conversations, they talked and smoked and sipped their drinks.

Every time the jukebox launched into a slow, romantic tune, Charlie was on his feet and leading her to the dance floor, where they moved together like they had known each other all their lives. Now his cheek pressed solidly against her hair and she snuggled close to his chest and shoulder, as if she belonged there. And right there in his arms, Annie began to dream dreams she had never before allowed herself to dream. She ached to be kissed and let her mind roam around a series of scenarios where she could let herself be caught alone with him long enough for that kiss to take place.

He tilted his head back and looked at her, causing her heart to stutter again. "What are you thinking about?"

She blushed. "Flying," she lied. How could she tell him the truth? Alone in an airplane — in the clear blue sky with the green earth below, in a machine that had the power to get her up there and to get her back to earth — Annie soared. And she knew she had control of her destiny. But in the arms of Charlie Richardson, what she felt had nothing to do with control and everything to do with want and need and losing control, and she dared not let him suspect that.

He pulled her very close and buried his nose in her hair.

Oh, God, she thought. My knees feel like water. I'm a goner.

As the party drew to a close and they were saying goodbye as a group, Charlie leaned over and whispered to her, "Come outside with me." His Adam's apple bobbed as if he had trouble getting the words out.

Dumbly she nodded and allowed herself to be led outdoors. Florene's smiling green eyes were the last thing she saw before the door closed behind her and they were out in the cool Texas night. The stars were in picking distance.

"Annie…" Charlie's voice sounded strained. "Oh, hell," and he pulled her close and kissed her, softly but with a growing intensity. And what surprised Annie was the intensity with which she kissed him back.

And then behind them the door flew open. Their friends spilled out into the night just as Charlie took a deep breath, threw his head back and shouted, "Yee-hah! I'm going to marry you, Annie Gwynn."

They all heard, of course, and they all clapped and cheered. Annie, both mortified and soaring above the earth all at the same time, realized that her legs were so weak they were about to give way beneath her. Had she heard him correctly? By the reaction of the others, she had.

"Come on, Annie," she heard Florene say. "Your transport to Long Beach leaves really early in the morning. We've got to get you out of here before you run off with this boy tonight."

Annie found herself in the car with the other WAFS. She turned and looked out the back window and saw Charlie standing there, hands in his pockets, staring after her.

The other girls teased her unmercifully all the way back to the barracks.

"Gwynn, you are a deep one," said Florene. "So quiet, so proper. And who comes out of this evening with a proposal? Why, little Miss Tennessee, that's who! And they haven't really had their first date."

So stunned was she by Charlie's declaration — by the feelings being with him had aroused in her, Annie could hardly sleep and then barely dragged herself to breakfast the next morning before they were scheduled to leave.

By March 18, she had received three letters from Charlie Richardson. But none of them said anything about marriage — somewhat to her relief. Nor did he, in any of them, profess his undying love for her. That, she would have liked to hear. He chattered on about what he was flying and where and about how he hoped she would have a mission back to Texas soon. Maybe she had misunderstood. Maybe he had been teasing her. Playing with her. She wrote back to him the same kind of letters she received. Light. Non-committal.

Still, she was excited over the prospect of seeing him again when she and Cornelia were scheduled to depart early Friday morning, March 19, to deliver BT-13s to Dallas. Several of the male pilots in the 6th Ferrying Group were delivering BT-13s as well.

They all RONed in Tucson. The next day they planned to make Abilene, but were grounded in El Paso because of a dust storm. Sunday morning, March 21, they took off with Dallas as their destination. "Here I go on another Sunday flight," Cornelia said to Annie as they headed for the flight line. "Well, Mother, what you don't know won't hurt you."

When they stopped to refuel in Midland, they decided to grab something to eat in the airport snack bar. There, they ran into the male pilots also headed for Dallas and Cornelia started talking to them. When one of them suggested that they practice a little formation flying out over the wide open spaces, Cornelia said she would like to try it. Annie couldn't believe it — thought she was kidding or putting up a brave front. The young men were taught formation flying because they would need it later going into combat in fighters and bombers. The women, not headed for combat, had no use for it.

They were well into West Texas by mid-afternoon when one of the young aerobats, apparently bored with the uneventful flying that made up most of ferrying work, decided to practice some of his hard-won maneuvering skills. Annie watched as he did some slow rolls, then some barrel rolls, then an inside loop and an outside loop and a couple of falling leaves. He flew off to the north, did a 180-turn and flew back. Then he flew south, did another 180-turn and flew back. He buzzed her aircraft a couple of times, but never came as close as that jerk Al had in the PT-19 over Pennsylvania.

Then Annie noticed one of the other planes near Cornelia's — off to the left, north of the rest of them. He flew up on Cornelia's right wing and stayed there. Seemingly bored with straight flight, he pulled up and executed a barrel roll, and then another. As he came over and down the third time, his landing gear struck the left wing of Cornelia's plane, sending it tumbling out of control in the clear Texas air.

Annie gasped as the world suddenly went into slow motion. She wanted to reach out in the air and grab Cornelia's plane and put it right. "Pull out, Cornelia," she screamed, her voice echoing around the enclosed canopy of her own BT-13.

Then she realized that, in watching Cornelia's plane, she had neglected her own and she had, inadvertently while looking down, moved the stick forward. Her craft, too, was now diving toward the red earth below. She pulled up, felt the controls mush, realized she had almost stalled, and — regaining her sense of balance and flight — returned the stick to neutral.

Cornelia's plane was still falling in that slow sickening flat spin every pilot dreads. "Get out!" Annie shouted through clenched teeth. "Bail!"

Sensing that she'd better check where the other planes had gone, she scanned the skies above, below and around her. She located the other five planes — circling crazily. Then the voice of the flight leader came through the radio, screaming at them all to get back on course before they ran into each other.

The rogue plane that did the deed had recovered, but sickeningly close to the earth. Annie saw him begin to climb for altitude. She searched the sky for the telltale white mushroom that would tell her that Cornelia had jumped. There was none.

Annie watched in horror as her friend's airplane crashed into the red Texas dirt. Tears running down her cheeks and sobbing, she began to look for a place to land. The radio in the basic trainer again crackled in her ear. "Do not attempt to land. Repeat. Do not attempt to land. I have given the S.O.S. Help is on the way. Repeat. Do not attempt to land."

Then the flight leader gave them new orders. The rest of the flight was to go on to Love Field, some 180 miles away. The flight leader said he was going down low to see if the pilot of the downed trainer could have, miraculously, survived.

"Please, I want to come, too. She's my friend," Annie said.

"Negative, Gwynn, follow orders."

She watched the leader's plane fly low over the yellow and blue wreckage.

Thank God, Annie thought. No sign of fire. She continued heading east in the direction of Dallas.

"Can you see anything?" she asked the flight leader.

"I can see the pilot inside the cockpit. The canopy is closed. There's no movement. And there is, fortunately, no sign of fire. Go on to Dallas, Gwynn, I'll take care of the rescue people."

Annie, numb, wanted to scream and cry out, but knowing she couldn't, she obeyed the command. She took one last glance at her friend's downed plane and whispered, "Oh, Cornelia. Why you?" And then she set the course ordered by the flight leader and flew on to Dallas.

The Flying Safety Section of the Ferrying Division of the Air Transport Command took charge of the crash investigation. Annie heard, much later — when all the piecing together had been completed — that the investigators found no evidence of pilot error on Cornelia's part.

"I could have told them that," she sobbed to Nancy. "He collided with her in mid-air. He just had to show off. But he couldn't properly handle his own airplane when he needed to and he caused her to die."

The official verdict: Cornelia must have been knocked unconscious in the collision with the other airplane. Otherwise, a pilot with her experience would have either been able to pull out of the spin or jumped. To Annie's knowledge, the possibility that the canopy might have been jammed never came up for discussion. She also realized that the fact there was no fire probably meant Cornelia had cut the switch and she had to be conscious to do that.

Annie begged for leave to go to Nashville for the funeral, but Nancy Love gently told her no, even though she would like to let all of the WAFS attend the funeral, the Army could not spare nearly twenty-five of its ferry pilots for the time they would be out of service. The word around the 6th Ferrying Group confirmed that Cornelia Fort was the first U.S. woman pilot to die while on active service to her country. Already, the publicity surrounding the accident was more than Nancy Love or the Ferrying Division brass could bear.

Having all the WAFS in attendance at the funeral would just add fuel to the fire. The curiosity factor was simply too great.

Nancy, B. J. Erickson, and the major in charge of Operations at Long Beach flew a C-47 to Nashville for the funeral at Christ Episcopal Church. Ill at ease speaking on an emotional subject in front of a crowd of strangers, Nancy declined to offer a eulogy. Instead, she wrote to Cornelia's mother and sent each of the WAFS a copy of her message.

> *My feeling about the loss of Cornelia is hard to put into words. I can only say that I miss her terribly, and loved her. She was a rare person. If there can be any comforting thought, it is that she died as she wanted to — in an Army airplane, and in the service of her country.*

B.J. suggested that Annie, the closest to Cornelia, be the one to check on her personal belongings and see that they were properly packaged to be sent to the Fort family. So Annie braved her dead friend's room.

Open on her desk was Cornelia's five-year diary, in which she recorded short daily observations. Annie thought her friend must have just finished an entry and left it open to pick up when she returned. But when she picked it up to mark the spot in the diary and place it in the box, Annie noticed the date on the page was March 21, 1940. She read the entry.

> *My beloved father, Dr. Rufus E. Fort, died today. I cannot believe my strong-willed, loving father is gone, but, there it is. The truth of the matter is, he is no longer with us and we will have to carry on without him. Oh, daddy, we will all miss you so.*

Annie looked again, not believing what she saw. Cornelia had left the diary open to the page dated March 21, 1943 — the day she met her own death. Annie shuddered at the deadly coincidence, and, carefully writing a brief explanation on a piece of Cornelia's stationary, she marked the page with it, closed the diary, and placed it in the box.

A week later, Annie requested a transfer. She fought the overwhelming urge to request Dallas because Charlie was there. But for how long? He would be sent elsewhere for B-17 training, and did she really want to chance reality setting in and spoiling the only romance she had ever had? Better to keep it long distance, she thought. She wrote out her request to return to Wilmington — and her reasons — and gave it to Nancy Love.

> *I hope you don't think this shows great weakness on my part, Mrs. Love, but I am finding it impossible to concentrate and work here in Long Beach where, everyday, Cornelia's absence is overwhelming to me. I feel such a tremendous sense of loss. Not only was she my closest friend in the WAFS corps, I watched her die and I don't think I can continue to live with those memories here. Please, may I return to Wilmington, or at least go to Dallas or Romulus?*

A few days later, her transfer back to Wilmington came through.

# CHAPTER ELEVEN

"Look at it, Clare!" Nancy tapped her index finger on the paper lying on the desk in front of her. "It's right there in black and white. Our percentage of successful, on-time, safe deliveries is much higher than the men's. And our pilot-error percentage is back to zero, now that they've determined Cornelia's crash can't be laid to pilot error."

"So what's the problem?" Clare asked, puzzled.

Nancy had just come from an ATC meeting in Washington and was in Wilmington to check up on her squadron there before returning to Long Beach. "The brass is unhappy about the lack of efficiency among the ferrying groups. They spelled it out to me as, 'It's the men who are screwing up, Nancy, not your girls. You've got a good record. How do you do it? What's your secret?'"

"That's easy and it's not a secret," said Clare. "Some of the guys stop off, maybe even go out of their way, to see girlfriends en route."

Nancy frowned. Clare had noticed her doing more of that lately and faint lines were beginning to etch their way onto her once smooth forehead.

"I used your exact words, Clare, and told them if they 'took away the fellas' little black books,' everything would be fine. I don't think they believed me. They think I've got some deep dark secret and I'm not sharing it with them."

"Well, I wouldn't discount our women hoping for an RON that will allow them to see the boyfriend or the hubby. You made it possible for me to see Will. Del Scharr flies into Saint Louis to see Harold every chance she gets. Betty certainly makes sure she's on every Long Island flight. And you sure don't turn down opportunities to go to Washington."

"True, but the point is, the women don't change flight plans and roam all over the country to do it," Nancy said.

"Exactly."

"I tried telling them that we're still proving ourselves. The men don't have to. But I'm not sure they wanted to hear that. They don't understand that women have to be better in order to even be allowed in the game."

"I think there's something more that they can't possibly understand."

"What?"

"All of us — to a woman — are so in love with the thought of flyin' those big, beautiful Army airplanes, that's all we want to do right now and we won't do anything to jeopardize that. We know how lucky we are to have the chance to fly them at all."

"Comes down to the old right versus privilege thing," Nancy said. "Men figure it's their right to fly big, powerful airplanes around the sky. Women look on it as a privilege."

"That's about the size of it, chief."

"Well!" The word had a triumphant ring to it. The frown disappeared and Nancy's lovely face once again wore a broad grin. "Here we go again. The brass has decided to let good ol' Nancy and her girls show them the way to a more efficient delivery schedule — little black book or no little black book."

"Another test?"

"Right. And, if we make good, our success will be waved in front of the guys' noses, as in 'See, the girls can do it. Are you going to let a bunch of females out-do you?' But then, that seems to be a part of our role anyway, so why complain. We get to fly their airplanes in the bargain."

"What's the test?"

"Deliver six PT-26s from Hagerstown to the Canadian RAF in Calgary, Alberta, by Easter. That's more than twenty-five hundred miles and Easter is nine days away. I promised Baker and Tunner we'd get them there."

Clare let out a long, low whistle. "That doesn't allow for any weather along the route. Are you taking the flight yourself?"

"Nope. I've already talked to Betty. She's in charge."

"Who's going with her?"

"You are, for one. Also Batson, McGilvery, Bernheim, and Gwynn — she needs the distraction. And just between you and me, there may be a little something extra in this for us if we pull it off. Something beyond the satisfaction of saying we did it."

"What?"

"I'm not at liberty to say, but if anybody can do it, Betty and you girls can."

"Eeeeyow!" Clare whooped, as she climbed into the cockpit of her PT-26 that Palm Sunday morning. "We're goin' all the way to

Montana and on to Calgary, Canada!" The other five laughed. They were used to Clare's sudden outbursts of enthusiasm.

They left Hagerstown early and ran out of daylight in Joliet, Illinois. Clare noted thankfully that, as they flew west, the weather improved. Spring definitely had sprung! Besides, these airplanes had canopies so they didn't have to contend with wind in their faces and icicles forming on their runny noses.

That night at the hotel, Betty informed them that they would be up at four in the morning. "We're going to get an early start. I want us sitting in our cockpits with the engines running when the sun breaks the horizon. Now get some sleep. Tomorrow's a long day."

"Today was a long day… we flew seven hundred miles!" came the tired, wounded chorus from the other five.

"Four a.m."

Despite considerable grousing and threats to sleep in, their consciences got the best of them and the five were sitting in the hotel lobby — as ordered — at four the following morning when Betty appeared fresh and ready to fly another near-record day. A charismatic leader in spite of her diminutive stature, Betty commanded a healthy respect from her charges. They did not want to let her down.

They took off as dawn broke. Destination — North Platte, Nebraska. A 600-mile flight.

Clare drank in the cornfields of Iowa and the wheat fields of Nebraska like she had never seen corn and wheat fields before. Crossing the Missouri River below Omaha provided the highlight of her day. She was back in her element — the West.

They were up at four again the next day and this time made Great Falls, Montana, a whopping 850-mile flight from North Platte, and this — Betty pointed out to them proudly — in airplanes that had an average ground speed of one hundred miles per hour.

Before finding a hotel, Betty got all the Customs forms filled out. Great Falls, one hundred miles from the Canadian border, housed the ATC's 7th Ferrying Group where training planes were processed for delivery to Canada and for aircraft bound to Alaska and, eventually, Russia. Their six airplanes were bound for an RCAF pilot training facility somewhere in Alberta.

The next day, up at four again, they flew along the majestic snow-capped Canadian Rockies and into Calgary.

While in Great Falls, Clare had treated herself to a ten-gallon Stetson. She wore it, perched atop her unruly curls, in the cockpit from there to Calgary. "And I'm wearin' it all the way back to Wilmington on the train. Just wait 'til people get a load of *my* Easter bonnet," she informed the others.

They had delivered the planes from Hagerstown to Calgary in a record four days — and four days before the Easter deadline. Nancy had to be basking in that glory by now, Clare thought — but quietly so. Nancy didn't go around boasting, even of her handpicked girls' accomplishments.

On the train ride back, they had a lot of time to think and to talk, and they took apart and put back together the entire women's flying program. Much of the conversation centered on the news that Cochran's first WFTD class, 43-W-1, would swell their ranks in early May. The twenty-three graduates were to be divided among the four existing women's squadrons.

"But did you hear the latest?" Betty said.

Clare decided that it helped that Betty went out on occasional ferrying trips with them. Back at New Castle, she tended to be a bit closed-mouthed, as any good commander must be. But when out with the other women doing the job they had all been hired to do, she loosened up.

"What, now?" the chorus of five voices answered.

"Cochran has reduced the total required flying time for recruits entering her program to the thirty-five hours required for a private license."

"My Gawd," said Clare, "she got our original five hundred reduced to two hundred for her first class, one hundred for the second, and seventy-five for the third. What's going on?"

"Nancy thinks that Jackie truly wants to open the program to any girl with the desire to fly and who can prove she has the necessary skills," Betty answered.

"What's that going to do to the WAFS?" Annie asked.

"My guess is that it won't affect the ferrying program for a long time," Betty said. "Certainly, young women all over the country will flock to the flight schools to learn to fly in hopes of qualifying for the new training school. But even after they've got their licenses and are accepted, training them to fly the Army way will take a minimum of six months. Maybe more. By the way, you know Cochran's moved her program from Houston to Avenger Field in Sweetwater, Texas?"

"Yeah," Clare said. "I'll bet Jackie will really be swamped with applications now."

"You know what really bothers me?" said Nancy Batson. "I heard Cochran's girls are flying AT-6s — those six-hundred-horsepower advanced trainers with retractable gear — and we're restricted to flying primary trainers. Are they ever going to let us transition into anything bigger? Hasn't the fact that Nancy flew the P-51 and you the P-47 had any effect?"

Betty shrugged. "I don't know. The girls in Long Beach are flying Basic Trainers and the girls in Dallas are moving into AT-6s. My gut feeling is things might be about to change for us as well."

On the eve of Easter Sunday, the six flyers climbed wearily out of two cabs that had brought them from the train station in Wilmington to the base in New Castle. The train ride back had taken three days and they all were travel weary.

"Just lead me to the showers and then to my bed." Clare, still wearing her Stetson, voiced what she knew the others felt with three days of unrelieved travel grime on them.

Upon their return, Colonel Baker passed out official commendations, which reflected positively on the entire WAFS organization as a ferrying unit. In just over six months, Nancy noted in her congratulations to the girls, the women of the WAFS had gone from "a group of civilian volunteers, not sure what they were getting into but willing to try, to a professional paramilitary cadre of ferry pilots capable of the delivery of airplanes, safely, on time and on demand, anywhere in the United States and Canada."

But the commendation wasn't the "little something extra" Nancy had alluded to earlier, Clare discovered, four days after their return. On April 26, ATC deputy chief of staff General C.R. Smith sent a letter to Ferry Division Headquarters.

> *It is the desire of the command that all pilots, regardless of sex, be privileged to advance to the extent of their ability in keeping with the progress of aircraft development. Will you please insure that the terms of this policy are carried out insofar as it applies to ferrying of aircraft within the continental U.S.A?*

And with that — weight, horsepower and multiple-engine restrictions were history.

"Aw'right!" Clare did an Indian dance around the barracks. "We're gonna get to fly the big stuff!"

News from the battlefront helped insert the exclamation point Clare put on those words. While the six were on their trip to Canada, American bombers, committed to a policy of precision daylight bombing, had carried out their first attacks into the heart of Germany. Pursuit planes were desperately needed to protect those bombers by flying with them all the way to the target and then home. But the pursuits, to date, did not have the range for the long trips. Newer, long-range pursuit planes were in the design and testing stages, and they were the ones the women might eventually get to ferry. They were the airplanes that would be needed to protect those bombers when Berlin itself became the target.

That night after dinner, the women of the 2nd Ferrying Group sat in the lounge of the New Castle Officers Club and indulged in that time-honored favorite pastime of all pilots, hangar flying. And, cautiously, they began to share their dreams of flying the big ones. Now that it looked like they were going to fly bigger trainers and eventually twin-engine craft and maybe pursuit, they were willing to admit to their longings. Eventually the conversation drifted into how and why they all learned to fly.

Clare, in rare form, regaled the younger WAFS — Annie, Midge, Gert Meserve, and Nancy Batson — with the tale of how she conquered her fear of flying and became a pilot "when you guys were still in grammar school." Even though she now had nearly three thousand hours in her logbook, Clare still had vivid memories of the day she went up in an airplane for the first time. Only seventeen, she had taken to hanging out with her older brother and his friends at the airport.

"I thought I was gonna lose my cookies right there," she told the gathering. "I had my eyes squeezed shut real tight, worrying about my stomach, when I thought, this is ridiculous, I'm up here, I might as well look around 'cause I'm never gonna do this again. So I opened my eyes and, my Gawd, it was beautiful. The trees were turning and this whole landscape of Colorado evergreens and aspen-gold Fall was spread out in front of me and I thought, well, maybe this isn't so bad. So I kept my eyes open the rest of the flight and forgot about my stomach and enjoyed myself. But I still wasn't sold. Right after that, one of my brother's friends crashed trying to land. I watched him hit and I watched him burn. I was sure sick that day. I'll never forget the sound of his screaming — or the smell. And I vowed I'd never go up in another airplane."

To their empathetic nods and murmurs of understanding, she continued, "I felt weird, too, because the guy had kinda come on to me. He was just a casual acquaintance of my older brother — treated me like any pest of a little sister. Then, one day, he looked at me with this funny grin on his face and said, 'You think some guy's gonna take you flyin' and light a fire in your pants, kid?' I didn't know what he meant by it, but it made me feel kinda creepy."

She had thought it a silly, hurtful remark at the time. Then, as she reflected on it more, even given her limited knowledge of men and sex at that point in her life, she thought she caught a suggestive meaning behind the words. But within days, the man was dead — burned to a crisp in an all-consuming fire. "Turns out… the airplane had lit a fire in *his* pants and it had burned him beyond recognition and that thought haunted me for a long time."

Everyone was quiet for a few beats until…"I had a similar experience," Midge said from her place on the other side of the table. Clare thought her voice sounded strained.

"Not over an airplane, though. Still, it disgusted me and made me feel dirty."

Clare waited. Finally, when Midge didn't continue, she asked, "How old were you?"

"Fourteen."

An uneasy silence engulfed the table where their drinks sat and where some of them leaned on their elbows as they listened to each other's tales.

"Do you want to talk about it, Midge?" Betty asked, gently.

"No." She leaned back and folded her arms. "Go on, Clare. I'm sorry I interrupted you."

Clare looked around the group, caught an almost imperceptible shake of Betty's head, and quickly made up her mind to get the conversation back on a lighter vein.

"Well, I'm here to tell you, the trauma sure didn't last very long. I was back out the next week. This new guy, just graduated from Parks Air College in Saint Louis, told me that if I was going to hang around airports, I might as well learn to fly and he'd give me my first lesson free. Now mind you, this was the middle of the Depression. Free *anything* sounded good, so I took him up on it. He had this OX-5 — remember the old Travelair, no brakes, no tail wheel, just a tailskid? You had to learn to taxi. The instrument panel consisted of an oil gauge, an altimeter and a gasoline thing bobbing up and down."

Betty and the other older girls nodded their heads.

"Well, we got up in the air and were flying around and he was having me do all these maneuvers. Him in the front seat yelling things like 'get the nose down' or 'get that wing up.' All the time, I thought he was actually flyin' the plane and I was just movin' the controls with him. Turns out, he wasn't flyin' the plane, I was. I soloed in four hours and forty minutes and I've been flyin' ever since."

That night, Clare lay on her cot unable to sleep. She couldn't get what Midge had said out of her mind. Something from the kid's past had surfaced that had nothing to do with Jacqueline Cochran.

The girl had a life. She wasn't a puppet. And for the first time, Clare saw Midge as more than a single-dimensional person — more than someone she had taken an instant dislike to. Of course, her reason for disliking Midge was that she was a threat to Nancy. But, maybe she wasn't so bad after all. Nancy didn't seem worried about her, nor did Betty.

I need to get to know her better, Clare reasoned, get past that façade she's got built around herself. Besides, with the girls coming to join us from the Texas flight school, we need all the *esprit de corps* we can muster. The newcomers, she knew, had already received training in basic and advanced single-engine trainers, they had had night flying as well as instrument flying. With all that experience, they were ahead of many of the original WAFS. But now, with Colonel Tunner and the ATC lifting the ban on transition to bigger, faster, airplanes, the WAFS could expand their horizons.

Up until now, Clare had ached to get her hands on an AT-6, the advanced trainer Jackie's girls had begun flying in Texas. Now, it looked like not just the AT-6, but, thanks to Betty's flights that began in February, the P-47 might be within range.

All this news about the girls coming from Texas, reduced hours to qualify for Cochran's school, and transitioning to bigger aircraft had served to remind Clare of one more concern that added to her wakefulness. Something Nancy had said to her two weeks earlier.

"Once Cochran gets her promised five hundred women pilots trained and graduated, technically, she will be out of a job. The merging of the new graduates with the WAFS is the beginning of the end for her."

"And Nancy Love will be sitting pretty as the head of the women's air force that Cochran dreams of commanding," Clare had said.

"No way will Jacqueline Cochran put up with that." Nancy's worry lines had popped out on her forehead. "The battle for control of the women pilots attached to the Army Air Forces is on."

Finally, Clare fell asleep counting the P-47s she now knew she would eventually be flying — in only a matter of time.

# CHAPTER TWELVE

Not being assigned to the "Easter" mission left Midge feeling out of sorts. She had heard, via the grapevine, that she was to go, then Annie Gwynn — recently returned from Long Beach — got the assignment instead. Scuttlebutt hinted that Betty thought Annie needed something like that to take her mind off Cornelia's death.

Midge had noticed that, even with the transfer back to Wilmington, Annie still seemed to be in the dumps. But Midge, feeling put upon herself at being passed over for such a crucial flight, was only mildly sympathetic. She certainly would have welcomed the chance to put a commendation in her performance jacket. Now that would have been something to show Jacqueline Cochran.

A few days after the Calgary flight, Betty called Midge into her office.

"I've got two PT-19s that need to go to Texas. I'm sending Teresa. Her husband's back there on temporary duty. It'll give her a chance to see him for a few hours. I want you to take the other one."

PTs again, Midge thought with a disgust she dared not show in front of Betty. That she wasn't checked out yet on any of the bigger planes rankled her. But now things were looking up. The timing of a delivery to Texas couldn't have been any better. Cochran was currently headquartered in Fort Worth. Teresa would be absorbed in seeing her husband and that would give Midge a chance to check in with Jackie. And Major Barry Metzger was also in the Dallas-Fort Worth area. He had temporary duty in Texas and, knowing that the WAFS were ferrying airplanes down there, he had written to her: *Maybe we can get together for a drink, if you ever get sent this way. I've really missed you.*

She laughed. As transparent as cellophane, he simply wanted to get her in the sack again. Yet she found him irresistible. Why?

The following day, she and Teresa headed south via Lynchburg for Charlotte, where they RONed the first night. The second day, they refueled in Atlanta and flew into Birmingham for their overnight. Birmingham's infamous smog kept them grounded part of the next morning, but they finally got off, refueled in Jackson, and made Shreveport before dark. The next day, they flew into Dallas' Love Field. The following day they would deliver their trainers to a base in some remote part of the state and then make their way back by bus to Dallas to catch an American Airlines flight to Washington. There they would board a train for Wilmington and grab a cab back to the base.

With the evening to kill in Texas' twin cities, Teresa took off to meet her husband. Midge called Cochran's office in downtown Fort Worth and was invited to come over immediately. Jackie lost no time in filling her in on the great progress she had made and how her plans were unfolding. "We have four hundred women in training at Avenger Field and the first class just graduated in Houston. My biggest problem is with this Texas socialite, Oveta Culp Hobby, who has been made the head of the Women's Auxiliary Army Corps. They've made her a colonel!"

Jackie explained that a bill was headed to Congress to grant the WAACs full military status and to change the name to Women's Army Corps or WACs. To top that off, she said, militarization of the women pilots under the Army had hit a snag and she had been offered the opportunity to place her girls as part of the WAC if that went through.

"They want to take MY girls and put them in the WACs under HER command. Pilots, Midge. For God's sake, you don't treat pilots like a bunch of stenographers and file clerks. Pilots belong in the Air Forces. We can do better than the WAC and I intend to hold out for that. So I'm flying to Washington tomorrow to meet with General Arnold to hear more on this latest scheme. Believe me, I'll put a stop to it just like I put a stop to that Love woman building an empire for herself on my turf. No one is going to command these women flyers we're training but yours truly."

Jackie paused, made that inverted V with her fingertips and looked at Midge over them, almost is if really seeing her for the first time since she entered the office. Then she smiled, dropped her hands to the desk and leaned forward in her chair. "So, tell me how things are going with you and the WAFS. How are you getting along with Betty Gillies now that she's your C.O.?"

"Betty and I get along just fine. I like her. She has a way about her that let's you know she's the boss without making you think she's anything other than a friend. Nancy asked her to personally guide me through the early cross-country flights until I got a bit more experience."

"How is she as a leader, compared to Nancy Love?" Midge knew from Jackie's voice — silken and low, almost seductive — that she was getting the third degree from the expert of the steel-hand-inside-the-velvet-glove technique.

"Well," Midge said, instantly on her guard, "Betty seems a little more at home with command than Nancy. I always have the feeling that Nancy would much prefer to be out flying airplanes than sitting behind a desk pushing papers and making assignments. Not that Betty doesn't love to fly, mind you."

"No, of course she does," Jackie said. "I've known Betty for several years. Never had much occasion to spend any time with Nancy, however. I heard she checked out in a pursuit and is busy chalking up transitions to other bigger aircraft. Do you know what all she's flown?"

"Not really. She hasn't been around New Castle much since the first of the year."

Midge felt like a traitor, though she had told Jackie nothing she probably didn't already know.

"Is she flying bombers, do you know?"

"I don't know."

"I hear now that Betty Gillies has flown the pursuit, Tunner has finally given the go-ahead for the rest of you to transition into the bigger planes. I thought they were going to keep you flying primary trainers forever."

"Well, for awhile, Colonel Baker was against the WAFS flying heavier stuff."

"That rather explains why Nancy moved on to Dallas and Long Beach, doesn't it? I hear things are considerably more relaxed at those bases. Are you sorry you didn't get sent to one of those other bases — away from Wilmington?"

Midge thought a minute. "Yes and no. The weather in Wilmington is lousy and obviously Texas and California are more desirable places to be for many reasons, weather being a big one. And, yes, the girls in Texas and Long Beach already are flying bigger airplanes — BT-13s and some AT-6s. But the squadron left at New Castle is the best. They're all very dedicated and excellent flyers. Six of them just got a commendation from Colonel Baker."

A commendation that could have been hers, Midge thought but didn't say so out loud. She wished she could do something to make Cochran think of her as something more than her personal lackey.

Cochran seemed to digest what Midge had said and shifted her position slightly in her chair. Midge sensed another tack.

"How are they going to react to my girls when they show up and are integrated into the squadron?"

"That's a hard one to answer, Miss Cochran. We've gotten quite close as a group over the last few months. I imagine the other three squadrons feel the same way. But if these girls are as good as you say they are, and as dedicated, then I think they'll be accepted and made to feel at home. From what I hear, they're badly needed. They tell us that planes are rolling off assembly lines faster than we can ferry them."

"Yes, bombers and pursuits. I've been wondering if this relaxing of the constraints on transitioning to heavier aircraft will actually mean you'll get to ferry them. They may prefer to keep the women flying trainers — albeit the bigger ones. Then they can shift all the male ferry pilots to flying the big stuff. That should make Baker and Tunner happy. Everybody but Nancy Love, anyway."

"You know, Bill Tunner doesn't like me," Cochran said, suddenly changing the subject.

Midge wasn't sure how to respond to that. She had heard Nancy and, more lately, Betty singing Tunner's praises, so she hesitated to say anything at all.

"I've heard that Nancy Love's husband, who, as you probably know, is a colonel and General George's assistant deputy chief of staff at the Air Transport Command, called me a bitch." She chuckled to herself. "Well, I've been called worse. As the saying goes, they ain't seen nothin' yet."

Midge thought of Barry and the Dragon Lady... but said nothing.

"You're awfully quiet all of a sudden. Don't you like me talking about your friends?"

"I don't know Mrs. Love that well, and Betty and Colonel Baker are my commanding officers. What else can I say?" Midge was surprised at herself, finding her tongue to say that much.

"Are you getting too settled over there with the WAFS, Midge? Do you want out? Do you want to come here and work directly for me? I can place you somewhere with my flight training school or with the women's air corps organization."

"I..." Midge stammered, visions of her chance to fly the promised bigger airplanes, maybe even pursuits, stalling before her eyes. "What kind of a job, Miss Cochran?"

"Well, Midge, I'll have to think about that awhile, see how things play out over the next couple of months. But Nancy Love's day in the sun is about to run into nightfall. There's only going to be one organization of women pilots in the United States and my organization is going to be the one. Naturally, I'll be the head of it. That's when I'll bring you back into the fold, Midge, unless you let me down between now and then."

"Let you down? I don't understand."

"Just keep in mind where your loyalties should be, Midge. This war is going to be over some day, and we'll all have to pick up our lives where they left off and forge new ground. A good job will be worth even more than before the war.

"By the way, how did the girls react to Cornelia Fort's unfortunate death? Such a lovely person. Even if she did come from all that money, I liked her. That girl had a head on her shoulders and was going places. I could have used her in my organization."

"We were all devastated, of course. Cornelia was loved and respected by every one of the WAFS. I never heard her say an unkind word about anyone. In fact, she defended you on several occasions last fall when many of the others thought you were trying to sidetrack the WAFS and get them broken up or disbanded."

"Yes, Cornelia would have done that." Jackie paused then obviously made up her mind that the meeting was over. "Well, Midge, I have a social engagement that I need to get to and I'm sure you have plans for a big night on the town in Fort Worth or Dallas. By the way, I hear Barry Metzger is in town and he's a lieutenant colonel now."

Midge held her breath. Did Cochran know or suspect that something had been going on between them. She was so adamant about young women staying clear of romantic entanglements with married men.

"Is he? I thought he was in California?" Midge lied.

"Temporary duty. He and his wife got back together, I understand."

"Yes, that's what I heard. Well, I'd better be going."

"Stay in touch, Midge."

"Yes, Miss Cochran, I will."

Midge's call to Barry Metzger, made from Love Field before she went to see Jackie Cochran, earned her that invitation to drinks and dinner at the Stockyards Hotel in downtown Fort Worth. But she was sure he had plans for her for the rest of the evening as well.

"You're looking ravishing, as usual," Barry said as he leaned down and kissed her on the cheek. Then he guided her to a secluded table in the dark lounge and sat next to her, taking her hand. "I've missed you, Midge." He ran his thumb seductively around her palm.

"Have you, Barry? I hadn't noticed, since I so rarely hear from you."

"Please, Midge…" Casually, he took her hand and placed it between his legs. "Now do you see how much I've missed you?"

"Barry!" She felt her cheeks burning as the waitress appeared just as she removed her hand from beneath the table. Midge knew that, to the girl standing there in her starched white apron and skirt, it appeared that she had been the initiator of the move.

The girl smirked as she took their order. Then she was gone.

"Just wanted you to know how I feel about you, Midge." Barry had a disgustingly triumphant smile on his face.

"And just how do you feel about me, Barry? I've never been quite sure."

"That I can barely keep my hands off you right now. It's all I can do not to take you right here in this bar, on the floor, right out in public."

Not only were Midge's cheeks red, unwanted perspiration was beginning to pool. She couldn't entirely blame her WAFS wool uniform skirt and jacket coupled with the nearly summer temperatures in Texas. Her own internal temperature was causing most of the problem.

"Barry, don't …"

"Don't what?" His voice had an insolence to it.

Midge wondered if he was drunk. She had never seen Barry Metzger drunk.

The waitress returned with their drinks and put a stop to any further exchange until they were served. When she left them alone, Barry sipped his Scotch and water while Midge toyed with her rum and Coke, the drink she had learned from Betty Gillies to like.

"Let's drink these and go upstairs, Midge." Barry had his seductive smile back in place. "I've got a room." He reached inside his jacket, pulled out a key and dangled it in front of her. "I've even ordered champagne on ice for us to drink after we've sated ourselves of each other. If that's possible. God, how I've missed you." He put one arm around her shoulders, leaned over and kissed her hard on the mouth. Suddenly she realized his other hand had gone up her skirt.

"No!" she blurted out, louder than she had intended, and shoved him away. She panted hard with the shock and the embarrassment. "No!"

"Calm down, people are staring."

"You're the one who needs to calm down. We haven't seen each other in over a year and you haven't said three words to me other than to invite me to bed. You'd have given a whore a longer line of talk than that. Well, this time, you better keep your oversized ego under control and your inflated cock zipped inside your pants 'cause you're not getting into mine."

She stood up, grabbed his drink and dumped it in his lap. When he looked down at the wet spreading stain and the ice cubes, she reached for her drink and poured that over his head. Then she walked out of the room and out the revolving doors to the street.

She shivered in spite of the early evening heat. What had happened to her? Why was she suddenly repulsed by Barry Metzger's attentions? Was it because she suddenly realized that she had worth as a person, something she never felt before? Was that what Jacqueline Cochran had been trying to tell her? Was that what Nancy Love and Betty Gillies and the others had been trying to show her by example?

Whatever the cause, she suddenly felt dirty in the presence of Barry Metzger. And his hand up her WAFS uniform skirt had been the last straw. She saw it as an insult to the entire corps of dedicated women flyers.

But now, here she stood in downtown Fort Worth, very much alone. She wanted to cry. She envied Teresa, right now either in the arms of her husband or cutting into a big Texas steak in the company of the man she loved. A woman in an unfamiliar uniform wasn't going to be allowed, alone, in any decent restaurant in town, so Midge decided to go back to Love Field, get a meal, a shower, and turn in early.

She realized she was experiencing what she had felt the first night her stepfather climbed the stairs and entered her room. Her mother was in the hospital following surgery. He sat down on her bed and told her that she was the woman of the house for now, and there were things she had to do to keep him happy.

Midge shuddered, remembering Barry's hand up her skirt. Remembering another hand groping beneath the sheet she had pulled tightly to her chin.

She really didn't want to see or talk to anybody right now.

# CHAPTER THIRTEEN

Three letters from Charlie were waiting for Annie when she got back from Calgary. One, forwarded from Long Beach, expressed his sympathy at the death of her friend. He had planned to see her when she got to Love Field on March 21, but Cornelia's death had changed everything and thrown the whole base into mourning. Florene's plans for a party were immediately cancelled, and Annie and the male ferry pilots were sent back to Long Beach on the first transport out. Now two months had gone by since they had met and they had yet to see each other again.

Should she go to Betty Gillies and ask for a ferrying mission to Texas?

Torn between her attraction to Charlie — her overwhelming desire to see and be with him — and her years of disappointment when it came to the opposite sex, Annie struggled with even admitting her interest in a man. She needed to talk to someone, but Cornelia, her confidante, wasn't there.

That evening she knocked on Clare's open door.

"Hey, Annie, come on in. Set a spell. That was some flight we had all the way up there to Canada."

"Clare, I have to ask you something."

"Shoot, kid. What's up?"

"I met this lieutenant in Texas on one of our trips from Long Beach." At Clare's gentle, knowing smile, Annie looked at the floor, embarrassed. "He's going to be a bomber pilot."

"The grapevine said you'd met somebody."

"Oh!" Annie squirmed a bit at hearing the word was out. But she took a deep breath and plunged on. "Do you know if Betty has any deliveries planned to Texas?"

Clare laughed. "You'd like to volunteer, I'll bet."

"Yes."

"Well, I know Jamesy and Culpepper just took two PTs down there. I'm pretty sure there's another Texas delivery in the offing."

"Do you think I dare ask her?"

"Yes, you can talk to Betty. She's pretty perceptive when it comes to matters of the heart."

The next day, Annie worked up her courage and went to see Betty, who happened to be about ready to assign four pilots to take PTs to bases in Texas. She agreed to put Annie on the mission. She did, however, add a word of caution. "Annie, this is none of my business. You're over twenty-one and I'm not your mother, but be careful. I know right now you're probably head over heels in love, or think you are, but wartime relationships begun in Canteens over soft lights and dreamy music, and the hasty marriages that sometimes follow, have a way of going sour in the cold light of day. Just because there's a war on, don't be in a hurry to make any irrevocable commitments."

Annie looked into her Commanding Officer's bright blue eyes and saw a friend. Others among the younger women had remarked that Betty, like an older sister, had their best interests at heart. Now she had occasion to see for herself. She thanked Betty for both her advice and her concern.

Four days later, Annie, Clare, Nancy Batson and Gert Meserve were in Texas. Annie sent a telegram to Charlie for fear a letter wouldn't get there in time. Florene, who heard from Charlie that they were coming, took her cue and planned a party at the Officers' Club the night they were due to be at Love Field. Anticipating the party, Annie, Nancy and Gert packed dresses and high heels in their B-4 bags. Clare declined, telling them she had a date to meet an old friend.

That night, Florene patiently helped Annie with her hair and makeup. She swept Annie's light brown pageboy behind her ears and caught it with a silk ribbon that matched her blue dress. And, for the first time, Annie wore eye shadow to enhance what Florene termed her hyacinth-blue eyes.

Annie had never bothered much with makeup. Makeup couldn't hide her height or her broad-shouldered, big-boned, rangy build. Her face, which she thought of as only minorly attractive at best, wasn't enough to compensate for those other off-putting factors when it came to men. Besides, she thought her face too round and her hair coloring too plain and ordinary.

Now, examining herself in the mirror in the WAFS quarters at Love Field, Annie took heart. The girl who stared back at her appeared to be quite attractive — if apprehensive. If only I could conjure up some self-confidence, she thought. What on earth could Charlie possibly see in me?

For an instant, in spite of the pleasing mirror image, she thought about hiding, running away, pleading a case of cramps like she almost had the last time. She considered asking Florene to tell Charlie that she wasn't interested in him and to please go away, that she was engaged to someone else, anything to avoid seeing him, talking to him, being close to him. Most of all being alone with him. But underneath all that, when she dared to admit it to herself, she really *wanted* to be with him — alone. Her heart speeded up at the thought.

Florene had posted Dorothy Scott to keep an eye out for Charlie and let Annie know when he arrived. She felt like a high school girl on her way to her first prom — waiting for the boy to come and meet her father and pass inspection; for her mother to call her downstairs to receive her gentleman caller who stood nervously in the living room, a corsage box clutched in his sweating hands.

Her check ride with Lieutenant Tracy to qualify for the WAFS hadn't been nearly so terrifying.

Then Dorothy appeared at her door. "He's here."

Annie picked up her purse, walked out and closed the door behind her. She felt the cool rustle of the blue silk skirt against her legs as she walked in her now strangely unfamiliar high heels. Too many months in slacks and coveralls and wearing low-heeled oxfords — not to mention the heavy boots for winter flying. Please let the Break Room be empty, she thought, no spies. But when she got there, Nancy, Gert and others lounged about in the chairs acting like they had nowhere to go, no better place to be. She knew very well they were going to Florene's party, too.

Apparently, Charlie had disappeared

"I think he's embarrassed," Gert said, laughing. "He took one look at us and broke for the front door."

"Damn," Annie muttered under her breath and she turned on her heel. She heard laughter behind her as she shut the door.

He stood several feet away under a tree. When he saw her, he strode forward, then stopped abruptly. She went down the wooden stairs and out to him. The way he looked at her, she felt like she must resemble something good enough to eat, but that he was afraid to sample the first bite.

"Hi, Charlie," she said, surprised at how even her voice sounded because, surely, her heart now pounded loudly enough for him to hear it.

"Wow! You look beautiful, Annie."

That stopped her. Words she didn't expect to hear. She took a deep breath, trying to stave off panic. "I've missed you, Charlie," she managed to get out. "I tried to get back sooner, but this is the first chance I've had."

At some point, he had taken her hand. Annie realized she had unconsciously stuck it out as if being introduced for the first time. Clumsy oaf, she berated herself. But he took it, held it, and, just like last time, did not let go. He said nothing about missing her. No comment on his declaration when they parted two months earlier. Oh, God, she thought, he doesn't know what to say and neither do I. He's sorry he said what he said before and can't think of a way to get out of it. Oh, you fool, you fool. How could you let yourself believe a simple one-time encounter could turn into a romance?

They stood and looked at each other. "Let's go to the party," he said, huskily.

He doesn't want to be alone with me. He'll get me inside and dump me on one of his friends and find somebody else. Plenty of girls in there — pretty and fun to be with. Annie wished she had never asked Betty for this assignment. She'd made a very big mistake.

Once inside the O-Club's smoky, low-lit interior, Annie sensed a replay of their first encounter. The music blared fast and loud and energetic couples were swinging around the dance floor at a frantic pace. Charlie, of course, wanted none of that. He led her first to the bar to get their drinks and then to a table as far away from the music and the crowd as he could get.

"Aren't we going to sit with your friends?" she asked, startled.

He looked stricken. "I thought we could be alone, at least for awhile, but if you want ..."

Annie could hardly believe her ears. He really wanted to be alone with her.

"No, no, it's OK, Charlie, I just thought ..."

He smiled at her. Those eyes the color of mountain lakes in July looked out at her like a man had never looked her at before. Maybe things were going to be all right after all.

They sat and sipped their drinks, made small talk about their flying, and looked into each other's eyes. She told him about the trip to Calgary and, when he asked, she talked about Cornelia.

"That guy should be court martialed and shot," Charlie said, when she finished the story of Cornelia's last flight.

Surprised at his vehemence, Annie said, "I heard he got off with a reprimand because they need pilots so desperately. They couldn't afford to lose him."

"That's what I heard, too. But what he did is counter to everything they teach us." He reached for her hand again and searched her eyes. "Annie… it could have been you."

No one else had said that to her, though she knew it to be true. She looked at Charlie with open adoration. Now she knew he truly cared about her well-being.

Then the G.I. band swung into *Stardust* and Charlie was on his feet, pulling her up with him. Once on the dance floor, everything came flooding back — like they had lost no time at all. Had never been apart. As he took her in his arms, she saw a tiny bloody spot where he had nicked himself shaving. Without thinking, she gently kissed it and inhaled the spicy fragrance of his aftershave.

He pulled his head back and looked into her eyes, a tiny smile forming on his lips. Then he pulled her close, rested his cheek on her hair and they began to dance, so close she could feel his tightly honed muscles moving against her. Annie let herself go and the two of them moved in perfect harmony over the dance floor. And once again, when the music stopped, he held her close and she felt the pulse racing in his throat, moving in concert with her own heartbeat.

Fast music began again and he detached himself, reluctantly she thought, and they moved back to their table. Others had joined them by now. Florene threw her a knowing look and Gert gave her a grin and a surreptitious thumbs-up, but Charlie seemed aware of no one but her.

Annie couldn't believe this was happening to her. Not big, awkward Annie Gwynn, the tomboy who lived down by Overall Creek, who preferred riding horses and flying airplanes to doing girl-type things like shopping for clothes, going to slumber parties, and chasing boys.

They didn't miss a slow dance.

Much later that night, Charlie walked her back to the barracks. She stopped and tilted her head back and looked up at the wide expanse that was the Texas sky, velvety black but looking as if someone had deliberately taken a straight pin and poked a million holes in the plush fabric for the stars to shine through. She kept her head back so long, a wave of dizziness swept over her. Then Charlie's lips touched hers and a new dizziness took over and she melted against him.

Just when she thought she would dissolve into a puddle right on the spot, he released her and they walked on. "I'm going to Lockbourne to B-17 school. Columbus, Ohio. That's close to Delaware isn't it?"

"Yes," she breathed.

"From there, it'll be on to England and a chance to look at Germany from 25,000 feet."

"When?" she asked, her voice quaking.

"June… to Lockbourne, that is." He stopped. They had reached the barracks. Several other couples were standing in the shadows nearby, all locked in deep embraces.

"So, do you think you could get over to Ohio sometime?"

He was so very close, Annie could feel his breath on her cheek. She turned into his arms. 'Yes," she said, as their mouths met again.

"Annie," he whispered. Together, they moved into the shadow of the barracks until she felt its wooden frame solidly against her back. Their mouths were together again and Annie thought her legs were going to desert her, right there in the warm clear night with nothing but Texas soil beneath them and Texas sky over them. Her mind reeled. Her body was telling her one thing, but Betty's words came back. "Don't make any irrevocable commitments." Surely one time wasn't an irrevocable commitment — except in her mind, in her family's beliefs, in the way she was raised. But this was wartime. Didn't that change the rules? He said he was going overseas — eventually.

Their mouths locked together, it would be so easy to give in to the strange and incredible urges she felt. Just one time? Irrevocable commitment?

"Charlie," her voice tore at her own heart. Surely it tore at his as well. "Charlie. Stop, please."

And he did.

They looked at each other, shaken.

He started to speak.

"Shush, Charlie." And she put her finger to his lips, her heart sinking at the look on his face. "I — I need to take this slower, that's all."

He had dropped his big bomber pilot's hands to his sides. "Oh, Annie …" his voice was ragged.

"I should go in now," she said lamely.

"I know."

"Lockbourne?"

Gently, he took her face in his hands and kissed her softly on the lips. "Lockbourne." And he was gone into the night.

Lockbourne. That would have to be enough for now.

# CHAPTER FOURTEEN

"Helen Mary is going to check out in the P-47 tomorrow, Teresa's next in line after that, then you," Betty told Clare. "So go ahead and get started on your AT-6 transition. Solo front seat first, then the back seat. Lieutenant Starbuck is expecting you."

"Back seat, eh. They weren't kidding." Clare tried not to show her excitement. She had been waiting for this.

"The back seat is as close as we can get to what a P-47 feels like without flying one," Betty said. "It gives you some sense of that big engine in front of you. You can't see anything but engine cowling, it's so massive. You really learn to get your S-turns down in that big fighter."

"What does it feel like?"

"Clare, it's like nothing you've ever flown before. And, of course, you're up there alone from the beginning — solo. You'll have to fly it to believe it. You've been cleared to do it, so go for it. And enjoy."

Clare looked steadily at Betty for a moment. "Are we really going to get to fly these things, or is this just an exercise to prove that a few women are capable of flying pursuits, then they'll pat us on the head and say thanks, but only us *guys* get to fly these babies for real!"

Betty toyed with the miniature OX-5 that sat on her desk. "OK, here's what Nancy told me: Helen Mary, Teresa, and you are going to be sent up to Farmingdale, Long Island, to the Republic Aviation factory where they make the P-47s. You'll live in temporary quarters there and ferry those big pursuits across to Newark, New Jersey — approximately fifty miles as the crow flies — where they will be loaded on ships bound for England. Then you'll haul yourselves back to Farmingdale and do it all over again."

"This is amazing," Clare said.

"They call these planes Jugs, by the way, because of their bottle shape. The men who are checked out in the Jugs will be ferrying the rest of them to the modification center in Evansville, Indiana, and then they'll fly them back to Newark or on to California, depending on which theater of war they're intended for."

"So just the three of us are handling the Newark run?"

"Yes, for now. Call it an experiment. They need pursuit pilots and this is an easy way to get a few more without shaking up everybody in the ATC by having a whole bunch of women flying around in the Army's prize possession. If we do well — and this is a *big* if — more of the girls may get a chance at pursuit transition as well."

"I heard some of the girls in Long Beach might get to fly P-51s."

"B.J., Evelyn Sharp and Barbara Towne are getting the same opportunity to check out in those planes in Long Beach that you three are getting here with the Jugs. And up in Romulus, Del Scharr and Barbara Donahue will get a crack at the P-39. But for now, on the East Coast, it's the three of you — once you're all up to speed. And the sooner the better, so get crackin'.'"

"What about you?"

"I'm your backup and relief. I'm needed here to run the squadron, so I'll come up there a few days a month to give you three gals periodic breaks or in case one of you gets grounded with a bad cold or something. Esther is capable of running the squad while I'm gone, so I'll get more flying time then."

Clare sat shaking her head. "You know, Betty, when I joined this outfit nine months ago, I never, in my wildest dreams, imagined that Mrs. Varsky's little girl Clare, from Colorado Springs, U.S.A., daughter of a steel worker and housemaid, would be flying the most powerful pursuit airplane in the United States arsenal."

"I know," Betty grinned. "Hard to believe, isn't it?"

"You bettcha." Clare paused. "Is this all a big secret?"

"Not a big secret, per se."

"What does that mean?"

"We're just not to broadcast it. It's not to be kept from the other girls. That'd be hard to do anyway. But don't talk about it unless asked. And, if asked, just say it's somewhat of an experiment."

"How did you determine who got picked?"

"It's based pretty much on seniority, number of hours in the air and prior experience. You, Helen Mary and Teresa unquestionably have all three. If all goes well, Meserve, Batson, Gwynn, Culpepper, McGilvery, and Bernheim will follow."

"I heard you had a height problem and had to get some help reaching the rudder pedals on the pursuit. That true?"

Betty laughed. "I'm five one and a half. So yeah, I had a problem."

"What did you do?"

"There's this test pilot at Grumman, where Bud works. He's not a whole lot taller than me. I knew he handled all kinds of aircraft.

So I called him up and asked him how he managed. He said he had made a special set of wooden blocks to fit over the rudder pedals so he could reach them more easily. When I told him why I asked, he offered to make me a set. I now have a portable set of wooden extenders that I carry into any cockpit where I may need them."

A few minutes later, out on the flight line, Clare preflighted her AT-6 then climbed into the front seat. Lieutenant Starbuck climbed into the back. Other than her two flights as co-pilot with Nancy in the Lockheed Hudson bomber, the sleek silver AT-6 — with its retractable landing gear, 600-horsepower engine and cruising speed of 145 miles per hour — was the biggest thing Clare had ever flown.

"Well, lieutenant, let's get the front seat work out of the way so we can move on to the more exciting stuff," Clare said.

When she got back to the barracks late that afternoon, she found a telegram waiting for her.

> *Sweetheart.* Stop. *Am shipping out in 48 hours.* Stop. *Have 24-hour pass.* Stop. *Will be at DuPont Hotel Wilmington 6 p.m. tonight.* Stop. *Love, Will*

"Oh my Gawd!" she cried, crumpling the telegram.
Annie appeared in her door moments later. "Clare, what's wrong?"
"It's Will. He's shipping out."
"Who's Will?"
Clare noticed the puzzled look on Annie's face and realized the girl didn't know. "Will's my husband, Annie."
Annie stared at her, then found her voice. "Oh, Clare, I didn't know. Are you going to get to see him before he leaves?"
"He's due here," Clare stopped and checked her watch, "in about an hour."
"Well, you'd better start getting ready."
"I don't think I can get off base."
"You just march yourself right down and talk to Betty. You know she'll give you a twenty-four-hour pass. Your husband's shipping overseas, for heaven sakes. Who knows when you'll get to see him again?"
Clare stood staring at Annie, suddenly unable to move.
"Now, Clare," Annie urged. "You're going to need every minute you can get to get yourself looking beautiful for him."
Clare almost laughed at Annie's choice of words. A couple of weeks ago, she had watched the others coax this nervous, lovesick

girl into getting beautiful for her smitten lieutenant. Now the shoe was on the other foot. Clare headed straight for Betty's room at the other end of the hall, hoping to find her there and not already off at the Officers' Club enjoying cocktail hour.

She found Betty in her room just about to take a shower. Clare asked if she could come in and then closed the door behind her.

"I know you're not supposed to give passes on this short notice, but…" Clare prided herself on her short-and-to-the-point way of speaking. She handed Betty the telegram.

Betty scanned the contents and looked up. "Go! I'll cover for you if anything comes up. Now get out of here. I'll try to stop Esther before she leaves the office and have her drive you to the DuPont."

An hour later, with Annie sworn to secrecy so that no one else knew she had left and why, Clare, carrying a small suitcase and dressed in civilian clothes, slipped out of the barracks into a car driven by Betty's administrative assistant, Esther Manning Rathfelder — one of the original WAFS who, now several months pregnant, had been grounded. She lived off base with her officer husband.

In the early morning hours, Clare startled awake from a sound sleep. The humid air of late June in Wilmington wafted through the curtains, but only a rare passing car disturbed the quiet of the slumbering city. Will slept peacefully beside her. Whatever had jarred her awake had not bothered him. She slipped from the bed and stood naked in the moonlight that streamed in the window.

Even though they'd been married exactly a year, they had spent so few nights together. Now, looking at Will sleeping, Clare remembered so well when she first laid eyes on him— that day he walked into the office at the airfield and asked about flying lessons. Up to that point, Clare had been juggling men since the days she started hanging out at the airfield with her brother. Guys had fallen all over themselves to get her attention, to teach her everything they knew about airplanes and flying, to get and keep her interest. But until Will, Clare's interest ran more to the flying than to the man.

The third child and first girl in the mixed ethnic, second-generation American family, Clare always felt pulled two ways. Her red-haired Czech father exercised his old-world, patriarchal control over her and her two sisters — as borne out the morning he informed her that, whatever her age, as long as she lived under his roof, she would be in her own bed by midnight every night. Clare always wondered what her father would have done had he found out she was sleeping with Will.

Clare had inherited her father's red hair, but it was from her Italian mother that she got the thick curls, dark brown eyes, and full-busted figure. Her mother also exhibited a far more understanding attitude toward her daughters.

"Clarissa, *bambina, mia cara*, you should be thankful your papa is so strict with you. I should have had such a papa, but mine died, rest his soul, on the boat coming to America. My mama had to raise me and your Aunt Sophia by herself. She worked long hours cleaning houses, like I do today. She had to fight off the men who thought her loose because she worked in their houses and had children but no husband. She taught me about men and what not to believe when they spoke the soft words."

Clare had had her share of soft words. Maury — who thought because he taught her how to do her first barrel roll in the sky that he had the right to teach her about rolls in earthbound hay. But that she reserved for her first true love, Sam. So unusually tall for a pilot, so handsome, and so smooth. She was nineteen, he twenty-two. He stole her heart and her virginity, and then left her to go fly the bush in Alaska.

She cried for a week and then decided no man was worth that kind of misery. She vowed never to get involved again unless she could make the rules. When he came back two years later and tried to pick up where they left off, she laughed him out of the hangar. From that day until Will, Clare only slept with one other man — Hal, strictly of her own choosing and to fill her own needs. Physically, they had been good for each other, but emotionally they knew to keep their distance. A fulltime relationship would have been disastrous to them both. They were competitors on the aerobatic stunt circuit. Each trying to do the other one better — stretching the stunt out to one more roll, climbing to ever higher altitudes, pulling out of a spin closer and closer to the ground. Then one day, Hal didn't pull out in time. Clare didn't fly stunts for over a month after that, but eventually she found she could forget Hal better by flying than moping on the ground.

Patience, she had paid dearly for. The patience to hold the stick back just the right amount of time to induce the spin, patience to coax out of a stunt that additional roll that brought the crowd to its collective feet screaming, patience to wait for Tunner and Baker to decide that she and the other women could fly pursuits, patience to endure Will's being gone and in danger as he flew his P-47 over the European mainland in range of German guns.

She stood watching him sleep. How did I get so lucky to have him pick me out of a crowd, Clare wondered for, perhaps, the thousandth time.

She moved back to the bed and lay down beside him, snuggling close. He stirred and his arm went around her.

"I love you, Clare," he whispered.

She eased her body over onto his.

# CHAPTER FIFTEEN

Midge noticed immediately the square set to Betty's jaw as she clinked on her rum and Coke glass with her fountain pen and cleared her throat.

"I've got announcements." Betty waved a piece of paper in the air. "This just came from the War Department today, July 5, and it is signed by General Stratemeyer, per the command of General Arnold. It's dated June 28, 1943. General Stratemeyer is chief of Air Staff to Headquarters AAF. He has established the office of Special Assistant and Director of Women Pilots in the office of the Assistant Chief of Air Staff, Operations, Commitments and Requirements. It then lists twelve things this director — who, by the way, is Jacqueline Cochran — will do in this position. But," and Betty paused, "nowhere does it say how any of this relates to the women in the Ferrying Division. In other words, us."

A buzz erupted from the women sitting at two round cocktail tables in the small lounge off the main bar at the Officers' Club at New Castle Army Air Forces Base.

"Damn that Cochran woman..." Clare said. "She got to Hap Arnold."

Betty rapped her knuckles on the surface of the table. "Quiet... there's more."

She's upset, Midge thought, and I don't blame her. Miss Cochran has done what she said she would do and walked roughshod over Nancy, Betty and all the WAFS — me included.

"Cochran has closed her offices in Fort Worth," Betty continued, "and is moving to Army headquarters in Washington. General William Tunner, head of the Ferrying Division — yes, he's been promoted to brigadier general — has named Nancy Love Executive for WAFS. Her job will be to direct the women of the Ferrying Division, Air Transport Command. That's us, ladies, the women ferrying the Army's airplanes."

The buzz grew louder. "What does that mean?" Clare demanded.

"I just talked to Nancy on the phone. General Tunner told her that he considers her responsibilities to the women attached to the Ferrying Division equal to Jackie's. On General Tunner's orders, Nancy already has moved permanently to Cincinnati, the new headquarters of the Ferrying Division."

Midge sat alone in her room in BOQ 14 after dinner and tried to reason out what, if anything, this turn of events might do to her status either with the WAFS or with her boss. Cochran's comments to her when they last met had been cryptic. "I'll bring you back into the fold. I can place you somewhere with the women's air corps organization that we are building now."

Cochran's boast that she would head the only organization of women pilots in the U.S. Army proved to be true. And she somehow knew this back in May. Was now the time to move back into the fold, Midge wondered. The WAFS had accepted her readily enough. Betty had been like an older sister, helping her learn the ropes. Midge knew her piloting skills were now far superior to what they had been, thanks to Betty. Everyone treated her like an equal, except for Clare, who kept her guarded distance. Midge racked her brain to remember some slight she might have given, unintentionally, but could think of none. Irreverent, funny, totally at ease with other people, Clare pulled no punches.

I can't worry about it, she decided. Her major concern now was why she wasn't getting the opportunity to transition into P-47s. Clare, Teresa, and Helen Mary were leaving tomorrow for Long Island where they would be stationed indefinitely ferrying P-47s. But Betty had said nothing about any of the rest of them.

The very thought of climbing into the cockpit of that sleek flying machine made Midge's mouth water. To ride a machine that powerful, to feel the thrust of its energy all the way to your inner core, had to generate the same exhilaration Midge associated with good sex. The minute she had laid eyes on the shiny pursuit she had felt an all-consuming desire to fly it. She snuck down to the flight line every chance she got to watch the male ferry pilots take their transition.

Then, one by one, Helen Mary, Teresa, and Clare, like Betty Gillies before them, had made the trip to the factory on Long Island for their introduction to the P-47. When each returned, she had transitioned on Wilmington's lone P-47. Jealous hardly described Midge's feelings watching them. She could taste her lust for the machine. Rumor had it that Gert was next. But Betty had said nothing to her and Midge knew the others had gotten a verbal go-ahead from the squadron leader before they approached the instructors for transition.

Maybe she should take the initiative and ask Betty if she could transition. Or move things along by familiarizing herself with the cockpit and the tech orders. Lord knows sitting around the barracks would get her nowhere. She decided to walk down to the flight line. This early in July, it would be light for two more hours. Maybe she could talk to the crew chief in charge of the Thunderbolt and pick up some more pointers. The guys on the flight line knew her. They knew all the WAFS and liked them.

She found Jerry Fuqua checking a wheel strut. Watching him was Hank Bascomb, one of the new ferry pilots, just back from overseas where he had been flying P-38 escort for bombers out of England. He, too, had checked out in the P-47 a couple of days earlier. His new assignment: up to Farmingdale to ferry the pursuits to Evansville and then the modified Jugs back to the East or on to the West Coast. Hank had been hanging around her ever since he got back, trying to get her to go out with him. Midge didn't particularly like him, but she had had a few drinks with him in the O-Club. She would have preferred to run into his buddy Greg Schultz, but in this case, beggars couldn't be choosers. She wanted to sit in that cockpit, needed to begin to familiarize herself with the feel of the Jug. Jerry might have let her do it, but she thought she could con Hank into talking her through the cockpit procedures. She hailed both men and went over to talk to them.

Hank greeted her with, "Well, look who's here, Miss Hot Shot herself. Got your orders to fly this baby yet?"

"I'm working on it." Midge delivered a stunning smile in his direction. And in no time at all, she had worked herself into the cockpit. All it took was accepting a date with Hank to go dancing Saturday night before he left for Farmingdale.

"You know, you can fly this baby," Hank said, perched on the wing root, leaning his head in close to hers. As he talked, he pointed out dials and switches. He reached across her to toggle a switch on the right side of the cockpit and, as he pulled his hand back, let it brush across her breasts.

"Oh, there's no doubt about that," Midge said, controlling the anger that welled quickly in her throat. She swallowed it down and kept talking. "It's just that Betty hasn't given me the go-ahead. Only four of the WAFS have been allowed to check out so far here at this base."

"What's really holding you back? You scared?" he needled.

"No, I'm not scared. We're supposed to have permission to begin transition."

"Well, you know," Hank ducked his head in a little closer to hers, "I'm supposed to be taking this baby up right now for another half an hour check-out time 'cause I got cut short by weather yesterday. Who'd be the wiser if you took it up instead? I can get the time in tomorrow. The weather's clear now."

"Wait a minute, you're telling me to take this airplane up. I haven't even checked out in the back seat of an AT-6 yet."

"You can fly it from the front seat, can't you?"

"Well, sure ..." she lied. She had had one flight in the Texan to date, and was not checked out, but Midge was confident she could fly it. She could pull the gear up on a Staggerwing, and though she had yet to raise the gear on a Texan it should be no problem.

"That's all you need. This thing's a big pussycat when you get her up. Yeah, she lands hot and heavy, but you've got a long runway here." He looked skyward. "Perfect night. Won't be dark for an hour and a half. Plenty of time to take two, three turns around the pattern. I'll walk you through everything right now if you want to try it. Of course, if you do it, you owe me more than one date."

Midge looked into the laughing eyes of the pilot crouched on her wing. He had just promised her a chance to do that which she coveted. Could she get away with it? What harm would there be in a couple of times around the pattern, just to get the feel of it? She'd keep quiet about it and she thought he would, too, if she made that part of the date deal.

"Okay, yeah, I'd like to do that. But you must keep it quiet. I don't want to get kicked out or anything."

"The soul of discretion." He crossed his heart.

"OK."

And just like that Hank gave her a quick course in flying the P-47. When he finished, she thought she understood everything and nodded.

"Jerry," Hank called to the crew chief, "I've checked her out. She's gonna take it up for a turn or two around the pattern."

"Uh, well, sir, uh, I don't think the WAFS are supposed to be flying that thing — unless Miz Gillies specifically gives the go-ahead."

"Sergeant, I know what I'm doing," Hank said, standing up and staring down the man he outranked. Hank wore the oak leaf clusters of a major, not to mention his combat ribbons.

"Yes, sir." Jerry didn't argue.

"Get the starter up here and then remove the chocks, Sergeant," Hank ordered, obviously enjoying himself.

"OK, Midge, you're gonna be twenty miles down range by the time you get the wheels up. Remember, twenty minutes, then bring her in. We want to get you down an hour before sunset — just like the rules say." He winked and patted her shoulder.

Midge quickly slipped into a parachute. The thirteen-foot, four-bladed prop loomed in front of her eyes. Hank jumped off the wing and Jerry stuck a battery charger into the side of the engine. Midge pushed the button on the stick to activate her throat mike and called the tower, then pressed the starter button and pushed the throttle forward. With a puff of black smoke, the engine roared to life.

She made a series of S-turns down the taxiway — the massive engine cowling blocked any view straight in front of her — and worked the rudder pedals, getting the feel of them. When she reached the end of the runway, she ran the checklist once more. Everything checked out. She sat frozen as fear chased her lust for flying this monster around an imaginary landing pattern in her head. Another airplane taxied up behind her. Time to go or abort. She pressed the mike button on the throttle, called the tower and was cleared for takeoff.

Midge pushed the throttle to the firewall and felt the airplane surge down the runway, pinning her backbone against the seat. She watched the airspeed indicator climb. The noise was deafening and the airplane shook, but before she knew it, she was off the ground and climbing. Just like Hank had said, by the time she got the gear up, she had left the airfield far behind. Soon, she found herself soaring somewhere over Maryland at five thousand feet and at nearly three hundred miles per hour.

She moved the stick and the rudders, very delicately, ever so slightly, in perfect coordination, and banked to the right. Then she moved it in the opposite direction and banked to the left. The response was immediate. "Sweet!" she said aloud.

Time stood still while she flew around getting the feel of the mighty machine in her control. She practiced a couple of imaginary landings at altitude — working her way through her mental checklist, touching each control and activating it as if going in for a landing — all the while flying at better than five thousand feet. They called it landing on the runway in the sky.

Traveling faster than she had ever traveled in an airplane before, she still couldn't feel the full impact of the speed at altitude. She would have to execute a landing before feeling the full power under her again, like she did at takeoff.

She looked at her watch. The angle of the sun was moving resolutely away toward the western horizon. Time to go back. She began looking for landmarks and wasn't finding any. Headed west slightly northwest, she did a 180-degree turn that put her on a southeasterly track. She began to descend, watching carefully in all directions for traffic. Then, when she picked up the beacon, she called the tower and eased herself into the rectangular pattern at the altitude ordered by the controller.

From the downwind leg heading southeast, she made the required perfect 90-degree turn to base leg. A true 90-degrees — the Army way. Moments later, she repeated the movement and turned to final. She stared down the runway and headed in.

As the plane sank, the massive engine blocked her view and Midge lost sight of the runway. She strained to look out one side and then the other, trying to gauge how high she was. She knew now why Betty Gillies used rudder extensions. Only an inch taller than Betty's five-one-and-a-half, Midge now realized the handicap her lack of height could be in a big plane.

The airplane felt extra heavy. She couldn't pull it up too sharply or she'd stall it, and because the nose was so big and so heavy, it took more strength than she had to keep it up. Now she also knew why you needed to transition from the back seat of an AT-6. That experience would have provided her with the feel, the knowledge to do this. Right here and right now she was too low and too fast going in and she knew it.

"Once you cut the power, it drops like a ton of bricks," one of the guys had told her. The men who flew it called the P-47 a "Bucket of Bolts."

Then the glare from the setting sun caught her square in the eyes, instantly blinding her.

Moments later, the sound of metal tearing against metal rent the air. The plane started to flip to the left. She fought the controls, compensated with hard right rudder, shoved the throttle all the way to the firewall and pulled up on the stick — not too much, just enough. There. Her hands were shaking. Slowly, the airplane gained altitude, shaking violently as it climbed.

And what the hell was that noise?

# CHAPTER SIXTEEN

Annie, sitting on her cot reading a letter from Charlie, heard the metallic scream of a low-flying aircraft in distress. She jumped up and ran to the window just in time to see a P-47 fly low over BOQ 14, a piece of metal hanging from the undercarriage.

I wonder which of the guys is in trouble, she thought. Annie knew it couldn't be one of the WAFS because the three destined for Farmingdale were packing, getting ready to leave for Long Island in the morning, and she had walked back from the O-Club with Betty only a few minutes earlier.

Annie ran to Midge's room figuring she would have heard it, too. But Midge wasn't in her room. The clothes she had worn to dinner were tossed carelessly on her cot. A quick glance at the cubicle where her clothes hung told Annie that her flight coveralls were gone. Was she down at the flight line? If so, she'd know who was up in that sick P-47. Annie ran downstairs, out the barracks door, and started jogging in the direction of the flight line.

Moments later a Jeep came racing by. The captain sitting in the right seat yelled something. The private driving hit the brakes and the officer turned around, called to Annie. "You a WAF?"

"Yes."

"Get in. One of your gals has got herself in a pickle up there in a pursuit."

Annie jumped in the back seat and the Jeep took off at breakneck speed. The roar of the wind in the open Jeep and her need to hang on precluded her from asking the captain who was in trouble as the Jeep headed for the control tower. When it skidded to a stop, Annie and the officer climbed out. "Come on, maybe you can help," he said. "Do you know her, the gal that's up there?"

"Who is it?" Annie already feared she knew the answer.

"Midge somebody."

"Culpepper. Midge Culpepper… yes I know her, but why…?"

"That's what Colonel Baker wants to know. A Major Bascomb just called and reported that she's the one up there. He told the colonel she took the plane right out from under his nose. Colonel Baker sent me to find out what the hell's going on. Is she one of your gals who's checked out on the P-47?"

"No," Annie said, breathing hard as they took the steps to the control tower two at a time.

"Then what the…"

"I have no idea, captain, but I can tell you this. Midge Culpepper did NOT just take an airplane out from under somebody's nose. I'll lay money some guy put her up to it — offered her the chance to fly it."

The captain stared at her, then grabbed the door to the tower and entered. She followed him into air traffic control where you weren't admitted if you didn't have clearance. The only light in the room came from the fading twilight outside the fishbowl windows that oversaw the entire airfield. Several pairs of eyes turned and focused on her and the captain as they entered.

"Colonel Baker's on his way. What happened?" the captain said.

"The P-47 called for clearance — forty-five minutes ago," the officer in charge began. "Woman's voice, but we got women checked out on that airplane. No raised eyebrows. She flew off. Gone half an hour, maybe. Heard her call the tower — all according to procedure. Gave her clearance to enter the pattern and land." He paused and looked at the other controller on duty with him. "Got anything to add to that?"

"No sir," the other man said, "'cept that, as she came in, she looked to be right on the money."

The first controller nodded and picked up the story. "She put the nose down. I'm guessin' to get a better glimpse of the runway. You know, to see around that big engine. That ol' Jug dropped on her and clipped that light pole down there." He gestured to a badly twisted pole, wrenched halfway out of the ground and lying at a forty-five degree angle like an accusing finger pointing toward the control tower. "Knocked out the electricity to the field — including the runway lights."

"We thought she was a goner." The second controller picked up the story. "Plane started to flip over on its back. She gunned it. She really manhandled that sucker, sir, 'cause the ship righted itself and, as it flew down the runway right in front of us, began to gain altitude — an inch at a time."

"That airplane was making the most god-awful racket you ever heard," the first controller said. "Metal on metal… the kind of screech you get when you drag your fingernails across a blackboard, but a thousand times louder." He shook his head. "Sounded like that Jug had a soul and it knew it was headed straight for Hell."

"She flew on out the end, rising as she went," the second controller added his finishing touch to the narrative. "Helluva flyin' job. Most of the cowboys 'round here'd be burning up in a heap of twisted metal at the end of the runway by now."

"I heard it," Annie said. "She came over the barracks. I saw something trailing from the underside of the plane. She flew on off to the south. Do you know where she is now?"

"Nope. Our radio's dead. She knocked out communications as well as the lights."

"Oh my God," Annie said. "You can't talk to her."

"Well, get on the phone to DuPont and find out if they can raise her," the captain said. "If not, find out if any of the nearby fields around here can. Anybody!" He looked at Annie. "You want to help your friend?"

"'course I do."

"Start making those phone calls."

"Yes, sir."

Annie took the list of phone numbers the sergeant handed her and sat down at the only phone in the tower. Soon she had contacted every airport within a fifty-mile radius of New Castle. Every one of them knew a wounded airplane was flying around out there in the coming twilight. All agreed to try to contact her.

"Assuming she gets back here, how's she going to land on a dark runway?" Annie asked between phone calls.

The captain stared at her. "Maybe we can get her to land at one of the other airports."

"That won't work, Captain," Colonel Baker's voice said from the doorway. Annie wondered how long he had been standing there listening. "We've got the only runway long enough to set that beast down."

Annie felt hope leak out of her like air from a punctured tire. Then the phone rang at her elbow. "New Castle control tower," she answered, listened a moment, then turned to Colonel Baker. "DuPont's got her on the radio, sir. They're talking to her right now."

A cheer erupted from the tense crowd in the small tower room.

She listened then relayed the message. Midge was flying around trying to use up the fuel in her tanks. She had considered bailing out but, in the coming darkness, couldn't tell what she might be jumping into.

"How does she sound?" Annie asked the man at the DuPont tower. She nodded, looked up at Colonel Baker and said, "He says she's in control of the situation. She understands that she needs to stay in the air while we figure out how to get her down."

"Have him ask her to do a fly-by in front of his tower and let him eyeball the damage to her airplane before it gets any darker," Colonel Baker said.

Annie passed that message on. And then they waited. When Annie heard his voice again, she snapped her fingers to get Colonel Baker's attention and repeated what he told her. "The entire belly of the airplane is ripped open — like somebody put a can opener to it." She paused, nodded. "A piece of metal's hanging from the back of the airplane. He thinks it might be fuselage skin hanging loose rather than something critical, but he's not sure. He says ignore it for now 'cause it's not going away."

Colonel Baker nodded. "Ask if we can keep the phone line open to him."

Annie nodded when she heard the ascent at the other end.

"We need to rig some lights to get her in," Colonel Baker said.

"How about the emergency generator, sir," the captain asked.

"Call Sergeant Andrews. Have him crank up the emergency juice."

"We'll have to hang up with DuPont, sir," Annie said. "This is the only phone line."

"Tell DuPont we need the line momentarily, but to keep his line clear so that we can call him right back."

The captain called for the emergency generator and again they waited. When the phone rang, Annie answered and handed it to Colonel Baker. "Yeah. OK, Andy, I understand. Yeah, I know you are. Thanks." And he rang off.

All eyes were on the colonel. He shook his head. "He had the emergency generator going full tilt. But when they tried to turn on the landing lights, it blew the fuses. They don't have enough spares."

Groans came from all corners of the room.

"Smudge pots, Colonel. Back in the old days we had smudge pots," the sergeant said.

"Get Kurowski on the line down in supply. See if he knows where those old smudge pots are stored."

Annie handed the phone to the sergeant. An eternity later, he hung up and said, "No smudge pots, sir."

The phone rang again and Annie answered. "She is? Okay, give us a few more minutes. Tell her we're working as hard as we can. Tell her Annie said that — yeah, Annie."

"She's just flipped on her last tank of fuel," Annie said to the gathered crowd of men.

"Anybody got any suggestions?" Colonel Baker asked. No one spoke.

"Couldn't we try to have her land at DuPont on their longest runway and have crash equipment standing by. That's better than any of the other options I can think of," the captain said. "I'll take the Jeep and drive over there and assist with the operations."

"That's it," Annie cried.

"What?" The eyes of every man in the room were turned on her.

Suddenly, she felt very small in spite of her five feet eleven inches. She squirmed a little. "Jeeps, sir." She looked directly at Colonel Baker. "Get every Jeep on the base over here and have them line both sides of the runway with their lights on. Lead her down between them. We had to do it at Pearl — at the civilian airport where I did my instructing. That's how we got a missing plane in one time when the power went off."

"Do it!" Colonel Baker ordered and gave Annie a rare smile. "Now, pass that along to your contact over at DuPont. Tell Culpepper what we're doing. Tell her to stay within range of the DuPont airport. Crank down her gear then try to work the flaps. Do another fly-by for them to check that the gear is down and locked and see if she has flaps. And tell her to turn on her landing lights."

Annie repeated the order into the phone. The answer came back moments later. "Part of the instrument panel isn't working, sir. She's throwing the right switches, but she doesn't know which ones are responding. If, on the fly-by, they tell her something isn't operational, she won't know what to do."

"Who's flown that goddamn plane?" Baker shouted.

The men looked at each other.

"Get somebody who can fly a Jug up here, pronto. Tell him we're going to need emergency landing instructions and that we've got a potential control panel problem."

Annie relayed the message to Midge through the DuPont tower that they were looking for a pursuit pilot to help her with emergency-landing procedures.

They waited. Annie could feel the growing anxiety in the room, everyone feeding on each of their individual fears.

"She's cranked the gear down," came the voice over the phone. Annie began repeating everything he said. "Appears to be locked… wait, she's got flaps!… she's got landing lights!"

Again a cheer erupted in the control tower.

"Tell her to get over here and await further instructions. We're working on runway lights," Colonel Baker barked. Annie repeated the instructions into the phone.

Minutes later, they all heard the tortured sound of the P-47 now beginning to circle above.

In the lull, as they waited for a pilot to talk Midge through the emergency landing and for the Jeeps on base to assemble along the runway, Annie had time to think. Inevitably, her mind went back to Pearl and her emergency landing in the Cub — but for a totally different reason. She hadn't been flying a wounded airplane that morning and she had gotten herself and her student down safely. The wounds came later when the Jap machine gun bullets ripped to pieces first her Cub trainer and then the body of the young man entrusted to her by his loving grandmother. She couldn't save Tom Witten. Nor could she save Cornelia, who had spun out and died right in front of her very eyes. Reason told her she was not to blame for either death. Nevertheless, she felt guilty being alive when Tom and Cornelia weren't. She had a chance to redeem herself — if only Midge, with her help, could get down safely.

The door to the tower control room opened and Lieutenant Tracy strode in. Baker told him quickly what they needed. The flight instructor nodded, took the telephone from Annie and began to talk to the man in the DuPont tower. It would be tricky. They still had no idea how much control she would have when she started down.

"What about fuel, sir," Annie asked Colonel Baker.

He frowned. "If she starts to run out of fuel before those Jeeps get lined up, we'll have to tell her to get the plane away from the populated area, find some place to jump and still send the plane out of harm's way for those on the ground below her — hopefully in Delaware Bay."

Annie thought about that and shuddered. After trying to use up most of the volatile gasoline on board to avoid a fire and explosion when she landed, now Midge still might have to ditch the airplane and hope that she bailed out over dry, flat, unobstructed land. No small task. Hopefully, that wouldn't have to happen.

With that, Annie saw a miracle. The lights of a hundred Jeeps snaked their way to the runway and positioned themselves at intervals that would guide the wounded aircraft down. Now the final act of the drama truly began, with Lieutenant Tracy relaying emergency-landing procedures to Midge via the control tower at DuPont. Moments later, they saw the landing lights of the airplane descending through the gloom of deep twilight.

The P-47 headed straight in, lined up for its trip down to the runway. All eyes were glued on the landing lights; everyone held their breath, some saying a little prayer for the lone woman fighting for her life in the cockpit of that dying airplane.

The lights dropped lower and lower.

"Bring it over the fence and drop it in," Annie whispered as if Midge could hear her. Even the field's longest runway might not be long enough if Midge left too much of it behind her.

Realizing she had been holding her breath, Annie let it out slowly, trying to relieve the tension she now felt throughout her body. Every nerve tingled. Every muscle tensed. She tried to imagine herself in that cockpit, ready to pull back at the precise moment of the final flare, yet not knowing when that moment would arrive because she had never flown this airplane before, and not only that, the airplane was mortally wounded. Annie knew all this had to be going through Midge's mind as the plane sank closer and closer to the runway, flying irresolutely toward that corridor of light created by the headlamps of a hundred Jeeps.

The fighter's lights were very low now. Once again Annie sucked in her breath and held it.

Then the wheels touched down hard, bounced before settling on the runway. Then they stayed. The big pursuit barreled past the line of Jeeps.

Please, let the brakes work if she needs them, Annie thought. And, as if on cue, the airplane began to slow. With a swell of pride for her friend, Annie watched as Midge, in full control of the ground roll, made the last turnoff, rolled onto the taxiway, and fell in behind the "Follow Me" Jeep. The attendant fire trucks and ambulance, sirens screaming, brought up the rear of the unlikely parade — all the way in. With the help of the ground crews' signals, Midge rolled the plane right up to its designated parking spot and cut the switch.

Annie and the men emptied out of the tower and ran down to the flight line where Midge sat very still inside the cockpit of that immense fighter airplane. Then Annie got a good look at the undercarriage. "Oh my God. Why she isn't dead, I'll never know."

"Amen to that," Jerry Fuqua, who now stood beside her, said.

Midge climbed out — a little shakily, Annie thought. When her friend's feet touched the ground, she ran forward and hugged her. Then Midge turned around to look at the damage.

"Oh my God," she said, seeing the ripped away underside of the airplane she had just spent two hours in. She seemed to falter, sink inside herself.

"Steady," Annie said. "You did yourself proud. Don't lose it now."

With that, a mechanic climbed up on the wing, jumped down into the cockpit and promptly went right through the floorboard. The only thing remaining of the belly of the airplane — what had separated Midge from a thousand or more feet of open air — was the flimsy Masonite flooring. The rest had been sheared through on impact with the light pole. Seeing what had just happened to the mechanic, Midge and Annie stood frozen in their tracks.

"I'm glad I didn't know," Midge finally managed to say.

# CHAPTER SEVENTEEN

Clare had just finished her second two-week temporary duty at the Republic factory in Farmingdale when Nancy Love told her about the B-17 flights.

The Air Transport Command was planning massive deliveries of B-17s to England via the route known as Snowball — from Gander, Newfoundland, or Goose Bay, Labrador, across the North Atlantic to Prestwick, Scotland. Some of General Tunner's men were balking. They considered the route dangerous. He was seeking a way to convince them that it was doable and decided to call on his two top women pilots. He asked Nancy and Betty Gillies to deliver one of the bombers in an armada in early September. Nancy asked if she could prepare two backup women pilots, just in case, and got Tunner's OK.

Knowing Clare was finishing up at Farmingdale, Nancy got her orders to bring a P-47 to Evansville, then travel to nearby Cincinnati so she could talk to her. "Remember the conversation we had back in April about the delivery to Calgary and the problem the men were having making deliveries on time and how it has become our job to show them how?"

"Of course."

"Well, we've got another one."

"I'm all ears."

"Are you familiar with the term 'Snowball'?"

"The route from Goose Bay, right? Across the North Atlantic to England — no, Scotland..."

"Right."

"What strikes you as the most dangerous aspect of flying that route?"

Clare thought a minute. "You're flying over the water most of the time, but the biggest problem, I guess, is the weather — blowing snow, icy cold, foggy, and bad visibility. But haven't we been flying 'Snowball' since Lend Lease days?"

"Yes. So the conditions don't seen prohibitive to you?"

Clare frowned and let out a small sigh. "If you let it, flying can be scary. But if we don't want to fly badly enough to discount the scary part, maybe we shouldn't be flying at all. You have to anticipate and prepare for emergencies." She paused. "What's this all about, Nancy? Why did you have me come all the way to Cincinnati to ask me questions you already know the answer to?"

"General Tunner is worried because some of his male ferry pilots have been complaining about flying the North Atlantic run. They claim conditions in winter — which will be here before we know it — are extremely dangerous. Now, as far as Bill Tunner is concerned, these flights have become routine and there is no reason for complaints. Some of the men don't see it that way, so he's looking for a way to prove it to them."

"I'm beginning to get the picture."

Nancy nodded. "He considers the Calgary flight a big step forward for the women pilots. We proved deliveries could be made on time if you stick to the schedule and the route and don't allow distractions to get in the way. Well, he's got the same idea here. He's banking on the men not being able to stand being bested by a bunch of women. Guess what he said to me? 'I've decided to let a couple of our girls show them just how easy it really is.' He wants Betty and me to deliver a B-17."

"Good Gawd, Nancy, a bomber... that's fantastic!"

"That's not all. General Tunner agreed to let us have a backup woman's crew — pilot and co-pilot. With any luck, they might get to make the trip as well."

Clare held her breath.

"I want you to pilot the second ship."

"Who's my co-pilot?"

"Who do you want?"

"You mean I can choose?"

"Obviously, given necessary hours and experience, it needs to be one of the original WAFS and one willing to follow orders. As you know, we have a few freethinkers around. They won't do."

Clare grinned. She assumed that Nancy referred to Midge who, after her unofficial and near-fatal flight in the P-47, had been grounded and put on desk duty. She was slowly being eased back into active flying — PT-19s and PT-26s. "Either of the girls flying pursuits with me in Farmingdale would be good," she answered.

"Ah, that presents yet another problem, Clare. With Betty and you taken out of their ranks for awhile, we can't spare the other two. You'll have to look elsewhere."

"Well, then I'd like to take Annie."

"Yes." Nancy nodded. "She's done an outstanding job. She took an emotional nosedive when Cornelia died, but she came back from that quite well, I thought. And Colonel Baker tells me she was instrumental in getting Culpepper down safely. He said she showed a very cool head in the midst of that disaster."

"She's a keeper."

"OK, you talk to her. If she agrees, we'll cut her orders. The two of you will be assigned to me from now until the flight is over and we're back on U.S. soil. Figure about two months — five weeks for training and three weeks to make the trip, spend a few days in England, and secure passage back. And, Clare... be sure to tell Annie this is to be kept quiet."

"Mum's the word." Clare hesitated. "So... Nancy, any chance I might get to see Will while we're over there?"

"I'll work on it."

In the midst of their transition into the B-17, Nancy received notification that her women pilots would no longer be known as WAFS. Women Airforce Service Pilots, or the acronym WASP — coined by Jackie Cochran — was the new name by which both the Women's Flying Training Detachment and the Women's Auxiliary Ferrying Squadron would be known.

No longer were all the Army's women pilots performing ferrying duties. Cochran had sent twenty-five of the Texas training facility's July graduates to tow target school. Now another twenty-five–from the August class–also were destined to tow targets for gunnery recruits in training in North Carolina. And the word was out that other non-ferrying assignments were on the immediate horizon. No, the designation "ferry pilots" no longer would adequately describe the Army's women flyers. The term Airforce Service Pilots had a more all-inclusive ring to it.

"We were WAFS until we woke up the morning of August fifth and learned that someone had changed our name while we slept," said Betty Gillies.

"So what's in a name?" Clare said to Nancy. But, to herself, Clare had to reconcile the thought that Jacqueline Cochran had just tightened her grip on all the women pilots flying for the military.

"We can still call ourselves WAFS," Nancy responded, tight-lipped. "And, as the executive for the women ferry pilots attached to the ATC, appointed by General William H. Tunner, I fully intend to do just that. Let's get back to work. We've got bombers to fly."

A week later, Clare watched an incredibly blue Grand Traverse Bay rise up to meet them as their instructor, Captain Red Forman, skillfully maneuvered the limping B-17 onto the runway. Half an hour earlier, Nancy, flying from the left seat, and Forman, in the right, had tried to land the four-engine bomber at their original destination in Ludington, Michigan. When they realized on final approach that the runway wasn't long enough for a comfortable landing of the big plane, Forman took the controls, shoved the throttles forward to full power and pulled out. In the process, the number-four engine detonated and Forman had to feather the prop. Now, they were on final approach for a landing at the closest alternate runway that would accommodate the crippled B-17, which was the runway located at the Traverse City, Michigan, airport — under the exclusive domain of the U.S. Navy.

They were only a few days into their training and building time under Forman's watchful eye. On this and all their flights, he occupied the right seat while Nancy and Betty traded off flying from the left seat of the big plane. Forman was Bill Tunner's chief pilot, longtime friend, frequent co-pilot, and all-around right-hand man. And it so happened that, on this trip north, they also were carrying their boss, Tunner, and some of his officers on an administrative cross-country flight. Further filling up the space were Clare and Annie, who were beginning their B-17 transition, so they were on board to learn.

With the landing at Traverse City successfully negotiated, Clare hoped they would all have a brief R and R while the Navy mechanics hunted for the problem in engine number four. Lunch at a nice little restaurant on the bay would be nice, Clare thought, admiring the splendidly leafed-out hardwoods and the dusky pines of the north woods. But when she looked out the window again, already anticipating the sweet smell of pine, Clare saw that two rows of Jeeps now flanked the gradually slowing airplane. And the men riding in those Jeeps were armed.

"What the ..." Nancy said, looking out the left side of the airplane.

"They're over here too," Betty said from behind Forman.

The "Follow Me" Jeep led them off the active runway and onto the taxiway where they were signaled to stop. The Jeep leading the left column pulled up to the pilot's side of the airplane and the officer commanding the guard motioned for Nancy to open her window. She did. "You can't land here. You must take off immediately," he told her.

"We have General William H. Tunner, commanding officer of the Ferrying Division, Air Transport Command, U.S. Army Air Forces and his staff on board and we have lost number four engine. We need to deplane and make repairs."

"I don't care who you are or who is on board, ma'am, you can't stay here."

General Tunner appeared behind them in the cockpit door. He leaned down and called out the window, "What's going on, ensign?"

The young man stiffened at the sight of Tunner's brigadier's star, saluted, but he held his ground. "Sir, my orders are to tell you to take off immediately."

Tunner stared. Clare noted the flush that crept up his ears and thought he was going to explode, but the general held his temper.

"Please, sir. I have my orders," the ensign said.

Clare swore she could hear Tunner counting to ten before he swallowed his anger and answered, "And so you do. Captain Forman, Mrs. Love, we have three engines. Can you take off?"

Clare saw Nancy's jaw tense. She stole a look at Forman, who gave a nod of ascent with an almost imperceptible lowering of his chin. "Yes, Sir, we can take off," Nancy answered.

"Then do it." Tunner turned on his heel and disappeared back into the bowels of the airplane.

Nancy looked at Forman.

"You're the pilot in command. I'm here to help," he said.

"Betty," Nancy's cool voice came back to them, "start looking for the next nearest airport that will take this airplane. Captain Forman, here's where we all earn these wings."

She waved a salute at the young ensign. "I suggest you move your Jeeps out of this airplane's path, unless you want to go with us," she said, and fixed him with a look that included the characteristic half smile she used when very displeased with someone. Clare knew those eyes had the look of an angry green sea and she almost pitied the young man now on the receiving end.

"Yes, ma'am." This time he saluted her.

"Prepare for takeoff." And she and Forman began the run-up.

Moments later, the big bomber began its lumbering rush down the runway on the thrust of three engines at full power, lifting off and just clearing those tall pine trees Clare had so much admired.

"Alpena, Michigan," Betty said moments later, and she called out the bearing and ETA.

On August 15, Nancy and Betty qualified as pilots on the Flying Fortress, the nickname for the B-17. Then on August 18, Clare and Annie did likewise. Just as Nancy and Betty had done, they hauled the big bomber around the sky using their hands and feet and refusing Captain Forman's offer of help. "We have to be able to do it ourselves," Clare told him, remembering what Nancy had told her about Jackie Cochran's tainted delivery of the Lockheed Hudson to England.

*****

*August 18 was the day that 376 B-17s from the US Eighth Army Air Force in England struck the Germans' vital ball-bearing factory in Schweinfurt and the Messerschmitt works at Regensburg. The Fortresses, minus fighter escorts, fought a desperate battle against enemy fighters and suffered heavy casualties. Thirty-six bombers were lost from the Schweinfurt formation and 24 from Regensburg. Fighters, not possessing the necessary range to protect the bombers, instead were used for diversionary tactics and took casualties as well.*

*The RAF had already learned the deadly lesson. Now it was the U.S.'s turn. Unescorted bombers cannot make daylight raids over Germany without taking severe losses in men and airplanes. The American commanders immediately began to reassess the wisdom of such raids. Production of pursuits to protect those bombers was moving into high gear in the airplane factories at home.*

*****

On September 2, the four women B-17 pilots, with their respective three-man male crews on board, left Lockbourne Army Air Base in Columbus, Ohio, and departed in two B-17s bound for England — two of two-hundred replacements for those downed Fortresses. The first leg of their trip would take them across the cold, foreboding North Atlantic. In her B-4 bag Nancy carried an official Air Transport Command letter of introduction to Major Roy Atwood, executive officer of the ATC European Wing in London. It was signed by Colonel Bob Love, Deputy Chief of Staff:

*I have known these people for a good while and they are thoroughly competent as pilots, as well as having a background in aviation activities. They are being sent to perform a certain amount of liaison with the ATA and other agencies interested in the ferrying of aircraft to the UK. ...I sincerely hope you will give them your highly accredited effort in showing them around.*

*P.S. Incidentally one of them is my wife...*

They RONed at New Castle, where they picked up the fleece-lined flight suits and oxygen masks required for the North Atlantic air route. In the nearly ninety-degree heat that enveloped the Eastern seaboard that week, fleece-lined anything seemed a cruel joke. From there, they flew to New York's LaGuardia airport for an overnight briefing and proper clearance. The next day, the bombers flew via Presque Isle, Maine, to the staging point for the trans-Atlantic flight, Goose Bay, Labrador, once a tiny Eskimo village on the tip of Lake Melville. Early in the war, the Canadian government had decided to build an air base there and invited the United States and the British to share the use of it. The base now served as air cover for transatlantic flights and as a staging field for ferrying bombers to Britain.

The four WAFS stepped onto that remote, wind-swept airfield the afternoon of September 4, 1943. That night, an artist known for his airplane nose art, painted **WAFS** in plain-Jane block letters on the port side of Nancy and Betty's aircraft, right under the pilot's window. Then below he added *Queen Bee* in flowery, feminine script. *The Princesses* marked Clare and Annie's ship, with **WAFS, TOO** painted in block letters.

The next morning, they sat on the runway working their way through the cockpit checklist. Clare watched as Nancy rolled her big Flying Fortress into position — number one for takeoff. Then, from the pilot's seat of number two, she saw a Jeep making a mad dash across the tarmac and headed for their airplanes.

"Uh, oh, Annie," she said, pointing out the window. "Somethin's wrong. He's movin' too fast, and the way he's wavin' his arms, he's got somethin' to tell Nancy before she takes off. Gawd, what could it be?"

"Maybe the weather's changed over the Greenland icecap and they want us to wait awhile," Annie said.

Clare looked at her. "I hope you're right, but I've got a bad feeling in my bones."

Two more Jeeps moved toward the airplanes. Each carried two passengers.

"Those guys are wearin' winter flight gear," Clare said as one of the Jeeps drew up beside Nancy's plane. The men in flight gear got out. The other Jeep then made its way over to Clare's airplane and, recognizing the base commander, she slid open her window.

"Orders cancelled," he shouted up to her. Some of his words were lost in the wind, but Clare heard enough to understand. "General Arnold. No women ... fly ... Atlantic. ... Step down. ... men take airplane."

A devastating wave of disappointment swept over Clare.

"You don't suppose there's a misunderstanding," Annie said, but her face gave her away.

"I doubt it, hon, not this time. It's midnight and Cinderella's airborne coach has turned into a pumpkin. We're not going to England after all," Clare sighed. "And I'm not going to get to see Will."

She unhooked her harness, stood, took her clipboard and made her way to the door where the replacement male pilots were just getting on. With Annie right behind her, Clare handed the paperwork to the new pilot and climbed down. They reached the ground just in time to see Betty and Nancy disembark from the *Queen Bee*.

They knew full well they would not be flying any more that day, so, following Nancy's lead, the women made their way to the makeshift bar at one end of the small mess hall. Each sat nursing her alcoholic beverage of choice until Clare, rarely at a loss for words, finally broke the silence. "You don't suppose the indomitable Miss Cochran got her sharp little claws in this, do you?"

"She couldn't know about it. Bill's kept a tight lid on," Nancy said.

"I'd put nothing past her," Clare said.

"Nor would I," Betty agreed.

"Not when you consider that she's still the only woman to ferry a plane to England," Clare said. "Granted, we weren't at war at the time and she didn't do the take-off and landing. But still, she did it, and the world knows about it."

At that moment, out of the corner of her eye, Clare saw the Operations Officer approaching them. He seemed hesitant. Then she noticed what looked like a telegram in his hand.

"Is one of you ladies Mrs. William Page Webb?"

Clare saw a mix of comprehension and apprehension flash across the faces of her three companions. For the second time that morning, Clare felt the bottom drop out of her world. Ice formed in her belly and it took everything she had to get out the whispered words, "I'm Mrs. Webb."

The Operations Officer handed her the telegram. The yellow paper shook in her hand. Her eyes blurred. She couldn't see the print.

"Here, Clare," Annie said, gently. "Let me read it for you." And the younger woman took the telegram, read it, digested it before saying, "It could be worse, Clare." Her quiet Southern voice sounded soothing. "Will's plane is missing and they believe it has been shot down. He's missing in action. It's quite possible he's been taken prisoner by the Germans."

# CHAPTER EIGHTEEN

"You're both going to Pursuit Transition School."

Midge thought for a minute she was hearing things.

Annie let out a "yeehaw" that sounded like a cross between a Rebel yell and an Indian war whoop.

It was a week before Thanksgiving and Betty Gillies had called them into her office. "You're due in Palm Springs, California, November thirtieth. We'll arrange transport. Classes begin December first. You two are part of the first class being sent out there. Congratulations!"

She had heard correctly. Betty, her smiling blue eyes matching her pleased grin, seemed to be waiting for a response. Midge looked at Annie, hoping her friend could come up with words for both of them because she was speechless. Pursuit School had seemed the most unattainable of goals after her P-47 debacle.

"What happened?" Annie asked.

Betty offered a simple explanation. "Pursuit production is way up. Deliveries are behind. We need more pilots capable of flying them right off the assembly line. Just like with the PT-19s last year, it means picking up the airplane at the factory and taking it to the shipyard or the fabrication center."

Annie was grinning. Midge knew how badly she wanted a chance to fly the hot single-seaters.

"It's good we can go together, Annie," she said, finally finding her voice.

Midge had to restrain herself from kissing Betty's feet. The woman who had been designated by Nancy Love as her mentor had retained a faith in her even when the others hadn't. She looked into Betty's eyes and, from the heart, said, "Thank you. I do have one question, though…" It suddenly occurred to her that she would be flying clear across the country in less than a week's time.

"What's that, Midge?" Betty asked.

"My aunt who lives outside of Saint Louis — the one I lived with until I came to New York — she's been ill. I had been hoping for a ferrying assignment that would allow me to RON there, but one hasn't come up. Could I possibly get a couple of days leave so I can stop off and see her?"

"I think that could be arranged," Betty said.

Midge caught a quick breath. Ask now, or you'll wish you had and be sorry, she thought. "Could Annie come with me?"

Annie looked at her in surprise.

"I've written my aunt so much about you, I know she would like to meet you."

"Maybe Annie would rather take a couple of days and go home. It is Thanksgiving, you know." Betty had a quizzical look on her face.

"Oh, I don't want to go home," Annie blurted out. "I mean, they aren't expecting me and it really isn't necessary. I had planned to work through the holiday, assuming we had planes to deliver. But I'd love to go to Saint Louis with Midge. That would be a welcome change."

"OK, then, it's fine with me," Betty said. "We'll get you out on a hop to Scott on Wednesday. Saturday morning, get yourselves back there. Something will be heading for Long Beach by then. From there, it's not much more than a taxi ride to Palm Springs."

For Midge, the last few months in Wilmington had been almost unbearable. If it hadn't been for Annie, she would have called it quits, taken her clipped wings and slunk back to Jacqueline Cochran's protective nest. The badly damaged P-47 she had taken without official sanction had marked her. She was an outcast — until today.

After Midge's accident, word came down that further incremental transition into pursuits by male or female ferry pilots stationed at any of the ferrying bases was temporarily suspended. Already Bill Tunner and his staff were looking at other, better training and transition options, for both the male and female pilots. Midge's accident served to speed up the discussions. But all the men who had hoped to begin transition, as well as a couple of the WAFS who thought they had been slated for transition, held the suspension of transition strictly against Midge and let her know daily how they felt about it. She considered asking for a transfer, but she didn't want to move away from Annie and Betty Gillies, her only two friends in the WAFS corps.

Now, more than four months later, the decree finally had been rescinded. Pursuit School was the answer they had been seeking.

Bring in a bunch of recruits and teach them in a group how to fly all of the Army's super fast birds. Rumor said they were hurting for qualified pursuit pilots.

Now, because Betty thought her to be a good pilot and because she had absolutely toed the mark ever since July 5, Midge had gotten the nod to attend Pursuit School. And Annie, known to have been one of the women in line for a try at pursuits and itching to get her hands on one, was going as well.

Though not injured physically, Midge had not escaped the episode in the P-47 unscathed. She could still recall every terrifying second spent in that wounded airplane giving off those ear-splitting screeches of agony. She had listened to the shrieking noise her entire time aloft, flying around using up fuel and waiting for those in command back at the base to prepare to bring her in. At twenty-four, she never expected to look death so closely in the face. But the ill-fated flight had taught her a couple of things about herself: one, she was a damn competent pilot or she'd be dead now; two, she could survive anything and come back.

The order prohibiting women from transitioning in pursuits did not affect the P-47 women pilots already assigned to Farmingdale. They had proven their mettle. Clare and the other two had left for Farmingdale the day after Midge's flight, so they hadn't been around to take part in the aftermath.

Midge had made the best of her time in Wilmington. She called on the survival techniques that had gotten her through her childhood. You lived with your mistakes and did not make the same mistake twice. She made up her mind she would neither resign from the WAFS nor give them grounds to dismiss her. She still had to prove to Jacqueline Cochran that she had the right stuff. Now, she also had to prove it to herself.

In the process, she and Annie had grown close.

That night, Midge waited in line for nearly an hour in order to use the only truly private pay phone on the base — the one outside the men's room off the bar in the O-Club. She would be seen, yes, but with the door to the booth closed, at least she wouldn't be heard. If anybody asked, she was talking to her aunt, telling her about her upcoming visit home. And she did make a call to her aunt, but it only took a couple of minutes. She owed her employer a report. Her next call was to Cochran at her Washington apartment.

Midge saved the news about Pursuit School for awhile, trying to determine her employer's mood and how things were going at WASP headquarters. She found the Director of Women Pilots in particularly good spirits. Jackie told her how she and Hap Arnold were working on the necessary details to launch the move for WASP militarization.

"It won't be long now, Midge. That will be the time for you to come back in the fold with me. I can get you that commission I promised you two years ago. I imagine Nancy Love's minions are wearing a little thin on you, anyway. You're used to better than that now, Midge — sleeping on metal cots, living in a barracks with hardly any privacy. No doors on the bathroom stalls. What a travesty."

"Miss Cochran, it's not as bad as it sounds. The doors were up long before I got here. Remember, I grew up in rural Missouri. I'm not that far away from the old outhouse days. I didn't have indoor plumbing until I moved in with my aunt in St. Charles."

And you spent your early days using an outhouse, too, Midge thought, remembering the stories of Jackie's childhood — the poverty she had vowed to escape from, and had. But rather than spend any more time picking apart the living quarters in BOQ14, Midge decided to let her boss in on the good news. "Miss Cochran... let me tell you what I called about. I have great news. I'm going to Pursuit School in Palm Springs."

The silence that followed at the other end of the line telegraphed to Midge that this news might not have been met with the enthusiasm she had hoped for. But after a few seconds, Jackie answered, "Well! That is good news. I'm sure you'll do well. I'm a bit surprised after what you did to that pursuit last summer, but they really are desperate for pilots to ferry those new planes, so I guess they are being more forgiving now.

"Is that all you had to tell me, because if it is, dinner is waiting. Floyd just gave me the high sign. We have guests and we're ready to sit down."

"That's it, Miss Cochran, I thought you'd be pleased."

"I am, Midge, I am. I know you will do superbly out there. You keep me posted and be sure and let me know where they send you after your schooling is over."

Midge hung up with a slightly bitter taste in her mouth. In the two years she had spent working for the cosmetics queen, before joining the WAFS, Midge had seen inside and behind that exquisitely made-up, fashionably dressed, expensively bought and kept bearing and persona that Jackie had so carefully constructed for herself. She presented that face to the world and you were expected to take her at face value.

"I was seven-years-old and I wanted a doll — a particular doll," Jackie had told her, voice low and the emotion and hurt barely disguised. "It was Christmas and the local commissary was giving away this doll in a drawing. I saved my pennies. By then I was working as a nursemaid and household helper to a woman who had just had twins. I bought two twenty-five cent tickets. The drawing was held Christmas Eve. I won the doll."

Midge had watched, fascinated, as tears rimmed those magnetic brown eyes.

"My fifteen-year-old sister had a two-year-old baby, Willa Mae. Mama and Papa made me give the doll to the baby. Midge, it broke my heart," thirty-five-year-old Jackie told twenty-one-year-old Midge in a moment of self-retrospection the night early in 1941 when they celebrated Midge's having earned her private pilot's license.

Jackie toyed with her glass of champagne, then raised it and toasted her protégé, who likewise raised her glass, waiting to see what was coming next.

"When I was working at Antoine's, after that baby was a grown woman and had a child of her own, I brought them up here to New York and helped them get a fresh start in life. My only requirement was that she had to return the doll to me. It's mine now, refurbished and with new clothes, and surrounded by a whole collection of lovely dolls. But she has the place of honor."

# CHAPTER NINETEEN

Annie noted the family resemblance when Midge's aunt welcomed them with open arms. Earleen Boswell was a small, plump woman with a washed-out version of Midge's rich chestnut hair — a preview, Annie thought fleetingly, of what Midge could be in twenty years if she should let herself slip into a backwater life style or frame of mind. But Annie didn't think that likely. Midge had a self-assuredness she didn't have — and that she envied. Living in New York could do that for you. Besides, she was petite like the girls Annie had grown up with, not an awkward five-eleven wearing a size fourteen at age fourteen, and still a size fourteen at nearly twenty-four.

"Annie, Midge has told me so much about you," Earleen said when the three of them were settled at her oilcloth-covered kitchen table, a cup of coffee in front of each of them. "She's so lucky to have friends like you and that Mrs. Gillies up there in Delaware. Though her Mama and I sure do worry about her flying those airplanes. Why, two girls and their instructor were killed down in Texas just a couple of months ago. They were part of Miss Cochran's school down there in Sweetwater." She switched her gaze to Midge. "By the way, Midge, how is Miss Cochran? You haven't mentioned her recently?"

Midge froze, her coffee cup halfway to her lips.

Annie stared, her eyes wide-open in disbelief.

"Aunt Earleen, Annie doesn't know about Miss Cochran," Midge said evenly. And, without faltering, she changed the subject. "How's Mama?"

"As good as could be expected with *him* around." Earleen waved the handkerchief she had pulled from her pocket. That was when Annie noticed her hands. They were gnarled, like an old woman's hands, yet Earleen was hardly fifty. Arthritis, Annie thought glumly. Midge's aunt ran a beauty shop in what used to be the garage. This woman was a beautician who worked with her hands and she already had a galloping case of arthritis.

"She's talking about my stepfather," Midge said to Annie, who nodded. After the mention of Jacqueline Cochran's name, she decided that she should keep quiet and let Midge and her aunt do the talking.

"He's not hitting her, is he?" Midge asked.

"No, ever since you called the sheriff on him, he's kept his fists to himself. But he talks bad to her, calls her names, tells people lies about her. I don't know how she puts up with it."

"You told her I was coming — but not him, right?"

"I did what you asked me to do, honey. Honus is supposed to bring her in tomorrow morning to help me get started on Thanksgiving dinner. He won't stay. Claims he can't stand a bunch of wimmen underfoot cookin' and gossipin'. He'll come back tomorrow afternoon when the football game's over on the radio, just in time for dinner."

"And he'll be drunk."

"That too. Anyway, should give you several hours to see your mama and introduce Annie to her before all the kin start arrivin' for turkey and trimmin's."

That night, Annie and Midge talked in the dark, stretched out on twin cots in what used to be Midge's room. Midge had told Annie about running away from home at fourteen and coming to live with her aunt and uncle in St. Charles. "I went to work for Aunt Earlene and decided right then that I wanted to be a hair stylist."

"Why did your aunt ask about Jackie Cochran?" Annie interrupted — finally getting up the nerve to ask. She sensed her friend's caught-breath hanging in the air as Midge took a few seconds to reply.

"I work for Miss Cochran," Midge said and sighed heavily.

Annie turned over and propped herself up on her elbow. "What do you mean you *work* for her?"

Annie never had been able to reconcile in her mind how Midge had come to learn to fly. She hadn't gone to college, therefore had not had the benefit of the subsidized, government-sponsored CPT course. For a young person to learn to fly without that was a very expensive proposition, certainly not within the reach of most ordinary people and particularly not in reach of a young woman going to school and earning her living washing hair at a hairdresser's.

Midge turned on the bedside lamp, sat up, plumped her pillow behind her, leaned back and began to tell Annie about her life before the WAFS. At beauty school, she had caught the eye of one of Saint Louis's most prominent hairstylists and the woman had hired her. A few months later, the hairstylist went to New York for a national beauticians' conference and took Midge along. There, Midge met

Antoine, who became so totally taken with her and her talents he offered her a job on the spot. Less than a year out of beauty school, Midge Culpepper of St. Charles, Missouri, had made her way to New York.

One day, Jacqueline Cochran came in unannounced to have her hair done. Antoine told the famous woman about his new protégé and suggested that Miss Cochran let her style her hair. She did, and the blonde aviatrix turned out to be as taken with Midge as Antoine and the Saint Louis beautician had been.

"I never have figured out what Miss Cochran saw in me," Midge told Annie, "but she started coming to me exclusively — always full of questions. She wanted to know about my life back home in Missouri, why I went into hairdressing, personal things, sometimes things I wasn't sure I should tell her. You have no idea how compelling she is. I told her anything she wanted to know. And then, one day, she asked me if I could type and take shorthand. Well, I could do both. Aunt Earleen had made me take all the secretarial courses in high school. 'Just in case,' she used to say. Just in case beauty school didn't work out is what she meant. Turns out, I was good enough at both that the business college and the cosmetology school both offered me scholarships."

Even in the low light Annie could see the slight flush of pride in Midge's cheeks.

"Would you believe I was class valedictorian?" Midge grinned. "The other kids with really good grades — and there weren't that many — were planning to go to teachers' college or business school. Nobody could believe that their class valedictorian was going to beauty school. They all looked down on it. Told me I should take the business school scholarship. But I decided to let myself dream. Besides, Aunt Earleen always told me I was a natural in the beauty shop so I chose that path."

Midge paused and seemed to be just staring into space. Annie thought maybe Midge was trying to make up her mind about something. Then, she seemed to decide and continued. "Anyway, after a while, Miss Cochran had me come up to her office on Fifth Avenue. She gave me a typing test and a shorthand test and apparently I did well enough that she offered to hire me at more than I was making at Antoine's. Needless to say, Antoine was not pleased, but Miss Cochran had worked for him and she had gone on to make him even more famous than before, so he forgave her and was quite gracious about my leaving. He even wished me the best. I've been working for Jacqueline Cochran ever since. I'm her administrative assistant."

"You say you *are* her assistant? I don't understand."

"Soon after I went to work for her, she sent me off to take flying lessons — all the ratings. She wanted me to be capable of flying her plane — to be her co-pilot in the Staggerwing. I traveled everywhere with her. When the war came along and she began to formulate plans for a women's flying corps, she promised me a place in it."

"Then why are you in the WAFS flying for Nancy Love? Why aren't you down at Avenger Field or in Washington with Cochran?"

"Good questions, except that the WAFS got there first — before she got her flying school. She wanted to know what was going on with Mrs. Love's program, so she decided to have me try to qualify in the WAFS."

"So you're a spy."

Midge grimaced. "No, I don't think I'm a spy. All I do is keep her posted on what's happening — from my perspective as a member of the squadron. I'm not on the inside. I'm not in on decisions and policy. Everything I've ever told her, she's already known about."

"Certainly she doesn't need so-called intelligence now," Annie said, disbelief in her voice. "She's the Director of Women Pilots. She's in the left seat. Why hasn't she taken you back under her wing to work in Washington?"

"She's offered me such a position. I told her I'd rather fly. You see, I've come to love the WAFS — well now the WASP — and what we're doing, ferrying airplanes out of New Castle. We're needed. And you and I wouldn't be friends if it hadn't been for the WAFS. Betty Gillies has been wonderful to me. The only person who doesn't seem to like me is Clare, and she's up in Farmingdale now. Of course, since the incident in the P-47, people have given me a wide berth. But I've learned to live with that — thanks to you."

Annie shook her head. "You still work for Cochran... meaning she's paying you?"

"Yes."

"Midge, that *is* spying." Annie was almost in tears.

"I need the money," Midge said quietly.

"But what could possibly make you sell yourself like that?"

Midge hesitated. Is she trying to come up with an excuse, Annie wondered, a lie of convenience, a cover up? Then Annie saw the tears welling in Midge's eyes.

"Listen to me, Annie," her voice was barely above a whisper, "you've seen my aunt's hands. She struggles every day to do the only job she's trained to do. My Aunt Earleen lives in near poverty. My uncle's been dead for three years now. What happens to her the day she can't do hair anymore, or some big-time upscale beauty shop sets up near here and takes all her customers away?" She sniffed and shook her head. "And my aunt has it good compared to my mother, considering that no-good she lives with. He hasn't worked since he married her. She gets by clerking at the grocery store. I'm the oldest of five kids. When I left home, she still had my two little brothers and my two little sisters to raise with that S.O.B. hanging around doing God knows to Sissy and Louise."

Annie gasped.

"Oh, yeah, that's why I really left home."

Now Annie saw the pain in Midge's face, sensed the despair in her voice, and heard the horror in the words that poured from her mouth.

"The night my mother went to the hospital with a miscarriage — because he beat the shit out of her — he came to my room. Told me to be quiet and not wake my sisters and to come with him. With Mama in the hospital, I was now the woman of the house. I thought he wanted me to fix him something to eat. He took me to his and Mama's room and he …" her voice broke. She took a deep breath and plunged on. "He did things to me he shouldn't have. He did it every night until Mama came home from the hospital. The minute she got back on her feet, I lit out for Aunt Earlene's and I never went back."

Annie felt like she had been punched in the stomach.

"Does your mother know? Does your aunt know?"

"Aunt Earleen knows. I finally had to tell her so she'd let me stay here. We told Mama some cock and bull story that the only way I could get the schooling I needed would be to stay in St. Charles where I could go to a good high school rather than that country school where all the backwater kids went. Which is true." Midge's eyes pleaded with Annie to believe her.

"I don't know if Aunt Earleen ever told Mama the truth or not. She may have. Even if she did, my mama went right on living with that scumbag. Aunt Earleen and I got the other girls out of there on the same premise. They came to St. Charles to live with her and go to school. Sissy's married now. She's two years younger than me. Louise just turned eighteen and is in beauty school in St. Louis. That's what Miss Cochran's money is going for, to keep Louise in school and to give Mama and my aunt money to put away for old age." Midge stopped. She took a ragged breath.

"I never see that paycheck. I live on what the WAFS pay me. The other check comes straight to Aunt Earleen and she takes care of it."

When they finally turned out the light, Annie lay staring into the darkness trying to absorb and come to terms with everything her friend had told her. Their lives had been so different. She looked up to Midge, Clare, Nancy Batson, Betty, because they had a self-assuredness she didn't. Now Midge's revelation of what her life really had been like had rocked Annie out of her genteel Southern complacency.

Since meeting Charlie, Annie's self-esteem had improved. With the knowledge that Charlie cared for her — loved her for who and what she was and wanted desperately to marry her — Annie had a new perspective on life, though she still could not find the words to tell her parents about him. The love she and Charlie felt for each other — still a very private thing— was something she couldn't share. She couldn't bring herself to face her mother's inquiries. "Who is he, dear? What do you know about him, about his parents? We had so hoped you would marry someone from Nashville or at least Davidson County. Someone with a similar background."

The night before she and Midge left Wilmington for St. Charles and then Palm Springs, Charlie had called to tell her that they had been told to expect to be shipped overseas the end of January. Charlie was pressing her to set a wedding date. "The minute I graduate from Pursuit School, I'll head for Columbus," she told him. "That will be early January."

She didn't have a ring, but that didn't matter to Annie. She had what she needed, the knowledge of Charlie's love. Still, when she wasn't around Charlie, her insecurities resurfaced rapidly. In Midge, she had found someone who made her feel better about herself, not worse. Now she knew the chinks in Midge's armor, and getting used to that was going to take some doing.

# CHAPTER TWENTY

Clare dropped her B-4 bag in the entryway and listened to the odd stillness of the empty flat. Her WAFS roommates stationed in Farmingdale all had gone home for Christmas — Helen Mary and Betty to their husbands and children in New Jersey and on Long Island, respectively, and Teresa to be with her husband, Dink, at his current posting. All had yet to return. She had, in fact, come back earlier than she had planned.

Christmas at home with her family had been a disaster. Whenever the song *White Christmas* played on the radio, Clare choked up and had to leave the room. The Christmas before, she and Will had both wangled twenty-four-hour passes. She had ferried a PT-19 to Dallas to be with him and they had stood in line to see the popular new movie *Holiday Inn* and had sung *White Christmas* walking back to the hotel.

Though she had petitioned Washington and the Army repeatedly for news of Will's fate, no word had come. He'd been missing for more than three months now and the war raged on as if no end were in sight. She found the words of the joyous season, Peace on Earth, empty and had gotten so disturbed by her feelings she ended up walking out of midnight Mass on Christmas Eve. The day after Christmas, she made the excuse that she had to get back to ferrying and left Colorado two days earlier than originally scheduled.

Now, back in Farmingdale and away from her family and the gaiety she had found herself incapable of sharing, Clare flopped down in what passed for an easy chair in their sparse quarters and looked around the drab living room with its brown and beige rental property furnishings.

They weren't allowed to hang pictures on the walls but had tried to personalize the place with homey touches — photos and favorite knickknacks on the pressed-board credenza. Clare had contributed a Venetian blown-glass angel and a lace doily made for her by her Italian grandmother. Teresa, the daughter of florists and herself a talented flower arranger, made it a point to keep some kind of fresh flowers in evidence, but now her last bouquet before exiting for the holidays sat wilted on the small coffee table.

Clare rose, picked up the vase, carried it into the kitchen, dumped the dead flowers in the garbage, poured the stale water down the drain, and rinsed the vase. Her unopened mail lay on the kitchen counter. She sifted through it. A letter in Nancy's handwriting caught Clare's attention and she ripped it open.

> *Dear Clare,*
> *Bob is coming to Cincinnati for New Years Eve — the Army is actually giving him three days leave. Will wonders never cease! He flies into Sunken Lunken the afternoon of the 30ᵗʰ. There's a New Year's Eve party in the ballroom of the hotel — the Netherland where my apartment is. It will be mostly Ferry Command people.*
>
> *We want you here with us. I am assuming you have no specific plans and the place to be on New Year's Eve is with loved ones. We're poor substitutes for Will, I know, but we refuse to take no for an answer. In fact, you will find orders enclosed signed by Bill Tunner for you to bring a P-47 to Evansville for modification on December 30. You are to proceed from there to Cincinnati via ground transportation and join us here for the holiday. You will take a modified aircraft back to Newark on January 2.*
>
> *Listen to "Mother Nancy" and do this — for us if not for yourself. We miss you.*
>
> *Love, Nancy*

Tears stung Clare's eyes as she re-read the message. She had no plans. Besides, orders were orders.

A general atmosphere of hope pervaded the end-of-the-year holiday that December of 1943 — and Nancy couldn't stop talking about it.

"We've turned the corner, Clare. We're winning the war," Nancy said, as they sat in her office the afternoon of December 31, catching up and waiting for Bob.

Clare leaned back and took a drag on her cigarette. "OK, so things are looking up. You haven't told me how life is treating *you*. Are things going well for you here in Cincinnati?"

"Actually things are going very well. Our pursuit training experiment in Palm Springs is an unparalleled success. Annie Gwynn, Midge Culpepper and the others have done an outstanding job. In fact, they graduate tomorrow. The second class graduates January 10 and a third begins January11. And that's just the beginning."

"Is this your idea?"

"No, it's Bill Tunner's. As you know, flying pursuits is a specialized skill. The men headed overseas to fly any kind of combat airplane, other than a pursuit, don't need that particular skill. Only pursuit pilots need to know how to fly them — pursuit pilots headed for combat and the pilots who ferry them from the factory to the docks.

"Two things have happened. One, we can't waste the combat pilots' time having them ferry pursuits when they are needed to fly in Europe and the Pacific. Two, there are so many pursuits coming off the production line right now, we can't keep up with the deliveries."

"And women, who aren't needed to fly combat, can deliver pursuits exclusively, fulltime," Clare volunteered.

"Right. So we're going to be sending as many women pilots to pursuit school as want to go and can qualify. A few non-pursuit-qualified girls will stay to ferry the non-pursuit aircraft we need to move and the rest will be transferred to flying jobs in the Training Command."

"Looks like I'm going to stay right where I am then, in Farmingdale."

"Yes, Clare. The best thing we ever did was let you three gals check out in the P-47 and send you to Farmingdale before anybody realized how important this would become."

"Betty knew. She told me straight off that we needed pursuit pilots. I suspect if that hotdog Midge hadn't racked up that P-47 in New Castle, we'd have had more pursuit pilots in all the women's squadrons by now."

"She's ambitious. I can't fault her on that. And she's one of the best when it comes to handling an airplane. She proved that when she got that wreck down safely."

"I don't see how you can put up with her. You know who she is and what she is."

"Not really. We know she worked for Jackie, but I've seen nothing that indicates that she has betrayed the original WAFS program in any way. And now we're all under the same umbrella anyway. If she's so thick with Cochran, why hasn't she bolted the ranks and gone back to work for the woman herself in Washington? Surely there's a brighter future for her there. She could make a lot more money. You know that being a ferry pilot is like being a vagabond. You don't know where you're going to sleep the next night and if you'll get a good meal or a lousy one — or go to bed hungry."

Clare stared at her friend for a minute. "This job has changed you, Nancy."

"How? How has this job changed me?" The frown, that Clare had noticed more and more on her friend's lovely and once serene face, reappeared.

"There! That frown. You didn't used to do that. Now, most of the time when I see you, you've got your brow furrowed."

"It's the curse of command."

"Precisely. You got into this business because you love to fly, you're good at it, and you thought you might as well offer that skill to the organization that needed it most."

"So?"

"So since our flight to England went sour, you haven't done much flying."

"Look, Bill Tunner brought me to Cincinnati to serve on his staff. He must like what I'm doing. He, and the others, have kept me busy here with operational duties — which I also happen to be good at."

"But wouldn't you be happier out flying?"

"Yes, of course I'd be happier out flying, but somebody's got to keep this organization functioning."

Clare heard an edge to Nancy's voice, but felt this might be her best chance to find out what was going on. Besides, she and Nancy had always leveled with each other. No point in changing now. "So... what's Cochran doing down in Washington?"

"Well, now that she has her graduates out towing targets, flying radar-blocking flights, flying bombers — after we did it, of course — and, in general, making themselves indispensable to the Army, she's clamoring for officer training for the girls. She's hot on the trail of getting the WASP militarized. That's been her big push all along and she's got Hap Arnold buying into it. Looks like we're going to be sent to Officer Training School."

"Us?" Clare said, surprised. "OTS?"

"Yes. It's not official yet, but if I know Jackie Cochran, it's coming. She's gotten everything else she's gone after."

"I don't like that idea," Clare said. "If I'm really 'in the Army' what will I do when Will comes home? I could be posted somewhere and not able to leave to go with him."

"Well…" Nancy waved her hand dismissively, "it may not happen. As long as we're volunteers, we have choices. But I'll tell you this. If OTS is offered to us, you'll be in the first class. If we're going to be officers, you'd be one of the first I'd pick."

"I'm not sure if that's the best news or the worst news I've heard today."

The phone on Nancy's desk rang. "Yes. Oh, hi sweetie. Yes, Clare's sitting across from me right now." She paused. "OK, we'll be right down." She hung up the phone.

Nancy locked her desk and rose from her chair.

"Let's face it, Clare — whatever happens to Jackie Cochran, she'll take us up or down with her. That's why I have to stay here and monitor and manage and keep the organization functioning for Bill Tunner." The frown disappeared from her brow and her lovely eyes twinkled. "But now it's time to close up shop, meet Bob and head home. It's party time."

\*\*\*\*\*

*In the air war, 1943 ended on mixed messages. The RAF had launched "The Battle of Berlin" and continued their night bombing raids on the German capital, but the USAAF maintained its preference for daylight raids, with fighter escorts if possible. But at the end of 1943, even the current model P-51Bs lacked the range to accompany the bombers all the way to Berlin and back. That was to change early in 1944 with the introduction of the P-51D model to the European Theater of War. As for the bigger picture, the Big Three — Roosevelt, Churchill and Stalin — met in Tehran the end of November 1943 and out of that summit came the Allies' commitment to a second front in France by summer 1944.*

\*\*\*\*\*

Joining the Loves and Clare at their table were an officer from General Tunner's staff and his wife, plus a divorced major also from Tunner's department. They met the other men stationed in Cincinnati with the Ferrying Division and several connected with Lunken Airport. General Tunner himself had gone to Memphis to be with his family for the New Year.

Clare wasn't exactly bored, but she found herself looking forward to the end of the party and returning to Nancy's apartment where she could simply enjoy being with her two friends.

"Would you like to dance?" the major asked Clare.

Clare looked at him. A couple of inches taller than she, he had brown eyes, black hair and a trim, fashionable black mustache, a la Clark Gable. A tiny scar creased his left cheekbone giving him a raffish look. All the others were engrossed in swaying gently to the music of Guy Lombardo and his orchestra, being broadcast from New York.

Misgivings rose to the surface of her already thinly stretched control, but she had accepted the invitation to be here, so Clare figured she'd better make an effort to have a good time. At least appear to be having one. "All right."

He pulled her close, but, to Clare's relief, he didn't try to crush her against him. They danced to the end of *Stardust* and moved immediately into *That Old Black Magic*. After some mental effort on her part, Clare began to relax. But later on, when the music had stopped and the countdown to midnight had begun — ten … nine … eight — her mind had room for only one thought. *Will, where are you?*

Clare looked at the major, saw hope in his eyes — hope that she would continue dancing with him, hope that she would kiss him at midnight, hope… But Clare, poised on the brink of 1944, felt devoid of hope.

"I can't do this," she cried, and fled, taking refuge in the ladies room, where she locked the stall door, sat down on the commode, and sobbed.

Ten minutes later, Nancy knocked on the door. "Clare. Please come out."

Clare pasted a smile on her face and opened the door. "The wrong guy wanted a kiss at the stroke of twelve," she said.

"Maybe this wasn't such a good idea after all." The frown creased Nancy's forehead again.

"Nancy, I'm a big girl. And, under the circumstances, I'm glad I'm here. It's good to be with friends on New Year's Eve."

At ten minutes after two in morning of the New Year of 1944, Nancy and Clare, dressed in robes and slippers, sat facing each other in easy chairs, feet up sharing an ottoman, each with a snifter of Cognac in hand. Bob had gone to bed.

"No further word, then?"

"No. I still don't know anything. The other pilots in the squadron saw his plane take a hit. But you know that between its armor plating and that big engine, the P-47 is virtually indestructible. They claim the pilots live through crashes, but heaven help whatever or whomever they crash into. All we know is that he flew off and no one knows where he went."

"Where was he hit?"

"Belgium."

"So he could be a prisoner of war."

"Or he could have been picked up by the Resistance. In which case, he may not surface until the war's over."

"Why, when you knew you loved him, did you wait so long to marry him, Clare?"

Clare stared into the middle distance for a minute before answering. "Because he's so much younger. I kept thinking he'd eventually lose interest, the minute one of those cute little Airport Annies looked slantwise at him. I didn't believe him when he told me he wasn't interested in anyone else. Besides, I knew people already were beginning to talk about us. He made no bones about courting me, no matter how I tried to keep it on the QT. He never strayed. He never even looked at one of those young girls, like I thought he would. Will has an old-fashioned streak. He always said he wanted to marry me and make an honest woman of me. Why?"

"Because he loves you, Clare, or he wouldn't have insisted."

"I know that now. And then I went off and joined the WAFS when I could have gone with him to the various training camps."

"And what would you have done with him in training and not allowed out of camp? You'd have died of boredom, particularly knowing what the rest of us were doing."

"But we'd have had more time together than we ended up having before he shipped out." Clare caught herself just short of breaking. "Now, I don't even know if he's alive, if he'll ever come home to me."

Nancy got up from her chair and came over to sit down on the arm of Clare's chair and put her arm around Clare's shoulder. "I can't tell you everything will be all right because we both know that would be a lie. But, never ever forget that I love you, dear friend, and I'll always be here for you — whenever you need me."

# CHAPTER TWENTY-ONE

Midge's assignment, upon completion of Pursuit School, turned out to be Long Beach with B.J. Erickson's squadron, part of the 6th Ferrying Group, where her primary mission would be to ferry P-51 Mustangs — built right down the road at North American Aviation — all the way across the U.S. to Newark for shipment across the Atlantic.

Annie's assignment — at the other end of the country — meant her return to Wilmington and, from there, on to Farmingdale where she would join Clare, Teresa, Helen Mary Clark and eventually other Pursuit School graduates ferrying P-47s. Midge felt a tug of regret. She had grown to depend on Annie's friendship.

Graduation was January 1, 1944. B.J. Erickson, aware of Annie's wedding plans and Midge's desire to be Annie's maid of honor, promised to get them deliveries to, or close to, Columbus, Ohio.

Midge had not yet met Charlie. She could hardly wait to see this man who had won her shy friend's heart. In some ways, she felt she already knew him, Annie talked to her so much about him.

"I never seemed to click with boys in school," Annie told her one night when they sat up late, sitting outside on the barracks steps at Palm Springs, talking quietly and looking at the stars. "I was big and awkward — some of my so-called friends called me 'horsey' behind my back. By the time I began to slim out, as my grandmother always said I would, I had been teased about my size enough that I had no self-confidence whatsoever. And by then I had fallen in love with airplanes and flying and had my head in the clouds."

"You know, your so-called friends were full of shit. There's nothing wrong with your looks, Annie. Surely some of the boys at school were interested?"

"Oh, I had an occasional date, usually because somebody needed an extra girl and I was available. My mother accused me of being standoffish, insisted that's why the boys didn't ask me out. I didn't think I was standoffish. I just never knew what to say to them."

Midge pondered that. "What happened with Charlie that made everything different?"

"Turns out, he's as shy around girls as I am around boys. We found we could talk to each other about airplanes and flying and gradually other stuff came out, too. And, when we danced, well, we just kinda fit together. Everything clicked. It felt good — right from the beginning — and the backwardness went away. You know, the night we met, he blurted out that he wanted to marry me. But then he didn't say another word — for months. I began to think I had dreamed it."

"When did he finally pop the question for real?"

"It took him until July. You know, we haven't seen each other that many times and ...." Annie fell silent.

Midge, sensing Annie wanted to say something else, waited. When she finally spoke again, in a hushed voice, she stammered, "I don't have a lot of experience when it comes to men, Midge. I need some, uh, advice."

Midge's eyes widened at the distress she heard in her friend's voice and at the improbable, though quite possible, thought that flashed through her mind. "You're not pregnant, are you?"

"No! Oh, good heavens no!"

Annie hesitated and then admitted, "My problem's the exact opposite. You see... Charlie and I haven't, well ..." Her voice now barely above a whisper, "Remember back at Wilmington? Esther Manning got pregnant and she had to stop flying when she couldn't get the stick back. I don't want that to happen to me — get pregnant and have to stop flying."

"Oh, my," Midge said, suddenly realizing Annie's dilemma.

"It's not that I don't want ... that is...." She paused, looked at Midge, seemed to wrestle with whether to share the rest, then blurted it out in a voice racked with anguish. "The last time I went to Lockbourne, in October, we went into Columbus. We decided to get a hotel room."

Though Midge couldn't tell in the darkness, she knew Annie's face was beet red and she felt a surge of empathy.

"I couldn't do it, Midge. An officer and this cheap-looking girl were right in front of us, and the leering looks the man at the desk and the bellhop gave them. I couldn't do it. I turned and walked out. It's probably just as well, because I realized, almost too late, that I know nothing about birth control. I've only heard some of the other girls talk about some things..."

Midge felt Annie's eyes on her. Sensed the plea that hung there in the desert air.

"What should I do, Midge?"

Midge sighed, put her arm around Annie's tensed shoulders. "I'll tell you everything I know. But you need to see a doctor. Now listen carefully."

The day following graduation, Annie and Midge made their first pursuit deliveries — a pair of P-51s to Columbus, Ohio. Two male ferry pilots from Romulus would take them on to Newark.

When they landed at Lockbourne, they were greeted by Charlie — who swept Annie into his arms — and by a group of newspaper reporters and photographers who flashed battery after battery of flashbulbs in their faces. Word had gotten out about the upcoming wedding of two B-17 pilots — a WASP pilot, who had been within minutes of ferrying a Flying Fortress over the Atlantic when Hap Arnold made his momentous decision NOT to allow women pilots to ferry into the combat zone, and a young Lockbourne graduate destined for overseas duty. The story made great newspaper copy. The small, quiet wedding Annie had hoped for had become a base-wide affair with national news-coverage implications. The base commander had even volunteered to give her away. She and Charlie had expected simply to stand up in front of the base chaplain — with Midge and his best friend and co-pilot, Steve, flanking them, say their vows and get away as quickly as possible for a very short honeymoon.

Midge watched as the preparations whirled around them. Protecting her friend, shielding Annie from the worst of the hubbub, became her primary mission. The wedding in the base chapel, scheduled for noon the following day, would be followed by a festive luncheon in the Officers' Club.

When the big moment came, Midge and Annie, both dressed in their newly cleaned and pressed WAFS dress uniform jackets and skirts and carrying small bouquets of flowers, stood at the back of the chapel facing a long red carpet that stretched all the way to the altar. Charlie's classmates as well as other air base personnel packed the pews. Seventeen WASP who Jacqueline Cochran had selected for B-17 transition at Lockbourne sat in the chapel as well.

"This is it, honey," Midge whispered to her. "Who knows when we'll see each other again after today."

"Like we WAFS have said from the early days in Wilmington, see you in some Alert Room at some airbase somewhere in the South," Annie said, her shining eyes misting slightly. She took a deep breath. "Thank you Midge, for everything. For being my friend."

"Thank you for going home to Missouri with me and listening. And most of all for understanding about Jackie Cochran," Midge said. "I'll miss you. Be happy, you and Charlie. Blue skies and tail winds."

When the organ launched into Purcell's *Trumpet Fanfare*, Midge gave her friend a quick hug. Before she turned to precede Annie down the aisle, she saw her friend's eyes come to rest on Charlie, who had just entered from the right and now stood next to the chaplain, looking back down the aisle. His eyes met Annie's and the love that Midge saw pass between them at that unguarded moment struck a powerful but sweet blow to her inner core. As she walked down the aisle in time to the majestic wedding music played on the chapel's small but powerful pipe organ, she wondered if, when and where she would ever find a love like theirs.

At the ceremony's conclusion, Annie and Charlie exited the chapel into the crisp winter air. Photographers, not only from the *Columbus Dispatch* but also from the Chicago and New York papers as well as the Associated Press, awaited them.

One other noteworthy wedding guest flew in and deplaned from her distinctive Staggerwing Beech, carrying her fur coat over her arm and issuing orders right and left. Jacqueline Cochran could not let something as auspicious as this wedding go by without her blessing. At the luncheon reception, she gave a champagne toast that outdid anything Midge had ever heard her say in public before: "What could be more fitting than the union of two of the United States Army Air Forces' most talented and capable pilots? This brave young man will soon leave for England in his B-17 and fly in freedom's cause against the evil powers of the Third Reich. This equally brave young woman, who knows her way around a B-17 cockpit as well, leaves from her honeymoon to take up residence in Farmingdale, New York, where she will ferry P-47s off the assembly line, past Miss Liberty's watchful eyes, and on to the shipyards in Newark, where those aircraft will be put aboard ships also bound for the hostilities on the European continent."

Jackie had ordered a limousine that stood by ready to whisk the bride and groom away to the Fort Hayes Hotel in Columbus, where she had reserved for them — and paid for out of her own pocket — the honeymoon suite.

When the reception was over and Charlie and Annie were safely on their way, Jackie stopped momentarily to speak to Midge. "I also have a suite at the Fort Hayes tonight. Please join me there for dinner, Midge. We have a lot to talk about."

What did Cochran want? What would she ask of her? And would she be obligated to do as Cochran asked? All those questions ran through Midge's head as she rode the elevator up to the suite a floor below where she knew Annie and Charlie, at that moment, either were dining together or lying in each other's arms. Midge swallowed a momentary gorge of jealousy as she knocked on the door.

"Come in, Midge," Cochran greeted her warmly. A white-coated waiter stood beside the serving cart that contained their dinner under domed stainless-steel lids. "Would you like some champagne, my dear? Henri is ready to pour you a glass."

Dinner uncovered and served, Cochran dismissed the waiter.

"They are a lovely couple," she said as they ate. "Have you and Annie been friends since the early days in Wilmington?"

"We really got to be good friends after my infamous flight. She didn't condemn me for it like some of the others did. She seemed to understand. She wanted to fly pursuits, too."

"And now she'll get her chance out on Long Island. Are you disappointed you weren't assigned there with her? Or are you pleased with Long Beach?"

"I've admired B.J. Erickson since our early days in Wilmington. I'm very happy to serve under her. And from Long Beach, I'll get to fly mostly Mustangs, and I like that."

Cochran frowned and idly ran her finger around the moist rim of her champagne goblet, causing the crystal to sing. "I want you to come back and work with me now, Midge. Hap is getting ready to go before Congress and seek militarization for the WASP. I'm going to need someone of your talents, and with your knowledge of the inside workings of the women's squadrons, in order to prepare him. And here's what I'm willing to do. You can spend two months with B.J. Erickson and her troops and get the feel for flying with a different squadron, fly as many Mustangs as they assign you to. But the first of March, I need you in Washington. If I can see my way clear to let you go back to ferrying in the future, I'll do it."

The trap had sprung and Midge knew it. As badly as her newly acquired pursuit-pilot skills were needed, Cochran's wishes would prevail. The time when Nancy Love or Betty Gillies could have intervened and gotten her assigned exclusively to a ferrying squadron had slipped irrevocably away. Ever since Jackie had been named Director of Women Pilots by Hap Arnold six months earlier, she had wrested control of such individual decisions away from the two women who had birthed and nursed the WAFS and made them a viable piece of the Army's war machine.

If Midge even tried to say no, she would be flying directly into the face of her powerful mentor's wishes, to say nothing of the paramilitary structure under which the WASP now existed. Besides, she liked and respected Jacqueline Cochran in spite of her idiosyncrasies. And, they had an agreement. She also knew what Cochran was like when someone stood in her way. While working for her, Midge had seen her employer rail against her competition— in the cosmetics business, in flying circles like the Ninety-Nines, in the races in which she competed, and finally against Nancy Love, who had, inadvertently, walked into what Jackie clearly considered her exclusive territory. Jacqueline Cochran never came out second best.

Yet, as Midge had told Annie, Cochran had never wronged her. At times, she'd even bent over backwards for her. Now, Cochran had made good, yet again, on a promise made two years ago. Though her heart felt like a lead weight in her chest, Midge didn't hesitate even for a split second.

"Whatever you say, Miss Cochran."

Midge went to Long Beach. Mid-February, she received an urgent call from Cochran in Washington. "Midge, we've got to move now for full militarization." Cochran explained that General Arnold had closed the primary flight training schools across the country as well as the Civil Aeronautics Administration War Training Service — the old CPT program. He also had transferred 35,000 officers waiting for flight training over to the ground forces.

"He says America has enough pilots to finish the war and is more in need of infantry now," she added.

Midge knew what that meant. "Those thirty-five thousand wannabe pilots are headed for the walking army. They won't take that lying down. We're going to hear from them."

"We already are," Cochran said. "That's why I'm calling you. General Arnold has been hit with a tidal wave of resistance from these men. They're going to lose their deferments. They're telling the press and their Congressmen that the reason they're losing their jobs is because the Army is using women pilots and now those same women are about to become commissioned officers. This couldn't come at a worse time."

As Midge tried to think of an appropriate response, Cochran cut back in. "I need you now, Midge. I am preparing a report for General Arnold to take to Congress in March and I need all the time and help I can get. You know I'm not good at writing. You are. I've already spoken to Miss Erickson. She knows that you're being transferred to my direct command. I need you here in Washington as soon as you can get transport here. Bring all your gear. The transfer is permanent."

# CHAPTER TWENTY-TWO

Annie, of course, hadn't counted on the Nashville *Tennessean* running a three-column photo of her and Charlie that also included Jacqueline Cochran on the front page the day following the wedding. Their quiet phone calls, first to her parents and then to his, made from the hotel that afternoon after the wedding, had taken the worst of the shock away, but this kind of publicity compounded everything. She could just hear her mother's friends' comments now.

Remembering the rush she and Cornelia had received from the press when they returned from Hawaii, Annie thought she should have seen it coming. The girl who had miraculously come out of Pearl Harbor alive now flew B-17s and P-47s. And she had just married a B-17 pilot destined for combat in Europe. Of course the newspapers made the most of it, in her hometown and everywhere else.

The phone call home also had reminded her of the rift, begun when she broke away from the tight bonds at home and left for Hawaii, and widened by her inability to communicate since joining the WAFS. She had succeeded in driving a wedge between herself and her family. She heard the hurt in her mother's voice: "We didn't even know you were seeing someone." And in her father's comment: "We'd have tried to come if we'd known — Columbus, Ohio's not the other end of the world."

Her repair work at home would have to wait a little while, however, because right after their three-day honeymoon, Annie and Charlie each had to report back to active duty. They still didn't know when he would leave for overseas, and she knew it would be a month before she could wangle another three-day pass to spend time with him or — if he had been shipped overseas by then — to go home.

Word caught up with her at Republic Aviation on January 26, when she returned from Newark to pick up another P-47. Charlie's squadron had been ordered to England. They were due into New York's LaGuardia Field later that afternoon and scheduled to leave the following day for Gander and on to Scotland from there. Just as she had done for Clare the previous summer, Betty OK'd a twenty-four-hour pass for Annie. They would have one night together.

To Annie, her life seemed to be ending rather than barely beginning. She hadn't realized what Charlie's going overseas would do to her, emotionally. Suddenly, all the barriers she had built up since December 7, 1941, to shut out the war crumbled. Under other circumstances, the reason she delivered P-47s to the docks could easily be cloaked in the sheer thrill of the thrust that glued her tailbone to the seat, the guttural snarl of the engine as it flaunted its awesome power on the takeoff surge, the acrid smells of the fuel and burned rubber and overheated metal that excited the inner core.

Once, not so very long ago, she could have brushed aside the knowledge that real bullets and bombs lay at the other end of each pursuit's journey. Not now. Now Charlie would be in the thick of the fighting — in harm's way of those enemy bullets and bombs — and she could not hide from that.

She lay curled in Charlie's arms. But her head resting on the white T-shirt he had pulled on after their lovemaking suddenly brought back the memory of pools of red blood staining Tom Witten's white T-shirt. She shuddered.

"Rabbit run over your grave," he teased.

"No, and don't make fun of me." She cuddled even closer to him, felt his long sinewy arms tighten around her.

He kissed the top of her hair. "Annie, Annie, I'd never make fun of you." And he tilted her chin back and kissed her softly on the lips.

Before she melted completely into him, which she knew she would do if she didn't speak now, she pushed on his chest with her hand. "Wait."

He looked at her with surprise. "What is it?"

"We don't know when we'll see each other again." She took a deep breath. "I've changed my mind about wanting a baby — *your* baby. What if…?"

"Shusshh." He caressed her hair. "Annie, we've talked this out. You have a job to do. A job you love. If you couldn't fly, you'd go nuts. And I'm not going to be around for awhile to keep you from doing just that."

"But Charlie..."

"No. Listen to me, Annie." He took her face in his big, rough, bomber pilot's hands, so strong but so incredibly gentle. "I will come back to you. I promise. And we'll have plenty of time to have all the kids you want — and we'll take them all flying. But not now. I don't want to be over there in England worrying about you here.

I know you. You won't be happy if you aren't flying. And you've finally got your wish to fly pursuits. Besides, I want to be sure that someone competent is getting those armor-plated monsters to the shipyard so they can come over and protect us when we fly our daylight bombing runs."

He kissed her nose. "Next one of those Jugs you deliver, you put a note in there to the combat pilot who gets to fly it. Tell him: 'Get a Kraut for me — one less to shoot at my husband when he comes over to bomb the stuffing out of them.' No kidding, Annie. You do that for me, OK? And sign your name. I'd give anything to see that guy's face when he reads a note from a girl back in the U.S. telling him she flew his ship."

Annie looked at the grin on his face, grabbed his ears and pulled his lips to hers. Moments later, they had ceased their laughing and were, once again, lost in their wonder over each other and the impossible chain of events that had brought them together. They shut out, for a time at least, the knowledge that they did not know what the future held for them — together or separate.

*****

*That same night, British and American troops landed at Anzio, south of Rome. It wasn't France, but the Allies had taken the ground war one step closer to Germany.*

*****

A month later, with Charlie safe in England, Annie got her pass and went home. Once again, her father picked her up at Berry Field.

"I wouldn't tell your mother this, but I think I understand why you didn't tell us ahead of time when you decided to get married. Your mother wouldn't have let you settle for a quick wedding without us being there. She'd have tried to talk you out of it. Into doing it here. Into waiting. Unless you, uh," he cleared his throat, "that is, uh, had to do it quick for, uh, any reason."

"Daddy, stop right there. Don't go getting any wrong ideas. The only reason we were in a hurry is because we knew Charlie's orders to ship out could come any day. We just didn't know when. It became a race with the clock for me to finish pursuit school and get back in time for a wedding before he got his orders. As it turned out, we made it with very little time to spare."

Her father looked relieved. "Is he a good man, Annie? He must be or you wouldn't have looked at him twice."

"Oh, Daddy, he's a wonderful man. And he loves me. That's all that counts."

"We didn't know what to tell people, Annie, it was all so sudden," her mother said when they had settled in the living room over coffee.

"Mother, he had orders sending him overseas."

"I know the war has changed things, people marrying when they hardly know each other. It's just so hard to understand."

"I love him, Mother. It's that simple."

"How long have you known him, dear?

"I've known him almost a year." And Annie tried to describe Charlie to her parents. "He's a gangly farm boy, really. Big hands, big feet, big heart. He's not sophisticated like so many people around here, but he's very genuine."

"And have you met his parents?"

"No, I only talked to them on the phone, just as Charlie talked to you. They sound like wonderful people. Charlie has an older brother who's in the Navy and a younger brother who's still in high school. They own a ranch outside Amarillo. Charlie learned to fly because all the ranchers out there learn to fly. They're so far from everything."

"Did he go to college?" her mother asked.

"Yes, Mother, Texas A and M. He graduated in forty-one, same as I did. He worked on his father's ranch before he left to join the Air Corps. He plans to return there after the war."

"That means you'll be living in Texas, then." She mother seemed to stiffen at the idea.

Annie smiled. "Yes, Mother. But first we've got to get this war over with."

"I still wish you could have been married here — in a church wedding, a proper wedding." The small frown resettled on her brow.

"Elizabeth, you promised…" Annie's father said.

"I only said I wish…" Her mother's lower lip dipped into a pout.

"Mother, we had a chance at a few days of happiness together and we took it. And we had a church wedding. I can assure you the Methodist chaplain at the Lockbourne base chapel put God's blessing on us." Then Annie winked at her mother. "We did the rest ourselves."

"Annie!" Her mother's girlish giggle broke the tension between them.

Annie couldn't believe she'd had the nerve to say and do what she did, but since her marriage, she suddenly found her confidence beginning to grow and assert itself — something she had, prior to this, felt only in the air at the controls of an airplane.

In her room that night, alone with her thoughts and the memorabilia of her childhood, Annie lay on the antique canopied double bed with the lace cover thrown over the crazy quilt made for her by Grandmother Gwynn. Her ceramic and metal horse collection still stood on the wall shelf and the horseback riding ribbons, earned over many summers, hung from the cork board and the trophies occupied the display case below. But the interest in horses gradually had given way to airplanes, evidenced by several models that hung from the ceiling of her room. When the opportunity to actually learn to fly came to her via the Civilian Pilot Training program at the University of Tennessee, Annie was ready.

"I need forty dollars," she had told her mother on the phone.

"I don't know, Annie, that's a lot of money for something so frivolous."

"It's not frivolous, Mother. I want to learn to fly."

"But, Annie, flying is so dangerous."

When Annie hung up, she called her father at work. The following day, a money order arrived from Gramma Gwynn for forty dollars. Her father had come through for her. He had gone to his mother, who responded immediately to her favorite granddaughter's wishes. And so Annie and nine male university students enrolled in the CPT program. Annie, to hear her father tell it later, "flew those boys into the ground."

And her graduation present from Gramma Gwynn had set her on the path toward her instructor's rating, which, of course, led straight to Pearl Harbor.

Annie stared at the ceiling and thought of Tom Witten… of Cornelia… and of Charlie.

# CHAPTER TWENTY-THREE

Midge, seated between Jacqueline Cochran and Nancy Love, watched as General Henry H. (Hap) Arnold strode through the door into the committee room, took his seat at the witness table, and prepared to testify before the eighteen-member House Committee on Military Affairs. It was March 22, 1944.

"Hap can depend on this committee to give him what he wants," Cochran whispered to her. "They trust him to know what we need to win the war."

Midge wasn't so sure. Since coming to Washington on Jackie's command a month earlier, Midge had heard enough gossip to give her cause for worry. But she momentarily forgot her concerns as a hush fell over the room.

Representative John Costello from Los Angeles rose to introduce H.R. 4219, the bill authorizing Army Air Forces commissions for women pilots already on duty and aviation cadet status for the women trainees at Sweetwater. Passage would mean the women were eligible for the same privileges, insurance, hospitalization and death benefits as those awarded to male flying officers and cadets in the AAF.

Hap Arnold began his presentation. "Gentleman, for some time it has been apparent that there is a serious manpower shortage. We must provide fighting men wherever we can, replacing them by women wherever we can."

Midge knew this to be a dramatic departure from Arnold's original stance on women flying for the Air Corps. After all, Arnold had dragged his feet for more than a year when Cochran first presented her idea to him. Midge still could not believe the man's turn-around and she credited her boss's tenacity, along with Nancy Love's ability to produce those first thirty crack female ferry pilots as promised, with tipping the scales. Now, the general had become their biggest booster.

"It is not beyond reason to expect that some day all of our Air Transport Command ferrying within the United States will be done by women," Arnold continued, and went one step further to say that he knew of no reason why women should not replace men in all the duties they were now performing — ferrying, towing gunnery targets, transport of non-flying personnel, courier duty — stateside. He explained that these dedicated young women were now performing those duties without the benefits available to the men currently performing the same jobs.

"From our point of view, with the present terrific manpower shortage, we should use every means we can to put women in where they can replace men. This bill will help to do that, but it will also make far more effective the employment of the present WASP that we have in our service."

When finished, Arnold — very much in control of the situation as far as Midge could see — sat back and waited for questions.

A committee member dropped the first bomb. "What about the recently terminated nine hundred CPT instructors and their five thousand trainees who have now been released?"

"The AAF has closed the primary cadet training schools. What about those eight thousand flight instructors who are now out of a job?" asked another.

Arnold explained that any man with flying experience would be given every opportunity to qualify in some phase of military aviation — pilot, copilot, navigator, bombardier, gunner. "If they cannot qualify according to our standards in one of these capacities, then we offer them other training in the AAF. We cannot lower our pilot standards because a man has had a few hours in the air."

Midge had heard that argument before. The WAFS, and later the WASP, had to pass the exacting flight physical required of all Army pilot trainees. Many male pilots flunked that very test. That the women who now flew for the Army had passed the test wasn't public knowledge, but the high command of the Ferrying Division and Air Transport Command knew, to a man, the physical and mental shape the women had to be in to pass all requirements and earn the right to ferry aircraft for the Army. Retaining high standards of performance also reached into the training program. The WASP now underwent seven months of training at Avenger Field, rather than the four Cochran originally envisioned.

As the questions became more pointed and the questioners more aggressive, sympathy seemed to build in favor of the out-of-work flight instructors. In contrast, an antagonism toward the WASP began to surface. General Arnold, who now appeared to Midge to be quite flushed, indicated he wished to go into executive session.

The three women were not allowed in. Nancy excused herself to go to the Ladies' Room. And with Arnold behind closed doors, Cochran released her fury to Midge: "Those goddamn cowards. They hid behind their deferments, chose non-combat jobs as civilian flight instructors rather than volunteer for the combat-bound jobs. Now they're squealing because their cushy little berth has been yanked out from under them. Well, I'd like to see some of those fellas willingly take a redlined dive-bomber for a run through the ack-ack over the beaches down in North Carolina. Some of those planes aren't fit to be flown, but my girls are flying them anyway because there's a war to be won. That's patriotism, Midge. That's dedication. That's professionalism."

Midge thought it surprising for Cochran to admit to anything being wrong with any of the planes her girls flew. Because she had spent all of her duty time in the Ferrying Division, Midge had been flying new airplanes right off the assembly line, not war-weary redliners. She most certainly hadn't been shot at. Even though they called it gunnery "practice," they still used live ammunition.

When Arnold came out of the closed session, Jackie rushed over to talk to him. Midge and Nancy watched as the two of them bent their heads together. Then his aides pulled Arnold away and Jackie returned to her chair.

"Hap says he really unloaded his anger over the flight instructors' protests in there. He's really PO'ed at them. Calls them obstructionists," she told them. "And listen to this. He also told the committee he prefers — *prefers* — the WASP over the civilian men flyers because the women are willing to fly any mission, including those the men feel are beneath them. He also told them that the women have proved they could fly airplanes that have gotten reputations for being dangerous — like the B-26 and the P-39. He told them... he *really* told them." But then her smile waned and that determined look, so familiar to Midge, replaced it. Jaw set, brown eyes flashing.

Nancy remained non-committal, her brow furrowed.

"It's obvious we've got enemies on The Hill. We need to marshal our forces and get to work," Cochran said.

Back in Cochran's Pentagon office after General Arnold's testimony on Capitol Hill, Midge realized the extent to which the events of the day had shaken her boss. Cochran paced the office, planning and strategizing, while Midge listened and awaited the instructions she knew were coming.

"Midge…" Cochran's her right hand hammered the air for empha- sis, the smoke from the cigarette she held making diaphanous silver gray columns and circles, "draft a letter and get it out to every mem- ber of the WASP, fast — the ones on active duty and the girls now in training at Avenger Field. We want to know if they favor militariza- tion or not. Make it a poll. We're gonna show Congress what kind of women they have out there flying their airplanes!"

She hesitated, brow furrowed, then plunged on. "But Midge, we need the right slant. Write it so that they can't help but favor it. I don't want any resistance in the ranks and I don't want any sur- prises."

Cochran stopped, took a drag from her cigarette, made a face, and then ground it out in the pristine marble ashtray that graced the top of her desk. "Ugh! I never have understood what people see in these things," she said.

Midge, pen poised over her steno notebook, awaited the next in- struction with a sudden, irrational sense of impending doom.

"And get this order out to all the ferry squadron commanders! No WASP is to be sent on a ferrying mission that takes her any- where near Washington, D.C. I don't want any of them running into a bunch of smart-aleck reporters and saying the wrong thing."

Midge wondered if Cochran feared the thought of criticism from within most of all. She knew for a fact that many of the original WAFS did not want to be militarized. Some, like Betty Gillies, Hel- en Mary Clark, and Lenore McElroy, had young children and if they were militarized under the same regulations as the WACs and the other women's military organizations, anyone with children under age sixteen would have to resign. She also knew a few of them val- ued, so highly, their individual freedom to do as they wished when they wished, that they would resign rather than submit to Army reg- ulations that would put them under orders with no recourse but to obey.

This is going to be interesting, Midge thought, as she sat down at her typewriter and began drafting the poll scheduled to go out as soon as she could get it finished.

# CHAPTER TWENTY-FOUR

"Pack your bags, Clare," Nancy said over the telephone. "You're in the first class at the School of Advanced Tactics down in Orlando, Florida."

"What? When?" Clare was not nearly as thrilled over the prospect of going to Officers Training School as Nancy sounded. Rumor had it that an invasion of the mainland of Europe was in the works. In Clare's mind, that could mean Allied troops reuniting with downed flyers being sheltered by partisans and, eventually, contact with prisoners being held by the Germans. She felt this was the first encouraging news she had received since Will's plane had gone down eight months ago. When he came home, she didn't want to be in the Army, obligated to remain on duty. No telling where he'd be sent, but wherever and whenever — a hospital, a rehabilitation center, discharge from the Army — she wanted to be there with him.

"Transport's been arranged from New Castle on Tuesday," she heard Nancy saying. "You and Batson need to get from Farmingdale to Wilmington in time to meet up with Betty and me and the others for the hop to Orlando. I'll be flying in from Cincinnati to go down with you."

"Are we being militarized?"

"Not yet. General Arnold made the presentation to Congress a few weeks ago. Things didn't go as well as he and Cochran had hoped. But she's going ahead with plans to get us ready to be officers. Remember, she believes in frontal assault wherever possible. By the way, the fittings and measurements we had a couple of months ago for new WASP uniforms?"

"Yeah."

"Well, they're ready. You can pick yours up when you get to Wilmington. "

"So our WAFS uniforms are out now?"

"Well, let's just say while we're in Orlando, we'll wear Santiago blue rather than WAFS gray. See you Sunday." The line clicked at the other end.

"Damn!" Clare said.

*****

*On April 15, 1944, 448 U.S. 15th AAF B-17 Flying Fortress and B-24 Liberators, flying out of Italy and escorted by 150 P-51s, pulled a daylight raid on the Ploesti oil fields in Romania. That night, the RAF attacked the rail line on the main line that linked the Romanian capital, Bucharest, to both Budapest and Belgrade.*

*****

On April 19, twenty-five WASP reported for Officer Training School in Orlando. Sixteen women from the early classes at Houston and Sweetwater joined original WAFS Betty Gillies, B.J. Erickson, Barbara Donahue, Florene Miller, Delphine Bohn, Del Scharr, Nancy Love, Nancy Batson and Clare.

"They're getting us ready to be officers, should that come to pass," Nancy told the assembled group Tuesday night at an informal meeting. "We're going to learn everything from military law to aircraft identification. Classes are eight hours a day, six days a week, starting tomorrow morning."

Settling into the classroom routine, Clare found the lectures on the instruments of war, particularly the demonstrations of top-secret bombsights and radar equipment, fascinating. Not so appealing were the whiffs of mustard gas and cyanide they encountered during a course in chemical warfare.

"Just when do you suppose we're going to encounter a jungle where we might need this class in jungle survival?" she asked Nancy one night when they were sitting around their quarters studying for a quiz the following day. "Since they won't let us fly outside the boundaries of the continental United States and Canada, there are no jungles that I know of where we fly. I can certainly understand learning to identify poisonous roots and berries and how to cook rattlesnake because we do fly over the desert out west, but *jungle* warfare?"

"Don't knock it, Clare. You never know when you might be forced down somewhere. You know that. You've made a few forced landings in your flying career."

"Yeah, but they were all on the high plains of eastern Colorado."

"Just consider your horizons expanded," Nancy said.

Clare and the others endured the four weeks with a resigned but amiable attitude. They found classroom duty boringly tame compared to flying. The news that the Congressional hearings on their militarization weren't going well depressed them not because they looked forward to being in the Army but because the things being said about them on Capitol Hill and in the newspapers turned out to be downright nasty.

Clare picked up a national magazine at the PX and passed it around. "Jackie Cochran's glamour girls," trumpeted the lead story. "35-hour female wonders." The story went on to suggest that these "pseudo pilots swap their flying togs for nurses uniforms and do some REAL work!" The WASP program was called a "blunder," a "fast play," and a "racket."

"How do you like that?" Clare said. "Most of us here have a couple thousand hours in the air but, no, not a word about that. Because Cochran lowered the required hours to enter the WASP program, now the press is making it look like we're all a bunch of spoiled little girls playing in the big boys' airplanes."

"Just because some of the girls only needed thirty-five hours to get in the program doesn't mean they haven't gotten the best training available and are now using it to help win the war," one of the Houston graduates added.

On the positive side, Gert Meserve sent Clare a copy of the Farmingdale paper that claimed the WASP were the country's "best kept secret weapon."

In spite of support from respected newspapers like the *New York Times* and *Herald Tribune* and the *Boston Globe*, more sensationally inclined rags jumped on the rumors that the WASP were nothing more than a glamorous publicity ploy designed to promote undeserving women at the expense of deserving men. And the press even tried to resurrect the "cat fight" stories about Cochran and Love that first had surfaced the previous summer when Jackie was named Director of Women Pilots over Nancy. Now one anti-WASP newspaper gleefully reminded readers of the so-called power struggle between the two that Clare knew to be mostly fiction. Her friend Nancy, she assured others when the subject came up, had no interested in power whatsoever, only in flying airplanes and in getting the job done and the war won.

Even worse than the bad publicity, the WAFS were still reeling from the shock of Evelyn Sharp's death on April 3. She had picked up a P-38 Lightning at Lockheed near Long Beach, California —

destination Newark. She RONed in New Cumberland, Pennsylvania, near Harrisburg, and when she took off for Newark the next morning, one of the engines quit. She managed to keep the plane right-side up and flying level, but couldn't gain enough altitude to clear the hills off the end of the runway. She put the stricken aircraft into a left rather than a right turn in order to avoid several houses. The plane stalled and she pancaked it, wheels up. Evelyn hit the canopy and broke her neck.

That's three, Clare thought at the time. Three of the original WAFS are now dead, having given their all to their country. Cornelia first, then Dorothy Scott last winter while at Pursuit School in Palm Springs, and now Evelyn. Three friends gone in a little over a year, and she still didn't know whether Will was dead or alive.

# CHAPTER TWENTY-FIVE

Annie caressed the thin, crinkly page of V-mail dated May 27 and smoothed out the creases. Charlie's cramped scrawl filled every available space. He wrote every other day, as did she.

> *Had a close call on takeoff early this morning. We had a 400-foot ceiling. I had just made a climbing turn on the gauges when the horizon went out. I rolled right out and went on needle, ball and airspeed. Stayed on them 'til I broke out on top.*
>
> *Doesn't help much to say how much I miss you, but I do. How could two people have so little time together and yet those days — and more especially the nights — fill up my memories of Stateside. I do love you, Annie. How did I get so lucky?*

She sat very still on her twin bed, staring at the letter. Then she closed her eyes and tried hard to remember what it felt like when he held her. Just thinking about it made her warm all over and she wrapped her arms around her body and hugged herself, swaying from side to side.

Clare found her sitting like that.

"Quit makin' love in your mind, Annie. The invasion's on! Our guys have landed on a beach somewhere in Normandy, France — they're calling it Omaha for some reason, probably security or something. We're on our way. We're finally gonna win this war!" And she pulled the taller girl from her perch, and the two of them danced around the small bedroom.

Moments later, Teresa and Helen Mary joined them, Teresa carrying a bottle of champagne.

"A toast to the invasion. June 6, 1944, a day that will live in fame and glory!"

\*\*\*\*\*

*The Allied air forces had put 13,743 aircraft into the air over the English Channel and the French coast at Normandy June 6, 1944. When the day was over, the Allies ruled the skies over the invasion beaches. Air power definitely was going to be key to the battle for France. Reports were that the Luftwaffe's air losses were so severe that it had about 185 serviceable aircraft to put into the battle. American P-47s and P-51s that the WASP had been delivering to the docks at Newark in increasing numbers for several months were part of those 13,743 aircraft. Their role in the invasion had been significant and would become increasingly critical in the months to come. And many more awaited delivery.*

\*\*\*\*\*

A week later, Annie delivered a P-47 to the modification center in Evansville. But instead of taking a modified Jug back to Newark, she was assigned to take one to the West Coast. There, she was to take transition in the twin-engine P-38 and, when checked out, bring one back to Newark.

P-38 Lightnings were powerful aircraft. They boasted twin 1,425-horsepower and liquid-cooled engines located in torpedo-shaped enclosures called nacelles that extended back in parallel tail booms. The single-seat cockpit sat suspended between them. Annie knew, from listening to other pursuit pilots, that some of the Lightnings also had a reputation for having faulty nose gear. Because of this, the manufacturer had installed polished disc-shaped aluminum reflectors on the inside of each engine nacelle. This enabled the pilot to "see" a mirror image of the nose wheel from the cockpit and determine whether it was down and properly locked into position.

The hydraulic system that operated the landing gear had a backup system in the form of a hand or "wobble" pump. In addition, a carbon dioxide cartridge — the button to activate it handily located under the pilot's seat — could be used to explode the nose wheel out of its casing if neither the hydraulic system nor the hand pump worked. After digesting the information and going through transition, Annie decided that flying the P-38 cross-country shouldn't be all that unlike flying a P-47. They were all new, untried airplanes, right off the assembly line with maybe ten minutes of a test pilot's time in the log.

With her check-out successfully behind her, Annie waited for her assigned airplane at the Lockheed factory the morning of June 18th but coastal fog kept her grounded until mid-afternoon, at which time she took off for a short first-day hop over the San Jacinto Mountains to Palm Springs. From there, she could get an early start east the following morning as the nearly 11,000-feet-high peaks to the west would block the bad weather and give her blue skies for flying. She spent the night in the quarters occupied by the WASP of the 21st Ferrying Group, recently activated there, and had dinner with two ferry pilots she knew. The morning of the 19th she headed east again — destination Wichita, where she RONed.

By five the next afternoon, Annie had set the P-38 Lightning down at Lockbourne, filed her RON with Cincinnati and notified Betty in Wilmington. The Operations Officer handed her a note with an invitation to dinner from Nancy Love, who had flown up to Columbus for a meeting that afternoon.

During the evening's conversation, Nancy passed on some potentially disturbing news. Things weren't looking very good in the halls of Congress. The WASP might NOT get their militarization. "We should know tomorrow," Nancy said.

Annie spent the night at the Fort Hayes Hotel — where she had spent her honeymoon — but this time, as she stretched out to go to sleep, she was in a room far less grand and she was alone.

Early the morning of the 20th, Annie was not far out of Columbus when she noticed the coolant needle on the left engine oscillating. Not good, she thought. Could mean possible engine failure. It had been only two and a half months since Evelyn Sharp crashed to her death in a P-38. That thought made Annie edgy. She didn't want to take any chances, so she radioed her problem and asked for clearance to do a one-eighty, come back to Lockbourne and land. The tower cleared her for a straight-in approach.

She put the gear handle down and listened to the reassuring hydraulic hum of the wheels in motion. Two green lights popped up on the control panel, but the top button glowed red. That meant the two main wheels were down, but the nose wheel had failed to lock into position.

"Uh oh..."

A quick check of the aluminum reflector confirmed her worse fear. The nose wheel, not locked in place as it should be, appeared instead to be hanging loose in the wind. She informed the tower.

"Suggest you do a low-level fly-by, One-Seven-Niner," the voice from the tower intoned — crisply calling off her airplane identification number, that impersonal barrier between the human being in the control tower and the human being at the controls of the airplane in question. "Let us get a visual on that nose wheel. We'll tell you whether it's up or down."

I know damn well it isn't down, Annie grumbled to herself. I can see that for myself. Why else did they put those mirrors out there. Certainly not for us to apply lipstick! But she held her tongue and didn't pass her caustic thoughts along to the control tower. Clare would have told them off good and proper, Annie thought, but the manners her mother had taught her often got in the way of her speaking her mind.

She pushed the button on the yoke and activated the mike. "Roger."

She lost as much altitude as she dared then, when the tower had given her clearance, executed a fly by.

"Yep," said the tower voice. "It's just hangin' there."

"I already knew that," she said, trying to hide the peevishness in her voice.

"Suggest you try the wobble pump."

"Roger." Annie regained some of her lost altitude and then proceeded to try to pump the wheel down manually. No luck. Half an hour later, her nearly continual pumping had failed to dislodge the stuck nose wheel.

"One-Seven-Niner, suggest you leave the pattern and climb to five thousand and see if you can get that thing to engage properly," came the instructions from the tower.

"Roger." Annie flew off to the northeast, away from the city, as instructed.

Looks like I need to do some creative flying, she told herself. Maybe if I try a sharp dive and then pull up abruptly I can shake the daggone thing loose.

She began a series of dives followed by sharp pull-ups to try to pop the nose wheel out by centrifugal force. Periodically she reported her non-progress to the tower. Her plan wasn't working. Finally, the tower reported to her that her maneuvers had produced a series of phone calls to the airfield. People had reported an airplane dive-bombing their houses. Three farmers complained that her aerobatics were frightening their milk cows.

"How are you doing, One-Seven-Niner?" the operator asked again a few minutes later.

For the first time, Annie heard mild concern expressed for her personal safety. She laughed and in her Southern-most drawl said, "I'm still flyin' north of Columbus and still pumpin' and still have a red light."

"Well, we've started to gather a crowd here at the airport," he reported back.

"Oh that's just great. I may crash on the runway because of a faulty nose wheel and I've got a crowd of thrill-seekers there to watch me do it."

"You're not gonna crash, Gwynn," a new voice said from out of nowhere and identified himself as an Air Transport Command officer. He had been listening like everybody else on that frequency — the only frequency in operation. "I just talked to your C.O., Nancy Love. When she found out which WASP was having the problem and what the problem was, she said for us not to worry, that you'd do just fine."

Maybe Nancy'd like to come fly this thing down for me if she thinks it's so easy, Annie wanted to say, but didn't dare since, by now, every airplane in the immediate vicinity of Columbus had heard her exchanges with both the tower and the ATC officer. She looked at her fuel gauge sinking lower and lower. She'd been diving and pulling up and pumping until her right arm was now so sore from overuse she could hardly move it. The engine coolant needle was stabilized — that was a relief — but the red light was still on.

She had been in the air long enough that her fuel was nearly gone, so she decided, as a last resort, to try the $CO_2$ cartridge. She remembered that the tech orders specified the cartridge be used only in an emergency. The instructor at Lockheed had told her, quite explicitly, *never* to activate the explosive cartridge because it had to remain in place for the combat pilot who might need to save his life someday.

Well, thought Annie, for her to take this airplane in with an unlocked nose wheel spelled certain disaster, therefore it had become a life-threatening emergency for her. *I'm the pilot whose life needs saving.*

Evelyn Sharp weighed heavily on her mind.

She put the aircraft in a climb to gain needed altitude, all the while keeping an eye on the fuel gauge. Then she informed the tower of her next maneuver. She put the plane into a steep dive, hauled back as hard as she could on the wobble pump, then reached under her seat and pushed the button. The cartridge exploded with such force, she thought it might have blown the nose wheel right off.

"Please let it still be there," she said out loud.

When she looked down at the instrument panel, the third green light had come on and the reflectors showed the nose wheel to be pointing straight out.

"It's locked," Annie said into the mike. Slowly, she let her breath out. She had no idea how long she had been holding it. "I'm coming in."

"Why don't you come around again and let us check it out for sure."

"Nope. It's down and locked. I can see it and I've got three green lights. Besides, I'm nearly out of fuel." She remembered Midge and her landing in the crippled P-47, and the fact that she had about a teacup of fuel left when they tried to measure it after she got down safely. "I'm comin' in."

"You got a lot of people down here waiting for you," the voice said.

Cleared for a straight-in approach into the wind and almost no crosswind to contend with, she lined the P-38 up with the runway and began her final descent.

Landing the Cub at John Rodgers Airport at Pearl Harbor flashed through her mind. No homicidal Zeros on my tail this time, thank God!

The sleek aircraft sank lower and lower. Annie watched the runway rise to meet her — always a beautiful sight, she thought. She had the yoke pulled all the way back into her stomach when the main wheels touched down, followed moments later by the errant nosewheel, and the 14,100-pound pursuit glided gracefully onto the runway without so much as a hiccup and kept rolling.

"Pretty as a picture," Annie said out loud to herself, grinning ear to ear. Out of the corner of her eye, she caught some movement. She slowed the airplane to make the turnoff to the taxiway and saw a Follow-Me Jeep racing along beside her. A guy in coveralls hung out the right side and gestured for her to stop.

"What the hell! What have I done now?"

Carefully, she braked and the P-38 rolled to a stop. At that point she noticed a couple of fire trucks, the hash wagon, a crash truck, and a police car trailing along behind her.

"G-get out," the man yelled as the Jeep pulled to a stop just off the wing. He waved his arms. "I'll take it in."

Annie took one look at the man's pop eyes and red face and the sweat stains under the armpits of his coveralls and, with great effort, kept a straight face. Talk about hysterical females! "No," she told him calmly, "I think I can handle it just fine."

With that, she gunned the engine and moved the airplane beyond the stopped Jeep and the rest of the entourage, turned off, guided the twin-engine pursuit onto the taxiway, and headed for the hangars. She parked the aircraft, cleaned up the controls and cut the switch. When she stepped from the cockpit down onto the wing, flashbulbs popped all around, nearly blinding her.

"Here, let me help you down," she heard a voice say, and then strong hands caught her around the waist and lifted her clear of the wing and onto the ground.

"You did some pretty creative flyin' up there," the uniformed man wearing captain's bars said as he put her down.

"I was prayin' for you, honey," said a woman in a Red Cross uniform standing next to him. Reporters and photographers surged around her, yelling her name and asking for quotes. "What happened up there? Were you scared?"

When Annie thought about it later, she decided that she had been too busy to be scared. But by later that evening, once again safely ensconced in a comfortable bed at the Fort Hayes, Annie realized that her right arm hurt so badly she might have trouble going to sleep. She called down to the desk and asked if they had any aspirin. When she gave her name, she found out that she was, once again, famous in Columbus, Ohio. The distaff side of the B-17 bomber pilots' wedding of last winter had now become The Heroine of the Pursuit Corps in the eyes of the local press. A bellhop brought her a pitcher of ice water and two aspirin. "Way to go up there today, ma'am" he said.

The next morning, she found the Columbus *Dispatch* outside her door.

GIRL PILOT DIVES ON COLUMBUS, LANDS CRIPPLED P-38 screamed the front-page headline.

The airfield called at nine to tell her that the mechanics had gone over the airplane, all repairs had been made, and she could take it on to Newark. Annie put in a quick call to Betty Gillies to give her an update. "I'll be there this afternoon."

"Have you heard the news?" Betty asked.

"What news?"

"Congress killed the WASP bill. Cochran is scurrying around trying to call off the next round of girls on their way to Sweetwater now to begin training. Those already en route will get nothing more than a ticket back home. Pretty sad, eh?"

"Yeah, Nancy told me the other night that things looked bad. So that's the end of trainees, but what about us?"

"Don't know. We're layin' low here, waiting to see what Cochran does next. I'd say, for now, this doesn't affect us. We'll just do our jobs and keep a low profile."

"Sounds good to me."

Annie took off from Columbus headed for Newark. When she got there and started to put the gear down, the same thing happened again. The nose wheel refused to lock and the red light came on.

"I'm not fooling around this time," Annie told the tower. "Give me my clearance. I'm coming in." And before anyone could protest, she fired the replacement $CO_2$ cartridge she had demanded the mechanics install, saw the green light come on and confirmed in the mirrors that the nose wheel was, in fact, down and locked. Then she executed as smooth a landing as the one she had made in Columbus. When she stepped down from the wing — this time without the blinding glare of flashbulbs — she informed the ground crew, "You've got a lemon on your hands. You'll need to reinstall the $CO_2$ cartridge — and I sure feel sorry for the combat pilot who has to fly this crate."

Annie opened the door to the flat in Farmingdale and dropped her B-4 bag and briefcase in the vestibule. "Anybody home," she called, expecting — with all the publicity her plight in Columbus had generated — that they would all come running to hug her and ask her how it felt to be famous and what really happened up there.

She saw Clare's face first and she knew, instantly, something was very wrong.

"Clare?"

Tears formed in Clare's eyes. "Oh, Annie."

"Clare? Is it Will?"

But Clare didn't answer, other than to shake her head.

By then the others had appeared behind Clare and they were all staring at Annie with the same mixed look of apprehension and despair.

Annie noticed that Clare had a yellow piece of paper in her hand. She held it out to Annie — and she knew. "Charlie!"

She felt herself sinking to the floor where she stood. The other three surged forward and caught her.

"His plane is missing, Annie… that's what the telegram says," Clare said. "Just like Will." And she folded the sobbing Annie in her arms.

# CHAPTER TWENTY-SIX

"We're going on the offensive, Midge," Jacqueline Cochran announced on July 1st.

Anybody else would be in hiding licking their wounds following the kind of monumental defeat her boss and her program had suffered, Midge thought. But not Jacqueline Cochran — she came out swinging.

"Hap wants a recommendation on what to do with the women who are already on duty and those in training right now. The current classes will be allowed to finish and the last of them are due to graduate in December. That means nearly a thousand women will be on duty flying by January first. It's up to us to nudge Hap's decision along with some research of our own."

So attuned now to Cochran's needs, Midge knew what she had to do and went to work immediately. Cochran set the goal — to have the report on General Arnold's desk the morning of August 1. That meant Midge had a month to compile and write a complete history of the WASP program. The report would conclude with Cochran's recommendations for the future.

*It is timely to evaluate the service of the WASP against a background of nearly two years of accomplishments and to determine their future in the light of today's known factors*, Cochran, with Midge's help, wrote as a preface to the report. *The usefulness of the WASP cannot be measured by the importance of the type of planes they fly, for their job is to do the routine, the dishwashing jobs of the AAF that will release men for higher grades of duty. At present each WASP saves one less-qualified man from being withdrawn from civilian life or releases one already-trained pilot for other duties.*

They said nothing about the problems with the civilian male pilots other than that they had lobbied against the WASP bill in Congress.

"We've got several alternatives, Midge," Cochran said as they prepared to close up the office in the Pentagon and head home one evening late in July. With the report nearly finished, they needed only to draft her final recommendations. She ticked off the options: "One, deactivation; two, accept what we did get in medical and insurance benefits, but seek nothing more; three, keep things exactly the way they are; four, continue to press for militarization."

"We're not going to get that last one, Miss Cochran," Midge said, the fatigue of her deadline assignment evident in her voice. "At least, I don't see any signs of movement in that direction."

"Well, I disagree," Cochran snapped. "I think it is the only path to pursue."

Midge's heart sank when she heard that. Suddenly her boss's bulldog determination to get her way threatened to stand in the way of the seven hundred women flyers now performing the jobs they were trained to do as part of the overall war effort. And there were more than four hundred still in training in Sweetwater.

"Don't push them to the edge, Miss Cochran," she said, aware that her advice had not been sought and probably wasn't wanted. "They might decide to take your first recommendation, and just deactivate and get rid of us all."

"They wouldn't dare. Hap won't let them." Cochran paused and leveled a cutting look at Midge. "And I don't remember asking for your opinion. Who do you think you are, criticizing me? Nancy Love? You picked up some bad habits during your time with Miss Society and her rich, influential friends."

Midge lifted her head and met the look in those blazing brown eyes straight on. Suddenly, she found courage she didn't know she had. The courage she had found a year earlier when the wounded P-47 threatened to extinguish her life. The courage to fight back.

"Miss Cochran, that's unfair. I've lived this dream along with you for the past three years. I've put this report together for you. I know what it says and what has been said about us. You know, and so do I, the mood of the country and the direction this thing is headed in. We're winning the war, which means men are going to come home and we women are going to be dispensable. I think it's a mistake to give them the opportunity — any excuse — to dispense with us sooner than absolutely necessary."

Jacqueline Cochran stared at her for what seemed to Midge an eternity. "I ought to fire you for insubordination."

"No, Miss Cochran..." Midge reached deep once again and used her last ounce of dignity and courage. "You ought to thank me for leveling with you. Someone has to."

A gulf opened up between them — only the width of Cochran's desk in actuality, but it might as well have been the Atlantic Ocean. It struck Midge that they thought too much alike, were products of too much the same environment and station in life. The difference — Cochran's acquired wealth had raised her so far above her roots that she could never go back. Midge, to the contrary, greatly feared that she might have to do just that. If she blew her connections with the powerful Director of Women Pilots now, she could be back in St. Charles, Missouri, tomorrow night.

Midge lowered her gaze. "I'm sorry," she said, not really meaning it but knowing it must be said. "I had no right. I'm sure I don't have benefit of the whole picture, which you surely must. I'll leave. You'll have my resignation on your desk in the morning. Right now I'm too tired to type it out."

She turned to go.

"No! Wait." Cochran's voice had a sharp, almost shrill edge. Midge thought she might even have detected a hint of fear, but she couldn't be sure. "I'm not firing you and I won't accept your resignation. Like you said, you've been with me through all of this and I realize that you must have formed opinions and you are entitled to them, misguided though they may be. I'm not so small a person as to forget the years of loyal service you've given me. I lost my temper for a moment."

No "I'm sorry" accompanied the statement. Jacqueline Cochran never apologized. But she did seem, for a moment, to be considering her next move. Then, as if she had made up her mind, she gave Midge her trademark winning smile. "Go home, get a good night's sleep. We have a lot more work to do and we'd better get started first thing in the morning. We have to finish this report."

"Thank you. Good night, Miss Cochran. I'll see you in the morning, then." Midge took a deep breath and walked out of the office.

When she got home, Midge let the built-up tears of anger, frustration and fear flow. She had given in to the necessity of keeping her cushy job for her own sake and, as she had once explained to Annie, for the sake of her mother, her aunt and her sisters. But looming even larger was that recurring sense of impending doom. Jacqueline Cochran and General Henry H. Arnold were on a collision course and, where her boss seemed blind to it, Midge sensed a fatal mid-air in the making and knew a deadly fall-out could be the only result.

When the phone rang a few minutes later, Midge sat unmoving, sunk deep in the only easy chair in her tiny apartment. Her eyes

were closed as she kept replaying the afternoon's scenario, searching for any other possible outcome. The last thing she wanted to do
right now was talk on the phone. It might be Cochran calling to tell
her that she had changed her mind and would, after all, accept her
resignation.

Finally, she reached for the phone after the fourth ring.

"Hello."

"Well, you sound like the voice of doom," Barry Metzger said
from the other end of the line.

Midge didn't answer.

"You're so happy to hear from me, the cat's got your tongue?"

"Hello, Barry."

"Is that all? 'Hello, Barry.' Can't you do any better than that? Of
course, the last time I saw you, I had rum and Coke dripping into
my eyes."

She couldn't believe he was actually making a joke about their
meeting in Fort Worth. "I'm surprised you even want to speak to
me," she said, finally.

"Water — or should I say Coca Cola — over the dam, darlin'. You
know I always want to talk to you."

"Barry, why are you calling me? It's late." She glanced at the clock
on the table beside her as she spoke, confirming that it wasn't quite
as late as she thought. Only nine. But she had to be back in the office
in exactly twelve hours.

"Not that late, sweetheart. What are you doing?"

"Where are you, Barry?"

"I'm a half a block from your apartment in a phone booth."

"How did you find me?"

"Easy. Ask anybody at the Pentagon where that cute chick who
works for Dragon Lady Cochran lives. They know — or can find
out."

"What do you want?" The cute chick remark cut.

"Why, to see you, of course. I'm only in Washington tonight. Have
to fly back to the West Coast in the morning. I'm looking for a soft
bed, darlin' and yours is still the softest and most tantalizing one I
know of — anywhere."

As much as she needed a diversion after her confrontation with
Cochran and the depression it had brought on her, Midge found Barry's approach unsettling — typical, she thought. The men in this war
lit where they felt like it, like bees hunting pollen on a flower. She
had heard some of the women talk the same way. "Take it while you
can, honey. Tomorrow you may die." A little far-fetched for a ferry

pilot, but several of the women had, in fact, died. Look at Cornelia Fort, Evelyn Sharp, Dorothy Scott. They died so young — twenty-three, twenty-four. On her last birthday, Midge had turned twenty-four. God, I hope they lived a little before they went, Midge thought. There's so much out there to see and do and have. But is Barry the price I have to pay? Is one night of escape worth the price? She made up her mind.

"Barry, I'm tired and I have a lot to think about. The answer is no." And she hung up the phone feeling that she had burned one more bridge in her fight for her self-respect.

Midge finished the report on time and Cochran delivered it to General Arnold the morning of August 1. She ended it with an ultimatum: *If the WASP could not be commissioned into the Army Air Forces, serious consideration should be given to inactivation of the WASP program.*

Midge, knowing it to be useless — a true exercise in futility — did not try a second time to talk her out of it. And she followed her boss's orders to release a copy of the eleven-page, single-spaced-on-legal-size-paper report to the press.

Newspaper articles began to stack up on Midge's desk in the succeeding weeks. Cochran wanted a record of all of them. The Wisconsin Department of the American Legion, at its annual convention, called for "the immediate and honorable termination" of the WASP. It claimed millions of taxpayer dollars were being wasted on the frivolous program. Influential columnist Drew Pearson wrote that General Arnold was "sidetracking the law" in an attempt to use the women pilots while 5,000 trained men pilots sat idle. Even the civilian flight instructors, still trying unsuccessfully to get the Army to accept them, kept the heat on with letters to the editor, which resulted in editorials in newspapers, large and small, across the country.

At the same time Cochran's report was released, General Tunner left for India to take command of The Hump Airlift — that vital air route from India across Burma to China that allowed food, fuel and other necessities to be delivered to the Chinese Army to insure that they kept up their fight against the Japanese. With his departure, the women ferry pilots lost their biggest supporter. Fortunately, General Robert E. Nowland, who replaced Tunner, also believed in the worth of his women ferry pilots.

But by mid-August, the number of WASP ferry pilots, which had reached a high of 303 in the spring, had been cut in half. The 150 women not qualified on pursuit, or who were nowhere near to having sufficient hours to hope to qualify for pursuit training, were sent back to the Training Command to be reassigned to a unit where they would get more flying duty. Of those remaining, more than a hundred already were qualified to ferry pursuits and another twenty soon would be. Nowland did everything he could to keep "his girls" flying.

*****

*August 25, 1944, American troops marched into Paris and liberated the city held for more than three years by the Germans. The Marines were turning the tide in the Pacific in the battle for the Mariana Islands. Soon the B-29s would be within striking distance of the Japanese mainland.*

*****

All the news Midge clipped about the war was good and all the news she clipped about the WASP was bad. And then one morning in September, Cochran walked into the office. By the look on her face, Midge knew what had happened.

"Hap has deserted us. He's shut the program down," she said and slammed the door.

Midge helped write Cochran's emotionless letter to the WASP that informed them that they were being deactivated and the program terminated on December 20, 1944. She tried to persuade her boss to be more personal, to show some caring and concern. Finally, Midge concluded that Cochran looked upon that as showing weakness. That, or she was simply incapable of dealing with this final defeat.

When the wording of the letter met Cochran's approval, Midge laid the final draft on her boss's desk for her signature. Then she returned to her own desk and typed out her resignation:

> *Dear Miss Cochran,*
> *I cannot, in good conscience, remain here. I suspect that you will, in fact, be closing up shop soon and will have little need of my services. I thank you for the opportunities you've given me. I have learned much from you, but I think my apprenticeship is now over. It is time for me to leave the nest and fly on my own.*
>
> *Nancy Love is desperate for every pursuit pilot she can muster. The factories are turning out fighters*

*faster than the current crop of male and female ferry pilots can deliver them. If Betty Gillies will have me, I'm going to return to Farmingdale to help ferry P-47s.*

*Sincerely,*
*Midge Culpepper*

On October 8, 1944, the same day Cochran and General Arnold's letters were delivered to WASP stationed at 120 bases around the country and the young women still in training at Avenger Field, Midge walked into Betty Gillies' office at New Castle.

"I'm back to fly whatever you've got, wherever it needs to go. At least until we have to go home on December 20th."

# CHAPTER TWENTY-SEVEN

September 22, 1944 was a beautiful fall day at Republic Aviation on Long Island and Clare was sure she had never before seen so much Army brass gathered in one sitting. She and Betty Gillies and the rest of the WASP contingent also sat in the reviewing stands, enduring the boring, never-ending speeches, awaiting the big event, *the christening*. In minutes, the deed would be done and the pilot scheduled to ferry the next airplane to the docks in Newark was Teresa James. Teresa would fly "Ten Grand" — the ten-thousandth P-47 to roll off the line.

Suddenly a hush fell over the crowd as the men and women of the day-shift rolled the monster fighter plane through a paper curtain and out the hangar door. Within seconds the air was filled with loud cheering as the workers pulled and pushed the aircraft to where Jacqueline Cochran stood on a lift-truck platform, waiting to break the celebratory champagne over the nose of the 12,500-pound Jug. The aircraft in place, the crowd quieted to watch Cochran swing and hit the plane. An explosion of green glass and fizz filled the air, followed by bubbly liquid dripping from the propeller hub. Cheers and whistles erupted and continued as Teresa, dressed in flying gear and with her long dark curls billowing in the breeze, moved forward and began to pose for photographs.

"Give us a big smile." "Show your teeth." "Come on, a little cheesecake." "Over here, big wave, big smile, that's right." Pop! Flash! Teresa endured the shouted requests, and kept flashing her broad smile.

"Cheesecake," Clare said, disgustedly, to Annie. "How the hell they expect a girl in a flight suit, strapped into a parachute, to give them a sexy, cheesecake pose is beyond me. They're all nuts. Nothin' but sex on the brain."

Annie laughed. "Teresa seems to handle it OK."

Finally, when the press and the Army public relations people were satisfied, Teresa hopped up on the wing, threw her leg over the side, and climbed down into the cockpit. More photos followed, flash-bulbs popping. Finally, the lineman inserted the starter and the air-plane roared to life. Ten Grand rolled away from the crowd, down the taxiway and toward the runway with Teresa grinning broadly, waving wildly from the cockpit — its Plexiglas canopy still open.

Moments later, Teresa and her airplane were cleared for takeoff and the crowd watched as she swung the Jug into its takeoff roll down the runway. It lifted smoothly into the air and she circled the field once, dipping her wings in salute before soaring off to the southwest toward the ship waiting at the docks in Newark.

Since June 1944, the WASP had been doing all the P-47 deliveries from the Republic Aviation factory. The men had either gone over-seas or on to other stateside ferrying squadrons. It's our show, Clare thought, smiling inwardly, remembering how long it had taken for Betty and then the rest of them to inch their way into the cockpits of these splendid Thunderbolts. On this celebratory day, they had no idea it would all be coming to an end in three months. By the time December 20 rolled around, the WASP in Farmingdale would have delivered 2,500 of the big Thunderbolts.

Two weeks after Teresa's flight in Ten Grand, the letters from Co-chran and Arnold came. Now, everything would be downhill and, from all appearances, it would be a rapid descent. "Damn," Clare said aloud, causing Annie and the others in the Alert Room to look up from their letters.

"Yeah, damn," Annie echoed.

Since Charlie's disappearance, Annie had become a shell of her former self. Gone was the easy smile, the ready sense of humor. She had no appetite. In her more normal moments, she could just muster a rueful laugh over the fact that she had fought what she called "the weight problem" her whole life and now, finally, the pounds were falling away. But for the wrong reason. She'd trade every pound for news of Charlie's safe return.

As autumn deepened, the workload increased. The flight of Ten Grand seemed to have spurred the workers at Republic to new heights and production records exceeded all expectations. P-47s rolled continuously from the assembly line and every pursuit-qual-ified WASP that Betty Gillies could muster jumped at the chance to ferry them either to Newark or to Evansville for modification. After mid-October, no more new ferry pilots came from Pursuit School. Thirty-seven women pilots made up the roster of Betty's squadron — most of them pursuit-qualified.

As the days grew shorter, tempers followed suit. The early animosity between Clare and Midge flared when Midge — newly reinstated in Farmingdale — tried to defend Cochran by explaining how devastated she had been when Arnold killed the WASP program.

"The bitch never gave us a second thought," Clare said angrily. "She wanted to be a colonel and command a goddamn women's air corps. When she couldn't have that, she acted like a spoiled brat who didn't get her way. She sold us out."

"That's not true," Midge insisted. "She really believed that we should be militarized and she fought to make that happen."

"I, for one, could care less about being militarized," Clare said. "Such nonsense, sending us to OTS. A waste of time when we could have been ferrying airplanes, doing what we were brought here to do — what we were sorely needed to do."

The women felt betrayed, stunned by their dismissal. Many couldn't bring themselves to make plans for where they would go and what they would do after December 20. Instead, they lived day-to-day and for the next airplane they would ferry, somewhere. The future didn't exist for them and Annie, Midge and Clare were among the most despondent.

Many of the women hoped for some further word from Washington, a change of heart. When Midge tried to tell them that no such reprieve would be coming, they turned on her as the bearer of bad news. By-mid November, they began drafting letters to General Arnold, Jacqueline Cochran, the Secretary of War, even President Roosevelt, volunteering to fly for free. All of them knew that the production of P-47s would not stop when they were deactivated and, because of their exclusive hold on ferrying from Republic, there were now few available male ferry pilots around who could take their place. Clare knew that soon, pursuits would be stacked up ten-deep waiting to be taken to the docks or the modification center. To her, it seemed that reality had totally escaped the supposedly great minds of the military establishment. Men, she decided for the umpteenth time in her life, could be very stupid and short-sighted — particularly where women, their motivations and their capabilities, were concerned.

One night in early December, the WASP currently on TDY at Republic and in residence in the Farmingdale flat decided to put up a small Christmas tree. As they began to hang their odd assortment of ornaments on it, Clare suddenly became overwhelmed with a deep, gnawing sadness. She excused herself and went to sit on her bed in the room she shared with Annie and now Midge, as well. And she began to compose yet another a letter to the War Department.

"Clare," Annie's voice startled her.

"What!" came her sharp retort. She wanted to be alone, to wallow in her own self-pity. Why else would she have excused herself from the forced gaiety in the other room. Forced, she thought, because she, Annie and Teresa, all three of them, were haunted by the disappearance of their husbands somewhere in northern Europe. And the others, if not troubled by personal tragedy, were engulfed in barely suppressed anger at Jacqueline Cochran and General Arnold and the Army in general for letting them down and letting them go.

One look at Annie's face, however, softened Clare's heart. She took a deep breath and put the letter down. "Sorry, Hon, what's on your mind?"

"What are you going to do after December twentieth?"

"Go home to Colorado."

"But, last year, you went home for Christmas and hated it. You told me you couldn't deal with the season. That your heart felt so heavy, you could no longer feel joy. Those were your exact words. What about this year? Do you think, after all that has happened — Will still missing, this stupid termination — that you can do any better there this year?"

Immediately, Clare understood. Last Christmas, Annie had been nearing graduation from Pursuit School and looking forward to getting married. Things were going right for her. Not wanting to go home for Christmas, she had gratefully stayed in California with the others at school, because they only had Christmas Day off. Now, this year, she had to deal with her husband missing in action, the job she loved being terminated, and the trip home she had dreaded last Christmas was about to become a reality. And this year, she had nowhere to escape to when the holidays were over.

"I've had a year to get used to Will's being missing — to not knowing. It doesn't make it any better, but some of the hard edges have worn off. My mother hasn't been well this last year. She's looking forward to me being home for an extended period of time. I can't let her down. She's supported me all along in my crazy obsession with flying. I owe her."

"When I went home in March, after Charlie went overseas, I began to make peace with my family. I guess it's tenuous, at best, based on me being so sure that, after the war, I'd be going to Texas to live with him. But now," Annie shuddered, *right now*, I don't know that that will even happen."

Clare saw the tears welling in Annie's eyes.

"Annie, Annie, you can't give up hope. I haven't."

"Oh, Clare, I try so hard… every day I tell myself 'he's alive and he's coming home to me.' But somewhere deep in my heart, I have this dread that it's not true… that he's dead. And for me to admit that out loud to you is like I'm pronouncing a death sentence."

"I didn't know you were the superstitious type," said Clare. "You thinking something isn't going to make it happen. Come on, now. No news is good news. He's in a POW camp somewhere and, when the war's over, he'll come home to you."

"How can you make yourself believe that? Is that what you honestly think when you think about Will?"

"Yes, it's what I *have* to think." Clare held out her arms to her friend — just as she had the day Annie had received the telegram. She stroked her hair and patted her back and, once again, let the younger woman cry until the worst of her unhappiness washed away, at least for a time.

The night of December 19, Nancy Love and Betty Gillies gathered the 37 WASP remaining in active service with the 2$^{nd}$ Ferrying Group at New Castle for "The Last Supper" — a banquet held at the Officers' Club. All were smartly dressed in their Santiago blue WASP uniforms — the official uniform ever since they had been delivered the previous spring.

Clare, Annie and Midge sat together at the first three seats immediately perpendicular to the head table where Nancy and Betty reigned over the proceedings. To the right of Nancy sat Nancy Batson, Helen McGilvery and Gertrude Meserve Tubbs; on Betty's left were Helen Mary Clark, Teresa James and Sis Bernheim to complete the head table.

After dinner, Betty gave her farewell speech. Then Nancy stood. "Not all of us are here from our early days back in the fall of '42," she began. "B.J. sends her love from Long Beach, Donnie from Romulus, and Delphine from Dallas — and several of the others who began here with us are now scattered to other commands or out of the service entirely."

Nancy glanced down for a moment and Clare thought she seemed to be faltering. But then Nancy raised her chin and looked out at the gathering. "Cornelia, Dorothy and Evelyn have flown on to what has to be a better place. And we have grown to greater numbers than we ever anticipated, thanks to the addition of all you graduates of Houston and Sweetwater who joined us later."

Clare knew Nancy didn't want to make this speech. Nancy hated speaking in public. But she felt compelled to make this one. Clare sensed that Nancy felt she had failed in her mission. That, somehow, she had failed the women she had invited into this adventure twenty-eight months earlier. Clare had tried recently to set her friend straight, looking at the realities of life and war and how things never turn out quite like we envision them. Now, she heard the fruits of their long talks in Nancy's heart-felt words:

"When we started in September 1942, I expected to have a squadron of fifty women, all of whom would deliver trainer and liaison type aircraft around the country, as needed. Little did I expect that the women in the Ferrying Division would eventually number more than three hundred and that more than a hundred of us would be delivering the hottest aircraft the Army has — the pursuits — to say nothing of the twin-engine aircraft that eventually became old hat to us.

"As you know, Betty and I — along with Clare and Annie — got a crack at the B-17. Almost made a trip to England. But that's history.

"All I can say to you courageous, dedicated women is… we did it! We accomplished everything we set out to do and far more. We accepted our accolades with humbleness and took our knocks with equanimity. We proved that women can fly anything the Army can build and we can fly them well.

"What we did has been called an experiment by some. I call it a worthy endeavor, a magnificent venture of monumental proportions, a success in all sense of the word."

She reached down and picked up her glass of rare French wine brought in especially for the occasion. "A toast to the most outstanding women I have ever known — will ever know. You are not only colleagues of the finest order, you are my friends. I salute you. I honor you. I love you all."

Nancy raised her glass. "To the WAFS and WASP: May your accomplishments live forever in the memories of all who know us and those who didn't."

Clare noted there was hardly a dry eye in the dining room as Nancy took a sip of wine and then sat down. As the others sat, Clare continued to stand. When every eye in the room finally focused on her, she raised her glass again. "To the one who started it all. Always a lady. One who never failed to keep the best interests of her girls at heart and who never let the lure of fame and power go to her head. Yes, here's to the *real* force behind the original WAFS and all the WASP of the Ferrying Division — my friend, Nancy Harkness Love."

# CHAPTER TWENTY-EIGHT

The train carrying Annie home to Nashville pulled out of Wilmington at 4:30 p.m. The sun, one day before the Winter Solstice, sank slowly in the southwest, casting its fiery glow on the network of iron rails, on the boxcars standing empty on side spurs, waiting to be loaded, and on the distant factory chimneys, turning the smoke belching from them a rosy hue. The glow reminded Annie of the fire the previous night.

The women of the 2nd Ferrying Group had finished their farewell dinner and enjoyed one last evening of dancing with the AAF officers stationed at New Castle, after which they reluctantly retired to BOQ 14 to finish packing. They were, after all, going home. And then somebody outside yelled "fire" and the sirens started to wail and they all ran to the barracks windows and looked out. Those already in pajamas pulled on robes, slippers, and coats; those still dressed grabbed their civilian coats — already laid out for traveling, and everyone piled out of the BOQ and ran to the building they had vacated two hours earlier.

The O-Club, their off-hours home away from home for more than two years, was ablaze.

They stood, transfixed, in the glow of the yellow flames. The heat of the destruction of the O-Club, Annie thought, proved a direct contrast to the chill that had pervaded the dismantling of the life they had lived for the last twenty-eight months. Tomorrow, nothing would be left of the WAFS/WASP program but the memories. And now, tomorrow, nothing would be left of the O-Club but the ashes — of their dreams and of their refuge.

"They think it started in the kitchen," said Clare, always the voice of reason. It occurred to Annie that it really didn't matter. Then she heard Nancy Batson shout, "Let it burn, let it burn." And she let out a Rebel yell.

"Yeah!" Raising her voice, Annie echoed, "let it burn!" Slowly, overwhelmed with a sadness she didn't understand, Annie turned her back on the conflagration and walked back to the BOQ to continue packing.

Now, when she looked out the train window again, the sun had sunk below the horizon. She continued to stare out into the darkness — interrupted at times by the lights of a house or a car on a road nearby — listening to the rhythmic clack of the wheels on the unending tracks. And in the soft darkness, she began to reassess who she was and where she was going.

Six months — from the longest to the shortest day of the year, summer to winter in her soul, as well as in the temporal world — had gone by since Annie heard that Charlie's bomber had been hit during a raid over northern France's Cotentin Peninsula. That day, U.S. troops had captured the town of Carentan and prepared to battle for the port of Cherbourg. The drive inland from the beaches following D-Day was only two-weeks old when it happened.

Initial reports were that the Number Four engine on his B-17 caught fire when the plane took a hit. Chutes were seen leaving the plane. Then, witnesses said, the pilots miraculously got the plane under control and brought it in on a belly landing into a field, where it skidded out of control and came to rest finally in a bog. Though the fire spread after impact, anyone still on board had a good chance of survival — already saved from the certain death of a vertical dive and a nose-first crash into either the ground or the nearby sea. The six crewmen who bailed out landed safely.

An eyewitness told an Army chaplain that, just before the plane exploded, she had seen two flyers emerge from the burning airplane, one half dragging, half carrying the other. They moved away from the downed plane and in the opposite direction from where she stood.

It turned out the eyewitness was a young girl given to visions and authorities were now convinced that she had seen yet another vision leaping out of the flames when contemplating the burning, exploding bomber. The rescuers found no sign of life and no one among the partisans in the area ever admitted to sheltering two American flyers.

That was all she knew — all she had.

Her father was waiting for her at the Nashville train station. That he looked decidedly older startled Annie. The last time she had seen him was ten months ago, right after Charlie's departure for England. Annie fully expected her family to find her altered by the uncertainty of Charlie's fate and the strain of the WASP's last few months, but not the reverse.

She walked into her father's waiting arms. His embrace lasted far longer than usual. When they moved apart, she saw him wipe moisture from his eyes.

"What is it, Dad?"

"We're so glad to have you home, daughter — finally."

He sounded a bit embarrassed at the emotion he showed.

"We can only imagine what you've gone through." He looked away from her as he reached for her bags. She let him take the larger one, but held on to the smaller one. She had carried parachutes and overstuffed briefcases on many a ferrying trip. She was fitter than he was now.

The ride out West End Avenue through the gray Nashville winterscape didn't lighten the mood. Kirkland Tower, Vanderbilt University's sentinel, loomed on the left side of the road, rising above the bare branched trees that lined the U-shaped entrance to the venerable school. Next came the spire of the Old Gym and then they were by the campus. A few blocks beyond, her father turned up Natchez Trace.

Thinking how foreign the city looked caused Annie to close her eyes and ask herself why? Why foreign? She grew up here. But for more than two years her world had been taken up with airplanes and the landscapes of runways, airport towers and barracks; of Army Jeeps, mess halls and thousands of uniformed men; of the patchwork quilt that was the fields, woods, mountains, deserts and plains of America as seen from the air. The warm red brick of ivy-covered university walls, the empty, black-barked trees that most of the year displayed a leafy umbrella of green, the quiet suburban streets like the one they now made their way down, were a study in contrast to her reality and belonged to another world.

But now it was her world again.

When she stepped over the familiar threshold and reentered the family life she had left behind, she was struck by the aroma of cedar that filled the room. A cedar fire glowed in the fireplace and next to it stood a magnificent Tennessee cedar complete with strings of colored lights and tinsel. Annie looked closer and saw the delicate ornaments of her childhood, her favorites. She smiled and breathed a pleased sigh as she turned to her mother, standing near the tree.

"We tried to make it look like you would remember it," said her mother, her hands unconsciously twisting the hem of her apron, a smile with just a hint of uncertainty creasing her face. Annie felt her reserve slip away, surprising herself as she crossed the room quickly and enveloped her mother in a bear hug.

"Oh, Annie."

"Mother, don't cry. I'm home."

"But Annie, so much has happened. And you're so thin."

"Shussh! Time for that later. What I really need is a cup of your coffee and then some breakfast. I'm famished and I can smell cinnamon rolls and bacon. Don't keep me waiting."

Every night, leading up to and for several days after Christmas, the family sat around the radio in the living room listening to reports from the War Department mixed in with Christmas music, the highlight of which was the Christmas Night performance of maestro Arturo Toscanini and the NBC Symphony Orchestra broadcast from New York. Filling the news was word of the critical battle underway in Belgium, referred to as "The Battle of the Bulge" and taking place around a town called Bastogne.

\*\*\*\*\*

*The Germans had broken through the Allied lines, surged forward, and surrounded several thousand lightly armed men of the 28th Infantry and the 10th and 101st Airborne. A German courier delivered a message to their commander, Brig. Gen. Anthony C. McAuliffe, calling for the surrender of the American troops. McAuliffe wrote one word on the paper and sent it back to the German commander. The words was "Nuts!"*

*The troops held on through Christmas day. On December 26, General Patton's 4th Armored Division broke through and raced to Bastogne. The sleet and low clouds that had kept Allied air power grounded and unable to come to their aid finally lifted. The siege of Bastogne was over.*
\*\*\*\*\*

Throughout that long week, Annie had checked the Nashville newspapers for word of the WASP dismissal, but there was nothing. The news from Bastogne and The Battle of the Bulge had driven any lesser happenings off the pages of newspapers around the country. Then two weeks later came some good news.

\*\*\*\*\*

*U.S. troops had landed at Lingayen Gulf, Luzon, 110 miles north of Manila. And a week after that, news came that the Burma Road was about to be reopened. On January 17, the Polish capital of Warsaw — under the yoke of the Nazis for five years — fell to the Red Army as it moved swiftly across Poland. And then on January 27, came the shocking news that the Russians had captured what turned out to be the Nazi's biggest extermination camp, Auschwitz. The Red Army was a mere 100 miles from Berlin.*

\*\*\*\*\*

Annie hid her discontent better than she could ever have hoped. Her mother refrained from prying questions and comments that might bring their long-standing differences to the surface. As the world embarked on the New Year of 1945, and the news from the battlefront improved, Annie consciously throttled back on her craving for activity and sank into winter hibernation. But by late January, with the festive feelings of the holidays behind them and the upbeat turn in the news, her restlessness resurfaced. She was too used to the hectic pace of the Ferrying Division and inactivity chafed her already raw feelings. I've got to find a job or go somewhere else, she thought. But this is where Charlie knows he can find me. And what will I tell mother?

She went out to Berry Field and talked to the old-timers who remembered her and the new ones who didn't. Didn't they need an experienced ferry pilot? Of course she was already aware of the answer. The military could not employ women and the civilians were not hiring. But one of the ATC men, when he heard she was a WASP, told her about Reconstruction Finance Corporation, a contractor the government was using to sell its surplus warplanes. RFC had to supply its own ferry pilots. Annie remembered hearing something about RFC before deactivation — that this might be an opportunity to do some ferrying work. But at the time, all the WASPs ferrying P-47s out of Farmingdale thought they would be kept on after December 20 and had paid little attention.

She got the contact's name and put through a long-distance call to him. That night, she broke the news to her parents that she was going out to Blythe, California, to ferry airplanes for the RFC. The heartbroken expression on her mother's face almost caused Annie to renege on her plans, but her father said, "If that's what you need to do, daughter, then do it." And that saved them all from embarrassment.

"You're dealing with a lot right now and your mother and I — though we will always support you — won't interfere or try to get you to stay when you know you have to go," he added quietly.

Annie felt an unnatural weight lift from her shoulders.

Two days later in a repeat of the scene two and a half years earlier when they put her on the train for Wilmington, Mr. and Mrs. Gwynn saw their daughter off at the train station again. This time, she was heading west. And her future was as uncertain in February 1945 as it had been in September 1942. The only differences this time — the tide of the war had changed decidedly in the favor of the U.S. and Annie faced the prospect that, at 24, she could be a widow.

A week later, Annie had found quarters in Blythe with three other WASP. "We've got a real live WASP nest out here," she wrote Clare and Midge. "Why don't you all think about coming out here and joining us? RFC needs ferry pilots. Granted, the stuff we're flying is pretty beat up — and it doesn't pay much — but at least we're flying."

She picked up several flights in downtown Los Angeles, a half block from the Biltmore Hotel, where the bidding sales on the surplus planes took place. One day, she and her roommates, having nothing assigned to fly that day, put on their WASP uniforms — something they were still allowed to do — and went downtown to see what they might scare up. They watched a man bid on four AT-6s and when he had successfully completed his buy, they approached him, identified themselves as WASP and asked if he needed ferry pilots. He did.

That afternoon, they delivered the four AT-6s to Tucson, Arizona, then caught the bus back to Blythe that night. They were each a hundred bucks richer. The man had even paid their bus fare.

A week later, Annie went downtown alone, approached the man who had just bought a P-51, told him she had flown several in the fall of 1944, and could he use a ferry pilot who could handle that Mustang? He hired her and later that day she took the P-51 to Tacoma, Washington.

On the morning of March 1, with an even dozen deliveries under her belt, she and five other ferry pilots were in Fort Worth to pick up six familiar, open-cockpit PT-19s. They headed back to California by way of Tucson. Their airplanes — primary trainers that had been used to introduce raw cadets to the mysteries of flight — were beat up and showed it.

"Good thing I'm not superstitious," Annie quipped to the others. "This makes number thirteen for me with RFC."

Over Mica Mountain, near the town of Paradise in southern Arizona, Annie felt — and at the same time she heard — an explosion. She had no clue what had happened, except that it was bad. "What the …!"

A quick check of the gauges told her nothing. But she knew she was headed down. She cut the switch, hoping that would prevent the gasoline from igniting when she landed the stricken aircraft. She did a quick scan of the terrain for a place to put it down and trimmed the airplane to optimum glide.

She located the other planes, but since primary trainers didn't come equipped with radios, she had no way of telling them she was in trouble. She could only hope they would notice her falling behind and realize she was in a gliding attitude, which she fought to maintain.

The terrain below was desert but rough — boulders large and small stood between the prolific cacti that littered the ground. She watched as her altimeter spun steadily downward. Then ahead of her she spotted a narrow, winding dirt road which, in the distance, she could see led to a small desert town. Careful not to stall and put the trainer into a spin from which she did not have the power to recover, she eased the nose up just a fraction, hoping to gain a few more feet for her glide path — enough to make that road, which was growing steadily closer.

"Just a little further, baby, please!" Now she had the road in her sights — not a very straight stretch, unfortunately, and it had barbwire and rocks and saguaro cactus on both sides. The tall saguaros seemed to be reaching their long arms skyward to beckon her in.

Even with her feet solidly on the rudder pedals, Annie felt the intuitive urge to pull her feet up to stretch the glide — just as she had tried to pull her bicycle up when she soared across Overall Creek. Now the rugged dirt road was dead ahead, rising up to meet her. Gently she pulled the stick back, stopped, waited a heartbeat, and a little more.

Now! She flared and a half-breath later felt the main wheels touch the surface, followed an instant later by the tailwheel. With the stick pulled back into her stomach, she held the airplane straight with the rudders. The ride was rough, but the airplane rolled, unimpeded. When it finally came to a stop, the wings were unmarred by contact with the red boulders or any of the brush and spiny cacti that grew along its rollout path.

Annie let out a sigh of relief.

Two of her companions appeared moments later, circled overhead and made hand signals. They were telling her they would send help and to sit tight. Already she could see the rooster tails of dust coming from the direction of the town. She waved and pointed toward the approaching vehicles. She climbed out on the wing and settled down to wait.

Soon three pickups and a couple of cars pulled up. As she jumped to the ground, several men, women and children crowded around her. She reached up and pulled off her goggles and leather helmet, letting her hair fall in her eyes. As short as she wore it, it was obvious that this was no crewcut airman.

"It's a girl," Annie heard several voices gasp.

Annie smiled. "Hi, my name's Annie."

The people of the little town of Paradise couldn't have been more helpful. Two men cut the barbed wire of the fence along the road a hundred feet or so down from where she had landed. Then all the men put their shoulders to moving the small plane off the road so that what little traffic came through there could get by. After Annie had climbed back into the cockpit and stowed everything in preparation for the mechanics that would be sent to look at the plane, one woman took her home for dinner and let her use the telephone to call RFC in Los Angeles. Annie tried to reimburse her, but the woman and her husband wouldn't hear of it. Annie spent the night in the family's guest room and the next morning, they drove her out to the downed airplane to meet the mechanics who had driven down from Tucson.

"If you can fix it, I'll fly it out of here," she told them.

"This airplane ain't goin' nowhere for a while, little lady," said one of them. "Three of your spark plugs blew. Came right through the engine here and out over here. Look, you can see the hole they blew out."

Annie looked and shuddered. She knew the PT-19 was beat up, but this was beyond reason.

"I'd say you might as well head back to Tucson and hop a flight to the coast. Let them decide what they want to do about this crate."

"Number thirteen," Annie said, shaking her head. "I should've known."

# CHAPTER TWENTY-NINE

"Midge," Annie's voice came over the telephone. "This Colonel Metzger the Army is sending to bring home our POWs held by the Russians... is that *your* Barry Metzger?"

The uninvited past invaded Midge's small Washington D.C. apartment. Though she was glad to hear from Annie, the mention of Barry's name always sent a shock wave through her. Stunned that Annie even knew of Metzger's assignment, she hesitated long enough to let her words sink in.

"Yes," she answered. "Why?"

"Charlie and Will are still missing. Clare and I haven't heard a thing in months. But hundreds of our POWs have already been repatriated and more are being processed every day. We'd like to volunteer for Metzger's team. If we can get to Germany, maybe we can find something out. Would you be willing to recommend us to him?"

The date was April 30, 1945. News was breaking hourly and rumors were flying predicting the imminent fall of Berlin and the Nazi Reich with it. Already, there was speculation about the Occupation and plans for bringing the troops home. And, yes, American POWs were being repatriated every day.

"Midge, you there?" Annie asked.

"Yeah, I'm here." Midge's mind whirled. "Annie, how do you know all this? I just heard of it today."

"Nancy Love called Clare this morning and told her about Colonel Metzger's assignment and suggested that we contact him. Of course I recognized his name right away. Would you consider asking him if he would talk to Clare and me? Include us on his team? We're both prepared to head to Washington on a moment's notice."

"Annie, I haven't seen Barry Metzger since April, two years ago. And we didn't part company in a very friendly manner."

"Yeah, you told me you dumped a drink in his lap."

"And one on his head!" Midge often thought of her actions that evening with a great deal of pleasure. That was the beginning of her road to independence — from him, from Jacqueline Cochran, from any of the forces that tried to hold her in their grip. Could she call him now, out of the blue, and ask him to help two of her friends?

"Did Clare ask Nancy and Bob for help?" Midge asked. "They have far more pull than I've ever dreamt of having."

"Bob has been transferred to ATC's West Coast Wing in San Francisco. He's already out there and Nancy is back in Boston to sell their house and then join him on the West Coast. But, yes, Nancy told Clare that she and Bob would make every effort to get Metzger's cooperation. Since we have such a small window of opportunity... well, here I am, asking for your help."

Midge wrestled with the enormity of the request from her perspective and the simplicity of it from Annie's. "I'll see what I can do and get back to you tomorrow."

"Midge, I'll be eternally grateful — as will Clare."

Annie's call upset the equilibrium Midge had carefully constructed in her life since December 20. After the WASP deactivation, she had returned to Washington hoping to find a job. The move paid off, and, thanks to Nancy and Bob Love, Midge was now working for the Air Transport Command. Once she had found a hard-to-come-by apartment, she brought her sister, Louise, east to live with her. Midge got Louise a job as a shampoo girl in one of D.C.'s elite beauty salons where she could continue her apprenticeship. Jacqueline Cochran surprised Midge by putting in a good word with the owner.

Midge found it hard to believe her former boss had forgiven her but, whatever the gulf between them, Cochran obviously bore no ill will toward the rest of Midge's family. With no explanation, she had continued to send the monthly subsistence checks to Aunt Earlene and Midge's mother, though Midge had not been on the payroll since October 1944. The woman had a deep generous streak that surfaced on unexpected occasions, and Midge was thankful for it because it had given her the latitude to make a fresh start.

For the first time, Midge felt she had taken hold of her life, concentrating on her work with the ATC, and put ferrying aircraft out of her mind as well as what it had been like to work for Jacqueline Cochran. Deep in the recesses of her mind, she knew that someday the war would be over and she would have to think about the future. *But oh please, not yet. I'm tired and I can't cope with that right now.*

Annie was a friend — no, Annie was her *best* friend. And though she and Clare had never gotten along, Midge had come to respect the woman for who and what she was. A thaw between the two had come to pass in the hours leading up to deactivation when the three of them had said their tearful goodbyes at the base in Wilmington.

After an almost sleepless night, Midge called Colonel Barry Metzger the next morning, from her desk at ATC headquarters. He was cordial, but with a reserve Midge was unaccustomed to when talking with him. He heard her out, went silent for a moment — she wondered what he was thinking, but dared not interrupt — then said, "Tell them to get themselves to Washington ASAP. I've been working out the details on this operation and I'm close to having the team I need, but I still need a couple more good people. They just may be the solution. I'll see… meantime, let me know when they arrive. I assume they'll be staying with you?"

Hotel rooms were hard to come by in wartime Washington. Unlike when they were ferrying airplanes for the Army, Clare and Annie no longer had ferry pilot priorities to help them secure lodgings. Nor did they have a per diem to pay for those lodgings and meals while in Washington.

"Yes, they'll be with me." And so she gave him her home phone number as well as how to reach her at ATC. The phone clicked at the other end without Barry's bothering to say goodbye.

The following day, Midge again dialed Metzger's office.

"Colonel Metzger," he barked into the phone.

"It's Midge. They'll be here the day after tomorrow."

"Good! I'm still working out the details. I should have everything in place by the end of the day. I'll get back to you." He hung up.

He called mid afternoon: "Tell them to pack light but smart, I have no idea how long we'll be over there." He spoke rapidly and with staccato emphasis. "And I need to see you tonight."

Midge held her breath for a moment — her mind whirling, her heartbeat shifting into high gear. She groped for an answer.

"Midge!" Metzger's voice was insistent. "Don't play games with me. If your friends want to go to the war zone with hopes of finding their husbands, you're part of this deal, like it or not! I'll pick you up at seven. And don't worry, I already know your address." The line went dead.

The setting — the crowded bar of D.C.'s Mayflower Hotel — had a *deja vu* feel to it and Midge sensed the eerie similarity to Fort Worth two years earlier. She and Barry once again sat side by side, each toying with a drink. His Scotch and soda, hers a Manhattan, her new drink, now that she had outgrown rum and Coke. He put his hand over hers. She tried to withdraw it, but he enveloped her hand in both of his, smiled an odd smile, and shook his head. "Don't pull away, my darling. I've been waiting for this for two years."

Midge felt her heart thudding, but was it excitement or fear?

"What is it you want, Barry?"

"I thought that was obvious." He smiled and lifted her hand to his lips, brushing them across her palm. "I want you."

"Barry, you have a wife and I have no intention of being someone's mistress. I'm grown up now. I have my own life to live."

"Think again, dearest. You don't want to refuse me." He was so close. His eyes held hers.

"Do you mean that you won't help my friends unless I sleep with you?"

"I wouldn't put it in quite those terms, but if you want to help your friends, come back to me now. I have no intention of letting you get away a second time. In fact, I'm prepared to marry you to keep you."

"Marry me! You're already married!"

He let out a sigh. "I was just getting to that. Connie and I are history. She's filed for a divorce in Reno. In less than six weeks, I'll be a free man. That means you and me, love. If you want marriage and a ring, then marriage and a ring it will be."

Midge shook her head, unbelieving. But he was smiling at her. He wasn't mocking her — at least she didn't think he was. The change in his demeanor troubled her.

"We're meant to be together, Midge. You know that. Remember how good we used to make each other feel." His hand brushed her cheek. She felt off balance.

"Now, let's finish these drinks and head upstairs. I already have the key." And he pulled it out of his jacket pocket just enough for her to see. "I've been waiting for you, Midge."

The last three and a half years swam before her eyes. No, he hadn't changed. The technique maybe, but not the man, she was sure. She had put her infatuation with him behind her. She didn't trust him. She was over him. But what about Annie and Clare?

He stood up and offered her his hand. "Come."

She slid from the booth, picked up her purse, and took his hand.

Two nights later, Annie and Clare were in Midge's apartment. Annie and Midge sprawled on the threadbare couch and Clare sat in the lone overstuffed chair. All held bottles of Budweiser in one hand and waved a cigarette in the other. They were in their pajamas, getting reacquainted after four months apart and living lives very different from what had been their daily routine while flying for the Ferry Command.

Finally, Annie asked, "So, what is going to happen, Midge? All you told us was that Colonel Metzger wants to see us tomorrow."

"Actually he wants to see all three of us."

Midge felt their eyes on her.

"Why all three of us?" Clare asked.

Midge had dreaded this moment. She weighed how much to tell them — particularly Annie, who knew of her complicated relationship with Barry Metzger. And she was embarrassed to admit any of this to Clare.

"OK, here's what's happening. Barry's job is to oversee the repatriation of the American POWs formerly held by the Germans, now being held, illegally, by the Soviets in Poland." And Midge proceeded to tell them about Barry Metzger's assignment as he had explained it to her:

As the Soviet forces began to advance west into German-held territory in early January1945, the Germans ordered forced-march evacuations of the POWs held in their camps located in Poland and East Prussia. Their aim was to move their POWs back behind German lines. The whole operation became a disaster as the Russian Army moved faster than the Germans expected and winter snows impeded the progress of the POWs. Some prisoners made it to Germany, but others escaped, others were simply abandoned by their German captors and left to fend for themselves. Estimates ranged in the thousands of American and British POWs roaming free around Poland.

And so, as the Red Army swept through, they picked up many of those POWs and now held them in collection centers. Though the U.S. was promised immediate access by the Soviets at the agreement at Yalta in February, that hadn't happened — until now. Finally, the situation had thawed.

Major John Proski — Military Intelligence Service, fluent in both Polish and Russian — was being sent to negotiate with the Soviets for the immediate release of the former American captives of the Germans. Metzger would be responsible for processing these prisoners once the Russians freed them.

Metzger had assembled his team, but needed three more capable people to handle the paper work of the repatriation process. He had planned to take three WACs to do the job, but had agreed —on the request of Bob and Nancy Love, as well as Midge Culpepper, to take three civilians instead — as long as it was the three of them. In a matter of days, they would accompany Metzger and Proski to Germany aboard a B-17 that Metzger had requisitioned for his personal use.

Annie and Clare stared at her in amazement. "What about your job with the ATC?" Clare asked.

"I've been transferred to Barry's staff. He took care of that with one phone call."

"You're not telling us everything," Annie said flatly. "You're giving up everything because he won't do this for us unless you do."

"No, Annie," Midge protested, "I'm not giving up anything. This is a plum assignment, a positive..." She broke off as she saw Clare shaking her head.

"You don't have to do this," Clare cut in. "You can't do this. You're selling yourself."

Midge sighed. "It's done."

"You're sleeping with him again, aren't you?" Annie said.

Midge couldn't meet her eyes.

"Of course she's sleeping with him. It's written all over her face, Annie," Clare said. "Midge, this didn't have to happen. We'd have found another way."

"Oh Midge." Annie's look held a hurt Midge didn't want to see.

"But I need to tell you the rest." And she told them of Barry's marriage proposal.

"Midge, he's married!" Annie said.

"No, Annie, it's OK. His wife is divorcing him. As soon as it's final — in six weeks — we'll be married."

Clare sniffed at that. "And you believe him?"

"I have to," Midge said shortly — and regretted her quick tongue. "Yes, I believe him."

Annie shook her head. "But Midge, why do you want to marry him? You told me you had come to despise him. Don't do this Midge — please."

Midge reached out and gently wiped away the tears that were running down her cheek. "We've settled some things. It will be OK, Annie, believe me."

The three were silent, not looking at each other. Then Clare picked up the pieces and said, "Well, Annie, looks like we're finally going across the pond in a Flying Fortress! OK, so we're going as passengers, but we're going to find Will and Charlie." She took a drag off her cigarette and then ground it out in the ashtray. "Here's to us — to the three of us!" She raised her beer in the air and the other two did the same.

# CHAPTER THIRTY

Just after dawn the morning of May 8, 1945, a B-17G Flying Fortress sat on the end of Runway 4 at Washington National Airport, waiting to carry Colonel Barry Metzger and his hand-picked POW repatriation team to Goose Bay, Labrador, and from there across the North Atlantic to Prestwick, Scotland, and on to Paris. Clare, Annie and Midge sat side-by-side on the canvas auxiliary crew seats along the right side of the fuselage, midway back in the waist of the airplane. There was no heat in the back compartments so the three women wore waist gunner's electrically heated suits and had a supply of army blankets close by.

Metzger and Major John Proski, also in heated suits, occupied the two auxiliary crew seats across from the radioman in the next compartment forward. The radio operator's cramped desk was located directly behind the bomb bay. Since this was a noncombat mission, no bombs were loaded that day, nor was there a bombardier on board. The flight engineer rode aft of the copilot and the navigator rode in the Plexiglas nose. Everyone wore oxygen masks as they would be cruising above 10,000 feet. Each passenger and crewmember carried a parachute.

As they sat waiting for takeoff, Clare felt more than heard the drop in engine resonance that indicated the pilot had pulled the throttles back to idle. She felt Annie, sitting on her right, come alert and knew she had caught it, too. An eerie *deja vu* invaded her thoughts, reminding her of when she and Annie had sat on the runway at Goose two years earlier, ready to take off for Scotland. The disappointment of that day was still vivid in Clare's mind. She hoped history wasn't about to repeat itself.

Suddenly someone was banging on the rear door, near the tail on the right side of the plane. Clare, nearest to the door, unfastened her harness, got up, went to the door and opened it. In stepped a corporal. He handed her a message. "For Colonel Metzger, uh, ma'am," he said, saluting her. "The war's over," he brandished his fist triumphantly in the air and let out a war whoop. "The Krauts have surrendered! Telex just came in. The lieutenant said get it to the colonel before you guys took off. You're probably the first peacetime flight to head for Europe."

Clare managed to thank the corporal who then ducked out the door. She closed and locked it, then — shouting so that Annie and Midge, both wide-eyed, could hear her over the idling engines — "Listen up! This is a telex dated May seventh, from Allied Headquarters in Rheims, from General Dwight D. Eisenhower:

> *At 2:40 this morning in an upstairs room of the Rheims [France] College Moderne de Garcons, where French children played table tennis before the war, General Alfred Jodl, of the German high command, today signed the surrender of 'all forces on land, sea and in the air who are at this date under German control.'*
>
> *The cease-fire covers the Soviet front as well as Western Europe and comes into effect at 2301 hours tomorrow [May 8]. It was witnessed by General Bedell Smith for Eisenhower's Allied command.*

"That's today, ladies! May 8th, 1945. VE Day!"

Whoops of glee erupted and the three women hugged each other as best they could, though Annie and Midge were still belted in. Clare quickly conveyed the message forward to the men on the plane. The radioman followed her back to her seat. "Get ready for takeoff," he shouted to them, grinning, then saluted smartly, turned and disappeared into the labyrinth that lay between them and the cockpit.

Clare sat back down and belted herself in. Moments later, she felt the engines begin to rewind, the roar building as they strove to reach takeoff pitch, and then, ever so slowly, the Fortress inched forward into its takeoff roll, gathered speed, and began its journey down the runway and into the air for its first leg of the trip to where the fighting had just ceased. Clare never failed to revel in the magic buzz that whole takeoff sequence brought to her inner core.

In Goose Bay that night, the liquor flowed. The ground crew there had liberated several bottles of champagne to add to the whiskey and beer already available. Deadly mixture, Clare thought, and shook her head.

Seems the men stationed at Goose had been anticipating this celebration. The combined crews of the B-17 and the Goose Bay outpost toasted Eisenhower, they toasted Hap Arnold, they toasted Patton, Churchill, Stalin. They drank to the health of the new President Harry Truman and to the memory of their fallen leader, President Franklin D. Roosevelt. They "spit in Tojo's eye" as each of the celebrants expectorated mightily into the roaring fire in the fireplace. And they all laughed because, finally, there would be tomorrows.

Neither Clare nor Annie felt much like drinking and made do with a single glass of bubbly. The men, however, seemed intent on celebrating themselves into total oblivion. Midge kept her eye on Metzger, who hovered over the pilot and copilot and, in a belligerent voice that everyone could hear, ordered them to switch to Coca Cola. When Clare looked over at the two pilots again, she noticed that, behind Metzger's back, they were spiking their Cokes with whiskey.

She looked up to see Major Proski approaching. He seemed to have been nursing the same whiskey and soda all evening — the exception to the male revelry.

"We were just barely introduced this morning. John Proski…" He offered his right hand.

"Clare Varsky," she said, accepting his handshake. "Actually, it's Clare Webb. I need to remember to use my married name now that I'm no longer in the service."

He nodded. "Colonel Metzger told me that he had volunteer civilian women on his team. I thought at the time, surely Red Cross work would be more interesting than interviewing gaunt, hungry, lice-infested GI POWs. So… I understand you have a vested interest in this effort?"

Clare smiled at his candor. "Both of us." She nodded toward Annie. "Her husband, Charlie Richardson, and mine, Will Webb, are pilots, shot down over enemy territory and missing in action. That's all we know. We hope to find out what happened. If …" she faltered, "if they're alive. If so, where they are."

"And what is Miss Culpepper's interest in this?"

"She's a close friend of Annie's and mine. We all served as WASP together, and she knew Colonel Metzger. Annie and I asked her to approach him about us being part of his team. She opted to come along."

"Tomorrow I'd like to talk to you and Mrs. Richardson, write down all you know about your husbands' disappearances and who you've talked to."

"Absolutely. Thank you," said Clare.

"I'll find out everything I can. I promise."

At nine that night, knowing they were scheduled to take off at dawn and they would have to be up by four a.m., Annie and Clare decided they'd had enough. Clare looked around for Midge, who was billeted with them. Metzger, sensitive to flaunting his relationship with Midge in front of the crew, had insisted on that and Clare begrudgingly gave him at least one positive point for being a gentleman. Now she spotted Midge engaged in an animated argument with Metzger, who was red-faced, gesturing, and unsteady on his feet. Then Midge threw up her hands and walked away. When Clare gave her the high sign, she joined them, and the three women said their goodnights to the still partying male crews.

"They've all had way too much to drink, particularly Barry," Midge said.

Clare was the first of the women to arise, and when she wandered into the galley to get a cup of morning coffee, she was met by a bleary-eyed Metzger and two green-faced pilots who were slumped in the metal folding chairs. Before she could get her coffee, the pilot, 1st Lieutenant Michael Johnson, groaned, staggered to his feet, went down on his knees, and retched all over the floor.

"We've got a couple of sick pups," Metzger said, glowering at Johnson.

"You don't look too good yourself," Clare shot back.

This time he glowered at her, pulled a chair out and sat down.

Clare went over to the fallen pilot, leaned down and offered him her hand. "Here, do you need to hit the latrine or do you want to sit down?"

"I'll sit." He took the hand she offered and climbed shakily to his feet. "Thanks."

"Find me a bucket and mop," Clare told another bleary-eyed man she recognized as a ground crewman. "I'll clean this up."

"Yes ma'am!" He stumbled off. But when he returned with the mop and bucket, Johnson pushed himself to a standing position and said, "I'll do it. It's my mess."

"OK... if you think you're up to it." Clare poured herself a cup of coffee and sat down by Metzger, who leaned heavily on the table, his head in his hands.

"They can't fly in this shape," he said.

Clare assumed he was speaking to her. "And it's going to be awhile before they are sober enough to fly. They need to sleep it off."

"Yeah, but we need to go now, while the weather's good. It's supposed to turn nasty. Storm brewing. We need to stay on schedule."

Clare looked at him steadily for a minute. "Tell you what, Colonel Metzger... I'll make you an offer."

Metzger looked up, frowning. "What?"

"Annie and I were checked out on the B-17 two years ago and we each have about fifty hours cockpit time. We can fly your plane for you — if you're willing."

Metzger stared at Clare. "Why would I want to do that?" His voice was surly.

"Because you're in a pickle and I'm giving you an out."

"You women aren't allowed to fly military planes now. General Arnold's orders."

"General Arnold will never know. Annie and I are perfectly competent pilots on this aircraft. Your guys won't want it on their record they were too hung-over to fly, and if we don't tell, nobody else is gonna blow a whistle. It shouldn't take us long to review procedures and surely Lieutenant Johnson can hold his head up long enough to help us with that. You've got a schedule to keep. We can make that possible."

Clare met Metzger's gaze straight on and felt his dark look turn quizzical. He blinked first. She remembered Midge's comment that he wasn't one to waffle. He made up his mind quickly and moved forward.

"You're on," he said, proving Midge right. "We'll have a crew briefing in twenty minutes. I'll drag the rest of these guys out of bed."

When the crew and passengers began to board an hour later, Clare and Annie were already in the pilots' seats running the cockpit check. At 6:05 Atlantic War Time, May 9, 1945, Clare — with Annie's left hand hovering over her right hand — pushed the four throttles forward to the stop and put the Flying Fortress into its takeoff roll. Effortlessly, the B-17 lifted off into the wind out of the west, steadily gaining altitude. "Gear up," said Clare.

"Gear up," Annie repeated after flipping the switch.

When she had acquired the necessary climb-out altitude, Clare, keeping the bomber at full power, put the big four-engine aircraft into a gradual climbing 180-degree left turn. It would take them thirty-seven minutes to reach a cruising altitude of 20,000 feet, where the winds were forecasted to be out of the west and blowing at about 120 knots per hour. Once they had their nose pointed east, that tail wind would get them to Scotland faster than originally projected.

"Here we are," Clare said to Annie as they climbed through 10,000 feet and prepared to don their oxygen masks, "we're finally getting that trip across the pond. Won't Nancy and Betty be envious?" When they reached cruising altitude, she activated her throat mike and said, "You want to take it for awhile? I need to stretch my legs."

"Sure," said Annie.

"Your airplane."

"My airplane." Annie took hold of the copilot's yoke.

Clare took her hands off the pilot's yoke, leaned back and stretched her arms, shoulders and back. "Ummm, that feels good." She swung her legs to the right, pushed out of the uncomfortable bare metal and mesh seat and steadied herself as her cramped legs protested. Before leaving the cockpit, she grabbed her portable oxygen bottle.

Down the narrow catwalk and through the gaping, empty bomb bay, Clare squeezed past the radio operator, nodded to Proski, and noted that Metzger was sound asleep, his mouth open and snoring in loud bursts. She laughed to herself and continued back to where Midge lay across the three seats, wrapped in a blanket and staring into a middle distance, lost in thought.

When she saw Clare, Midge held up two fingers, pointed toward the back of the plane, closed her eyes and laid her head on her hands. The two pilots were sleeping it off in the back. Clare gave her a thumbs-up. With that the plane was buffeted by a sudden gust of wind. Clare grabbed the webbing above Midge's seat to keep from being thrown into her. The buffeting continued and Clare realized that bad weather had caught up with them. She gestured toward the cockpit, turned and began to make her way, carefully, back toward the front of the airplane.

She slid into that now-familiar left seat, removed the portable oxygen, fastened her harness, and reconnected her earphones. Then she looked out the windscreen. "Geez! Where did that come from?" They were being chased by dark, roiling, rapidly building clouds. "The weather briefing we got said we were well in front of it."

"I know, Brett's been on the radio looking for an update, but nothing's come through yet."

"Want me to take it?" Clare asked

"I'm OK for now, but I'm glad you're back up here. It's really starting to get rough."

Just as Clare spotted the southern tip of Greenland far in the distance off the left wing, the big airplane was rocked by another wave of high winds. She noticed Annie's grip on the yoke tighten as she fought to keep the plane level in the fierce gusts. Brett, the radio-man, appeared over her shoulder.

"OK, I got a recall message. This storm is moving faster than they thought. We're to turn north and land at BW-One."

Clare and Annie stared at him. "Bluie One?" said Clare. "Green-land. Are you sure?"

"Yes, ma'am, they don't want us to try for Reykjavik. It's that bad. So we have to get on the ground. I've got the message right here. Freak storm. Organized itself quicker than they thought and they're not sure how long it's gonna last."

"OK," Clare said, "ask again to verify, and ask Marty to find BW-One for us."

"Roger."

"I'll take it back, Annie," Clare said, and they passed the controls between them again.

Marty, the navigator, appeared with a slip of paper. "OK, here's the new heading," and he handed it to her. Clare noted it and put the airplane in a gentle 100-degree turn north. Then she turned the nose of the airplane into the wind, blowing from the northwest, and held the airplane there, crabbed into that wind.

The next time Brett came into the cockpit he handed Clare the landing instructions. She read them, looked up at him — her eyes holding a question in them.

"That's what they gave me," he said and shrugged.

"OK. Annie, here's the deal. Brett will contact the weather station at BW-Three. It's located at the mouth of the fjord that leads to BW-One. There's a whole bunch of fjords down there and finding the right one is downright impossible. They will ID the right one and give us our coordinates and heading. At that point, we drop down and fly up the fjord at an altitude of a thousand feet. The mountains on either side are thousands of feet high. Oh yeah, and there's a bunch of dead-end offshoots and no place to turn around. Appar-ently it's so narrow in places you think you can't get between the walls, so we've gotta thread the needle— gotta get it right the first time. And, of course, we'll have a left quartering tail wind a good bit of the time."

"Wow!" said Annie, wide-eyed. Clare continued, "Fifty miles in-land, we're to look for the wreckage of a ship. When we spot that, watch for the field on the right 'cause we'll be right on top of it. Need to make a thirty-degree turn to begin our approach. There's only one runway and it slopes up toward the glacier. Go arounds aren't advised."

"Uh huh," said Annie, grinning. "Well, this is what we spent all those hours with Captain Forman perfecting, so we could do it if we had to."

"OK, Brett, go back and fill Colonel Metzger in on this latest development. Tell him we're taking this baby down to one-thousand feet, up the fjord and onto a Greenland glacier," Clare said. "We'll let everyone know when they can shed their masks. And tell him to enjoy the ride."

And so she began to put the Fortress into a gradual descent.

It wasn't long before Mike Johnson, the pilot, entered the cockpit. "Clare, I'm feeling a lot better. Do you want me to take it in?"

She looked back at him. He still had that greenish, sickly cast to his face, his eyes were bloodshot, and a day's growth of stubble told her he hadn't shaved that morning. Probably couldn't hold the razor steady. But for some reason no doubt connected to pride, he still wanted to fly this 55,000-pound airplane with ten souls aboard. "Have you landed here before, Lieutenant?"

"No, I haven't had that pleasure, but I've landed at BW-Eight. It's similar."

"Tell you what. Annie and I have got it." Clare patted the yoke affectionately. "She feels good. We'll put her down."

He hesitated and Clare thought he was about to argue with her. She turned and looked at him again. "Yes, Lieutenant?"

"Roger!" He gave her a three-quarter salute.

Brett came back. He had the heading for the fjord. Clare nodded. "We're almost down to a thousand," she said, checking the altimeter for the umpteenth time. Both she and Annie took a minute to look down and eyeball where they were headed. There they saw the several inlets that were the beginnings of the many fjords leading inland. Only one would take them to Bluie One.

"Wow!" Annie repeated.

"Yeah!" said Clare as she made one more 360-degree descending turn to lose the rest of the altitude. Then, making the final turn at 1,000 feet to start the run up the fjord, she and Annie glanced at each other. "Here we go…" they said together, both knowing it was to be the flight and the landing of their lives; their last flight at the controls of a B-17; their flight to destiny. And no one would ever know about it but the ten people onboard.

In minutes they were flying in a magnificent canyon of mammoth icy crags. At a thousand feet, the surface of the fjord appeared to be but a few feet beneath their wings. The water was a deep, vibrant azure and reflections of the northern springtime sun bouncing off it nearly blinded them. And just as they were warned, at points the icy walls closed in on them, but the wingtips passed with ease as Clare wove the big airplane through the narrows. She caught herself holding her breath. "My Gawd, it is so beautiful," she said as the full impact of the arctic splendor unfolded before her eyes.

"I never dreamed I'd ever see anything this magnificent," said Annie.

Finally, the shipwreck appeared in front of them. As advised, they looked right and there it was. The runway. Clare put the airplane into a 30-degree right turn to a heading of 070. The 5,000-foot-long, 145-foot-wide runway glinted in the sun and stretched away from them, running slightly uphill. It was no more than a mat of pierced-steel planking atop a base of pea-sized gravel and it ended abruptly at the foot of a very large snow bank. The glacier.

Clare lined the bomber up with the centerline and allowed the plane to sink, bleeding off airspeed.

"Full flaps."

Annie lowered the flaps. "Full flaps."

"Gear down."

Annie hit the switch. "Gear down and locked."

Moments later they passed over the water's edge marking the end of the runway. Just past the end of the runway, Clare set the big airplane down in a perfect three-point landing and, her feet deftly working the rudders, let it roll out straight and true down the runway.

The B-17, a taildragger airplane with the little wheel in the back and the main gear in front, landed just like the little Travel Air OX-5 taildragger Clare had first soloed eleven years earlier. When it had slowed sufficiently, again working the rudders, Clare put the bomber into a gentle left turn that led to the taxiway. Moments later, she parked it where she was directed by the ground crew. Then she cut the switches and shut the airplane down.

"We did it, Annie."

# CHAPTER THIRTY-ONE

By early May, Bluie West One — 61 degrees 9 minutes latitude and 45 degrees 25 minutes longitude — enjoyed sixteen hours of daylight. Following dinner in the mess hall, Annie and Clare took their mugs of coffee and found their way onto a weathered plank deck that offered a view of the mountains and glaciers, retreating snow and the oncoming march of spring and greenery. The storm that had made them run for cover had gone south of them — along the route they would have been flying. Everything at Bluie One was calm and peaceful. The sun was still high in the sky. Greenland was in the throes of trying to live up to its name.

Major Proski joined them for after-dinner coffee.

"So you two and Miss Culpepper were WASP pilots," he said. "I was aware there were women pilots in the Ferrying Division, but I didn't realize the B-17 was included in your qualified list. I thought you were all pursuit pilots."

"Annie and I are two of only a very few who were lucky enough to get a crack at the Flying Fortress," Clare said. "It turns out we were badly needed to ferry the pursuits, but we were *not* needed to ferry B-17s. They decided they needed the men to do that."

"I heard you all were relieved of duty. How were you able to make this flight?"

"We were deactivated and sent home back in December. We aren't supposed to fly Army planes, but when Colonel Metzger's pilot and copilot fell ill this morning — given that we needed to keep on schedule — Annie and I volunteered to fly until the men recovered. We all thought it would be a milk run to Reykjavik. The possibility of having to land at Bluie One obviously never entered our minds."

"Well… you certainly stepped in when needed. That was some flying job you did today. What a landing!"

"Thank you, Major, words like that are music to our ears," Clare said. "Colonel Metzger is well aware of our flight experience. However — and I'm sure he will tell you this himself — this is to be kept strictly between those of us on this flight, because we are all break-ing the rules, schedule or no. But you didn't come out here to talk to us about flying. Right?"

"True. Let me fill you in on my assignment — why I'm part of this team. As you know, Colonel Metzger's job is to oversee the repa-triation of our POWs currently being held by the Soviets in Poland. My job is to secure their release from the Red Army so that Colonel Metzger's team can do its job."

"Haven't a lot of POWs been processed already?"Annie asked.

"Since March we've been processing hundreds of former POWs on a daily basis, in Germany and France, but several thousand more men can't be accounted for. As the Russians swept through Poland, they picked up some of those men. They promised immediate access to them, but up until now we've had no luck getting our people in there to tend to their medical needs and to get them released. And so I'm on my way to Poland, hopefully to negotiate their release. It might be possible that either or both of your husbands could be there. Colonel Metzger asked me, as a personal favor, to do what I could to help you. So I want what information you have before I head east."

Clare glanced at Annie. "Do you want to start?"

Annie gave him Charlie's unit number and other identification and then told him the story of the bomber going down over northern France just before the battle for Cherbourg — about the six who parachuted to safety and about the two who were seen running from the burning plane just before it exploded. "But when rescuers ar-rived, there was no sign of either man. That's all I know, Major. There has been no further information. I wish I knew more."

"That gives me something to work with. What about you, Clare?"

Clare related what she knew of Will's disappearance. Returning from escorting B-17s on the disastrous August 17, 1943, raid on Schweinfurt, Will's 56th Fighter Squadron had taken their P-47s hunting, strafing everything in sight and doing damage to German installations where they could. Near Sint Niklaas, Belgium, one of Will's buddies had seen his plane take a hit.

"P-47s are heavily armored," Clare said. "I flew them, so I know. Seems as if the likelihood of Will, himself, being hit was small, but a control surface could have been badly damaged making the plane difficult to fly. The other pilot said Will was fighting to keep his plane under control. He rolled once and took off toward the coast. That's when his buddy lost sight of him. But no one reported a plane down between there and the coast."

The major nodded. "P-47s *are* known for protecting their pilots, so the odds are good that he landed safely or with minor injuries and was captured. Odds on him being picked up by the Underground also are good. I'll see what I can find out."

The next morning the weather at Bluie One was clear and reports east were good as well. The storm had blown itself out. Lieutenant Johnson and his copilot, fully recovered, were at the controls when the big plane took off.

Back in her passenger seat along the cylindrical wall of the plane's interior, Annie could not see out, but she sensed in her gut the bomber's roll down the runway and the smooth takeoff out over the fjord. She wished she could have seen it again from the copilot's perspective, but she had her memories of yesterday and the images were imprinted on her brain.

Deplaning in Paris, they were herded onto a truck transport to take them on the long journey to their headquarters at what had been a German airfield and where the Army had opted to set up this particular operation. There, they would meet the rest of the repatriation team.

En route, they all had a chance to see, first hand, the devastation of first the French and then the German countryside. When they passed through Cologne, they saw the now-destroyed Hohenzollernbrücke and Hindenburg bridges over the Rhine River, as well as whole blocks of stark, burned-out buildings. But they also noted that the tall spires of the thirteenth-century Cathedral of Cologne were still standing. Somehow, the RAF's bombs and those dropped by the U.S. 8th Air Force B-17s had managed to avoid the historic structure. The Rhine River valley offered some glimpses of spring coming to the war-torn landscape, but destruction was, seemingly, everywhere.

By the time they reached their destination outside Frankfurt, Annie was emotionally exhausted — so tired she thought she could sleep forever. But the next morning, they were up at six, met after breakfast with the rest of the team that had arrived two days earlier, and began to set up their work area and quarters. They were one of several teams that would be working in what had been a recreation center, a clapboard building on the sprawling former Luftwaffe airfield. Annie, Midge and Clare were to be located in one partitioned corner of the sprawling main room of the rec center. Other teams of three were partitioned off the same way.

Major Proski left immediately for Poland and, possibly, Moscow, while the rest of them got ready to receive and process the freed POWs. Then they settled in to wait.

Finally, word came that Proski had been successful in securing the release of the American prisoners held by the Russians in Poland. Send the trucks, he said, and with that a fleet of requisitioned Army troop transports set off for Poland, gears grinding. The line snaked for more than a mile.

POWs began to arrive in camp three days later. Men in ragged uniform remnants piled out of Army trucks that had made their way across Soviet-held Poland and eastern Germany in to the western zone and on to Frankfurt. First the men were deloused and sent to the showers. After that, doctors examined them and they were given clean clothing. From there, they went to the mess for a meal. "Not too rich to begin with," the docs warned, "and small portions until their shrunken stomachs can handle more food."

Most of the men ignored this cautionary advice and immediately went back for more, stuffing themselves with the predicted results. After eating, and in many cases recovering their equilibrium, they were sent to the recreation center where several teams, including Annie, Clare and Midge, interviewed them, took down their personal information and gave them new I.D. cards. After filling out endless forms, each man received stationary so he could write home.

When the POWs began to arrive, the three found themselves working from 7:30 in the morning until 7:00 at night, with a quick thirty minutes for lunch and a couple of bathroom breaks. Otherwise, they had no time to themselves. Annie scrutinized the face of every man who came through the door and she had already talked to all the WACs they were working with, giving them a look at a picture of Charlie.

At night, exhausted, they retired to the barracks that had been set up for the WACS who were working on the repatriation program.

One morning late in May, Annie took advantage of the momentary lull and stood up to stretch her long legs, cramped from being folded under the card table. "Think I'll get a cup of coffee," she said, but as she spoke, two more men came into their cubicle.

"Go ahead Annie, "Clare said. "Midge and I can cover for you and handle these two."

"Thanks." Annie headed into the kitchenette, poured herself some coffee and quickly returned to the main room. As she stood looking out the door, sipping her coffee and smoking a cigarette, the mix of the voices of her two friends and the men they were interviewing drifted in and out of her consciousness.

"… there were three of us. We were on a … we were ordered on a forced march — had to leave the camp in a blizzard. The camp was in Poland. Never been so cold in my life."

Annie tried to tune out the conversation but, in spite of herself, she found herself straining to hear.

"We'd been walking for days in the snow and were down to two guards. One day, they just disappeared. The three of us — Bud, Charlie and me — up and decided to walk out."

Annie heard "Charlie" and turned around, her attention riveted on the back of the POW Clare was interviewing.

"Charlie and Bud," Clare repeated, writing the names down.

"Yeah, Bud's from North Carolina and Charlie — big guy from Texas, a B-17 pilot. We stuck together. The Ruskies finally caught up with us."

By now Annie's heart was pounding and her full attention was focused on the former prisoner seated in front of Clare.

"What happened next?" Clare asked.

"Well, nothing. That was the problem. Finally, our senior officer went to the commandant and asked if we could be released to find our way to the American lines, but he was given what he called 'a surly *nyet*.'"

Annie was holding her breath now — wanting to run to the man, grab his thin shoulders and plead, "Where is he?" But she fought the urge and listened as Clare carefully steered the GI in the direction she needed him to go with his statement.

"Finally this American officer and a couple of non-coms arrived in a Jeep and they began meeting with the commandant. One of our guys who had drawn KP duty — getting coffee and cakes for the Russians and the American officer — said he overheard the Russians demanding money for each one of our POWs they released. Then one of the Russians said that he understood every American POW was worth two Russian POWs returned. Then a third one popped off that they really wanted the Russian prisoners back because most of them were cowards and traitors and would be shot. Geez, miss, can you believe that!" The man shook his head and took a deep breath. "Apparently, the American officer got what he wanted, because a couple of days later, these Army trucks showed up and they loaded us on them. Took several days and a lot of trucks."

"Are your friends with you now?"

"Bud and Charlie? We got separated, but I think they got the next truck. They should have come in right behind me."

"When did you arrive, sergeant?" Clare asked.

"This morning. We rode in the truck all night and slept sitting up. I've been through all the clean up and seen the docs. They won't let us come talk to you ladies until we're cleaned up and presentable." He grinned at her when he said that.

Clare laughed with him then led the man back to his story. Annie continued to listen even though every nerve in her body seemed to be firing off in all directions, telling her to move — to go, to run, to look for Charlie. But she was on duty. When three more POWs entered, she made herself return to her post and asked one to sit down.

Throughout the remainder of the morning they continued to come in, two or three at a time. The minutes crawled by and Annie endured them, all the while wanting to bolt through the door and out into the courtyard where she could see the men as they were being processed. Finally, it was lunchtime.

"I'm going out to look," she told Clare and Midge.

They nodded. "Good luck."

Annie began her trek through the courtyard and out into the rest of the compound, her eyes darting to each group of POWs she saw. She walked down to the delousing station and stood at a distance, watching a different group exiting the showers next door to the medical examining building. She worked up her nerve to approach them.

"I'm looking for a tall Texan — a bomber pilot," she told three men dressed in clean shirts and trousers.

"Will I do?" answered the shortest of the three.

Annie laughed.

"Yeah, how 'bout me?" chorused the other two.

Annie put on her best smile, reached deep down inside herself for that confidence that so often eluded her and said, "Well, guys, wish I could say yes, but this guy's special. He's my husband— name's Charlie. A B-17 pilot."

Several others had gathered around.

"Charlie Richardson?" said one of the newcomers.

"That's right. Charlie Richardson from Amarillo, Texas." Her heart was pounding so hard, she was sure they could hear it.

"I just saw him heading into the mess kitchen," the man said.

Annie threw her arms around him, sensed how very thin he was, gave him a quick kiss on his freshly shaven cheek, then took off running. She stopped, turned around and waved to them. "Thank you!"

she shouted, throwing more kisses, then ran the rest of the way to the mess kitchen.

"I wish my wife was here lookin' for me," one called after her.

"Don't keep him waitin'," another said.

The guys all cheered and whistled.

When she reached the mess hall she slowed, wondering how bad she looked now — hair flying every which way, red-faced, sweating, out of breath. So she slowed down, tried to catch her breath and compose herself. Then she pushed the door open and entered.

Inside, she scanned the crowded room. Men were sitting, eating, others in line with trays to get food, some with trays of food looking for seats. And that's when she saw him. He was carrying a tray. He was very thin. Her first thought was he really needed the food on that tray. She also noted that his six-foot-four frame seemed a bit stooped. But it was Charlie.

She moved toward him. The other men saw her and stopped, watching. The mess hall went suddenly silent.

Charlie seemed to sense the change in the atmosphere and looked around. He saw her and froze.

"Charlie?"

"Annie?"

The tray slipped from his hands, clattering to the floor, as he vaulted over the table in front of him and ran to her.

"Annie!"

Charlie's arms went around her. She knew he was safe and she was home.

# CHAPTER THIRTY-TWO

The day after Charlie's arrival, Midge gathered Metzger's team for dinner in the mess kitchen and Charlie told them all the story of his eleven months in captivity. He began with how he and his copilot had escaped from the burning bomber just before it exploded. He had dragged his wounded crewmate to safety.

A passing truck, driven by two German medics out looking for their wounded, had picked them up. They put the badly wounded copilot on a stretcher, took him back behind their lines to the field hospital and handed Charlie over to the military police. Because he was an aviator and an officer, he received good treatment. He was taken to Dulag Luft, an interrogation camp near Frankfurt, the first stop for captured Allied flying personnel. From there he was sent to Stalag Luft III in Sagan, Poland.

"I was there from late July until we were evacuated in late January," Charlie told them. "They tried to send us back to Germany. We heard they planned to put us in the path of the bombs falling on Berlin and tell the Allies that we would die if they didn't stop bombing the city. We marched through snow — it seemed like forever. But eventually I escaped along with two buddies. The German guards got careless about keeping track of us and finally we just walked away. We lived with a Polish farm family for awhile — worked the fields for them in return for food and shelter. But when the Russian Army got too close, we were afraid we would put the family in danger. So we gave ourselves up thinking they would turn us over to the Americans. That took a little longer than we figured on.

"Then this guy showed up," he nodded at Proski, "and a couple of days later, the trucks began rolling in to take us out."

"I knew about Stalag Luft Three," Proski told the group. "It was *the* camp for captured flying personnel. It made sense to me that, given the German's admiration for aviators, a B-17 pilot would be sent there. I kept thinking, hoping, that Annie would get lucky and we'd find Charlie." He paused and flashed a smile toward Annie. "And we did!"

Midge had finished getting Charlie's papers in order after his emotional reunion with Annie in the mess hall. The entire repatriation center rose to the occasion and cheered on the reunited pair. Then Metzger found Annie and Charlie a room in a nearby inn where they could stay and Midge helped them get settled that evening.

The following day, Metzger pulled Midge aside. "Charlie's been cleared for transport home, and I think she should go with him. There's no reason for him to hang around and I can spare her now."

"No way," Midge said. "Annie told Clare and me she expects to finish the job here, even if you send Charlie home."

"I find that very hard to believe," Metzger said.

"You've just never run into anyone with Annie's sense of integrity before," Midge said. "You need to work it out for them both to stay. Besides, we know most of the men have been returned or are en route by now. Our job will be over soon."

"So I've got to pull strings to allow Richardson to remain here with her, is that what you're saying?"

"That's what I'm saying."

"Look at the red tape it'll create."

"Listen to me, Barry, you've got a chance to be a big hero. Instead of worrying about a little red tape, call *Stars and Stripes* and get them to send a reporter over here to write up this love-story-come-true-in-the-midst-of-the-turmoil-of-war-and-repatriation.People will love it!"

Metzger stared at her, but when he thought about it, he decided she was right. So for the next few days, the disruptions continued as a reporter and photographer from *Stars and Stripes* came in along with a newsreel photographer from CBS as well as a reporter and photographer from *Life*. Charlie and Annie were interviewed at length, posed for photo after photo and talked into the newsreel cameras so that the people back home could see them and hear their story from their own lips.

Finally the last of the trucks deposited the stragglers.

While Clare, Midge and Annie completed their necessary documentation, Colonel Metzger and Major Proski wrote their final reports. The mission was declared a success. With their job finished, they began packing up and getting ready for the flight home to the States.

Nothing had come to light on Will Webb. It seemed he had vanished into thin air, along with his P-47. "He still may stumble into one of our Army command centers," Proski told Clare. "I've asked that Will's file be kept open."

After dinner the night before they were to leave, Midge was alone in the room she shared with Clare when she heard a knock.

"It's Annie. May I come in?"

"Sure, Annie, come on in."

"I thought I'd better see if I left anything here when Charlie and I moved into the inn. I've almost finished packing and had a few minutes."

Midge found the change that had come over Annie remarkable. For someone who claimed to lack self-confidence, she certainly had exhibited a lot of it the last couple of weeks — butting heads with Barry and showing her grit and determination at every step. Now, it was like he was smitten with her — in awe of her.

But now Midge was worried about Clare, which was strange since, before coming on this trip, she hadn't even liked Clare. The last few weeks had changed all that: after all they'd gone through, she counted Clare as a good friend. She was convinced Clare was covering up a badly wounded heart, though she gave a good performance of keeping her equanimity. On the surface she was the breezy, bordering on brassy, Clare they all knew. But Midge sensed she was crying inside. She had lived with her for more than a month now and watched the intensity with which the woman applied herself to her work.

"Talk to me about Clare," Midge said to Annie.

Annie's composure faltered. Her mouth trembled. She seemed to lose her buoyancy. "I know she's torn up that she's had no luck finding Will. But I don't know how to reach out to her. I've got Charlie back. Surely that fact alone is a source of silent hurt to her — though she would never admit it. I'm afraid that whatever I say to her will sound self-serving."

Midge nodded. "You know, Annie, I look at you and Charlie and I see what love is supposed to be. I look at Clare and how she wants so desperately to find Will, and I see what love is supposed to be." Her voice caught. "I know now that I've sold short."

Tears began to roll down her cheeks. "I thought the physical attraction between Barry and me was enough. But God, Annie, now that I'm faced with spending the rest of my life with him, I know that I'll be doing it without love." She shuddered. "There... I've said it."

"Oh, Midge." Annie threw her arms around her friend. "You know, it's not too late. You aren't married yet. You don't have to go through with it."

"I made a promise. I've watched you fulfill your promises. I've watched Clare fulfill hers. What am I, Annie? Who am I? What am I going to do?"

At that moment, Clare walked in and found them both weeping. Silently she shut the door and put her arms around both her friends. She was crying, too.

Later that night, Midge lay on her cot and tried to find sleep, still wrestling with her new self-revelation and not knowing what she could do about it. Though she and Metzger were lovers, their relationship up to now had been a series of one-night stands. Dealing with Metzger at close range and on a daily basis over the last two months, she was discovering things about him that she didn't like. The more she was in contact with him in the real world, the more she worried that marriage to him was the wrong step.

The night in Goose Bay when he got drunk had helped open her eyes. Had it not happened again, she might have reconciled herself to a once-in-a-lifetime occurrence brought on by the wild celebration of the end of the war in Europe. But as the pressure of the assignment worked on them all, it had happened again — twice, in fact, and under normal circumstances— and she was growing more concerned. Barry Metzger, by all appearances, was a boorish, belligerent drunk.

At 2 a.m., she realized she had tossed and turned half the night away. They had to be up at six. She got up, quietly slipped into her robe and slippers, and went out on the porch to have a cigarette. Within minutes, Clare joined her.

"Can't sleep," said Clare.

Midge realized it was a statement, not a question. "Me neither."

"I've been thinking about what you told me earlier — why you and Annie were crying when I came in tonight. I knew you were struggling. I could sense what was happening between you and Metzger. Maybe because I lived through all the doubts before Will and I got married. He was seven years younger than me, you know. You should have heard the talk that went on back in Colorado Springs when we were 'an item' — long before I gave in and married him. I thought ours was just a physical attraction, but as I got to know him better, I realized it was love. It was still a long time before I agreed to marry him, and even after we married, my father never forgave me... first for 'livin' in sin' and then for marrying a man 'too young' for me — and, according to him, 'beneath me' to boot."

"I didn't know," Midge said.

"Yup… Will and I talked about Alaska a lot. It was going to be our escape when the war was over. Good place for two pilots to go, don't you think? I'm thinking about doing it anyway — going to Alaska that is. If Will ever comes back from the dead, that's where he'll look for me. I've been checking into potential jobs there — flying the bush. I have a nibble I think I'll follow through on as soon as we get back to the States." She paused. "Which, by golly, is just a couple of days away."

"Clare …" Midge's voice faltered. "Will … Annie and I … we wanted to say something …"

"Shushh, Midge, it's OK. I know. Yes, I'm hurting, but … this is hard to say and don't take it the wrong way … I've known all along that we probably wouldn't find him." She wrapped her arms around herself and stared off into the darkness. "The one thing I told no one but Major Proski is, there was one report, immediately after Will went missing, about a possible fighter plane crashing into the North Sea near the mouth of the Westerschelde River estuary off the coast of Holland. But it was never confirmed, no wreckage was ever found. Considering his position when he was hit, it seemed doubtful Will had enough fuel to fly that far, but he was a helluva pilot. Hell, I taught him! He might have tried for the coast so that he could ditch rather than run out of gas, fall into someone's backyard and kill a bunch of innocent civilians. Will was the kind of guy who would do that. So, though I've been forever hopeful, I've also known the odds are stacked against me."

"But it has to be tearing you apart," Midge said.

"Yes and no. I long ago learned to be a realist, to deal with what life hands me, and to make the best of it. The war is over, at least for me, and my husband didn't come home. I have a lot of company. There are a lot of war widows out there. What we have to do is pick up the pieces and go on. I'm gonna try to do that in Alaska, if and when the war with Japan is over. When you decide what you're going to do, if you need a place to start over, come see me there. I'll let you know where I end up."

"So you're OK?"

"I'm not sure that's the right word for it, but I'm surviving and I will be OK." Clare looked at her watch. "It's three in the morning. We have to be up in three hours. What do you say we try one more time to get some sleep?"

Back inside, Midge lay on her back, listening to Clare's breathing as it grew steady, slower and softer. Sleep still wouldn't come. Midge knew why. She had made up her mind, she just hadn't convinced herself yet that she had the courage to follow through. Moments before sleep finally took her, the realization came to her that she did have the courage.

# EPILOGUE

*June 6, 1946*

Annie had to have Charlie give her a boost to mount her mare, Dakota. Now that she was seven months pregnant, her ranch activities had been curtailed, but she enjoyed the two-mile ride to the highway every day to get the mail. She leaned down and kissed Charlie. "Thanks, hon. See you at supper."

Charlie waved and climbed into his truck to go back out on the range and join the fence-mending crew. He took the truck instead of his horse most mornings so that he could come home for lunch with Annie.

West Texas was already hot and the sun was straight overhead. Annie wore a wide-brimmed sombrero for protection. It had a chinstrap, so periodically she pushed it back behind her head and let the wind blow through her hair, making her feel the sort of freedom she was used to back when she was flying the open-cockpit PT-19s on ferrying trips out of Wilmington and Hagerstown. She really loved this daily ride. Turned out she and Texas ranch life were suited to each other. The girl who dared jump Overall Creek on her bicycle now galloped her horse over the sprawling acres of the Richardson family ranch. She and Charlie even owned an airplane — a war surplus L4-B, a Piper J-3 Cub just like the ones they both had learned on. The little plane gave the ranching Richardsons quick access to Amarillo when they needed to go to town. Until recently, Annie had been flying a little each day, but now she found she could no longer get the stick back.

"When the little tyke is big enough to sit up in the front seat, I'll take him — or her — flying," she had told Charlie.

Dakota was doing a leisurely walk when she topped the rise and Annie could see the mail truck just pulling away from the boxes. "Good," she said out loud, and the mare pricked up her ears as Annie urged her into a lope.

The mail held the usual bills and flyers, but what caught Annie's attention was a letter postmarked Alaska.

"Clare!"

Excited, she urged Dakota into an easy lope to make the trip home a little faster. Good horsewoman that she was, when she got back to the corral, Annie walked the mare to cool her off before letting her drink her fill at the water trough. Then she removed the saddle and bridle, curried her and turned her loose to graze. Finally, she sat down at the kitchen table and tore open Clare's letter.

*June 1, 1946*

*Dearest Annie — Charlie too,*

*Sorry to be so long answering your letters.*

*Lots of news. Midge is here — and she sends her love. She arrived mid-spring. I had given up on her, but it turns out it took her longer than she expected to put her life in order.*

*First and foremost, she did NOT marry Barry Metzger. They had it out after we all returned to the States. He was furious, I guess, but she held her ground. Our Midge is no longer a pushover — if she ever was.*

*She was able to get her old job back with the ATC, but that only lasted until September after Japan surrendered. Bob and Nancy came to her rescue again. Bob was in the process of becoming the president of a fledgling airline in Washington. He hired her to run his office.*

*She got her mother to leave that no-good she was living with and move in with her sister — Midge's aunt. I believe you met them both. Jackie Cochran helped her with that. Midge is lucky, she has good friends in high places. Sometime in February, she decided to move up here. I have wanted to open a flying service and I convinced her we could do this together. She brought her sister with her and Louise immediately found a job with a local beauty parlor and a boy friend!*

*Now hold on to your hat. Both of us have stayed in touch with John Proski. He's out of the Army now and has decided to come up and visit Midge and me. Midge thinks he's interested in me. I think he's interested in her. This little triangle ought to be interesting. Stay tuned for chapter two.*

*I'm lovin' my job. I AM flying the bush. That day you and I flew into Bluie One is the day I decided I had to fly in the wilds. I told you then it was my flight to destiny. I've never felt so free. The more I thought about it, I realized it was true for all three of us.*

*Don't ask me how financially solvent we are — we aren't. But we are working hard to make this business go. We've heard there are some other WASP up here doing the same thing. When I get a minute, I'm going to try to find out who and where they are.*

*Take good care of that little one you're carrying. It's nice to know that one of us is concerned about the next generation of flyers.*

*With love,*
*Your pal Clare*

# AFTERWORD

*Flight to Destiny* is a work of fiction. It is, however, based on a non-fiction book I wrote fourteen years ago, *The Originals: The Women's Auxiliary Ferrying Squadron of World War II*, published in 2001. In *Flight to Destiny* I have followed the story of the "Original WAFS" as closely as possible while still taking literary license to allow for the fictional characters and fictional happenings that move their stories — and therefore the book — forward. I used the same technique in my first WASP novel *Flight from Fear*, published in 2002.

How to portray Nancy Love, head of the WAFS, and Jacqueline Cochran, head of the WASP (Women Airforce Service Pilots) — real-life characters in a fictional story — was my challenge. They could not be my protagonist/antagonist because I would not presume to write in their heads. By creating the proverbial "sidekick" for each I was able to achieve the distance I needed and yet stay close to the source. Enter Clare Varsky and Midge Culpepper — close associates of those two powerful women in command positions. As alter egos, Clare (friend and confidante to Nancy) and Midge (employee of Jackie) are able to comment objectively and subjectively on the two leaders' actions, deeds and verbalized thoughts.

The other main character, Annie Gwynn, provides a connection to the real-life Cornelia Fort, who was the third woman accepted in the WAFS squadron. Cornelia was an eyewitness to the Japanese attack on Pearl Harbor, December 7, 1941. Fifteen months later, she became the first woman pilot to die actively serving her country in wartime. As Cornelia's sidekick, Annie is at Pearl Harbor on that fateful day and it is through her eyes that we get a first-hand account of the attack, which is based on an article written by Cornelia and published posthumously in *Cosmopolitan* magazine the summer of 1943. Annie is also an eyewitness to Cornelia's fatal, mid-air collision on March 21, 1943. So three fictional WAFS — who are not patterned on any particular member of the WAFS or WASP but have many of the traits found in the majority of the 1,102 women who served — are the heroines of this book. Consequently, the "Original" squadron of WAFS that Nancy Love founded and commanded, of necessity, grows from the historical 28 to 31. As one always does with fiction — as in drama played out on stage —readers are asked to suspend disbelief and allow the characters to weave their story.

In trying to be as historically correct as possible *and* make the story exciting, I chose to borrow pivotal events that happened to real WAFS or WASP and portray them as happening to my three heroines. Thus Nancy Batson's heart-stopping flight over Pittsburgh in November 1944 — tussling with a malfunctioning P-38 nosewheel — becomes Annie's frustrating flight over Columbus, Ohio, in June 1944. Florene Miller's gripping fight to control and fly the stricken P-47 in Dallas in November 1943 becomes Midge's life-and-death struggle with a P-47 over Wilmington in July 1943. Words used by Nancy and Florene to describe these events—in one-on-one interviews—helped me depict the drama in *Flight to Destiny.*

Nancy Love and Betty Gillies were to have flown the Atlantic in a B-17 in early September 1943 and were stopped before they could make the flight. In order to make that a part of this story — and it is an integral part with import that plays into the eventual resolution of the book — Nancy, on her boss General Bill Tunner's request, includes Clare and Annie in that mission. Four WAFS rather than two are given this opportunity.

The marriage of two B-17 pilots is taken from the story of one of the seventeen WASP graduates from Avenger Field that Jackie Cochran sent to Lockbourne AAF in Columbus, Ohio, to take B-17 transition in the fall 1943. There was such a wedding at Lockbourne in early 1944.

The October 1942 group flight of Piper Cubs to Mitchel Field on Long Island and the PT-26 group flight to Calgary, Canada, in spring 1943 were actual ferrying flights. Midge and Clare were added to the flight to Mitchel. Annie and Clare were added to the Calgary flight. But the events of the flights themselves are accurate.

Lastly, Annie's adventures ferrying airplanes after December 20, 1944, came from an interview with WASP Gayle Snell (44-9) and her experiences in those early months of 1945. Other than what Gayle related to me about ferrying after leaving the WASP, everything that happens in the story after December 20, 1944, is pure fiction. However, I did a considerable amount of research on the Prisoner of War situation in Germany in spring 1945, as well as on weather considerations when flying the North Atlantic in order to write a believable ending to the story. I also did extensive reading on the B-17 and took a ride in EAA's B-17, Aluminum Overcast, in 2009 — for the experience and for research purposes.

*Sarah Byrn Rickman*
*April, 2014*

# ACKNOWLEDGMENTS

Primary research for all of my WAFS/WASP books has been done at or with the help of the Blagg-Huey Library at Texas Woman's University (Denton), the home of the WASP Archives. My heart-felt thanks to Kimberly Johnson and her staff for all their help.

References to historical milestones during World War II, quoted throughout this book, are taken from *World War II Day By Day* (London: DK, a Dorling Kindersley Limited Book, 2001).

Description of the landing up the fjord to the glacier is inspired by "Bluie West One (BW-1)" by Howard Traeder, Pilot, 603rd Squadron, 398th Bomb Group Memorial Association — web page last accessed January 5, 2017: http://www.398th.org/History/Veterans/History/Traeder_BluieWest.html. And by two other websites also accessed January 5, 2017: http://en.wikipedia.org/wiki/Bluie_West_One and http://warbirdforum.com/bluie1.htm

# ABOUT THE AUTHOR

Sarah Byrn Rickman has been researching the WASP and closely following their activities for 25 years. In that time, she has written and published seven books about these women who flew for the U.S. Army Air Forces in World War II — two novels, three biographies and two histories. She has another WASP biography currently in the works and expects publication later in 2017.

Other Books by Sarah Byrn Rickman:

     • *FINDING DOROTHY SCOTT: Letters of a WASP Pilot,* Texas Tech University Press, September 2016 (biography/nonfiction)
     • *WASP OF THE FERRY COMMAND: Women Pilots, Uncommon Deeds,* * University of North Texas Press, March 2016 (nonfiction)

     • *NANCY BATSON CREWS: Alabama's First Lady of Flight,* University of Alabama Press, Tuscaloosa AL, 2009 (biography/nonfiction)

• *NANCY LOVE and the WASP FERRY PILOTS OF WORLD WAR II,* University of North Texas Press, Denton TX, March 2008 (biography/nonfiction)

• *FLIGHT FROM FEAR, A WASP Novel,* ** Disc-Us Books, Inc., Santa Fe NM, 2002 (fiction)

• *THE ORIGINALS: The Women's Auxiliary Ferrying Squadron of World War II,* Disc-Us Books, Inc., Sarasota, FL, 2001 (nonfiction)

Book Awards

* Combs Gates Award, 2009, given annually by the National Aviation Hall of Fame for creative projects that reflect an emphasis on the individual pioneers – the people – who defined America's aerospace horizons. *WASP of the Ferry Command: Women Pilots, Uncommon Deeds* is the final installment in the trilogy: "WASP of the Ferry Command, World War II." *The Originals* and the Nancy Love biography are the first and second books in the trilogy.

** Finalist: Original Softcover category, the WILLA Literary Awards 2003, presented annually by Women Writing the West for the best books published the previous year about western women and set in the west. Named for Pulitzer Prize winning novelist Willa Cather.

Sarah currently serves as an oral historian for the WASP Archives at Texas Woman's University and as editor of the official WASP newsletter. She has written numerous WASP articles published in national magazines and journals. Inspired by the WASP, she earned her Sport Pilot certification in 2011.

Sarah is a former reporter/ columnist for *The Detroit News* and the former editor of the *Centerville-Bellbrook Times* (suburban Dayton, Ohio). She earned her B.A. in English from Vanderbilt University and an M.A. in Creative Writing from Antioch University, Mc-Gregor.

She now lives in Colorado Springs, Colorado, with her husband, Richard, and their black Lab, Lady.